VOLUME 6

Written by Brandon Varnell

Art by Kirsten Moody

American Kitsune, Volume 6: A Fox's Mate

To see Brandon Varnell's other works, or to ask for permission to use his works, visit him at www.varnell-brandon.com, facebook at www.facebook.com/AmericanKitsune, twitter at www.twitter.com/BrandonbVarnell, Patreon at https://www.patreon.com/BrandonVarnell, and instagram at www.instagram.com/brandonbvarnell.

If you'd like to know when I'm releasing a new book, you can sign up for my mailing list at https://www.varnell-brandon.com/mailing-list.

ISBN: 978-1-53445-57-3 (paperback edition 1)
978-1-951904-33-3 (OELN Edition)
978-1-951904-31-9 (eBook)

DEDICATION

This page is made in dedication to my amazing patrons. Without them, my characters would never get lewded by so many wonderful artists:

Aaron Harris; Abraham Madsen; Adam; Alarinnise; Alex Burt; Armando Pastrana; Aaron Cortrighr; Austin; Brendan Smiley; Bruce Johnson; Bryce McClay; ByzFan; Casey G. May; Catcrazy9; Chase Corso; Charles Dorfeuille; Chett Nialo; Christopher Gross; Cody Woodard; CosmicOrange; Daniel Glasson; David Bell; Edward Grindle; Edward Lamar Stephenson; Edward P Warmouth; Eric Bailey; Feitochan; Forrest Hansen; Forrest Hansen; G___Sweet; Grant; Green and Magenta Beast; IronKing; Jacob Flores; Jared B; Jason Wilcox; Jeremy Schultz; Jessy Torres; John Patton; Jordan McDonald; Joseph Snyder; Joshua Hasbell; Manny G; Mark Frabotta; Mason; Matthew Wallace; Max A Kramer; Michael Erwin; Michael Moneymaker; Mike Dennehy; Minocho; MrRedSkill; Nathan S; Norodim; Nyxterrynne; Phoenixblue; Philip Hedgepeth; Rafael; Randgofire23; Raymond T; Red Phoenix; Reent Dopychai; Repooc Ilahsram; Richard Garret; Rob Hammel; Robert Shofner; Rooser45; Roy Cales; Samuel Donaldson; Sean Gray; Seismic Wolf; Smudi Corp; Tanner Lovelace; Thomas Jackson; Thomas Lindsay; Thomas Oconnell; ToraLinkley; Travis Cox; Vincent Frosceno; William Crew; Wizard4Hire; XY172; Zach Miller; Zach Strickland; Zak Whiteaker; Zenn Barger

CONTENT

WORDS YOU SHOULD KNOW:

Chūnibyou: A Japanese slang term which roughly translates to "Middle School 2nd Year Syndrome". People with chuunibyou either act like a know-it-all adult and look down on real ones, or believe they have special powers unlike others.

Kanji: One of the three writing systems in Japan using Chinese characters.

Tsundere: A Japanese term for a character development process that describes a person who is initially cold and even hostile towards another person before gradually showing a warmer side over time.

Yōkai: A class of supernatural monsters, spirits and demons in Japanese folklore. The wordyōkai is made up of the kanji for "bewitching; attractive; calamity;" and "spectre; apparition; mystery; suspicious."

Youki: The energy source used by yōkai

Nue: A legendary Japanese yōkai.

Rumi Takahata: A character from an eroge called Cat Girl Alliance.

Gundam: A science fiction media franchise created by Sunrise that feature giant robots (or "mecha") called "mobile suits," with titular mobile suits that carry the name "Gundam."

Yandere: A word commonly used to refer to a character in anime and manga who, at first glance, appears to be extremely cute and kind, but will later show stalker tendencies and even murder people who get too close to their love interests.

Gyakujutsu: Techniques used in feudal era Japan to combat against yōkai. There are only a few humans alive who can use these techniques now.

Shōnen: The demographic of manga for young boys. Shōnen literally translates to "young boy." Typically, this is referring to teenagers between 13 and 17.

Iaidō: A Japanese martial art that emphasizes being aware and capable of quickly drawing the sword and responding to a sudden attack.

Natsumo Shinobi: A fictional manga inside of the American Kitsune universe. This manga series was inspired by and parodies a real series called Naruto.

Kenjutsu: The umbrella term for all (koryū) schools of Japanese swordsmanship, in particular those that predate the Meiji Restoration.

Yamato Nadeshiko: A Japanese term meaning the "personification of an idealized Japanese woman", or "the epitome of pure, feminine beauty." It is a floral metapho that combines the words Yamato, an ancient name for Japan, and nadeshiko, a delicate frilled pink carnation called Dianthus superbus.

Baka: the Japanese word for idiot.

Kudagitsune: A minor fox spirit that kitsune conjure. They often serve as messengers and spies.

Yuki Rito: The main character to the manga/anime series To LOVE-RU and To LOVE-RU Darkness.

Doujinshi: Self-published manga often created by amateurs. Some amateurs go on to become mangaka, while some mangaka go on to create doujinshi.

CHAPTER 1

Homecoming

THE BODHISATTVA SAT upon his throne within the large entrance hall of his home. The throne, a construct made of the purest gold with intricate silver designs etched upon its surface, had been forged by the best Mountain Kitsune crafters. It had been a gift from the Great Mountain Clan, who had crafted it from precious metals found deep within the Pico de Orizaba Mountain.

As was the case with all kitsune abodes, the Bodhisattva's entrance hall was an expression of opulence. The marble tiles glittered as light filtered in through the many open windows that made up the left wall. Massive Corinthian columns sparkled in a combination of silver and gold, with artful designs depicting the history of the Bodhisattva.

Humans believed the Bodhisattva to be the Buddha and his many former lives. The truth was that the nine-tailed kitsune, the Celestial Kyūbi of the Great Celestial Clan, had always been the Bodhisattva. Each Celestial Kitsune who was bestowed the ninth tail by Lord Inari, God of Foxes, became the next Bodhisattva, an enlightened being that existed beyond the comprehension of mere humans and mundane yōkai.

Since the Shénshèng Clan's founding, every leader had been bestowed the ninth tail, just as it had been with the Gitsune Clan. They were the only two clans who retained the title of Kyūbi. The last of the three Kyūbi was always selected from one of the other Great Clans.

Kneeling before him was one of his sons, his second eldest and the one in charge of gathering and disseminating information. He never stayed in one place for very long, this boy. He often traveled between cities, states, and countries, though the Bodhisattva knew that his son had recently taken a liking to the United States. He'd said something about the women there being easy to seduce.

"We have also learned that Luna Mul, along with thirty of her clansmen, has been killed."

The Bodhisattva shifted in his seat. "Luna has been defeated?"

Luna Mul was the current head of the Great Ocean Clan. A kitsune with six tails, she was one of the more powerful kitsune in the world. Most kitsune never made it to their sixth tail. In a world fraught with danger, many kitsune were killed before even reaching their fourth tail.

"Yes, Father."

"By whom?" he asked, his frown imperceptible. "The last I remember, she and her clan were securing California for me. It should have been a simple task."

He had been hoping to use them as a means of gaining a stronghold within the United States. Long had the United States been a safe haven for yōkai who belonged to no clan. None of the great yōkai clans, be they kitsune, tengu, or Nurahiyon's Night Parade of One-Thousand Demons, resided there. It would have made the perfect stronghold, a bastion with which he could use to move his forces and further influence the world. And also...

It's the place where the granddaughter of that accursed woman lives.

"According to what we've discovered, Luna was using this as an opportunity to expand her slave-trading operation. This normally wouldn't have been a problem, but it appears that she ran afoul of the Sons and Daughters of Humanity."

The Sons and Daughters of Humanity, yet another thorn in his side. They were an anti-yōkai organization, one that did its utmost to kill yōkai wherever they went. So far, he'd managed to keep them out of China, but he knew that they were spread across most of the world.

"The Sons and Daughters of Humanity would not have been able to kill someone of Luna Mul's strength."

His son hesitated. "We did learn that Luna Mul was not killed by the Sons and Daughters of Humanity, but someone else."

Nodding, he asked, "Who killed her?"

Another moment's hesitation. "Our spies have confirmed that the person who killed Luna Mul was a human."

The Bodhisattva blinked. "What did you just say?"

"I said that Luna Mul was killed by a human—"

"No, no, I'm sorry," he interrupted. "I don't think I heard you correctly. What did you just say?"

He did not move at all. As if he had been carved from stone, The Bodhisattva looked down at his son with an unwavering, uncompromising gaze.

His son squirmed beneath him but pressed on. "Luna Mul was killed by a human."

The Bodhisattva needed a moment. "A human?"

His second son, Zhìlì, shifted nervously before nodding his head. "Yes."

"A human killed a six-tailed kitsune?"

"According to the report, he caught her by surprise," Zhìlì admitted. "He shot her with a standard military grade pistol while she was distracted."

From a purely physical standpoint, kitsune were one of the weakest yōkai races. If they weren't using reinforcement or some other physical augmentation technique, then they were no stronger than a human. A bullet to the head could easily kill a kitsune who was distracted.

The Bodhisattva withheld his scowl. "Guns. Inelegant creations suitable for a species of apes."

Zhìlì nodded, though whether in agreement or something else was unknown to him. "According to the report I received from my spies, Luna Mul was toying with two other yōkai: a River Kitsune who goes by the name of Kotohime, and the inu, Kiara F. Kuyo."

The Bodhisattva's right hand twitched. While he did not hold any fear of the inu species like many of his brethren, he still hated inu as a whole. He also knew of those names. Kiara F. Kuyo was a prominent businesswoman and owner of the largest chain of fitness centers in the United States. Then there was Kotohime, the bodyguard of Lilian Pnéyma, the girl that his youngest had desired with a fervent passion.

The Bodhisattva shunted aside his annoyance at hearing those names and thought about this new information. Luna Mul had always been an incredibly arrogant woman, too sure in herself and too secure in her own power. Yes, he was not surprised that she had been killed. He had even expected it to happen eventually. What surprised him wasn't that she had been killed, but who had killed her.

Humans were weak creatures, pathetically so. While he harbored no hatred toward the primate race, he didn't like their arrogant sense of superiority. They were a race who felt entitled to more than they deserved.

Ever since the creation of guns and the atomic bomb, humans had become too dangerous to openly challenge. Kitsune—nay, all yōkai had been forced into hiding. While they might have been able to defeat the humans if they rallied together, such a thing would never happen.

There were many different yōkai races, hundreds, in fact, and these races did not get along. It wouldn't have been an exaggeration to say that most yōkai hated each other. There were always wars going on between one race of yōkai or another.

Yes, yōkai were too embroiled in their own hatred toward each other to focus that hatred onto humanity. That wasn't even going into the hatred between the many different clans within each race.

His own race was a prime example. Few were the clans who got along with each other. The kitsune world was one of cutthroat politics and backdoor deals. Alliances were forged and backstabbing was most often the end result. While not true of all kitsune alliances, such as the pact between the Great Ghost Clan of Pnéyma and the Great Forest Clan of Wald, for the most part, the various kitsune clans did not get along. Almost all alliances made among kitsune ended in treachery.

Just like his brief attempt at allying with the Pnéyma Clan.

The Bodhisattva took a deep breath. What had happened to his son was regrettable, but it was also his own fault. The boy should have consulted him before going after that girl.

However, that did not mean that he would let what happened to his son go unpunished. He had already hired an assassin from a yōkai ninja village located within the United States—he didn't know where the village was located, as they kept themselves hidden like any good village of assassins—though he had not heard any word since commissioning them for the task. He wondered what was taking so long.

Shaking his head, the Bodhisattva dispelled those thoughts and focused back on his son.

"Tell me what you know about this human," he commanded. "I am intrigued and wish to know more."

**

I chased after her, running down the stairs, across the hall, to the entrance, and out of the convention center. The doors slid open and my feet hit the pavement.

She was running toward them, the three yōkai who'd just finished fighting. Two of them were down, and the last loomed over them, her raven locks of hair drifting in a breeze and her six tails writhing behind her like snakes.

She was ahead of me, screaming at the woman, her voice filled with rage and fear; rage at how her bodyguard had been hurt and fear at what this woman could do. The rage had overpowered her fear, or perhaps it was the fear that was fueling her rage. I didn't know.

Her two tails flailed forward to launch two balls, twin spheres of light, which grabbed the woman's attention and made her move. Two more were flung and subsequently blocked by a wall of water. The water undulated, then morphed, shifted, and changed from a wall into a spear.

A spear that was soon thrust through soft, pliant flesh. The ground was painted with blood. She stumbled forward, then collapsed like a marionette without a master.

I screamed, raised the gun in my hand, and fired.

Blood splattered across my face.

***

Kevin jerked awake with a start as the seat that he was sitting on shook. He looked around for a second, wondering where he was. It was only after a loud noise filled his ears and he spotted several buildings and a runway through the small window that he remembered; he was on a plane heading back to Arizona.

It had been three days since the San Diego Comic-Con that had gone horribly, horribly wrong. It had been three days since a group of kitsune and an anti-yōkai faction calling itself the Sons and Daughters of Humanity had fought and killed each other. Three days since he'd fought and nearly died against Ken.

Three days since he had killed someone.

Kevin pressed a hand to his face and squeezed his eyes shut. It did not bring any reprieve, however, as the moment his eyes were closed, he saw the woman that he had killed, her body jerking in spastic motions as bullets penetrated her flesh, blood spraying from her like a fine mist to paint the ground carmine.

The last three days had not been easy. Due to the extensive damage that Kotohime and Kiara had taken, plus Kotohime's bad case of youki exhaustion, they'd been cooped up in the hospital. Kevin was grateful that Lilian and the others had been there, or he'd have probably gone stir-crazy. His mate and his mate's sister had occupied most of his time with their antics, which had been a good thing. It kept him from focusing too much on the blood that now stained his hands.

Christine, Lindsay, Eric, the twins Alex and Andrew, and Heather had eventually arrived when they were found by Kuroneko's people. They'd apparently been stuck in Kiara's bus, which had been damaged to the point that Kiara had deemed paying for the cost of repairs to be a waste. She'd decided to get a nice little bonus check from her insurance company instead—little being a mild euphemism.

During that time, Kevin and Lilian had filled the twins in on the yōkai world—not like they could have kept it a secret after what happened at the Comic-Con anyway.

Alex and Andrew had not been as surprised as Kevin expected them to be.

Everyone was gathered inside the hospital room. Kevin and Lilian were sitting on a bed. Iris had been sitting on the same bed, but she had tried to grope Lilian, and thus, she had received a tail smackdown that sent her to the floor, which was where she remained. Christine and Lindsay were sitting on a pair of chairs. Eric was standing near the back. The twins, Alex and Andrew, were sitting cross-legged on the floor.

Kevin had just finished explaining everything to his friends: the existence of yōkai, who the Sons and Daughters of Humanity were, and the fact that Lilian and her family were all kitsune.

Neither Alex nor Andrew seemed surprised.

"We always knew that Lilian was weird," Alex admitted after Kevin finished his long-winded explanation.

The russet-haired boy seemed pretty calm about what he'd learned, all things considered. He just sat on the ground, his legs crossed, looking completely untroubled, though Kevin suspected that the young man might have been in shock, or perhaps the information that had been doled out had yet to sink in.

"Oi!" Lilian pouted at being called weird, not that it did much good.

"Yeah, anyone who's decided that you are the one for them and not me has to be off their rocker," Andrew added.

"Oi!" Now it was Kevin's turn to pout.

"Uh, brother, I think you mean anyone who decided to date Kevin over me has to be crazy."

"No, I didn't. Who the hell would want to date you?"

"If given a choice between you or me, every girl would choose me over you."

"You don't know what you're talking about."

"Of course I know what I'm talking about. Face it, Andrew, I'm better than you are in every way, shape, and form. No girl would choose you over me. You're a loser."

"That does it! You've frayed the last bit of my patience, and now you're going to get it!"

"Bring it, son! I'll break my foot off in your ass so hard you'll be shitting in a bedpan for weeks!"

As the fraternal twins began a scuffle in the hospital room, rolling around on the floor and pulling each other's hair out like a couple of middle school girls, Kevin and Lilian continued pouting.

"Lilian, I feel like none of my friends appreciate me."

"And I feel like they think I'm crazy."

Kevin gazed into his mate's eyes, feeling his chest glow with warmth, love, and compassion. "You're not crazy, Lilian. I'm the crazy one. Crazy for you."

"Oh, Kevin," Lilian said softly, her eyes growing warm and a little moist. "I'm crazy for you, too."

"Lilian."

"Kevin."

"Lilian!"

"Kevin!"

"I'll kill you both!" Christine shouted as Kevin and Lilian began hugging.

The feeling of something shuffling against him snapped Kevin out of his reverie. He looked down. Crimson locks of hair framed a gorgeous face that was reminiscent of a fairy tale princess. Her body was pressed into his, her legs thrown over his lap, and her right arm was nestled between his back and the seat. Her lips were parted in a way that enticed him to lean down and claim them in a kiss.

It was against the policies of the plane for people to sit like this, but Lilian had enchanted the attendant who walked down the aisles. Kevin normally would have bopped her on the head for that, but kitsune didn't like flying, or so he'd been told. Lilian had seemed fine with it, but that might have been because she'd been holding onto him like a lifeline the whole time.

While Lilian had acted mostly normal, Iris had been freaking out as the plane flew—at least, until she'd passed out in her seat. Speaking of…

Iris sat next to them, also asleep. Her long, shimmering strands of midnight hair resembled silken threads that glimmered like captured starlight. Thick eyelashes hid her eyes from view, and her pouty lips, painted a dark crimson, just begged to be nibbled on.

He looked away when he realized that the straps of her shirt had slid down her arms, the slight V-shaped hem falling with it, revealing tantalizing amounts of Iris's stunning cleavage. Kevin almost wryly noted that, even when sleeping, his mate's sister looked sexy beyond all reason.

He looked further into the plane. Kirihime, Kotohime, and Camellia were sitting together. Kotohime was awake, he could tell, even though her eyes were closed. Her posture, straight and proper, hands folded in her lap, let him know that she was keeping a wary ear out for potential danger. She'd been on edge ever since the battle with Luna Mul. Camellia was fast asleep, leaning her head against an equally dozing Kirihime as she snored away.

"Hawa-hawa-hawa-hawa... zzzz... hawa-hawa-hawa-hawa..."

Yes, those were snores.

A little way off, Alex, Andrew, and Eric also slept peacefully. Given all they'd seen, done, and learned, this didn't surprise Kevin. They must've been exhausted.

Alex and Andrew were, oddly enough, resting on each other. Kevin wondered how two people who fought so much could be so close. Then again, they were twins. Eric was mumbling in his sleep.

"Hehehe... I wanna squeeze them big fun bags... kukuku... let me suck on them, please..."

Kevin felt several drops of sweat trickle down his forehead. *That boy...*

In front of Eric and the twins sat Lindsay and Christine. They were a little behind his seat. Kevin snorted when he noticed that Lindsay was tightly hugging Christine, who was grimacing in her sleep. Christine would occasionally shove the other girl off of her. Lindsay would frown, shift around some, and then go right back to hugging Christine as if she were a teddy bear. He felt sorry for the yuki-onna.

Sitting in front of him, Lilian, and Iris were Heather and Kiara. They, much like Kotohime, were awake. They were talking about something, though he didn't know what. He could barely make out their whispers.

He looked back out the window. They were rolling across the runway. The landing must have been what had woken him up. Objects flashed by the window and several other runways were visible, until, eventually, the terminal that they would be docking at came into view.

The airplane slowed to a stop.

Seconds later, a soft *ping!* echoed throughout the airplane as the intercom came on: "We are almost ready to begin disembarking passengers. Please remain seated until our attendants are ready to direct you out. We would like to thank everyone who came aboard, and we hope that you had a great flight."

Everyone unbuckled and stretched in their seats, luxuriating in the feeling of freedom after the hour-long flight.

"Lilian." Kevin shook the girl awake. "Wake up, Lilian. We've arrived."

"Hmm... ah... huh?"

Lilian blinked several times, her long eyelashes fluttering as she turned her head like she was looking for something. When her eyes landed on Kevin, she smiled.

"Oh, Beloved... good morning."

Kevin's lips twitched. "It's actually the afternoon."

"Is that so?" Lilian mumbled. Her eyes were a little droopy. "Does that mean I don't get a good morning kiss?"

"It doesn't need to be morning for you to get a kiss," Kevin said as he cupped her cheek, leaned down, and kissed her. Her arms went around his neck as she returned it.

In the other seat, Iris woke up and stretched her arms above her head. Her mouth parted to release a sensual moan that had several of the men around them passing out, their eyes rolling into the back of their heads as they fell back in their seats. They were actually kind of fortunate, Kevin thought, since it meant that they didn't see Iris's breasts popping out of her shirt...

... Right, so maybe they weren't very fortunate. Poor men, passing out before they could even catch a glimpse of such glorious cleavage.

On a side note, Kevin had noticed that Eric had lasted long enough to see the already tight shirt stretch across Iris's boobs, and he, much like Kevin, could probably tell that Iris did not believe in wearing bras. The pervy young man was now lying passed out on the floor, a puddle of blood expanding beneath him as it flowed from his nose.

"Man down! Man down!"

"We've got someone suffering from Nasal Sanguination! Quick, call the paramedics!"

Kevin, Lilian, and everyone else grew silent as two paramedics rushed into the airplane. Kevin didn't know how they had boarded, considering the airplane wasn't even connected to the terminal yet, but he'd long since learned to ignore the weirdness that happened around him.

"Beboop! Beboop!"

The paramedic in the front released strange noises. Kevin thought he was trying to sound like an ambulance, but it sounded more like the squeals of a dying pig.

"Beboop! Beboop! Beboop! Beboop!"

They carried a stretcher between them, which they placed the passed out, still nose-bleeding Eric on before rushing back out of the airplane. They appeared heedless of the many eyes on them.

"Well," Iris started, crossing her arms under her chest, "that was weird."

Lilian and Kevin could only nod.

***

12

Because they didn't have the bus anymore, Kiara couldn't drive them home. She paid for several cabs to take them back instead.

Christine and Lindsay took a cab together, though Christine had been hesitant. The last Kevin saw of them, Christine had been banging on the window and shouting something as the cab drove off. He wondered if she was wary of the tomboy after being used as a hug pillow. Heather went with Kiara, and the twins got their own cab. Eric would've gotten a cab, but he'd been sent to the ICU after losing too much blood via spontaneous nasal combustion.

The Pnéyma family plus Kevin, Kirihime, and Kotohime ended up needing a special cab because there were six of them—too many to fit into one little cab. Kiara hired a hummer cab to take them home.

Kevin had to admit that being driven home in a hummer was kind of awesome. How many people could say they've ridden in a hummer?

It was late by the time they arrived home. Kotohime prepared them a late-night meal while Kirihime unpacked Camellia's, hers, and her sister's clothing and toiletries. Kevin, Iris, and Lilian did their own unpacking.

That evening, the family of six sat down to a lovely dinner prepared by their resident Yamato Nadeshiko; it was a Japanese dish of udon noodles, broiled fish, and pickled vegetables with miso soup. Rather than forks and knives, as would have been the standard utensils used in an American home, Kotohime brought out chopsticks.

Kevin had grown used to using chopsticks in his own house. He didn't even bat an eyelash anymore. That said, he felt like he was becoming a caricature of real people, like his entire life was being turned into an anime, because, honestly, how many other non-Japanese Americans used chopsticks near-daily like he did?

"Hey, Stud?" Iris grabbed Kevin's attention just as he was getting ready to place some broiled fish in his mouth. He looked up, sighed, and then set his food back down.

"Do you really have to call me that?" Kevin asked.

"Course I do," Iris said before getting on with her question. "So, have you ever had any cats before? And I'm not talking about the one that came on the trip with us. I mean have you had any cats before Lily-pad started living with you?"

Lilian, who was already digging into her food and had several udon noodles hanging from her mouth, looked up upon hearing the question. She slurped up the remainder of the noodles and focused on their conversation.

Kevin thought the question odd, but he tried to recall if he'd ever had a cat before.

"I... I don't know," he admitted, frowning. "Back when I was younger, I used to always bring animals home." His face scrunched up as he thought about the question some more. "I remember having several pet birds, a couple snakes, a skunk..."

"You brought a skunk home?" Iris asked, her face scrunching up as if he'd admitted to watching yaoi hentai.

"I couldn't just leave it to fend for itself," Kevin defended. "It was out in the cold and rain and it was eating from the trash can. That couldn't have been healthy for it."

"So you brought it home?" Even Lilian appeared a little incredulous now.

"Wouldn't you have done the same thing?" he asked.

"No," Iris said, Lilian nodding in concurrence with her sister. Even Camellia was nodding along with them. "No, I wouldn't. I don't want my place or my body smelling like shit."

Kevin pouted. "That's just a defense mechanism they use to keep predators away. So long as you show a skunk that you mean no harm, it won't spray you like that."

"Really?" Iris asked, deadpan.

"Really." Kevin maintained Iris's gaze for less than two seconds before being forced to look away.

Iris nodded. "Thought so. And you still didn't answer my question."

"Why do you want to know so badly?"

"Call it idle curiosity."

Kevin frowned and tried to remember some more. "I do remember owning a cat once. It must have been... five or six years ago, maybe? I can't really remember when, but I do recall bringing home a black cat when I was younger. I let it stay for somewhere around a month or so before the landlord and my mom realized I was keeping a cat in the apartment." Kevin paused, his eyes turning toward the ceiling as if he was remembering something else. "You know, now that I think about it, the cat that I brought to California with us looked a lot like the cat that I brought home back then." He frowned, blinking some more. "I wonder if they're related."

Iris and Lilian shared a look.

"I wonder what happened to that cat anyway?" Kevin asked. "I hope it's all right."

Several miles away, in another part of Phoenix, a certain nekomata sneezed.

"I'm sure the cat's fine, Kevin," Lilian assured her mate. "You know how felines are. They're always moving from place to place, never staying in one spot for long periods of time."

"I guess," Kevin said with a sigh. Sure, they hadn't known each other for very long, but he really did miss that cat.

Dinner soon ended. Lilian and Kevin forced Kotohime—who should have still technically been resting—to relax while they took care of the dishes.

Because of the late hour, the two did not sit on the couch and watch anime until the desire for sleep claimed them, but they instead went straight to the bathroom and got ready for bed. After going through their nightly routine (brushing teeth, washing face, flossing, etc.), Kevin and Lilian wandered hand in hand into their bedroom.

"You're troubled," Lilian said the moment he closed the door behind them.

Kevin's smile was more of a grimace. "Am I that obvious?"

"To me, yes," Lilian said, gazing at him with a compassionate expression that few people could have matched. Just being the recipient of her look made Kevin feel like warm putty. "You're still thinking about what happened at the Comic-Con, aren't you?"

Kevin's smile was tremulous. "Yeah…"

"Do you want to talk about it?"

Kevin thought about her offer. He hadn't told anyone about his feelings yet, and the temptation to open up was strong. So much had happened during that time, and he was struggling to wrap his mind around all of it: The battle between the yōkai and anti-yōkai forces, his shameful defeat at the hands of that blond fop, the battle of Kiara and Kotohime against the six-tails, and their subsequent defeat.

Lilian getting stabbed by a spear of water.

His rage as he watched her crumble to the ground.

The way he'd taken the gun in his hand and shot someone, killing them. It didn't matter if that person had been evil. It still made him sick to his stomach just thinking about it. Even now the urge to vomit remained strong. Even now he could see the bloodstains covering his hands.

"Maybe… maybe some other time," he said with a strained smile. "I don't think I'm quite ready to talk about what happened."

Lilian stared at him, her eyes gentle and benign, a sea of viridian surrounded by beautiful fair skin. She closed the distance between them so very little space remained. Tilting her head and leaning on her tiptoes, Lilian pressed her mouth to his.

Her kiss was soft and ephemeral, a gentle caressing of lips that caused his body to grow warm. Kevin relaxed. He rested his hands on her waist, feeling the warmth of her naked skin as they slipped under her shirt. He took her lower lip between his, and then switched to her upper lip where he gently suckled on it.

They pulled back after another kiss. Lilian's tender smile did wonders for his heart. The purity in her expression soothed him in ways nothing else had.

"When you're ready to talk, I'll be here," she said, and Kevin felt his heart constrict. Six months ago, these words would have been meaningless, but now they were his panacea.

"Thank you," he said, his emotional voice a soft whisper.

Lilian took his hands and pulled him onto the bed with her. Kevin lay down on his back as Lilian took residence on his left, snuggling against him. Her head rested on his chest. Kevin didn't wear shirts to bed anymore, so her ear was pressed against his bare skin. He wondered if she was listening to his heartbeat.

"Good night, Beloved," she murmured. "I love you."

"Night, Lilian. I love you, too."

Kevin felt it when Lilian fell asleep. Her tense body relaxed, the muscles in her legs, arms, and stomach went slack. Her breathing evened, which caused her chest to slowly push into him. She mumbled a bit, her warm lips kissing his chest before her head turned and she tried to snuggle deeper into his pectorals.

Kevin did not close his eyes. He couldn't—or more like he wouldn't. He had no desire to fall asleep, not when he knew what awaited him in his dreams. Anger. Blood. Hatred. Violence. A nightmare from which he couldn't escape was all that awaited him if he allowed himself to be taken in by exhaustion.

So he stayed awake, listening to the sound of Lilian's breathing, holding her close, until his mind became addled and his body relaxed against his will. He fought and struggled, but it was no use. The body could only stave off exhaustion for so long, and he *was* exhausted. His mind, his body, his heart, his very soul was worn and weary, desiring nothing more than to embrace the darkness.

Darkness came, and with it, Kevin re-experienced the moment that had turned him into a murderer.

***

Christine and Lindsay exited the cab parked right outside of the Diane residence. Together, they walked up to the decently sized house. Behind them, tires screeched as the cab sped off.

After much cajoling and several minutes of begging, Lindsay had convinced Christine to spend the night with her, claiming that she didn't want to be alone right now.

Christine honestly didn't want to be near Lindsay at the moment. It wasn't that she didn't like the girl, but rather, that she didn't like being used as Lindsay's pillow. While she would never admit this out loud, the only person that she wanted holding her like Lindsay had been doing on the plane was Kevin.

"I'm home!" Lindsay called out as she and Christine entered the house, closing the door behind them. They took off their shoes and put them onto the shoe rack off to the side. Footsteps echoed from down the hall, growing closer until a large woman appeared around the corner.

"Oh, Lindsay, darling!"

"Hey, Mom—ack! W-wait! Don't—murgle!"

"Oh, I'm so pleased to see that you've returned safely. When I saw the news about what happened at that convention thingy that you and your friends were going to, I grew so worried! Oh, dear girl, you should have called to let me know you were all right!"

Christine watched with the utmost amusement, enjoying the entertaining sight of Lindsay's face being smothered in her mom's large breasts. Mrs. Diane was a plump woman, not fat, but still large. She and Lindsay looked nothing alike. Only their blonde hair appeared similar, and even that was different due to their hairstyles. Lindsay wore a pixie cut and her mom had long, curly hair.

After assuring Lindsay's mother that, yes, they were perfectly all right and unharmed and that, no, they'd not been present during the "earthquake"—a blatant lie if Christine had ever heard one—the two adjourned to Lindsay's bedroom.

"Dinner will be ready in a few hours," Mrs. Diane had told them. "I'll call you when it's finished."

"Okay, Mom."

Breathing a relieved sigh, Lindsay flopped face-first onto her bed. Christine entered more gracefully, walking over to the desk, avoiding the scattered soccer balls that littered the floor. The desk was on the wall opposite the bed. She moved the chair back and sat down, her shoulders slumping as if they were weighed down by twenty-pound weights.

"Hey, Christine," Lindsay spoke softly, her voice muffled by the bed.

"Yeah?"

Turning her head to look at Christine, Lindsay asked, "Do you think Kevin is all right? He seemed kinda…"

"Depressed?" Christine offered when Lindsay seemed unable to think of an appropriate word. "Mopey? Angsty? Emo?"

"Yeah…" Lindsay grimaced.

Christine felt her shoulders slump further. "He did seem really down about something. I'm guessing something happened during the Comic-Con and he's not telling us so we won't worry about him."

That was just like a man, refusing to tell others anything to not worry them, heedless of the fact that by keeping it all in, he worried them even more. Honestly, if she didn't love him so much, she would have hit him.

Nyou can still hit him, nya.

Christine felt her cheeks burn like dry ice as a feline voice bounced around inside of her head. *You again? Don't you ever give up? Besides, I know where you're going with that, and I'm not hi-hitting on Kevin. He already has a girlfriend.*

So? I'm sure he wouldn't mind having a mistress on the side.

Despite not wanting to, Christine did imagine what it would be like if she was Kevin's mistress.

She sat on the bed. Kevin stood just a few feet away. She was dressed only in a translucent nightgown while Kevin was clad in a pair of boxers that did nothing to hide his erection.

"Are you sure we should be doing this?" Christine asked in a husky voice that sounded absolutely nothing like her. "Your mate will get upset."

"It doesn't matter," Kevin said.

He walked over to the bed, climbed onto it, and animal-crawled up to her. Christine lay down as he moved on top of her. She gasped when he leaned against her, pressing his erection against the junction between her legs.

"I can't take this anymore, Christine," he whispered into her ear. Christine shuddered. "I need you."

Christine whimpered when Kevin took her ear into his mouth and nibbled on it. She placed her hands on his back, and her nails scratched against his skin as if she was trying to find purchase.

"K-Kevin..."

"Christine," Kevin spoke her name in a low-pitched growl.

"Kevin."

"Christine..."

"Christine. Christine? Hey! Christine!"

"Gya!"

Christine screamed as Lindsay's face suddenly appeared in front of her. She lost her balance and tumbled off the chair, her arms windmilling until her head smacked against the floor. Trying to

blink the stars out of her eyes, Christine lay there until her friend's face appeared within her field of vision.

"You okay?" Lindsay asked

Heat rose to her cheeks as Christine stood up. "I'm fine," she mumbled, trying to play off what happened.

Lindsay didn't look convinced, but she also didn't argue. "If you're sure."

"I am sure." Christine calmed her racing heart. Damn that stupid cat for putting delusions in her head. "A-anyway, what were you saying?"

It took Lindsay a moment, but her eyes widened a moment later. "Right! I was talking about Kevin. I said that sounds just like him to keep everything inside so he doesn't worry us."

Christine nodded. Lindsay had known Kevin for a long time. They'd been together since elementary school, so it only made sense that she likely knew more about him than anyone else. Even Lilian probably didn't know Kevin like Lindsay did.

"Has Kevin done this before?" Christine asked.

"Plenty of times," Lindsay admitted. Grinning, she went back over to the bed and sat down while Christine took the chair again. "Kevin hates troubling other people with his problems, so he always suppresses his feelings when he's facing some kind of hardship. I remember when Kevin used to get picked on for being too different. He never told me what happened. I didn't even know about it until much later."

"Different how?"

"Come on. Don't tell me you haven't seen it," Lindsay said. "Kevin's not like most boys. He's too… responsible."

Christine nodded. She had seen it. Before Lilian had shown up, Kevin had always done things by himself. He lived by himself, he took care of his mom's apartment by himself, he cooked for himself, and he even had a part-time job to pay for his own activities. None of the other boys in their group did any of that.

Back then, when all she'd done was watch him from a distance, she had thought that Kevin acted too responsible. Teenagers like them should have been having fun, not working and cleaning.

Lindsay leaned back against the bed and sighed. "I remember the times when Kevin would have to take care of his mom when she was going to college. He'd always come to school depressed. Whenever I asked him why he was sad, he'd give me this really fake smile and say, 'Nothing. I just didn't get enough sleep,' or some other stupid excuse."

"Now why are you looking all depressed?" Christine asked, noticing the way her friend's shoulders had slumped the longer she talked. "Don't tell me talking about stuff that happened in the past is making you sad?"

"No, no, it's not that." Lindsay waved off her friend's words with a strained smile. "I was just thinking about how Kevin will be fine so long as Lilian's by his side."

Christine wrinkled her nose. "Ah."

Thinking about Lilian and Kevin put a damper on Christine's feelings. She liked Lilian. The girl was outgoing, open, and that made it hard to hate her... but she was also dating Kevin. That made Christine's feelings about the kitsune conflicted.

She always asked herself those "what ifs." What if she had been the first person to reach out to Kevin? What if she and Kevin had reconnected before Lilian showed up? Would they be where they were now, or would their relationship have deepened?

When she had confessed to him, Kevin had told her that the only reason he could even talk to her was because of Lilian, because Lilian had helped him find the courage to speak with girls. Christine often wondered, if she had been the one to help him overcome his nervousness around girls, would she be dating Kevin instead of Lilian?

Then she would remember that Lilian was more outgoing than her and that the chances of her helping Kevin overcome his weakness the same way the redhead had would have been slim, and then she became disheartened.

"What do you think about what happened at the Comic-Con?" Christine changed the subject.

"Which part are you talking about? You'll have to be more specific. A lot happened, you know," Lindsay pointed out.

"Of course I'm talking about the fight that happened. What else would I be talking about?"

"I guess I should have expected that." Lindsay shivered. "I remember what happened to my mom when Lilian was kidnapped, but I wasn't actually there when that happened. I had no idea that stuff like this happened in real life. It's scary. Is the yōkai world always like that?"

"You mean is it always that violent?" Christine asked for clarification.

"Mm."

"Hell if I know. What?" Christine shrugged when Lindsay looked at her. "I've never really been part of the yōkai world. I've lived around humans my entire life. Before coming to Arizona, I lived in Alaska with a bunch of orphaned human children. I didn't even know that I was a yuki-onna until my benefactor found me."

"Benefactor?" Lindsay asked.

"That's right, I never told you about my benefactor, did I?" Christine said. "He's the guy who adopted me. I don't call him Dad because he's never acted like one. Honestly, I can't see him as anything other than a pervy old man with a loli fetish."

Lindsay tilted her head. "Loli fetish?"

"But he does pay for my apartment and all of my necessities, so he's not all bad," Christine continued, ignoring the questioning stare of her friend. "We don't talk very often, though. I'm not even sure where he is right now."

Thinking of Orin made her wonder what that perverted old monkey was doing. Knowing him, he was probably hitting on some unfortunate young lady, or getting his ass kicked for hitting on said unfortunate young lady.

"Doesn't he at least call you?"

Christine shrugged. "Of course he does. He calls at least once or twice a year to make sure I'm doing okay."

"That's so sad." Lindsay hugged herself around the waist. "My parents are usually busy with their own lives, but I at least see them every day and know they love me." She suddenly shuddered. "My mom, at least, sometimes displays a little too much love for me."

Christine snorted in amusement. "Whatever, it's not like I really care about that. I've lived on my own for most of my life. Not being able to see a man I've only met a few times is no skin off my bones."

"Don't you ever get lonely, though?"

Christine looked at Lindsay and then averted her gaze.

"Sometimes," she admitted. "I've been alone all my life, so it doesn't really bother me too much, but there have been times when I wished someone was there for me. Ah! B-but it's not like I'm lonely or anything! I'm not! I just would've liked someone to occasionally talk to! That's it!"

"Hm. So you get lonely occasionally?" asked Lindsay.

"N-not in the least!" Christine felt a chilling coldness rise to her ears. They were most definitely turning blue. It wouldn't have surprised her if steam was rising from them as well.

"What about now? Are you still lonely?"

The coldness that had spread to her cheeks slowly vanished at her friend's questions. Calming herself with several deep breaths, she looked at Lindsay as the other girl stood up and walked over to her, and then glanced away.

"N-not recently," she said, stuttering only a bit. "Not since— kya! What are you doing?!"

Christine squawked as Lindsay pounced on her, sending them both spilling to the floor. She hit her head on the carpet, again, and then squeaked when she realized that someone was sitting on top of her. It was, of course, Lindsay. Her tomboyish friend was wearing the largest, creepiest grin that Christine had ever seen.

"I think someone needs a hug!" Lindsay sang as she leaned down, presumably to give Christine a hug.

"I do not need a hug! Get! Off! Get—kya! Stop that! W-what are you—WHERE ARE YOU TOUCHING?!"

It was during this moment, as Christine and Lindsay rolled around on the floor, looking almost like a pair of lovers in the middle of a hot make-out session, that Mrs. Diane opened the door.

"Dinner's ready, you two—"

She stopped.

And stared.

Neither Lindsay nor Christine noticed her peering into the room, thus they continued rolling around on the floor. To the impressionable mother, it looked like her daughter was having a *very* heavy petting session with her loli lesbian lover.

"I'll just... leave some food in the fridge for you two to grab whenever you're hungry," she said, slowly shutting the door behind her and walking the other way. She could still hear their voices coming from the other side of the door, however.

"Hahaha! Come on! What's wrong with a little affection between friends?"

"Just because we're friends doesn't mean you can—H-hey! What the—cut it out, Lindsay! Stop grabbing me—no—wait! Don't!—iyahn!"

***

"Nya..."

Cassy Belladonna looked at her depressingly empty fridge. Her stomach was rumbling and she was on a quest to find some food. Most unfortunately, there wasn't much—a slice of cheese, an almost empty carton of milk, and half of a fish. It was barely enough to make a halfway decent meal.

I guess this is what happens when you fail all your missions.

Feeling awfully downtrodden about her lack of foodstuffs and her failure to kill Lilian Pnéyma, Cassy took everything that she had left and prepared a paltry meal for dinner.

She sat down at her small, rickety table in silence. Her chair creaked precariously underneath her weight. She didn't weigh much, barely a hundred and ten pounds. The chair was just that old and decrepit, much like the rest of her residence.

Cassy lived in a studio apartment in the bad part of Phoenix. The worn walls had paint peeling off and the ceiling had several holes in it. She thanked the Shinigami that it didn't rain very often in Arizona. Even so, she kept several buckets on hand for when the stormy season came. Much like the walls, the floors were old, weathered, and ragged, while the carpet was rundown and missing chunks in several places. Her furniture, too, held the appearance of something that she had found in a junkyard.

This apartment didn't actually belong to her. The complex that it was located in was rundown, derelict, and abandoned. The person who had owned it died several years ago, supposedly murdered, and no one wanted to live in it afterward. It would have been demolished and constructed into something new, but because of its inconvenient location, the government had decided not to waste the money and left it standing—a ghost complex in the middle of the ghetto.

After her disappointingly sparse dinner, Cassy lay down on her ratty old couch, the torn fabric scratching her skin as she tried to get comfortable. She didn't have a bed, just the couch. It was, in fact, one of only six pieces of furniture in her entire apartment.

Before she could get too comfortable, a loud ringing penetrated her eardrums. Cassy winced as she sat up and fumbled around inside one of the pockets of her leather pants. She pulled out her cellphone, accepted the call, and placed it against her ear. Only one person could have been calling her. Only one person even had this number.

"M-Mistress Sarah," she stuttered, "I didn't expect you to call while I'm on nya mission, nya."

"On a mission? Truly?" The person on the other end was a woman with a young, yet harsh-sounding voice. *"Is that what you're calling it? You failed to kill your target, and now, instead of returning in shame like you should have, you're loafing around in Phoenix. I should have you locked up for insubordination."*

Cassy winced, but she still tried to defend herself. "B-but you never gave me the order to return!"

"Because I had decided to allow you this chance," her mistress explained. *"Since you were so eager, I thought I would let you prove yourself to me. Unfortunately, much like I have come to expect, you've proven yourself to be nothing but a sore disappointment. Not only have you failed to kill your target, but you spent more time hanging around that boy you're so fond of... while in the presence of your target, I might add."*

Even though she was only speaking to her mistress through the phone, Cassy couldn't keep the shiver from escaping her. "N-nya, th-that's because..."

"That is because you are a failure," Mistress Sarah spoke harshly. *"You've never once completed the missions given to you. Every single one of them has ended in failure."* A tired sigh came from the other end. *"I honestly have no idea how someone with so much talent can be such an abject failure, but there you have it."*

Cassy didn't know what was worse: Her mistress's harsh words, or the fact that everything her mistress said was true. "I-if you give me one more chance, I'm sure I could—"

"You have been given many chances," Mistress Sarah cut her off. *"Too many. Twenty-four missions I have sent you on and twenty-four missions you have failed. This is the last straw, Belladonna. I can't have you lowering the reputation of my village."*

"You're ordering me back?" Oh, that was not good. Receiving an order to return was the same as being told that she was a failure, which she didn't need anyone telling her. She already knew that she was a failure.

"No, not yet at least," Mistress Sarah said, but before Cassy could sigh in relief, the woman spoke some more. *"You are too talented to just take back. However, I have come to the conclusion that you lack the necessary ability to harden your heart and steal your mind to complete your assignments. That is why I have decided to assign you a tutor. He will teach you, train you, and work with you on this assignment. You will listen to him and do everything that he tells you to. I will not suffer another failure on your part."*

"Yes, Mistress," Cassy replied meekly.

"Good."

A soft *click* emitted from the other end and the line went dead. Cassy dropped the phone on the floor and lay back on the couch, raising her left arm and covering her face.

"Nya..." she moaned piteously. "It looks like my life is going from bad to worse."

In the stillness of her apartment, the only sound to be heard was that of the crickets chirping.

"I didn't even find out who she was sending, did I?"

***

Long after the sun had gone down and everyone else went to sleep, Kotohime remained awake.

She stood on the balcony, staring up at the night sky. A million stars shone with a brilliant luster, their formations creating shapes and patterns that Kotohime recognized but was not necessarily familiar with. The world of twilight was so different from daytime; it was a beautiful vision of the phantasmagoric night given form by the moon goddess, Tsukiyomi-no-Mikoto.

Hovering several feet above the ground in front of her was a kudagitsune, the small, ephemeral creature's tube-like wraith body giving it away. Kotohime extended a small scroll for the creature, which took the parchment into its mouth, swallowing it and causing the entire thing to disappear. The kudagitsune promptly took off into the night.

She waited until it was gone, and then walked back into the living room. She noted with some amusement that Iris was no longer on the couch. Kotohime assumed that the girl had snuck into Lilian-sama and Kevin-sama's bed again. It was something that she'd been doing a lot, especially recently. Whether she was doing this as a means of pranking her sister and her sister's mate, or simply because she didn't want to sleep alone, Kotohime had no idea.

As she stepped further into the apartment, a noise caught her attention. She paused and tilted her head, listening.

"Hawa-hawa-hawa-hawa... zzz... hawa-hawa-hawa-hawa..."

A small droplet of sweat formed on her temple and trailed down the right side of her face as Camellia-sama walked into the room. The woman's eyes were closed, her mouth was half-open, and she was completely naked.

Is she sleepwalking?

After further observation, Kotohime determined that Camellia-sama was, without a doubt, sleepwalking. Her gait was slow and stumbling. She'd bump into a wall, turn around and walk off in another direction, only to bump into another wall.

Kotohime trailed after the woman, unsure whether or not she should wake Camellia-sama up. The decision was soon taken out of her hands when Camellia-sama opened the door to Kevin-sama's room and walked in. The door shut behind her, leaving the hallway in stark silence.

"Oh, my," was all Kotohime could say

CHAPTER 2

Making an Attempt at Returning to Normality

I WATCHED AS LILIAN CRUMPLED TO THE GROUND, a water spear sticking out of her stomach and erupting from her back. A soundless scream tore from my throat, but I could barely hear it. My own heart pounded in my ears, uneven staccato bursts that pumped blood irregularly through my veins. I stared at the fallen form of my mate, the girl who'd pledged her life to me, and who I had pledged my life to in return.

Then I looked at the woman who had hurt Lilian. Her six tails swayed like velvety serpents, blacker than night except for the white tips on the ends. Long raven hair covered a face that, much like every other kitsune I'd come to know, was aesthetically appealing to the eye. Even her condescending smile was sexy in its own way.

I cared for none of that. This woman had just harmed my mate; she had just hurt the person who I had come to cherish more than anyone else.

The gun felt heavy in my hand.

I looked down at it, a standard military grade pistol, 9mm, black, and with a laser-sighted scope situated on top. I raised the gun and took aim at the woman whose back was turned. The sound of gunfire filled the air…

… and my hands became stained with blood.

***

Kevin awoke with a startled jerk.

His eyes flew open. He looked around wildly. He relaxed upon recognizing his room; the white walls and ceiling, the anime and sports posters taped to the walls, the bookshelf containing his massive collection of anime and manga, the sexy lace panties hanging from his ceiling fan. Yes, he recognized this place like the back… of… his… hand…

Wait. What?

Kevin blinked several times before realizing that, yes, there was indeed racy underwear hanging from his ceiling fan: Black panties with floral embroidery. Gauzy. He would have assumed that they were Iris's, but she didn't wear underwear. Lilian's then. He also noticed that there was more underwear hanging from the ceiling fan, too, several pieces of sexy undergarments that most would have considered highly inappropriate for a teenage girl to possess—never mind the fact that Lilian was actually a hundred and sixty years old.

"How did those get up there?" he asked no one in particular.

Someone answered him anyway. "I put them there. I've strung up several more along the other ceiling fans in the apartment, too."

"Ah, I see," Kevin said. He blinked, and then he looked down at a familiarly grinning face. "And why would you do that?" Another blink. "And what are you doing in my bed?"

Iris gave Kevin a wicked grin from where she lay resting against him. He didn't know how she'd done it, but somehow, the Void Kitsune had managed to slip in between him and his mate, worming her way into his and Lilian's mutual embrace. It was impressive; he hadn't even felt her when she'd done it.

What the heck? Is this girl a freaking ninja or something?

34

"It's been a while since I've done any pranks," Iris explained why she'd strung up Lilian's underwear, which he guessed made sense. Kitsune were pranksters, so naturally, they must have enjoyed playing pranks.

"As for why I'm in your bed," Iris continued, squirming against him. Her left thigh bumped into his morning wood. Her eyes danced mischievously as he tried to glare at her, even though his face was warm enough that he could practically feel its incandescence. "Well, I just don't like sleeping alone." Long black hair tickled his skin as she lay her head back on his chest. "You and Lily-pad are warm, and it's still chilly outside."

She and Lilian used to share a bed when they were younger, or so he'd been told. That had stopped after Lilian met a young—at the time—Kevin. After that, the redhead had decided that he was going to be her mate and stopped sleeping with Iris because, and he quoted, *"Human relationships are between a man and a woman only,"* or something like that.

Iris had argued with Lilian, but she'd been rather firm on this and denied her sister every time the subject was brought up. From what he knew, his and Lilian's first meeting had also been when Lilian decided to stop "experimenting" with Iris.

Kevin didn't understand the nature of their relationship back then, but he tried not to think about it. The last thing that he wanted to think about was a lesbian twincest relationship. Doing so would have only given him a headache.

"I see," Kevin said. "And why is *she* in my bed?"

Iris turned her head to see who Kevin was talking about. She paused as if startled by the sight.

Camellia lay on his other side. She was snuggling with him as if he were a giant hug pillow, and drool was leaking from her mouth onto his chest as she snored away.

"Hawa-hawa-hawa-hawa… zzz… hawa-hawa-hawa-hawa…"

Yes, those snores.

While Kevin tried to figure out how the heck this situation had happened, Iris was rather entranced by the vision before her. She had to admit, if only to herself, that the sight of her naked mother cuddled against Kevin's bare chest appealed to the more primal side of her.

Also, her mom had some really nice boobs. She hoped hers grew to be that big when she fully matured. How big were those anyway? A hundred and four centimeters? They must have been somewhere around there.

"Why are you looking at me?" Iris asked, shaking her head. "I didn't even know she was in bed with us." She paused. Her eyes turned up toward the ceiling fan, which she stared at in absent delight. Some of that underwear hanging from the ceiling was actually her mom's. "Come to think of it, how did she get in here without waking any of us up? Mom's a klutz. There's no way she should have been able to walk in without causing a massive ruckus."

"Hawa-hawa-hawa-hawa… zzz… hawa-hawa-hawa…"

They certainly wouldn't be getting any answers from the woman herself. Camellia didn't appear to be getting up anytime soon.

"Ne, Iris?"

"Mm?"

Iris looked back at Kevin, who was staring at her mom with an unfathomable expression. The look on his face was deeper than normal. Of course, his expressions had grown more contemplative in recent months. Perhaps it was a sign that he was maturing.

"Do you know why your mom became the way she is now?" he asked. Expressive blue eyes stared at her like an open book. She could practically feel the sympathy he felt for her mom radiating from him. "She wasn't always like this, was she? Something must have happened to make her become the way she is now, right?"

Iris frowned. Delicate fingers splayed against Kevin's chest as she slowly crawled out from between him and Lilian.

The normal sense of mischief that she felt was gone. This was not a topic that she particularly enjoyed talking about, nor was it one that she would've told to anyone else. But, perhaps she could tell this boy since he was her sister's mate.

As she deliberated, Kevin's eyes unbiddenly trailed over the inch of bare shoulders and glorious cleavage as her sleepwear, sexy negligée the color of twilight, slid down her curvaceous frame. He stiffened in more ways than one when light pink nipples peeked out from behind her loose-fitting clothes.

Iris smirked down at him, her lips tracing an artful curve that held a hint of mystery as if those lips were the holders of a most beautiful, dangerous secret. She opened her mouth to speak—

"Mom's condition is our fault," a voice said before Iris could answer.

Kevin and Iris turned to Lilian, now awake and looking at them both. She must have been awake for some time because there was no sleepiness in her eyes. Had she been watching them?

Lilian placed a hand on Kevin's chest, her fingers tickling his skin. She seemed to enjoy the way his pectorals twitched.

"Lilian," Kevin whispered, smiling at his mate.

She returned his smile. "Good morning, Beloved."

Iris was forgotten more quickly than Son Goku running away from needles.

Lilian moved in and pressed her lips to his in a kiss. Kevin welcomed her, deriving great pleasure from the feel of her softer-than-silk lips against his. His one free hand—the one not pinned between Camellia's glorious breasts—reached up to gently cup her cheek. He rubbed circles against her fair, unblemished skin with his thumb.

The kiss became something more when Kevin opened his mouth and Lilian slipped her tongue inside. It danced around his, and Kevin had no trouble dancing back, caressing and rubbing his tongue against hers, entwining them together like two slippery serpents.

Lilian moaned into his mouth. It was a sensual sound that caused his already awakened libido to skyrocket. Few things could drive him mad the way that Lilian's moans could—and most of those things involved Lilian in some way, shape, or form.

Lilian's legs rubbed against his, and the spine-tingling caress of her bare skin sent his body into a hyper-aware state. Her panty-clad crotch grinding into his thigh inflamed his desire. Her breasts as they pressed into his chest sent his mind into a downward spiral of pleasurable delirium.

His hand slid from her cheek to her neck. He threaded his fingers through her soft hair, then pulled her closer, so that he might partake in more of her oh-so-wonderful lips. As their kiss deepened, his hand slid down her neck, roamed across her back, and planted itself firmly on her left butt cheek, which he proceeded to knead like a baker kneading dough.

"Hawa-hawa-hawa-hawa... zzz... hawa-hawa-hawa-hawa."

It was too bad they were interrupted by some of those unusual snores.

Lilian reluctantly released Kevin's lips. The string of saliva that connected them broke when she moved away. She then turned her gaze toward the source of the snores, her mother, who was still snuggling with Kevin on his other side and drooling on his chest.

"Hawa-hawa-hawa-hawa... zzz... hawa-hawa-hawa-hawa..."

Lilian looked back at Kevin, a single, perfectly manicured eyebrow raised, as if asking, *"Dare I ask why my mom is laying in our bed?"*

Kevin properly interpreted her expression and shrugged. "I don't know how or when she got into our bed. I woke up this morning and she was just there."

"Mom does have a tendency to sleepwalk," Lilian said with a sigh.

"Does she really?" asked Kevin.

"Oh, yes. I'm actually surprised this hasn't happened sooner." Lilian paused. "Ah, but then again, there probably hasn't been a very good time to add a sleepwalking scene yet, you know, 'cause it's not really relevant to the plot."

"Right." Kevin nodded his head. "I suppose that sort of fanservice wouldn't really be important to the—wait." He looked at his mate strangely. "The plot?"

"We'll deal with her later," Lilian determined, and her smile took a turn for the sexy as her bright, gorgeous eyes, half-lidded in barely restrained desire, captured him again. Kevin's heart rate sped up when her face came so close to his that their noses were touching. "I want to spend some more quality time with my mate."

She leaned in even closer, close enough that her lips touched his with the barest of caresses. Kevin slowly closed his eyes as Lilian did the same. Just a little bit more and—

"You know, this is really sexy to watch and all, but it kinda makes me feel like you two are forgetting about me, and that's just not right," Iris said.

Their eyes snapped wide open again. They turned their heads to look at Iris, who must have moved away while they were kissing. She was laying on her side, closer to the edge of the bed. One hand was being used as a headrest. Her other hand had mysteriously vanished underneath the covers, which hid her hips from view. Judging from her half-lidded eyes, the blush on her cheeks, the seductive curvature of her lips, and the fact that her breathing had increased, Kevin could take an educated guess as to what her hand was doing down there.

"Morning, Lily-pad." Iris's smile was a combination of love and mischief. "How did you sleep?"

"Why are you in mine and Kevin's bed?" Lilian asked, her right eyebrow twitching.

"Why ask a question that you already know the answer to?"

Lilian's left eyebrow joined the right in twitching, but then she sighed.

"I suppose I walked into that one," she admitted.

"You definitely did," Iris agreed.

"Don't agree with me," Lilian grumbled, and then shook her head. She refocused her attention on Kevin. "Anyway, you wanted to know why Mom acts the way she does, didn't you?"

"Um, ah, y-yes," Kevin said, his cheeks growing warm. "I had almost forgotten about that."

Iris snorted in amusement. "Of course you did. Not that I blame you. If Lily-pad greeted me with a kiss like that, I'd forget all about whatever I was talking about, too."

More warmth rose to Kevin's cheeks. In the wake of Lilian's enthusiastic and rather welcome greeting, he'd completely forgotten that Iris was also in the bed with them... and their mom too. Seriously, who does that?

Lilian sent a look of mild disapproval at her sister, but she soon went back to focusing on Kevin.

"Anyway, Mom's condition is actually our fault," Lilian said, answering the question that Kevin had posed to Iris. "One of the things you must understand is that the Void and Celestial powers are diametrically opposed to each other. If Celestial powers are the powers of creation, then the Void is the negation of concepts. They aren't meant to coexist—certainly not within the womb of a woman at the exact same time. Our birth shouldn't have been possible."

Lilian sat up, her wondrous thighs straddling his waist. Kevin tried not to squirm when the back of her bum pressed into the pitched tent in his boxers.

"I think I understand what you're getting at," Kevin said, struggling to put his theory into words. "You two are sort of like the opposite of magnetic attraction. North will always attract south and vice versa, while north will be repelled by another north, same as with south. In your case, you and Iris are opposites, Celestial and

Void, north and south, but rather than attract, your powers repel each other in the same way that two magnetic poles of the same type would."

"Yeah, I guess that's one way of looking at it," Lilian said.

"That was a really unnecessarily complicated way of explaining it, though," Iris added. "It would be better to simply think of these forces in terms of elements. You know about the elements, don't you, Stud?"

"Of course I do." Kevin huffed, somewhat annoyed at being asked such a stupid question. Who did this foxy nee-chan think she was talking to? And why was he thinking about her using the Japanese term for sister? "I learned about the elements a week after Lilian started living with me."

"It was in book one," Lilian supplied helpfully.

"Right, right. I wasn't in that volume, was I?" Iris said, idly twirling a strand of hair between her fingers. "Alright, let's do a recap then. There are several elements that we yōkai use based on the pulse within our blood. The five elements of the lower tier are simple: fire, river, lightning, wind, and earth. Each of these elements has exactly two things in common. They each have a strength and a weakness to another element."

Reaching between her breasts, Iris pulled out a notepad and a marker. After scribbling on it for several seconds, she showed her drawing to Kevin. It was a diagram detailing the five lower-tiered elements. They were drawn in the form of a pentagon, with fire being on top. Two arrows were traveling along the pentagon, one on the outside going clockwise titled "strength," and one on the inside titled "weakness" that moved counterclockwise.

"Fire is weak against river but strong against wind, wind is weak against fire but strong against lightning, lightning is weak against wind but strong against earth, earth is weak against lightning but strong against river, and river is weak against earth but strong against fire. These elements create a sort of circle of weaknesses and strengths, ensuring that no one element is stronger than any other."

Iris paused to make sure that Kevin had absorbed everything. This was a pretty big info dump, so she wanted to ensure that she wouldn't have to explain this again. Explaining this crap wasn't her expertise anyway. She was a seduction specialist, not an Inari-damned teacher.

Kevin nodded. She continued.

"The same holds mostly true for middle-tier elements as well, though it's far more complicated than this simple explanation," Iris continued explaining in an oddly lecturing tone of voice. "Due to the esoteric abilities of the middle-tier, there are even more weaknesses and countermeasures and additional attributes that can be contributing factors when determining elemental strengths and weaknesses."

Lilian moved off him as Kevin sat up and leaned against the headboard while Iris drew another diagram. His mate followed his example, resting her back against his chest as she sat between his legs. Camellia mumbled a soft "hawa" before sprawling herself across his and Lilian's legs, her position highly reminiscent of an overgrown cat affectionately cuddling with its owner.

Iris showed Kevin another diagram. This one was vastly more complicated than the first one.

"These are the middle-tier elements: forest, ocean, magma, and ghost or spirit. Now, this is a lot more complicated than the lower-tier elements, which are simpler due to the fact that each element is incredibly basic. Forest is weak against magma and fire but strong against ocean and river. Ocean is weak against forest and earth but strong against fire and magma. Magma is strong against forest and earth but weak against river and ocean. They are the simpler three elements of the middle-tier due to their composition being strictly related to earthly elements."

"I like to think of them as the triad of the middle-tier elements," Lilian added.

Kevin's face scrunched up. "Isn't the Triad some kind of transnational criminal organization based out of Hong Kong? I think I saw a documentary on them once... or maybe it was a movie. I can't remember."

"I think it was in an anime, actually," Lilian said.

"Hmm... maybe..."

"Oi! Are you two going to keep talking or can I continue? Because if you don't want to hear my super info-dumpy, yet very genre-savvy explanation, then please continue."

Lilian and Kevin sheepishly looked at Iris. The sexy, raven-haired female coughed into her hand and grumbled about idiotic nerds before continuing.

"Anyway, that explanation is very basic. There are a lot of factors to consider when it comes to elemental weaknesses for the middle-tier, but I don't want to get into those right now."

"Lazy," Kevin said.

"Super lazy," Lilian added.

"Pipe down while sensei explains the other element," Iris snapped. "Anyway, the last middle-tier element is the ghost element, which is sometimes called the spirit element. It's what we call a non-elemental element. Of course, we call it an element, but it's really not. All beings who can use the ghost element have the ability to manipulate the lost spirits wandering the world and, if they have enough youki and training, they can control powerful forces from the spirit world."

"Like hellfire," Lilian said. "Hellfire is a spirit technique that doesn't create fire, but brings fire from the spirit world into the physical world."

"Right." Iris nodded at Lilian's addendum. "Anyway, that element has no real weakness, but it also doesn't have any strengths either. You could consider it a neutral element that exists outside of the main elements." A pause. Iris capped her marker. "And those are the lower and middle-tiered elements."

There was a moment of silence. Then…

"That was a pointlessly long explanation," Lilian said.

"Quite needless, if you ask me," Kevin added.

"Don't diss my explanation!" Iris snapped.

"But I think I understand," Kevin continued. "It's actually not that difficult to grasp. It just takes some time to understand the concepts."

It probably helped that he'd read so much manga and watched so many anime with similar powers and abilities to these kitsune that he could make the connections by using them as reference points.

"Hmm. Good." Iris smiled at Kevin. "I'm glad to see that you're more than just another set of muscles."

Kevin rolled his eyes. "Just because I'm into exercising doesn't mean I'm an idiot, you know. Anyway, after all this talk about elements and whatnot, I assume the top-tiered elements, Celestial and Void, are different from the lower and middle tiers, right?"

"That's right," Iris said, once more making herself comfortable by sprawling onto her side. While her left hand pillowed her head, her right traced idle circles on her naked hip. Kevin did his best not to look. "However, I've been talking for way too long and don't really feel like explaining the rest, so I'll leave that to Lily-pad."

Lilian frowned at her fraternal twin, but she began explaining the concept of Celestial and Void powers to Kevin.

"You already know that Celestial and Void powers are diametrically opposed to each other; they are each other's weakness and strength. Celestial powers will always be able to destroy Void powers, and Void powers will always be able to negate Celestial powers. A battle between a Celestial user and a Void user will always come down to who has more strength, more youki, more experience, and more powerful techniques."

As Lilian explained the differences between Celestial powers and the Void to Kevin, Iris glanced at her mom. The woman was still snoring. Drool was still leaking down her face. She really was an adorable ditz.

Meanwhile, Lilian continued her lecture. "The most important thing you need to know in order to understand Mom's situation is that these two elements cannot be combined for any reason. Combining two elements that are so incompatible can lead to nothing but mutual destruction. The absolute nothingness of oblivion will always reject the natural ways of the world as dictated by those of divine influence."

Kevin tried to wrap his mind around everything that Lilian was telling him. It was hard. He understood the part about them being opposites, but subjects like "oblivion" and "divine influence" confused him. Maybe it was because he simply didn't know enough about these two powers, or maybe there was more to learn about her world than he'd realized. He didn't have an answer.

"Now imagine, if you will, a boiling pot with these two forces being mixed together inside of it," Lilian said, and Kevin did exactly that. Lilian's green eyes softened when he winced. "You can imagine how... ugly such a thing would be, right?"

Kevin grimaced. "Yeah... it certainly doesn't paint a pretty picture."

"Right... so, now imagine that my mom is the boiling pot in which these two incredibly powerful, yet mutually opposing forces are being mixed together in order to create two new lifeforms."

Kevin's wince was more pronounced this time. He looked at Lilian, who now had tears in her eyes.

"Our birth should have never been possible," Lilian explained, her eyes downcast. "Our mom should have died when she became pregnant with us, yet she somehow survived and gave birth. However, you can't survive something like that and not expect to pay a price. That price was the near-complete destruction of her mind."

Kevin closed his eyes. He suddenly felt sick to his stomach.

"I'm sorry," he said, his voice a whisper. "I should have never brought this up."

Lilian's right hand on his cheek forced Kevin to open his eyes. She had shifted so that she was facing him, and though her smile was tremulous, it also spoke reassurances that eased Kevin's tumultuous emotions.

"It's okay," she said. "I don't really mind telling you this. I actually had been expecting to tell you this sooner, but so much has happened that we never had the time."

Her hand gently caressed his cheek. Kevin leaned into her touch and placed a kiss on her palm. This caused Lilian to release a pleasant hum as she moved her hand over his lips. She looked about ready to try sticking her fingers into his mouth.

From her place on the bed, Iris watched the two get all lovey-dovey again with a sigh. It seemed that even depressing subjects like this weren't enough to make them stop—or maybe it was because this subject was so depressing that they did it. Mutual reassurance and support and all that.

"Hey," Iris said as something suddenly occurred to her. "Do either of you find it odd that we just had a long-winded info dump about kitsune powers and how it pertains to Mom while lying on the bed in nothing but lingerie and boxers, and with the very woman we're talking about, who happens to be completely naked, sleeping on top of you two?"

Lilian and Kevin blinked. They looked at each other, and then at their distinct lack of clothing—Kevin wore a pair of boxers and Lilian was in a large T-shirt and lace panties—and then they turned their attention to Camellia. She was still dozing away while sprawled across their laps.

She was still naked.

"Hawa-hawa-hawa-hawa... zzz... hawa-hawa-hawa-hawa..."

She was also still snoring.

"I really want to be surprised and freaked out by this realization, but for some reason, I can't," Kevin admitted.

Lilian nodded her head. "I know what you mean. I personally blame the author. If you weren't put into so many perverted situations like this, you'd probably be experiencing more shock. Then again, maybe that's a good thing. It does get kind of annoying to watch you constantly freak out after a while."

Kevin had no idea what she was talking about. "What?"

"Nothing." Lilian dismissed Kevin's question with a wave of her hand. "Anyway, why don't we take a shower and get ready? We've got school today, and I don't want to miss breakfast because we were running late."

"Right."

The trio was just about to vacate the bed and get a start on their day when a loud, frightened shout, followed by several equally loud thumping sounds, resounded from somewhere within the apartment.

"My lady?! My lady?! Where are you?! MY LADY?!"

Kevin, Lilian, and Iris all facepalmed at the same time.

***

Breakfast at the Diane residence was awkward. Lindsay couldn't put her finger on it, but she could definitely tell that something was up with her parents—her mom, in particular, was acting really weird.

After waking up and taking a shower, she and Christine had gone into the kitchen, where her mother was cooking breakfast and her father sat at the dining room table, a cup of coffee sitting before him and a newspaper in his hands. While her father didn't seem to have noticed the odd tension that hung in the air, greeting her and Christine with his usual gruff "Good morning," Lindsay's mother had been acting odd—er, odder than she usually did.

Considering how strange her mother acted on the best of days, that she seemed to be acting even more eccentric was cause for alarm.

They sat at the dining room table. Christine was on her left, absently munching on a piece of toast. Her friend didn't seem to have noticed the abnormal tenseness in her mom's posture, nor the way her mom's eyes kept traveling from her to Christine. Lindsay wondered what her mom was thinking.

"So, um, Lindsay dear." Her mom coughed into her hand. Christine and Lindsay both looked at the plump woman. Her dad didn't so much as spare them a glance. "I've noticed that you and Christine are, uh, awfully close."

Lindsay blinked. What an odd thing to say. Was she just now noticing this?

"Well, of course. Christine is one of my best friends. It's only natural that she and I would be close."

Lilian was also one of her best friends, but she spent most of her time with Kevin.

"Best friends?" Mrs. Diane scrutinized her daughter far more than Lindsay felt comfortable with, leaning over the table and gazing at her with a narrow-eyed look.

Okay, now things are getting weird. Is Mom glaring at me?

"Uh... are we supposed to be something else?" Lindsay, despite being on the opposite side of the table, tried to lean back in her seat. She took a brief moment to curse how these straight-backed chairs didn't let her lean away from her mom's penetrating gaze. "What are we supposed to be if not best friends?"

"Oh, nothing, nothing." Her mom leaned back in her seat, her face relaxing as she laughed in a manner that made Lindsay question the woman's sanity. "Never mind me, dear. Just, uh, continue eating."

Lindsay decided to do just that. In fact, she decided to try her best to forget this whole conversation had ever taken place. Yes, there was no need to remember her mom's odd behavior.

"Ne, Lindsay." Christine leaned over to whisper in her friend's ear. Lindsay became disturbed when her mom started paying abnormal amounts of attention to them again. "Why is your mom acting so damn weird?"

"Heck if I know," Lindsay muttered, going back to her pancakes. "Just try to ignore her. It should make her stop."

"And if it doesn't?"

"Pray that she doesn't act like this forever?"

"... That doesn't inspire much confidence."

***

Kevin vacated the bus with Iris and Lilian. All around them, other students were disembarking from buses and cars and making their way through the school gates.

Desert Cactus High was a massive school that consisted of several large buildings. All of the buildings were modern-looking, square structures, though the library was shaped like a cylinder. It was an open campus, so the buildings were spaced apart. The whole school was surrounded by a gate.

Kevin looked at the school that he'd been attending for the last year and a half, at the people surrounding them. Everyone was laughing and chattering excitedly as they spoke, telling their friends about all of the fun they'd had over spring break—a trip to Mexico, visiting family out of state, and so on.

He clenched his hands into fists as he thought about his spring break.

The first gunshot exploded like a thunderclap in my ears.

Was it wrong that he felt jealous of his peers? Probably. It certainly wasn't right. Nor was it their fault that his spring break, despite having many truly enjoyable highlights, had been overshadowed by the darkness at the end.

Blood splattered against the pavement.

"Beloved? Are you okay?"

A worried voice sounded out beside him, followed by the feel of a soft, delicate hand wrapping around his. Lilian. Upon looking at his mate and seeing the worry in her eyes, Kevin forced the visions into the back of his mind. He couldn't let Lilian or the others worry about him.

"I'm fine," Kevin lied, forcing himself to smile.

"You sure about that? You had a pretty freaky face for a moment there, Stud." Iris, too, seemed a little worried. Kevin was surprised. She didn't seem the type to worry about him. "You looked constipated or something. Have you thought about taking laxatives to help with that?"

And just like that, Iris ruined the moment with her usual commentary.

Kevin twitched. "I'm not constipated, and I don't need laxatives."

"If you say so…" Iris didn't look convinced.

The group soon flowed into the school with the rest of the crowd. Desert Cactus High School was a large institute with over fifteen hundred students, so there were a lot of people jostling them as they walked. Lilian used the opportunity this presented to cling to Kevin's side, which was just alright with him—or it would have been if Iris didn't also try clinging to him.

"Why are you always latching on to me or Lilian?" Kevin asked.

Iris's smirk was quite devilish as she held Kevin's arm to her chest. "I just don't want to get lost in the crowd, Stud. There are so many people here. You don't want me getting lost, do you? Who knows what might happen."

She was trying to rile him up. Iris knew that he didn't like it when she did this. That was why she did it. Unfortunately, he wasn't sure what to do about it. Even though Iris was totally lying about getting lost, it was true that they were trapped within a large crowd, and it was better to stick together.

"Please ignore her, Beloved," Lilian said. "Iris is hoping to get a rise out of you."

"That's not a nice thing to say about your wonderful sister." Iris's lips peeled back in a sexy little grin. "You know that I would never do such a thing. I'm a pure and innocent maiden."

Lilian and Kevin snorted at the same time. Iris was anything but innocent. She was crass, lewd, and didn't have any issues putting herself on display if it meant getting what she wanted. In fact, she loved it when people lusted after her. She basked in the attention.

Just what she wanted out of this particular situation he didn't know, but there was probably some hidden design to her actions.

"It looks like the crowd is beginning to thin out," Kevin said. "You can let go now."

"Don't wanna." Grinning, Iris held onto him even more tightly.

Kevin forced himself not to twitch. "Lilian? Could you please get your sister off me?"

"Hm? Oh, sure thing, Beloved." Lilian smiled at him and promptly directed a pout at Iris. "You've had your fun, Iris. Now stop clinging to my mate. He doesn't like it."

"Hm… I don't feel like it."

Now even Lilian was glaring at Iris. She tugged on Kevin's arm. "Look. You've had your fun. It's time for you to stop messing with Kevin."

"Aww, come on, Lily-pad." Iris tugged back, grinning deviously as she pushed her sister's buttons. "You should learn to be a bit more considerate towards your sister and let her have some more fun. You know, I remember a time when we used to share everything together. Why can't we go back to those simpler times?"

Kevin could actually feel Lilian twitching against his arm. It was like the rumbling before an earthquake.

"I thought I already told you that Kevin isn't interested in going the harem route."

What?

Kevin blinked.

"What are you talking about?" Iris chuckled, her voice oozing condescension as if her sister had just said the dumbest thing ever. "Every guy wants a harem. Why else would harems be so popular among male audiences?"

"Are we really talking about this in school?" Kevin asked. He went ignored.

"The only one who's interested in harems here is you," Lilian retorted.

"Psh! Don't lie, Lily-pad. I know that you also think it would be hot. Come on. You can be honest with me."

Lilian hesitated for all of one second. A flash of something, perhaps reluctance, passed over her face. Then it hardened, becoming determined once more. "I am being honest. Kevin doesn't want a harem, so no harems! Now let! Go!"

"Nope!"

It didn't take long for the two girls to begin fighting with Kevin in the middle—literally. Each of them already had ahold of one of his arms, and they pulled him between them, yanking and tugging as if he was a rope in the middle of the fiercest game of tug-o-war ever.

Kevin groaned and whimpered as he found his arms being pulled on by the fraternal twins. For such delicate-looking girls, these two were way stronger than they appeared, and they weren't even using reinforcement!

"Come on, Lily-pad. Let me have some more fun."

"Absolutely not! It's my duty as Kevin's girlfriend to protect him. Now let go of my mate! And stop calling me Lily-pad!"

Kevin didn't know how he felt about her saying that it was her duty to "protect him." It felt like he'd just taken several hits to his masculinity points—not that he cared about MP. He just wanted these two to let go of him.

My arms are being ripped off!

A crowd formed around the trio. The two girls ignored the crowd, busy as they were playing tug of war with Kevin's arms. Kevin, too, ignored the growing number of people watching them, but that was because the pain of having his arms being ripped out of their sockets made it hard for him to focus.

Someone... anyone... help!!

***

Lindsay and Christine were dropped off by Mrs. Diane, who continued to act oddly all the way to school.

Christine didn't know what was wrong with her friend's mom. However, it felt like the woman was bearing a personal grudge against her. Every time Christine had looked at Mrs. Diane, the mother of one had been glaring at her through the rearview mirror.

It had been as creepy as fuck.

"Your mom creeps me out," Christine said as she and Lindsay entered the school campus.

There were already a lot of people at school. They had woken up a little later than normal, plus there was that issue with Mrs. Diane and her weirdness. Christine eyed the crowd like all of the people were a bunch of worms.

"Yeah... I'm really sorry about her." Lindsay rubbed the back of her neck. "I don't know what's come over her, but she seems to be really... paranoid about something."

"I don't care what she is," Christine grumbled. "I just don't want her staring at me like that anymore."

As they continued on their way to class, Lindsay was greeted by several people. She greeted everyone back with a smile and a wave, chatting with some and just grinning at others. Christine observed it all out of the corner of her eyes. Lindsay was well-liked by a lot of people. It was probably because she was friendly, outgoing, and sporty. It was a stark contrast to her.

Not that Christine cared about being popular. The only people she liked were Kevin, Lindsay, Lilian... and she guessed Iris could be included in that list too, loath though she was to admit it.

Suddenly, without warning, Lindsay stopped walking.

"What's wrong?" Christine asked.

"What do you think's going on over there?" Lindsay pointed at something several feet away.

Christine looked at the crowd that her friend was pointing to. There were a lot of people, and they seemed to have formed a circle around something. She couldn't see past all those heads. Pretty much everyone present was taller than her by at least half a foot.

I hate being so short.

Nya-ha-ha-ha!

Quiet you!

"Don't know." Christine shrugged.

"Wanna go see?" asked Lindsay.

"Not really—h-hey! What the hell are you doing?!"

"Come on. Let's check it out."

"I said I don't want to!"

Despite Christine's protests, she ended up getting dragged behind her friend as the tomboy waded through the crowd of people, using their smaller, more lithe bodies to slip past all of the others until they were standing inside of the massive circle.

And in the center of that circle was…

"What the fuck?" Christine's right eyebrow began twitching.

"Huh, never thought I'd see something like this," Lindsay muttered.

It was like watching two children fight over who got to wear the pretty dress first… only instead of a dress in the center of Lilian and Iris's tug of war, it was Kevin. The poor boy looked like he was experiencing excruciating pain. His face was scrunched up as he groaned, moaned, and whimpered. He looked pitiful.

"That looks painful," Lindsay muttered worriedly. "Christine, do you think we should help—"

"Hey! What the hell are you two doing?! Can't you see you're hurting him?!"

"—Kevin…" Lindsay finished with a mutter, then sighed. "Never mind."

Christine marched up to the pair of kitsune, stopping just a few paces away and staring them down. "Let go of him right this instant!"

Lilian and Iris stopped trying to rip Kevin's arms off and turned their attention to Christine.

"Why should we?" asked Iris. "And why are you even bothering us?"

"Th-that's—" Christine stuttered, her face freezing over like the Arctic. She recovered quickly, however, and presented a strong front once more. "As one of Kevin's friends, it is my right to be concerned about his well-being!"

"Che, whatever," Iris dismissed Christine's words. "Didn't you confess to the stud and get turned down in book four? You don't have any say in what we do with him."

"Th-that's only because Lilian got to him first," Christine hissed, steam now pouring from her ears and hoarfrost gathering around her as she lost control over her powers. Several people—including Lilian, Lindsay, Iris, and Kevin—started shivering. "Had I reconnected with him before Lilian, I would have been the one dating him."

A pause.

"N-not that I want to still date him or anything! Hmph! I've been over Kevin for months now."

Another pause.

"And what's this about a book four?"

"I have to agree with Iris on this one," Lilian added. "This is between me and my sister. Sorry, Christy, but could you please not interfere?"

"Like hell, I will!"

Thus the tug of war began anew, only this time, Christine was also part of the equation. There was no way she would let her friend be pulled around like this. While Lilian and Iris had ahold of his arms, she grabbed onto the front of his shirt.

Kevin, who was pretty much insensate by this point, found himself being tugged in three directions, and, unfortunately, something had to eventually give.

Fortunately for Kevin, the thing that gave wasn't his arms, which would have really sucked because he needed those arms. Because Lilian and Iris were battling each other more than they were Christine, who pulled Kevin from the front as opposed to his sides, they were the ones who ended up losing the tug of war.

Unfortunately, because Christine had been yanking on him with all her might and hadn't been prepared for when he slipped from Lilian and Iris's grasp, both she and he took a tumble. Christine squawked as she landed on her butt, the jolt of her tailbone hitting cement bringing tears to her eyes. Kevin, on the other hand, landed on his stomach.

As consciousness returned to him, Kevin found himself engulfed in darkness, with his nose pressed up against something cottony soft, and kind of musky. He couldn't quite tell what it was, as his brain felt a little fuzzy, but the feel of fabric against his nose and the scent was strangely familiar. It was different from what he was used to, but still, he kind of recognized this smell. Moving his head, his nose brushed against whatever this thing was.

That was when he heard a feminine gasp.

Kevin froze. His eyes began to adjust, and he finally realized what his nose was brushing against. He blinked several times as he stared at the pair of white cotton panties surrounded by two milky-white thighs. He could barely make them out due to the sparse amounts of light trickling in through what he now understood was a skirt… a very long skirt that could have only been worn by their resident goth loli.

"Oh, crap!"

Kevin attempted to scramble out from underneath Christine's skirt. In hindsight, this wasn't the best idea. Because he was so frantic and letting his fear rule him, he ended up doing more harm than good.

He became tangled inside of Christine's skirt.

"W-w-w-WHAT THE HELL ARE YOU DOING?!"

"Gah! I'm sorry!"

"DON'T APOLOGIZE, YOU DOLT! GET THE FUCK OUT FROM UNDER MY SKIRT!"

"I'm trying, but it's harder than it looks! I can't seem to find the exit!"

"Kya! What are you—WHERE ARE YOU TOUCHING ME?!"

"HOW AM I SUPPOSED TO KNOW?! I CAN BARELY SEE UNDER HERE!"

"AND THAT'S WHY YOU SHOULD GET OUT OF THERE!"

"I WILL IF YOU STOP SQUEEZING ME WITH YOUR THIGHS!"

"S-S-S-SQUEEZING YOU?! I-I-I AM NOT—SHUT UP!
SHUT UP, SHUT UP, SHUT UP!"

"G-guh... can't... breathe..."

While Christine and Kevin struggled to escape from their
embarrassing predicament, Lindsay joined Lilian and Iris as they,
along with pretty much everyone else in the vicinity—which had
grown to at least a hundred people since Kevin fell face-first into
Christine's crotch—stared at the pair.

"I feel like I should be bothered right now," Lilian muttered,
frowning. "Like, really, *really* bothered by what's happening."

That you should.

"Oh! It's you," Lilian greeted in surprise. "I haven't heard
from you in a while."

That's because it's hard to write blatantly obvious self-inserts
when the story is flowing so smoothly.

"Ah, yes, I can understand how that would be a problem."
Lilian nodded her head in agreement. Iris frowned.

"So, I'm guessing you're somehow responsible for this..." She
gestured to Kevin and Christine.

They looked like they were wrestling, with Christine's thighs
wrapped around Kevin's head while the young teen struggled to pry
himself out from underneath those thighs and the, by now, twisted
lolita skirt.

Ah. Yes, that would be my doing.

"Fanservice much?"

W-well, I sort of wanted to try my hand at this, you know, to
see if I could do it.

"Uh-huh..." Iris stared at the scene some more. "Well, it
certainly looks like something you'd see in those ecchi fanservice
anime. Still, why Christine?"

Why not?

"Touché," Lilian said.

Lindsay looked at her two friends oddly. "Who are you two talking to?"

"No one," Lilian and Iris said at the same time.

Kevin finally managed to get out from underneath Christine's skirt, a task which had been far harder than it should have been and for all of the wrong reasons. He sat on the ground, his hands pressed against the cement behind his back, gasping for air, his face fire truck red from a combination of oxygen deprivation and having his head squeezed like a lemon between a pair of surprisingly strong thighs. Christine wasn't in much better shape.

"I... I'm really sorry... about that..." Kevin said between pants. Who knew struggling to escape from a woman's skirt could be so tiring?

"It-it's fine," Christine mumbled, her face glowing like frozen lava.

"W-wait." Kevin started in surprise. "You're not mad at me?"

"W-well, i-it's not like this was... was your fault or anything," Christine stuttered a bit. "I mean, we were—that is Lilian, Iris, and I were sort of, well, you know..." As words tumbled from her mouth, the lolita-dressed girl became more and more embarrassed, until she eventually tried to sink her head into her dress. It was absolutely adorable.

"So cute!"

It was so adorable, in fact, that several of the teens present, who just so happened to have a loli fetish, were blasted backward when blood burst from their noses like Blastoise using Hydro Pump. They sailed through the air and crashed into the ground, their nasal sanguination spraying carmine fluids everywhere.

Strangely enough, Lilian, Lindsay, Iris, Christine, and Kevin, who were in the center of the massive jet streams of red fluid, did not get covered in blood. Several other people did, however, and they complained quite loudly.

"Ugh, this is seriously disgusting!"

"Did you people really just get a nosebleed over a little girl? Have you no shame?!"

"I can't believe this!"

"It's going to take forever to get these stains out…"

"S-so, you're not mad at me?" Kevin asked again, ignoring the complaints of everyone around him. Christine shook her head.

"I can't be mad at you." Christine began drawing circles in the ground with her left index finger. "It wouldn't be right if I got mad for something that wasn't your fault."

"A-ah, so I see." Kevin smiled. "Thank you."

Christine squeaked at the sight of his sunny grin, but she managed to also return it with a smile of her own, albeit it wasn't quite as bright. "Y-you're welcome."

"Is it weird that I feel insanely jealous right now?" Lindsay asked in a calm voice.

"I suppose that would depend," Lilian said. "Who are you jealous of?"

"Both of them."

Iris and Lilian stared at Lindsay very, *very* oddly.

"Dyke," Iris muttered.

"Did you say something?"

"Not a thing."

***

"Your love life is really screwed up, Stud," Iris said as she, Lilian, Lindsay, and Kevin resumed their walk to class.

A still blushing Christine had stuttered something about not wanting to be late and departed soon after the whole "face in panties" incident. The girl had been trailing frost and mist in her wake when she left.

"Please don't remind me," Kevin groaned.

"Seriously, you'd think stuff like this wouldn't happen after hooking up with my sister, right? Like your life would be filled with rainbows and bunnies and lovey-dovey crap, right? And yet here you are, having all kinds of ecchi encounters with other women." Iris shook her head in mock sadness. "I almost feel bad for you."

"Oh, shut up," Kevin grumbled. "At least half of those encounters are your fault. And I don't want to hear you calling them ecchi. This isn't a harem comedy, you know."

"Considering the author's thoughts on your love life, it might as well be." Iris grinned at him. "But hey! Think of it this way. You've been hitting so many flags from all the girls around you recently that a harem route might open up for you!"

"Yeah, well, the author needs to burn in hell," Kevin snapped. Then his right eye twitched. "And don't mention harems! Don't mention flags either! My love life isn't an eroge!"

"How about a galge?"

"It's not one of those either!"

"I agree with you, Beloved," Lilian concurred, holding Kevin's arm to her chest. She was, thankfully, the only one doing so this time. "The author should just hurry up and die. Maybe then we'll have someone else write for us and we'll get some halfway decent scenes."

O-oi! That's not a very nice thing to say.

"It's your fault for writing crap."

Mugyu...

"You shouldn't use other people's catchphrases," Iris commented idly. "You might get sued for plagiarism or something."

"Are you ever going to tell me who you're talking to?" Lindsay asked.

"Now where would the fun in that be?" Iris sent Lindsay a sexy little smirk, which caused the tomboyish blonde to flush scarlet and turn her head.

"Probably not," Lilian agreed. "Humans aren't meant to understand this stuff. It would make your brains explode... or something."

"Then why do you two keep doing this in front of me?" asked Kevin. "What am I? Chopped liver?"

"You're different." Lilian gave her mate a fond gaze. "You're my mate, which makes you special. Remember what Kotohime said? Long-term exposure to kitsune has granted you a limited version of The Power. That means you're immune to the potential dangers that being around us can cause."

"Ugh, somehow, it feels really wrong when you say it like that."

Lindsay frowned. "But wait. If long-term exposure causes this... power-thingy to manifest, then how come no one but Kevin has it? I've been around Lilian for nearly as long as Kevin, and I haven't gotten this strange power."

"What Lily-pad means to say is that long-term, intimate exposure with kitsune has granted the stud a limited ability to break the fourth wall," Iris explained, smirking at Lindsay. "She's not talking about standard meetings and greetings, but sexual encounters." The smirk widened when Lindsay's face burst into flames. "So, basically, unless you were to become intimate with one of us, or both of us, you wouldn't be able to get the powers that the stud has."

Another pause ensued. Iris's half-narrowed, succubus eyes danced with mirth as she gazed into Lindsay's wide brown ones.

"Maybe you'd like to join Lily-pad and me in our sexcapades?"

"What sexcapades are you referring to?" Kevin squawked, turning to Lilian. "What sexcapades is she talking about?"

"She's not talking about anything," Lilian assured Kevin. "There haven't been any sexcapades since I fell in love with you."

That appeared to reassure Kevin... until he realized something. "What exactly have you and Iris done together before falling in love with me?"

Lilian went silent, which was unfortunate, because it meant that Iris had free reign to speak. "What haven't we done? You remember how good I was at pleasing Lily-pad during our trip to California? You didn't think that was my first time playing with her, did you?"

Kevin's cheeks gained several shades of red. Lilian's cheeks were also red, but she was defiant enough to glare at Iris. Lindsay looked like someone had shoved her face into an oven.

"Well, if you don't want to get into some lesbian triple play with Lily-pad and I..." Iris continued as if she'd said nothing out of the ordinary. "Maybe you'd like to join Lily-pad, the stud, and me in a four-way orgy?"

"There will be no orgies! And don't ignore Kevin and me! It's rude!" Lilian shouted.

Kevin wanted to tease Lilian about the pot calling the kettle black, but his hormonal teenage mind was having trouble coping with the erotic imagery that Iris's words had invoked—and he wasn't the only one.

Within the confines of her mind, in a small section that contained all of her innermost desires, Lindsay was inundated with massive amounts of erotically sexual encounters of increasingly questionable ratings.

Less than five seconds after Iris's spoken words, Lilian and Kevin and Iris mutely watched as Lindsay was launched into the air like a cannonball. There were copious amounts of blood spraying from her nose like the jet propulsion system of a rocket.

"Huh..." Kevin muttered in shock. "I didn't realize women could get nosebleeds."

"Of course we can, Beloved," Lilian said as if he'd just mentioned something really stupid. "Women might hide it better than men, but we're just as, if not more, perverted than even some of the most perverted males."

"Except for that friend of yours," Iris added unnecessarily. "No one's more perverted than him."

Then again, Eric wasn't really a human so much as the embodiment of lust and perversion, so perhaps he wasn't the best person to compare someone else to.

"I guess that makes sense," Kevin admitted. "And I do recall you having several nosebleeds before."

Lilian's first nosebleed had been after one of their more stimulating encounters. He remembered Iris mentioning something, which, now that he thought about it, was quite similar to what she'd mentioned just now. Lilian had been sent crashing into the ceiling back then, such had been the power of her nosebleed.

Lilian blushed. "I had been hoping you would forget about that."

"Not on your life. I'm keeping that little memory tucked away for potential blackmail material."

"Are you sure you're not a kitsune?" Iris asked.

Several feet away, Lindsay finally hit the ground. Her body twitched several times as blood continued to pool out of her nose. Kevin took note of the dopey and somewhat perverse smile on her face.

"Well," he started, "I guess it shouldn't come as a surprise that you women are a bunch of perverts. After all, you and Iris both like walking around naked."

"Hawa," Lilian mumbled, her shoulders drooping.

***

Since Lindsay had passed out, the trio had to take the girl to the nurse's office before heading to class. They ended up running a bit late because of this. Kevin could only hope that their homeroom teacher, Ms. Vis, didn't flip out on them.

Entering the classroom as sneakily as they could, the trio noticed that class was well underway. Ms. Vis stood by the whiteboard in all of her pale-skinned, vampire-esque glory. That day she had chosen to wear a brown business suit with a skirt, black stockings, and heeled shoes. She appeared every bit the consummate professional as she lectured the class.

Kevin found this thought funny. He would never call this woman "professional." She was more like "obsessive-compulsive." Several people near the door noticed them, but a glare from Kevin made their mouths snap shut before they could speak.

"... This statement can be tested by comparing the price of each jar of salsa," Ms. Vis was saying as she wrote on the board. "If nine dollars over three jars of red salsa equals three dollars per jar versus eight dollars over four jars of green salsa equals two dollars per jar..."

As Ms. Vis continued her lecture, Kevin, Lilian, and Iris tried to sneak over to their seats.

"Hey, Teach, those three are late!"

They were, most unfortunately, not successful in this endeavor, as one of their peers decided to be a jerk and rat them out. Iris and Lilian made a silent promise to prank the fool for his indiscretion while Kevin just glared at the boy.

Ms. Vis whirled around, her eyes drawn in a furious expression. Her mouth was halfway open, no doubt to verbally ream them for daring to show up late to class.

Then her eyes landed on Lilian. All the emotional hardness on her face evaporated like a cold wind in June. What remained was only warmth. The trio shuddered.

"Lilian!" Like a prepubescent girl who'd bumped into her crush, Ms. Vis squealed as she rushed forward, arms spread wide to engulf the redhead in her fierce embrace.

Kevin and Iris wisely chose to move out of the way. Lilian, having been walking between them, was not so fortunate.

"W-wait! Ms. Vis! Don't—mfffed!"

Mutely staring at the scene with unwarranted solemnity, Kevin stood in place as Ms. Vis proceeded to shove Lilian's head into the valley of her modest chest. If the teacher was a little more attractive and less vampirish, this scene might have actually been pretty hot, like something out of an extremely perverse eroge that featured a yuri teacher and her female student.

"Oh, Lilian," Ms. Vis gushed. "You have no idea how pleased I am to see you again. Not being able to glimpse your lovely face over spring break was pure torture!"

"Mff mrff mff!"

"Get off me," was what Kevin presumed she had said.

"I heard you were in California when that earthquake hit, you poor dear. But don't worry. You're here now, and I'll make sure nothing bad happens to you ever again."

That was what the news had reported happened during the comic convention. Kuroneko had people inside of the news department, and they had reported that an earthquake had broken several water lines.

Kevin was surprised that the people had just accepted the report at face value. That said, he also understood that humans would more readily accept a logical lie than an extraordinary truth.

"Mrffle mrgg! Mmmffff!"

Kevin could not even begin to guess what she was saying that time. It sounded like she was merely stringing monosyllables together.

"Yes, from now on, you shall stay here. Where it's safe."

"MMMRRFFF!"

Lilian's muffled scream echoed throughout the classroom.

***

Lunch had come.

After gym class, Kevin, Lilian, and Iris met up with a recently awakened and extraordinarily mortified Lindsay, and a somewhat amused Christine. Then they proceeded to grab a table for lunch. While Lindsay and Christine had gone to the cafeteria to grab some grub, the trio had pulled out their traditional Japanese bento boxes, which contained their... traditional Japanese lunches.

"I can't believe you two," Lilian grumbled a complaint to her mate and sister respectively. "You two didn't help me at all."

"I really am a fan of Japanese pop culture," Kevin said as he stared at his bento box, his right eyebrow twitching and a vein throbbing prominently on his forehead. "Truly, I am, but this is going a little overboard. Who the heck makes people traditional Japanese lunches in America?"

"Kotohime, obviously," Iris said, idly picking at some of the vegetables with her complimentary chopsticks. "You should know by now that she's a very traditional Japanese woman, a Yamato Nadeshiko in every sense of the word. Of course, she's going to make us a Japanese lunch."

Kevin sighed. "I'm beginning to think I should start making my own lunches again."

"Mou." Crossing her arms, Lilian gave the two her most adorable pout, which was cute enough that if there was a cuteness scale, the redhead would have just broken it. "You two aren't even listening to me."

"Aw, I'm sorry, Lily-pad." Iris pulled her sister close and rubbed her nose into Lilian's hair, inhaling her scent. "Did I make you jealous by speaking with the stud instead of you? Would you like me to make it up to you? Perhaps with a kiss?"

"Uh, no," Lilian deadpanned. "However, if Kevin wants to make up for ignoring me, then a kiss would certainly be the best way to do it... at least until we get home."

While Iris pouted at Lilian, who pulled out of her grasp and scooted closer to her mate, Kevin let out a mild chuckle.

"A kiss, huh?" Kevin scooted closer to Lilian and turned until he was straddling the bench. "I suppose I could give you a kiss..."

Lilian's eyes lit up. Kevin sighed dramatically. "However, I'm not sure if I should. I mean, kissing in a public setting isn't very appropriate, and our school does have a 'no public displays of affection' rule. I'd be loath to break it."

Lilian groaned, causing her mate's lips to twitch. The groan ceased when he laid a hand on her cheek and turned her head toward him. Their faces were so close that their noses were almost touching.

"Still, I do owe you an apology for not helping you with Ms. Vis," Kevin murmured, though Lilian was no longer paying attention. Her eyes had become drawn toward his lips as he spoke. She could think of several things she'd like those lips to be doing. Talking was not one of them.

"So, how would you like to go on a date?" he asked.

"Eh?" The words snapped Lilian out of her stupor. "A date?"

"A date," Kevin repeated. "We haven't been on one for a while now, not since Christmas."

Lilian actually needed a moment to realize something. "Now that you mention it, you're right. It's been a really long time since we've gone on a date."

As one, Kevin and Lilian turned their heads to look at the reason that they hadn't gone on many dates. Iris stared at them, leaning against the bench, elbows propped up on the table. Her dark eyes were glimmering in amusement.

"I don't know why you're looking at me," she said, her wide grin showing off her pearly whites. "I've never stopped you two from going on dates together."

The twitch of Lilian's left eye was the physical sign of her irritation. "No," she said sarcastically. "You've just gone with us every single time, ensuring that we'd never be alone together."

"I had to make sure you two weren't getting up to anything that would bring this story past an M-rating," Iris replied.

"It all happened off-screen!" Lilian snapped.

"And if anything was going to go past an M-rating, it would have been something that you did," Kevin added.

"Hmm… true enough," Iris said, pondering his point. "All right, I guess I can let you two have one date to yourselves."

Like you ever had any choice in the matter, Lilian and Kevin thought at the exact same time.

Joining up with them after getting their meals was Alex, Andrew, Lindsay, and Christine. They sat down in their designated places. Alex and Andrew sat beside Lilian and Kevin, while Lindsay and Christine sat on the other side next to Iris. Upon seeing the lunches that had been prepared for Kevin, Lilian, and Iris, Lindsay just had to speak up.

"Okay, I know you're really into that anime stuff and everything, but do you really need to have Japanese lunches, Kevin? Isn't that taking your obsession a little too far?"

Kevin didn't like being called out on his love for anime. He disliked even more that Lindsay seemed to think this was somehow his fault.

Crossing his arms over his chest, he tossed his friend a mild glare. "I'll have you know that these lunches were not made to my specifications. I might love anime and manga, but I'm not so obsessed with Japanese culture that I would have someone make me traditional Japanese bento." He paused, and then reluctantly added. "No matter how cool it seemed at first."

Lindsay rolled her eyes. "Right, and that's why you've been having those bento-thingies for the past six months."

Kevin's cheeks inflated like a hot air balloon. "The reason we've been having bento lunches for the past six months is that Kotohime insists on making them. It's not like I ask her to make them for us."

"But you never ask her to not make them, do you?"

"…"

"Heh, she's got you there, Stud."

Kevin pointed at Iris. "Not another word out of you!"

"It is kind of odd, though, right?" Alex said after swallowing a bite of his sandwich, roast beef it looked like. Yum. "Don't get me wrong. It's totally cool that you're going full otaku and everything, but seeing you eating a Japanese lunch every day is weird."

"I'm not an otaku," Kevin grumbled.

"You're totally otaku," Alex returned fire.

"Your otakuness knows no bounds," Andrew added with a nod.

"Kevin, you're so otaku that the otakus in Japan are envious of how otaku you are," Christine said, and then blushed when everyone turned and stared at her. "W-w-w-what the hell are you people looking at?"

"Heh." Iris grinned. "I never thought I'd hear you say something like that. It sounds like you know an awful lot about otakus. Is there something that you would like to tell us?"

"W-w-wha—of course not!" Christine shouted. "D-d-don't look too into this or anything! I just don't want to be around Kev— I mean everyone else and not understand what you people are talking about. It's because you guys keep using all these weird terms like otaku and shōnen and desu. You guys are at fault for this! Y-you should take responsibility!"

"Responsibility for what?" Iris fired back, her eyes glowing with delight. "The way you say that makes it sound like one of us fucked you six ways to Sunday." She paused, blinked, and then grinned. It was quite the devious grin. "Or maybe that's what you want? Would you like to have the stud screw you six ways to Sunday?"

Christine's face turned a deep shade of winter blue. Lindsay suspiciously held a hand to her nose. Kevin and Lilian looked at the tomboy as blood leaked between her fingers.

"Wh—that's not—SHUT UP!"

While Iris mercilessly teased Christine until the poor girl looked ready to start flinging icicles, Alex and Andrew continued their merciless assault on Kevin.

"You put the 'k' in otaku."

"When people look up otaku in the dictionary, they see your face."

"You've even got an otaku meme on Twitter."

"Shut up! I am not an otaku!" Kevin stood up and slammed his hands on the stone table. He glared at his friends. "I'm not! Just because I like anime that doesn't mean I'm an otaku. And you two have no right to say anything!" He pointed an accusing finger at Alex and Andrew. "You watch and read just as much anime and manga as I do!"

"You make a good point," Alex admitted. "It doesn't change the fact that you are, indeed, an otaku."

Andrew nodded at his brother's words. "Only a true otaku would deny being otaku."

"No, they wouldn't! Otaku are people who proudly proclaim their status even though they know others will look down on them for it. That's half the reason they get such a bad rep in Japan, and even then, Japanese society has begun to accept otaku culture more readily in the last few years. I once read an article on Rocket News 24 that some people are beginning to think that being otaku isn't something to be ashamed of."

"And how could you possibly know that unless you were an otaku?" Iris teased.

Kevin grabbed his hair and threw his head back. "Arggghhh!"

"Poor Kevin." Lilian giggled. "Getting ganged up on by everyone."

"Ha…" Kevin sat down and pouted at his mate. "You're not really helping me out, you know. You should be backing me up."

"I can only back you up when something isn't true."

"Now you're just being mean."

"I'm sorry," Lilian said in mock contrite, her eyes glittering with mirth. "Would a hug make it better?"

Kevin sniffled. "Maybe."

Lilian spread her arms wide. "Okay. Come here, Kevin."

"Lilian."

"Kevin!"

"Lilian!"

"Would you two knock it off already!" Christine snapped out of her state of perpetual humiliation long enough to shout at the hugging couple.

Conversation continued to flow, changing topics over the course of lunch. Kevin talked and laughed along with his friends. However, despite acting just like he always did, a part of him felt separated from everyone else, isolated. Alone. He no longer felt like he belonged with these people. He didn't deserve to be with them.

That's right. How could I continue spending time with everyone after what I've done?

Kevin had blood on his hands now. He saw it every time he took a shower, carnelian covering his hands that didn't wash off no matter how hard he scrubbed.

Someone capable of killing another so easily doesn't deserve to have friends like this.

His right hand clenched into a fist. What right did he have to be friends with anyone? He was a monster. Only a monster could possibly kill like he had. Only a monster would...

Kevin's thoughts were halted as a warm, soft, and gentle hand moved over his own. He looked down, recognizing the fair skin and long, graceful fingers. He knew who they belonged to. He had held that hand hundreds of times already. He'd also sucked on those fingers, but that was a story for another time.

He followed the hand, up the arm, past the shoulder, and onto the enchanting face of Lilian, whose lips were set in an expression of compassion. She didn't say anything, but her desire to help him, to offer comfort, was so palpable that it felt like a physical thing.

Unconsciously, against his will, Kevin found his body relaxing. He couldn't afford to let these thoughts get to him. He needed to be strong, for Lilian if no one else.

His hand turned in hers and he gripped back. He offered her a soft smile, which was returned, though her eyes still revealed her inner thoughts. They also offered an invitation, one that Kevin saw clear as day within her startlingly beautiful irises.

"Whenever you want to talk, I'll be here," her eyes seemed to say.

"Thank you," Kevin said back.

"Hey, aren't we missing someone?" Lindsay suddenly asked. Kevin and Lilian stopped focusing on each other and turned to look at her. Even Iris had stopped teasing Christine to look at the blonde girl.

"Huh? We are missing someone," Lilian said. "Where's the butt monkey?"

"Who cares?" said Christine, her tone disgusted, as if she was repulsed by the very idea of talking about Eric.

"I'm with the snow woman." Iris ignored the looks that she received for her comment. "Who cares? It's Eric. He's probably peeking on some poor, innocent freshmen girls in the locker room or something."

No one disagreed.

***

"So I, like, totally found this gorgeous dress at the mall the other day. I was going to buy it, but my dad was all, like, no way, we don't have enough money, and I was, like, for realz? You're such a cheapo, Dad."

"Must be hard having a father who doesn't buy you everything you want."

"Was that sarcasm?"

"Of course not."

"How do you make your eye stand out so much?"

"It's just the way I put my eye shadow on. The trick is to…"

"Have you heard about how Justin Bieber was deported to Canada recently?"

"What?! No way!"

"Way."

He was standing within one of the lockers. His back was resting against the metal, and his leering eyes peered out from between the slits. Brimming with lust, Eric was given prime viewing seats to a show that every lecherous male would have given an arm, a leg, and their left testicle for.

They stood just outside of his locker, chatting amicably amongst themselves as they undressed. It was the freshmen girls who'd just gotten out of class and were now changing back into their regular clothes.

Once again, Eric had to bemoan the fact that anime and real-life didn't coincide with each other. For if they did, then surely all of these girls would have been getting naked by now. Ah, well. At least he was still getting to see some budding teenage bodies. That was enough to send his perv-o-meter rocketing sky high.

Hee hee hee! This is perfect! None of them even suspect that I'm here!

He didn't say anything out loud, of course, nor did he let out the perverted old man giggles that he was tempted to release. His master had told him that he needed to be stealthy, which meant no giggling, laughing, or mumbling to himself. It felt kind of wrong, not mumbling and giggling and making commentary on the girls as he peeped, but, well, he had to listen to his master. That woman knew what she was talking about.

And so he continued spying on the girls. Most of them were now in nothing but their underwear. Was this heaven? This must be heaven? There were girls wearing nothing but bras and panties, so this had to be heaven! He was in heaven!

Unfortunately, heaven didn't really agree with Eric, and thus, it all came crashing down soon enough. It started with a slight itching of his nose, followed by a strange tingling in his nostrils, like someone was tickling him with a feather. He tried to ignore it, but the feeling became more and more insistent. It was like that obnoxious feeling people got when they weren't sure if they had properly saved at the last checkpoint in a galge; it only became stronger with time.

Thus the inevitable happened. Eric couldn't hold it in anymore.

"Achoo!"

Time stood still. The noise inside of the locker room stopped. Everything became silent. Bone-chillingly silent. Deathly silent. The silence of a tomb.

Eric held his breath, skin breaking out in a cold sweat. He tried to hide his presence, to mask it by using the ninja techniques that he'd seen on Shinobi Natsumo. It was too bad that Shinobi Natsumo was an anime and not conducive to real life.

The door to his locker opened.

Eric received a full blast of killing intent from a horde of extremely pissed-off women.

"Uh…" Eric grasped at straws as he attempted to think of something, anything, that he could say to get himself out of this situation. "I don't suppose you'll believe me if I tell you that the reason I'm in here is because the guys from the track team thought it would be funny to stuff me in a girl's locker, would you?"

Several girls cracked their knuckles in response to his words. One of them, a girl that he recognized quite well by now, pulled a claymore seemingly out of thin air.

Eric whimpered.

CHAPTER 3

Existential Trauma

THE BELL RANG, a signal that school had come to an end. For the students who'd just returned from spring break, it was a godsend. No longer would they have to deal with the horror that was teachers giving boring lectures, no longer would they need to sit in class, contemplating whether stabbing their ears with pens would keep them from hearing such boring lectures. They were free.

Kevin, Iris, and Lilian walked out of their last class with the other students, traversing through the crowd. Before they could get too far, the group ran into someone none of them really wished to see.

"I see you have returned safe and sound from your spring break, Kevin Sweeft."

Juan Martinez Villanueva Cortes stood before them, leaning against the wall, arms crossed. As per the usual, he wore the matador outfit that belonged to the theater club, and his hair was bright and yellow and large, done up as it was in a horrendous-looking pompadour style. Of course, Kevin knew this was just his human form. In truth, this boy was actually a half-yōkai, a human/kitsune hybrid, to be exact.

"Ah!" Lilian pointed. "It's the pompadour guy!"

Juan's face exploded with color as he stomped on the ground, looking for all the world like a child having a tantrum. "It is not pompadour guy! My name is Juan Martinez Villanueva Cortes! Get it right!"

Iris leaned over to whisper in her sister's ear. "Who the hell is this guy?"

"It's Juan the pompadour—"

"That's not my name!"

"I don't think you two actually got any screen time together," Lilian continued. "I guess there just wasn't enough space or something. Not like it matters anyway. He's just a support character at best."

"Ugh!"

Several arrows appeared out of nowhere and speared Juan through the back. Each arrow had the words "Just a support character" written on them. The boy fell onto his hands and knees, his very being exuding a sense of depression like a raincloud.

"What do you want, Juan?" Kevin asked. He really didn't want to see this kid, especially knowing that Juan was responsible for Lilian's kidnapping at the hands of Jiāoào. If he had never told that pretentious little brat of a kitsune, then Jiāoào would have never been able to kidnap Lilian.

The boy stood back up, the aura of gloom disappearing and the arrows vanishing. He gave Kevin a haughty smirk.

"What makes you think I want something?" he asked. "I am merely here to inform you that I am pleased to see that none of you came to harm during your trip to California. I hear a lot of terrible events happened there. Tidal waves and localized earthquakes." Juan held a hand to his chest in faux relief. "Eet does this heart good to see that you've all returned safe and sound."

Kevin clenched his fists. Did Juan know about what really went down in California? Of course, he did. He had to. This person was an information broker. It was his job to know when something happened or would be happening.

Did that mean Juan might have also been responsible for them getting caught up in that disaster? Kevin shook his head. The possibility was there, but he didn't think so. Still, he'd best not let his guard down.

"Well," Juan started, moving past the trio. "Perhaps I shall see some more of you three later, but for now, I think I shall take my leave. Adiós."

Kevin and Lilian both frowned as Juan disappeared around a corner. Iris looked between the two and where the pompadour boy had left.

"That was odd," she said.

"I'll say," Lilian agreed. "He didn't call me flour for once."

A trail of sweat trickled down Iris's scalp. "That wasn't what I meant."

***

When the trio arrived at the front of the school, they found someone waiting for them.

Her brown hair fell down her shoulders in a messy bed of spikes. Feral eyes gazed at everyone who dared look at her wrong, which caused everybody there to give her a wide berth—except for several starstruck girls, Kevin noticed with some amusement. The charcoal-colored business suit that she wore, despite being at odds with her feral demeanor, suited her well. One of the sleeves was missing, however, displaying the stump that was her left arm as if it was a badge of honor.

Several months ago, Lilian had been kidnapped by Jiāoào. Kiara had gone with him to rescue her and had lost her arm in battle against a Void Kitsune. Despite missing an arm, she didn't seem bothered, and in fact, she was quite proud of it.

It must have been an inu thing.

Iris put Lilian between herself and Kiara as the group walked up to the woman, causing her sister to roll her eyes.

"Kiara?" Kevin greeted his instructor in the ways of asskickery. "Is something up? You almost never show up at our school." Immediately after asking the question, a theory occurred to him. "Chris hasn't done something stupid, has he?"

Kiara laughed. "No, Chris hasn't done anything—not that I'm aware of, at least. And I honestly don't think I'd care if he did. I'm actually here to pick you up."

"Me?" Kevin pointed at himself.

"Yes, you."

"Why?"

"Because we need to go somewhere," Kiara spoke with a tone that said her reasons should have been obvious. They weren't, but she wasn't in the mood to explain herself. "Now then, I've got a busy schedule today, so hop in and let's get going."

As Kiara entered her stupidly expensive sports car, a white Lamborghini with the Mad Dawg logo imprinted on the hood and car doors, Kevin looked at his mate and her sister.

Already knowing what he was going to say, Lilian smiled and said, "Don't worry about us. We'll head home on our own." Her mate going off with Kiara was actually fortuitous. She needed to speak with Kotohime about something anyway.

After sharing a kiss with Lilian, Kevin entered the car through the passenger's side and strapped in. Kiara then rolled down the car window and looked at the two fox-girls. While Lilian didn't flinch due to long-term exposure and the fact that her mate underwent training with this woman, Iris nearly pissed herself at the fanged grin that Kiara gave them.

"I'll be sure to bring your mate back to you safe and sound in a few hours," Kiara told Lilian.

"I'll hold you to that."

"Heh," Kiara smirked at the girl, then turned her attention to Iris, whose head just barely peeked out from behind the redhead's left shoulder. Iris froze when those feral eyes locked onto her. "Boo!"

"EEK!"

Iris shrieked and hid behind Lilian again. Kiara's howling laughter echoed across the campus as her Lamborghini peeled out of the school gates.

"Was that really necessary?" asked Kevin.

"No," Kiara said, her grin widening to reveal sharp canines, "but it was fun."

***

Lilian watched as the car containing her mate pulled out of the school gates. Then she turned to look at her sister.

"Fraidy fox."

"Tch!" Iris twitched and glared at her sister. "I'm not afraid of that s-stupid dog."

"Oh, you're not, are you?" Lilian smiled at her sister. "Then why are you shaking?"

Iris looked down at her knees to see that, indeed, she was shaking. Looking back at her fraternal twin, her expression morphed into a scowl. "I-it's got nothing to do with being afraid! I just... don't like dogs."

Lilian nodded. "Most kitsune don't."

Tossing her sister a strange look, Iris said, "I'm kinda surprised you're not afraid of that mutt."

"I was at first," Lilian admitted. She wouldn't deny it. Kiara used to petrify her. "But I got over it once I realized that Kiara didn't have the same hatred for kitsune that most inu have. You know that she and Kotohime actually have a history together."

Lilian didn't know what sort of history those two shared, though she knew they were familiar with each other from their conversations. She'd thought about asking Kotohime. However, her maid's past was hers to bear, and Lilian didn't want to intrude on what seemed to be her maid's private and very personal affairs.

"Huh, you learn something new every day, I guess." Iris scratched the back of her head before shrugging. "Aw, whatever! Let's just head home already!" Grinning, she threw an arm around her sister and nuzzled her nose into Lilian's red locks. "With the stud gone, that means I get to spend some time alone with my Lily-pad."

"I already told you that I can't do those things with you anymore." Lilian tried to push her sister away to no avail. "And stop calling me Lily-pad!"

***

As the two kitsune walked toward the bus, neither knew that they were being watched.

Chris Fleischer sat on a stone bench near the buses, his scowling face a mask of barely constrained hatred. His eyes burned furiously as they followed the two kitsune. He gnashed his teeth together until he tasted the coppery flavor of blood on his tongue.

Ever since his defeat at Lilian's hands, his life had gone down the drain. People no longer feared him. Students he once picked on even made fun of him! Worse still was that he couldn't do anything back. He didn't know what that fox-whore had done to him, but whatever she'd done, the strength that he had once prided himself on had all but vanished. These days he possessed no more strength than a normal human.

His mind churned with rage as he glared back at the gate that his sister's car had passed through. He knew the bitch had accepted that faggot as her pupil, Inugami knew why, and it made him hate her all the more. Why would she train that cocksucker when she had a brother like him? That boy was just some stupid fucking human.

There has to be something I can do to make those two pay for fucking up my life.

Chris didn't know what, but he knew, beyond a shadow of a doubt, that he needed to do something. Even if he had to sell his soul to the Shinigami, he would get his revenge.

***

Kevin would've liked nothing better than to enjoy his time in Kiara's slick car. He might not have been a car fanatic, and he might even think that owning something like a Lamborghini was a gross waste of money, but he was still a male. All men, no matter their opinions, loved riding in fast cars. How many people could actually say they'd ridden in a car that costs over $165,000 anyway? So yes, Kevin would have normally been ecstatic to ride in such a vehicle.

Too bad Kiara made enjoying the drive impossible.

"Holy crap!" Kevin shrieked as the Lamborghini caught air after zooming over a small hill. It hit the ground seconds later, shock absorbers taking the brunt of the impact, though Kevin could still feel his teeth rattling inside of his mouth. "What the heck is your problem?! AAEEEE!!"

Kiara laughed as she peeled around a corner, tires screeching and engines blazing. She slammed on the brakes, allowing her tail end to drift, and then slammed on the gas, making the tires squeal as they shot out of their turn.

"Come on, boya? Don't you like my driving? Where's your sense of adventure?"

"I lost it along with my intestines after that first turn you made," Kevin groaned. He felt sick. "I think I'm gonna throw up."

"If you hurl in my car, I'm going to hurt you."

"Then stop driving like a maniac!"

"Tch. You're no fun."

The sports car leveled out and slowed down, traveling at a normal speed. Kevin thanked the gods for this. Just where did this woman learn to drive? And where the heck were the cops when you needed them? Pulling 145 on a 45 mile per hour road was not a safe driving practice!

"So," Kevin started after mastering his stomach, "are you going to tell me where we're going now?"

"You'll see when we get there, boya. Don't be so impatient."

Kevin frowned at Kiara's reflection in the front window. She didn't usually act cryptic like this, which meant she wanted to surprise him with something. Knowing her as he did, whatever surprise awaited him probably wouldn't be good for his health.

He looked out the window to see buildings whizzing by. He recognized where they were, or at least their general location.

"Hey, Kiara."

"Hm?"

"Would you mind if we stop by somewhere before going to wherever it is you're taking me?"

Kiara didn't take her eyes off the road—fortunately—as she spoke. "And just where do you want to go? I'm sort of on a schedule, so I can't go too far out of the way."

"I just wanted to visit a friend's house for a second. I promise it won't take long."

Kiara agreed after Kevin told her where he wanted to visit. It was on the way, so it wouldn't take them long.

They soon reached a small cul-de-sac filled with middle-class houses; the kind of residences that looked almost identical to each other, save for small touches here and there. They stopped in front of one house in particular.

Kevin was shocked by what he saw.

"W-what the heck?"

A large moving truck sat on the curb; its back was open and several burly men in uniforms were offloading furniture that he didn't recognize and proceeding into the house. Kevin stepped out of the Lamborghini and moved to stop one of the men as they walked back outside.

"Excuse me," he said, stepping in front of the man who looked like he benched cows for a living. "But could you tell me what's going on here?"

The man, his bald head gleaming in the sun, raised an eyebrow. "Can't you see we're moving furniture inside? I thought it would be fairly obvious."

Kevin's right index finger twitched. "I know that. I meant why?"

The left eyebrow joined the right in being raised. "Because someone is moving in."

"What happened to the people who owned this place previously?"

"They moved, obviously." The man peered at Kevin in concern. "You all right, kid? Your face is looking a tad pale."

"I-I'm fine," Kevin muttered, offering a quick thank you to the man before getting back inside the car. As they drove off, away from the house, a mesh of confusing and jumbled questions entered his mind.

After the Comic-Con disaster, Kevin and the others had easily noticed the missing Justin, despite how unobtrusive his presence sometimes was. None of them knew what happened to their friend. He'd last been seen with Alex, Andrew, and Eric, but sometime during their escape, he had disappeared. They hadn't even noticed that he was missing until after arriving at the hospital that he and the others had been staying at.

They had asked Kuroneko if she knew what happened to him. However, even though she had searched all over, there was no trace of their friend, and the security cameras at the convention had been fried. With nothing left to go on, they had been forced to label him as missing.

"You feeling okay, boya?" Kiara asked.

No. No, he wasn't feeling okay. One of his friends was missing, and that same friend's parents had moved out of their house. He didn't know what that meant, but he felt like these two events were somehow connected, even if he didn't know how or why. How could he possibly be all right?

"I'm fine," Kevin said.

"You're a terrible liar."

"Ugh."

"I'm gonna have you do one thousand pushups during our next training session for lying to me."

"Urk!"

Kevin made a promise to himself as they drove down the road: Never lie to Kiara. It didn't end well.

***

Lilian and Iris arrived home to find about what they had expected. Kotohime stood out on the balcony, hanging up the laundry as she hummed to herself, and Kirihime and Camellia were...

"M-My Lady! Please come back!"

"Hahahaha! Catch me if you can!"

With sweat trickling down their faces, Lilian and Iris watched in mute shock as a bare-as-the-day-she-was-born Camellia ran from an overwrought Kirihime. The fox-lady chased after her mistress. She was furiously waving a towel in her left hand, which she was obviously attempting to wrap around Camellia, who the fraternal twins noticed was soaking wet. She had probably just gotten out of the bath.

"It's a good thing the stud's not here. If he was, then I have no doubt that something ecchi would have happened between him and Mom, probably some kind of boob fall or something, or maybe even a crotch fall," Iris declared.

"I'd like to disagree with you..." Lilian watched her giggling, naked mother run about with childish glee. "... but I don't think I can."

"Ah!" Camellia gasped as she noticed them. She stopped running and turned to Lilian and Iris, her already radiant smile growing in both brilliance and moé. "Iris! Lilian! Hello!"

"Hi, Mom," Lilian greeted. Iris just sighed.

"M-My Lady, watch out!" Kirihime shouted.

"Hawa!"

Lilian winced as Kirihime, unprepared for Camellia's abrupt stop, ran right into the voluptuous woman. The two crashed to the floor. Somehow, beyond Lilian's ability to comprehend, Kirihime fell on top of Camellia, whose face became buried beneath the maid's skirt. Meanwhile, Kirihime had fallen in such a way that her face was buried in her mistress's pelvis.

It was the perfect 69.

"H-hawa! Why is it so dark all of a sudden?!"

Kirihime, her eyes rounder than tennis balls, tried to say something. Due to the placement of her mouth, no words came out.

"Ahn!—K-Kirikiri, w-what are you—aaahn!"

The two younger kitsune watched as their mother's legs wrapped around Kirihime's head and pulled her deeper into the place between her thighs as if it was a reflexive reaction. The intensity of Kirihime's muffled grunts and groans increased, becoming louder and more frequent. This caused the gasps and moans from the surprised and confused Camellia to increase, which in turn caused her legs to tighten their hold around the other woman's head.

Lilian and Iris stared at the scene for a few more seconds before turning to each other.

"I'm gonna put our stuff away," Iris declared.

"Thank you," Lilian said. "I have to speak with Kotohime."

"Right."

The pair promptly walked off in separate directions, ignoring the scene of the three-tail's face being buried between their mother's thighs. While Iris disappeared down the hall leading to Kevin's room, Lilian went outside where Kotohime just had finished hanging up the last of the laundry.

She absentmindedly wondered what Kevin would say if he knew that their maid/bodyguard was hanging up his underwear where everyone could see it. It was probably a good thing that they usually didn't arrive at home for another hour or two.

"Kotohime?"

"Ara? Lilian-sama?" Kotohime turned around. Her kimono, a beautiful mauve piece with sakura petals swirling from the base in a spiral pattern up the fabric, gently swayed as she moved. The woman presented her ward with a magnificent smile and a polite bow. "I am pleased to see that you have returned home. I trust you had a pleasant time at school?"

"It was fine," Lilian said. The novelty of school had kind of worn off by now, but she still enjoyed the chance it presented to spend time with all of her friends.

"That is good." Kotohime rose from her bow. With her hands clasped in front of her, she looked the very picture of an ideal Japanese woman. "It always brings me great joy to see how happy you've become. I must admit, I had my doubts, but I believe that attending a human school has done you a lot of good. You seem much happier now than you were before."

If Lilian was not already positive that her maid didn't know the real reason for her joy, she probably would have said something. However, they both knew that the true reason for Lilian's happiness wasn't necessarily the school. Attending school just happened to be a byproduct of what made her happy.

Thinking about her happiness made Lilian remember the reason that she'd come out to the balcony in the first place. Straightening her posture, Lilian mustered her courage and looked Kotohime directly in the eye.

"Kotohime, I want you to teach me how to fight."

Kotohime blinked. "Ara?"

***

Kevin eventually discovered where Kiara was taking them after they exited the I-10 on West Warner Road. They parked in a mostly empty parking lot, in front of a two-story building constructed out of a combination of brick, steel, cement, and glass. Exiting the vehicle and following Kiara to the building, Kevin glanced at the sign on top of the door, which read *C2 Tactical.*

They walked between a set of large cement pillars and through the double doors. Upon stepping inside, Kevin saw why this place had been given such a name. It sold guns. Situated along the walls, on racks, and in stands were a large variety of guns: handguns, rifles, shotguns, etc. There were several types of firearms that he couldn't even begin to recognize.

Kevin froze. Kiara walked several steps into the store before realizing that her pupil no longer walked beside her. She turned, frowning at him. "Something wrong, boya?"

"N-no."

"Then hurry up and follow me."

Kevin walked into the store, ignoring the shudder that passed through his body. He followed Kiara as she walked up to a display case near the back. No one was there, but that changed when Kiara rang a small bell sitting on the glass display counter filled with guns.

"Hold yer horses, I'm comin'!" a voice shouted from behind a door on the other side of the display.

Some bumping followed and the door soon opened to reveal a middle-aged man with a beard and salt and pepper hair. He walked up to them, his black C2 Tactical shirt stretching over his expansive beer belly. Upon reaching the counter, he glanced at Kiara for barely a second before a grin that revealed smoke-stained teeth appeared on his face.

"If it ain't Kiara! How ya been? Haven't seen you in a while."

"You know I don't really care for guns," Kiara quipped.

"Ah-ha! Ain't that the truth. Yer into that hand-to-hand stuff," the man laughed, slapping his hands on the glass display, causing it to rattle as he leaned over. "Don't know why. Fighting bare-handed might look cool, but nothing beats a good gun by yer side. Can't do anything with yer hands if someone pops a cap in yer belly."

Kiara's smile was indulgent if a bit strained. "Yeah, well, you know me."

"That I do," he said before noticing Kevin. "And I'm guessing this is the runt you mentioned over the phone?"

Kevin's right eye twitched at being called a runt, but he didn't say anything. His eyes were locked mostly on the guns within the display case. His hands felt clammy.

"Yep." Kiara placed a hand on Kevin's back. "This is Kevin, my disciple and someone who I felt could stand to benefit from learning a thing or two about shooting a gun." If she noticed Kevin's shudder at her casual mention of the words "shooting a gun," it didn't show. "Boya, this is Jeffrey Sanderson. He's the one who tutored me back when I was learning about long-range weapons."

Kevin forced his eyes away from the guns to look at Kiara. "I didn't know you knew how to use guns."

"It would be stupid not to understand how to use a gun," Kiara told him. "If you don't know how guns work and how to use them properly, then how can you expect to beat people who do use them?"

That made sense. Kiara didn't learn how to use a gun because she wanted to use them, but because she wanted to understand their strengths and weaknesses so she could defeat people who did.

All yōkai, regardless of species, were susceptible to guns. While some like inu and oni had some resilience to projectile weapons, even they were not immune. It might have been the atomic bomb that caused yōkai to create a law about never revealing their existence to humans, but it had been guns that initially leveled the playing field between humans and yōkai.

Kevin's mind felt strangely numb as he filled out the paperwork that Jeffrey placed on the table for him. He was then led to a room near the back. Carpet shifted to glossy cement. The sound of their footsteps echoed loudly in Kevin's ears, a dull, incessant tapping that almost made him recoil. Jeffrey led them to a table near the back where several guns had already been laid out.

"Normally, we'd be going to the office room in the back, where you'd watch a movie on gun safety," Jeffrey informed Kevin, his voice echoing across the almost empty room. "But, I figured it would be easier fer me to just show you. Kiara said yer better at learning through first-hand experience."

What followed was an explanation of gun safety and the basic types of guns. Kevin barely heard any of it. His eyes had zeroed in on the array of weapons lying on the table. Long-barreled rifles with heavy magazines. Semi-automatics. Pistols. Double-barreled shotguns. Weapons with tactical scopes. There was a lot of variety in that selection, and all of it made Kevin quake.

"Now then." Jeffrey didn't seem to notice Kevin's lack of attentiveness. "Why don't we start off with something basic."

"H-huh?"

Jeffrey picked up one of the handguns, a black 9mm pistol. "This here is a Smiths & Wesson MP9 with a seventeen-round magazine and a four-point twenty-five-inch barrel, reinforced polymer chassis, superior ergonomics, ambidextrous control, and proven safety features. It's a great weapon fer a beginner to learn how to shoot."

After saying all this, the man shoved the gun into Kevin's hand. He looked at the gun, his eyes wide and his hands shaking terribly. Jeffrey placed a hand on his back and led Kevin to the shooting range, which was already set up with a paper target 50 feet away.

"Now then, when firing a gun, you need to have a firm stance. Keep yer feet exactly shoulder-width apart. Place yer leading foot in front and the other just slightly back. Then put both hands on yer gun…"

Kevin felt his body move as if it had a will of its own. He felt like an outsider as if there was someone else inhabiting his body, and he was merely watching as it followed Jeffrey's instruction. His hands rose up, gripping the gun and pointing it at the target. They were shaking badly. Sweat covered his hands, creating a wet, slippery surface against the handle.

My shout of rage and anguish proceeded several thunderclaps as I unloaded all of the bullets in the gun into the kitsune who had hurt my mate.

Visions plagued his mind.

Blood sprayed from the multitude of wounds that opened up like a fine mist. The woman's body jerked back and forth as if she was undergoing intense muscle spasms. The blood that jetted from her body like streamers splattered against the ground, staining it in crimson.

The shaking increased until his arms began to shake as well.

She stared into my eyes, her own wide and round, surprised, as if she could not believe what had just happened. Her mouth opened but no words came out, just a strange gurgling and a lot of blood. Then she fell onto the pavement, on her back. Her body twitched once, twice, and then it went completely still.

The gun clattered to the floor.

"H-hey! Careful with that thing! The safety isn't on!"

Kevin ignored Jeffrey as he spun around, shoving the older man out of the way with his shoulder. He ran out of the shooting range, and then out of the shop altogether.

His stomach rebelled against him the moment he exited the front door. Kevin fell onto his knees, one hand pressed against the ground while the other went to his stomach as he proceeded to empty out its contents. His body shook, shoulders wracking as vomit spewed from his mouth. Even after everything he'd eaten that day had spilled onto the ground, his body continued to dry heave.

The sound of doors sliding open reached his ears, but he paid it no mind. The sigh that followed, which was swiftly proceeded by a hand falling onto his shoulder, was harder to ignore.

"So, you're afraid of using guns because of what happened during spring break." It was not a question. "I suppose I should have seen this coming. You might be working hard to get stronger, and you might be getting better at fighting, but you're still just a kid."

Kevin didn't say anything, or more like, he couldn't say anything. Even if he had been capable of speech, what would he say? What could he say? Nothing. So he kept silent.

"Come on," Kiara said, lifting Kevin's right arm and slinging it over her shoulder. "Let's get you back home. We'll do this once you've come to terms with what happened."

***

The wind blew across the land, billowing blades of grass, making them sway in a gentle, constant motion. Presenting a stark contrast to the grass were the two figures standing on opposites sides of the small park. The tension between them hung thick in the air, a palpable, suffocating feeling. It was a good thing, then, that nobody else was present.

Lilian stared at Kotohime, a nervous trickle of sweat running down her scalp. Her fists clenched and unclenched, and her tails had turned into a flurry of activity, swaying and writhing in agitation.

Contrasting to the appearance of Lilian, Kotohime remained calm and collected, her gaze reminiscent of placid pools of twilight. Even when Lilian's body wavered and vanished like a ghost, those eyes did not change. Even when the earth bulged all around and chains of light shot up from the surface, the swordswoman acted without haste or worry.

A flare of youki, strong and swift, burst from her body. The chains shattered into nothingness, revealing them to have been illusions. Her body then turned, a counterclockwise motion as her blade, still in its sheath, lashed out and struck flesh.

"Kya!"

A cry of pain erupted from Lilian's mouth as she was sent sprawling to the ground. She quickly scrambled to her feet, however, and leaped several feet back to put some distance between them. Kotohime did not follow her, and instead, she chose to let her opponent recover. She kept a two-handed grip on her blade as she observed her ward.

"You should know that an illusion of that level will not work on me, Lilian-sama," Kotohime said as Lilian placed two fingers against her now bruised cheek. She jerked her hand back and hissed in pain. "If you wish to fool me by using illusory arts, then you must be more subtle about the illusions you weave."

"I know," Lilian grumbled as she climbed to her feet.

"If you know this, then you should also know not to break part of your illusion after casting it," Kotohime continued. "While your imagery is impeccable, the form that you tried presenting to me disappeared halfway through. What's more, your chains did not make any noise when they shot from the ground, which was a clear indication that they were fake. This also allowed me to hear your footsteps as you tried to sneak up on me from behind."

Lilian winced with each point that Kotohime struck home. "I know that, but it's difficult maintaining multiple illusions at once, especially when I'm trying to affect more than one sense at a time. At most, I can affect two, maybe three senses at a time, but I can only hold that type of illusion for about a minute, and that's only when I'm using a single illusion. I don't have enough power to affect more than one sense when I'm using a multi-layered illusion, or two illusions at once."

"Indeed. As a two-tails, you lack the power and control necessary to cast multiple illusions simultaneously. In which case, your focus should not be on crafting multiple complex illusions, but simple illusions designed with subtle misdirection in mind. Observe."

Kotohime ran toward Lilian, who tensed at the woman's swift approach. She didn't know what her maid and current teacher planned on doing, but she prepared for every eventuality that she could conceive. Closer and closer Kotohime moved. Her blade raised when she reached striking distance. Lilian moved aside as it swung down...

Crack!

"Owch!"

... and still ended up getting hit.

"Ow, ow, ow." Crouched on the ground, Lilian cringed as her hands felt the large, mountainous lump sprouting from her hair. It felt like a baseball underneath her skin! Tears gathered in her eyes as she looked up at Kotohime. "H-how did you do that? I could have sworn I dodged it!"

"An illusion," Kotohime responded, placing her sheathed katana at her side once more. "I merely created an illusion to make my blade look sixty-five centimeters off from where it actually was. Simple, but effective."

That meant that Kotohime had used a smaller-scale illusion to only change one aspect of herself: The position of her blade. By changing only the position of her blade by several centimeters, she created an illusion that was hard to tell was fake. Small illusions were harder to see through than large illusions.

Wincing, Lilian stood to her feet. "That wasn't a simple image illusion, though, was it?"

"Indeed it was not." Kotohime's smile spoke of how pleased she was that Lilian had recognized this. "With an illusion like this, there are three senses that need to be taken into consideration: Visual, auditory, and somatic, or sight, sound, and touch."

"Why touch?"

"I'm glad you asked."

Quicker than Lilian could see, Kotohime raised her blade and swung it down, stopping just before it could reach her charge. Lilian's eyes bulged as a blast of air struck her face. Her hair was buffeted away from her, and her eyes stung as the wind caused them to water.

Kotohime returned the blade to her side. "Tell me, what did you feel just now?"

"Well, I felt wind hitting my face," Lilian said. Kotohime remained silent, causing her to frown at the obvious prompt. Thinking harder, Lilian eventually discovered the answer. "Which I need to take into account when creating an illusion. When you struck, the wind caused by the air being displaced from your swing hit my face. A skilled fighter would notice if this didn't happen and realize that it was an illusion."

Kotohime beamed. "Exactly. Experienced fighters have the ability to recognize even the most minute and seemingly innocuous shifts in perception. If you create an illusion of yourself running toward me while the real you is running several feet from the illusory you, someone such as myself will be able to hear that difference due to the angle at which the sound vibrations are coming from. Likewise, if you create an illusion like the one I just showed you, we'll notice the different angle at which the displaced air is hitting our face and respond accordingly."

Illusions were a complex art that required making someone think that something was happening when it really wasn't. To do this, an illusionist sent their youki into the mind of the one they wanted to place under an illusion. The foreign youki would then affect that person's mind, creating a false representation of the real world.

However, because illusions were so complex, they required intense focus and imagination. Not only did illusionists need to focus on who they were casting an illusion on, but they also needed to visualize exactly what it was supposed to look like, how it would feel, what the other person would smell... everything. If they didn't do that, then there was a good possibility that the person would realize they were under an illusion and break it.

Lilian's frown spoke volumes about her thoughts. "I see. There is a lot more to crafting realistic illusions than I thought there would be."

Nodding, Kotohime said, "There is, but try not to let it get you down too much. This is not something that can be learned through lectures and study. Only real-life experience can teach you how to craft convincing illusions while in a combat situation."

Lilian grimaced. "So you're saying I need to fight more if I want to get better, is that it?"

"More or less." Kotohime's placid smile held hints of amusement. "But then, is that not why you asked me to help train you?"

"Yeah..."

"And speaking of training, may I ask Lilian-sama why she has come to me for help?" the swordswoman inquired. "I'll admit that I am pleased to see you asking me to help you become stronger. However, you have never asked me for help before. I had assumed that you had no desire to learn how to fight."

Lilian breathed out an exhausted sigh as she lowered herself to the ground. The grass was wet, but she paid it no mind and absently plucked several blades of grass from the ground, releasing them and letting them blow away in the wind.

Kotohime remained silent. She knew that Lilian would speak when she was ready.

"Honestly, I don't really want to learn how to fight," Lilian said at last. "I've never been interested in fighting, just like I've never been interested in my family's political games. All I've ever wanted to do was live to the beat of my own drum, to live how I want, without being bogged down by the many codes of conduct and etiquette the matriarch forced on me. More than that, I didn't want to get involved in the secret wars and political backstabbing that goes on in our world."

Lilian placed her hands on the ground behind her and leaned back, looking up at the cloudless blue sky.

"That's part of the reason I ran away."

"And the other reason was to find your mate, no doubt," Kotohime teased. "You know that you're very lucky to have run into him like you did. The United States is a big place. For you to end up in the same state as the one you decided to mate with is nothing short of astounding."

"I guess so."

A short interlude of silence pervaded the pair. Lilian frowned as she thought of what would have happened if she'd never bumped into Kevin. Would she have continued searching? Moving from place to place? Would she have ever found Kevin? Or would she have eventually been captured by yōkai who'd have had no trouble enslaving and breaking a young kitsune like her? The thought made her shiver.

"Anyway, I guess the reason I'm asking for your help is that I've realized something."

"Oh?" Kotohime looked at her ward with interest.

"Even if I want nothing to do with the kitsune world, with the yōkai world, that doesn't necessarily mean I can just ignore it. Our spring break showed me this. No matter where I go, no matter how far I try to run, this world is something that I'll never be able to truly escape from."

It was something that Lilian had always feared. She'd spoken to Kevin about it, but he'd always told her not to worry, that she should have more confidence in him. However, it wasn't confidence in him that she lacked now. It was confidence in herself.

"And also, I guess I'm doing this because I feel guilty."

"Lilian-sama?"

Lilian looked up at Kotohime, the smile on her face trembling. "Kevin is working so hard, training every day to get stronger for me, but the only reason he's doing it is because I've forced him to. It never really occurred to me until recently, but if I had never met Kevin, if he never found me in that alley when I was injured, then he would have probably lived a normal life, free of the danger that comes from being involved in our world. I pulled him into this world, the world of yōkai." She sat up straight and looked at her hands, clenching and unclenching them. "How could I force him to grow stronger in order to stand by my side if I'm not willing to grow as well?"

Kevin was learning to fight for her. Every day he went to Kiara and trained for her. He was growing stronger, becoming more capable, more able to protect himself, and all of it was for her. He was getting stronger every day and what was she doing? She was enjoying her life without a care in the world. She didn't deserve someone like Kevin if she was unwilling to step up.

Thinking of Kevin made her remember the past few days, and her mood began to lessen.

Ever since the convention, Kevin hadn't been himself. He acted the same way, and he could fool his friends and everyone else, but she knew that something was wrong. He tossed as he slept, he woke up in a cold sweat, and sometimes he would mumble in his sleep. He was suffering. It hurt her to see him like that. It hurt even more that he refused to speak to her about it.

The feeling of a hand on her shoulder startled Lilian. She looked up into the smiling face of her bodyguard, who appeared very pleased by something.

"It seems you have finally begun to mature, Lilian-sama," Kotohime said. "I am pleased to see how well you're growing. It appears that coming to the human world and getting your mate has been very good for you."

Lilian brightened. "You think so?"

"Oh, yes." Kotohime nodded her head. "And speaking of mates, perhaps we should head back home and see if yours has returned yet."

"Yes!"

***

Kirihime sighed as she exited the bedroom where her mistress had taken residence. After that embarrassing interlude in which she'd found herself being shoved face-first into her mistress's, uh, well, between her mistress's thighs, it had taken nearly an hour to get Lady Camellia dry and even twice as long to get her clothed. After that, she'd had to deal with her mistress's natural clumsiness. This meant running around, trying to keep the woman from tripping over her own two feet.

She truly loved Lady Camellia, however, sometimes that woman caused her so much trouble.

Fortunately, she could rest easy now. Camellia had fallen asleep after exhausting all of her energy, much like a child who, in their never-ending enthusiasm, ran around for several hours before passing out.

Since she didn't need to attend to her mistress, Kirihime thought it would be a nice gesture if she made dinner for everyone.

Her sister was currently working hard to help Lady Lilian grow stronger, and Lady Lilian and Lord Kevin were also working hard. Cooking dinner was the least she could do for them.

Gently humming an old Japanese lullaby that her sister had taught her, Kirihime prepared a stir-fry using the leftover meat she had from her last kill. She would have done some more hunting, but she didn't need any leather right now. She had all of the leather that she would need for her latest project.

"I wonder if Lord Kevin will enjoy the present I'm making for him," she thought out loud.

Lord Kevin was such a nice young man, respectful, compassionate, and possessing an unusual capacity for acceptance.

She'd heard the story of how Lady Lilian had first entered his life. She had been both shocked and appalled by how the young kitsune interrupted his daily lifestyle. While what she had done from a kitsune perspective was not wrong, per se, and Kirihime would never disapprove of her actions, her execution had been awful.

On the other side of things, Lord Kevin had shown remarkable kindness toward someone who had, for all intents and purposes, ruined his life. He allowed Lady Lilian to stay with him despite not liking her, treated her with respect in spite of the girl's constant— not to mention poorly executed—attempts at seducing him, and he had even protected her whenever she found herself in trouble. Lord Kevin's ability to accept others and his innate kindness were quite remarkable. She was very grateful to him, even more so since Kevin had eventually accepted and returned Lady Lilian's love.

The *click* of the front door opening made Kirihime perk up.

"I'm home," a tired voice sounded out. Male. It was Lord Kevin.

Kirihime smiled as she turned and walked into the living room, greeting Lord Kevin with a smile.

"Good evening, Lord Kevin—oh, dear, are you feeling well? You look pale."

Lord Kevin's face was, indeed, unnaturally pale. He always had sun-kissed skin from spending so much time outdoors, but now it was ghostly white. A cold sweat had formed along his forehead.

Lord Kevin gave Kirihime a conflicted smile. "I'm fine. Is Lilian here? And where's Iris?"

"Lady Lilian has not returned from training with my sister," Kirihime responded with a frown.

"Training?"

"As for Lady Iris, well, I think she is in your room." Kirihime walked up to Kevin and observed his unsteady gait with increasing worry. "Are you sure that you're all right? You look, well, forgive my saying so, but you do not look very... um, healthy, right now."

"Thank you for your concern, but I really am fine," Lord Kevin said with a smile that didn't reach his eyes. "I just have a lot on my mind."

"Would you like to talk about it?" When Lord Kevin just stared at her, Kirihime flushed and quickly amended her statement. "W-what I mean is that if you wished to talk about whatever it is you're thinking about, I am willing to listen. I know you're not as close to me as you are to Lilian and Iris, or even my sister, but I would like to support you however I can."

Lord Kevin stared at her for several long seconds, biting his lower lip in indecision. Kirihime couldn't help but notice how this made him look much younger than his usual demeanor presented. He always acted so mature. Seeing him like this made her realize that he was still very young.

"Do you... do you think I'm a monster?" Lord Kevin finally asked, much to Kirihime's shock.

"A monster? Of course not! Why would I ever think that?"

How could this boy possibly think something like that? Lord Kevin, a monster? The very notion was ridiculous.

"No reason," Lord Kevin said.

"Is this about what happened during the convention?" Kirihime asked. The grimace that her question elicited told her all she needed to know.

Maybe it was because of how despondent Lord Kevin looked, but Kirihime found herself pulling the young man into a comforting embrace. She turned his head on its side and drew him close, allowing him to use her bosoms as a pillow. He stiffened at first but eventually relaxed. He reached up and wrapped his arms around her waist as if hoping to draw comfort from her hug.

"Lord Kevin," Kirihime breathed out, lowering her head to rest her cheek on his hair. "No one here will ever think that you're a monster. Not me, not Kotohime, not Lady Iris or My Lady Camellia, and certainly not Lady Lilian. We all love you very much."

Kevin didn't say anything, and Kirihime did not ask him to. Being a kitsune, and one who was particularly inured to violence due to the circumstances revolving around her life, she couldn't imagine what he must have been going through.

A cough interrupted this otherwise touching moment.

Kevin and Kirihime froze. Slowly, oh so slowly, their heads turned simultaneously to see a deadpan Lilian, an amused Kotohime, and a grinning Iris staring at them.

"Uh…" Kevin thought fast. "This isn't what it looks like."

"Really?" Iris said, chuckling, her eyes filled with mirth. "Because it looks to me like you two are getting awfully cozy with each other—not that I mind," she added. "If you and Kirihime get together, it means I'll get Lily-pad all to myself."

"Be quiet, Iris," Lilian demanded with a stern glare before turning back to Kevin and Kirihime. She placed her hands on her hips and gave them a look that Kirihime couldn't quite identify, but nevertheless, she found it frightening. "Kirihime, I had no idea that you loved Kevin so much. Don't tell me that you're trying to become his mistress?"

"Ah!"

Kirihime's body unfroze itself, and she reacted in a manner that was most unbefitting of a maid.

"Kya!"

She shoved Kevin away, which caused him to stumble back, trip, and subsequently crack his head on the table. She ignored this, busy as she was waving her hands in front of her face in frantic motions.

"Th-this is not what it looks like, Lady Lilian! I-I would never think of stealing your mate! Honestly! I was just hoping to comfort Lord Kevin because he seemed so depressed. I think he brings out my motherly instincts!"

A pause.

"N-not that I want to be his mother or anything, you understand. He already has a mother. I-it's just that, if I did have a son, I think I would want him to be like Lord Kevin."

"Ufufufu... so my sister is beginning to feel some motherly affection towards Kevin-sama? How cute."

Kirihime blushed. Lilian sighed, and Iris? She made a face.

"I didn't even know you had motherly instincts. Aren't you a crazy yandere?"

Kirihime's blush was soon combined with a pout. "Th-that's not a very nice thing to say, Lady Iris. I'm not a crazy yandere."

"Indeed." Kotohime nodded. "My sister only has mild yandere tendencies, and they only really activate when she's fighting." Kotohime paused, her mien turning thoughtful as if something had just occurred to her. "Or when she's jealous. My sister can be quite possessive, ufufufu..."

"M-mou." Kirihime pouted some more.

"Ufufufu," Lilian giggled. "I was only teasing you, Kirihime. I know that you don't love Kevin like that."

"O-oh?" Kirihime was relieved, but then she realized that Lilian had just pranked her. She puffed up her cheeks like a squirrel that had several acorns in its mouth. "Th-that wasn't very nice."

"Speaking of the stud," Iris added, eyes trailing over to where Kevin lay on the floor in an expanding pool of blood. "We might want to get him some stitches or something. It looks like he cracked his head open."

"Inari blessed! Beloved!"

As Lilian panicked and rushed over to Kevin, Kirihime blushed.

That was totally her fault, wasn't it?

***

It was very fortunate for Kevin that Lilian and Kotohime were both talented healers. Not long after he cracked his head open did Lilian heal his wounds.

He woke up about half an hour later. An apologetic Kirihime had fretted over him, and, despite telling her not to worry about it, she'd tried to take care of him for the rest of the day. This didn't work out so well. Kirihime was so used to taking care of Camellia that she didn't know how to take care of someone else.

Fortunately, Kotohime had recognized this and convinced Kirihime to give him some space. The last he saw of Kirihime was of her walking to her room with slumped shoulders reminiscent of a sulking child.

Kevin stood on the balcony. The night sky hovered overhead, a million glimmering stars that looked like tiny pebbles.

He knew that, logically, the stars dotting the night sky were actually gigantic, bigger even than the Earth, but from where he stood, they looked like mere pinpricks within a vast ocean of dark velvet. It was almost amazing how something so large could appear so small. It made him feel minuscule in comparison.

Everyone else was asleep, or so he assumed. Lilian and Iris certainly had been when he left the bed. He knew that he should have been sleeping, too, as he had another day of school tomorrow.

I watched as her body fell to the ground. Watched as she twitched before going still. Watched as blood pooled around her and formed a small puddle. Watched as her eyes, vacant and sightless, gazed upon nothing.

But he couldn't go to sleep. Every time he closed his eyes, he saw that woman's body, saw her getting jerked about as bullets penetrated her flesh, saw the spray of blood, saw her twitching and spasming before going still, and her eyes staring at him accusingly…

He pressed a hand to his face, shuddering. When would this nightmare end?

"I was wondering where you had gone off to," a voice said from behind him.

"Iris," Kevin said weakly as the vixen in question walked up to him.

Her two tails, blacker than even the night sky, swayed enticingly behind her body, which was barely covered by her tiny negligée. He watched with a sense of fascination as her tails coiled around her legs and torso like velvety serpents.

Kevin shook his head. There was something seriously wrong with him if he was thinking about how hot Iris's tails were.

"Shouldn't you be in bed?" Iris questioned. "Your mate's probably missing your warmth right about now."

"What about you?" Kevin shot back. "I'm surprised you didn't use this opportunity to your advantage to try and cuddle up to your sister."

"I thought about doing that," Iris admitted shamelessly. Kevin almost shook his head, but doing so would have probably made him vomit at the moment. "But I suppose you could say my curiosity got the better of me. You interest me."

Her eyes, dark and mysterious and smoldering, burned into his like twin coals. Her lips curved into an artfully sensational smile. He turned away, trying to ignore the way his heart hammered at the sight.

Iris chuckled. "Even after all that's happened, you're still so innocent. How cute."

"Did you have a reason for coming out here other than to bother me?" Kevin asked.

"Lilian is worried about you." That single statement made Kevin wince. "You might think you're being kind by not letting her know what you're going through, but in truth, all you're doing is hurting her. She knows that something is wrong, and the fact that you aren't opening up makes her think you don't like her, or that you don't trust her."

Kevin whirled around in shock. "That isn't it at all!"

"Then what is it?" Iris asked as she stared at him with those unfathomably dark eyes. "How come you're not telling her what you're thinking? What you're feeling? Lilian has never been anything but honest with you. She's never hesitated to open up to you. Why can't you be the same way?"

Kevin turned around, unable to stand looking into those eyes any longer. He looked at the night sky. How much easier would his life be if he were a star?

"Well?"

"It's because I'm afraid," Kevin admitted softly.

"Excuse me?"

"I said I'm afraid," Kevin said, loudly this time. "I'm afraid that she'll hate me if I tell her what I'm thinking, what I'm feeling. I'm afraid that she'll think I'm a monster."

"Do you really believe she would do that?" asked Iris, sounding as skeptical as she looked. "Do you really have so little faith in Lilian? In the bond you two share? Because if so, then maybe you aren't the man I thought you were. Where's the person who stood up to me in the bathroom? Where's the man who broke my enchantment with nothing but pure willpower and grit? Did that person disappear? Did he ever exist? Was he just an illusion?"

Kevin remained silent. Iris didn't understand. How could she? She hadn't killed anyone. What did she know?

Iris clicked her tongue. "I guess the man I thought was so interesting really was just an illusion," she said, before walking back inside of the apartment.

Kevin didn't stop her. He didn't even turn around to look at her.

High above his head, the dark moon shone like a glimmering crescent.

***

Iris continued walking until she reached the hallway, where she abruptly stopped.

"You heard all that, right?" she asked, turning her head to look at the person standing several feet away.

Lilian was wearing cute pink pajama pants and a baby blue spaghetti strap shirt, the strings of which hung off her shoulders. On any other occasion, Iris would have gushed over how cute she looked. As things stood, now was not the time.

"I did," she said softly. "Thank you."

Iris sighed and scratched her head. "You don't have to thank me. I'm your sister. Helping you is what sisters do." Her expression turned serious. "But you know you've got your work cut out for you, right?"

"I know."

"But really, that boy." Iris looked back at the balcony where Kevin still stood. "To think he would be this interesting, kukuku…"

Lilian deadpanned. "Whatever you're thinking, stop it."

"I'm not thinking anything." Iris slinked up to her sister, grabbed her arm, and guided her into Kevin's bedroom. "Now, then, you promised me some cuddle time."

"Fine," Lilian sighed in resignation. "You can sleep with me, but we're only sleeping. Got it?"

Iris pumped her fist. "Score."

"… I'm already beginning to regret this…"

***

A knock sounded at the door.

Cassy had been expecting her superior to show up sooner or later. She didn't know who it would be, but it really didn't matter. She'd been dreading this meeting regardless.

She stood up from her couch and opened the door, sucking in a breath when her "tutor" was revealed to her in all his splendor.

The person in question was male, about a foot shorter than her, with spiky red hair that traveled down his back in a lion's mane and a muscular physique covered by a black one-piece with red lines traversing the fabric like the circuits of a computer chip. His eyes, golden and glowing like smoldering flames, peered out from underneath thick bangs. He wore an amused smile filled with condescension like he was looking down on her, which he was.

"Hello, Cassy," he said in a surprisingly deep voice for one so small. "I'll be your instructor from here on out." He gave her a smile filled with sharp, jagged fangs. "I'm looking forward to working with you."

CHAPTER 4

I'll Always Love You

PAPERWORK NEVER SEEMED TO STAY FINISHED. It was something that Kiara had discovered after her fitness centers had gone from a single building in downtown Phoenix to the massive company that it now was. No matter how much she completed or how hard she worked, it just kept piling up. It almost made her regret creating a multi-million-dollar corporation. Almost.

Sitting behind her desk, Kiara went through the two massive stacks of paperwork that came from being the boss of a large chain of gymnasiums. There was a lot that she needed to look over: Logistics, statistics, employee placement, and changes in Mad Dawg cardholder policies. While most of the day-to-day affairs were handled by managers and regional vice presidents, a good chunk of work still ended up on her desk. It was tedious, but she had learned to deal with it.

The beep of the intercom gave her a much-needed reprieve. She pressed a small button on the speaker and said, "Yes?"

"Ms. Kiara, Mr. Swift has shown up. I've sent him to the training room."

Kiara sighed. "Very well. I'll be down in just a second."

"Yes, ma'am."

As Kiara took the elevator down to the first floor, her mind churned over the issue that was Kevin Swift. For a little over five months, she'd been training him in martial combat. During that time, he'd made some impressive leaps in both physical prowess and skill. So much so, in fact, that she had almost forgotten one simple fact:

Kevin Swift was not a warrior.

He did not take joy in combat like her. His reason for fighting was simply the desire to stand by his mate's side and protect her from those who would seek to do them harm.

This desire was admirable, to be sure; however, Kevin's lack of intent and desire to harm his enemies left his heart vulnerable. The boy had talent, but he lacked the ability to harden himself against the inevitability of death. He didn't seem to understand that, when faced with an opponent who wanted to kill the people you loved, it was sometimes necessary to kill them first.

She stepped into the training room where Kevin awaited her. He was dressed in the uniform that she had decided he would be wearing as of two months ago. It was a standard white gi with a dark belt and four ounce gloves. He was doing several warmup exercises that she had personally taught him.

Nothing seemed wrong. Nothing appeared out of place.

Kiara knew better.

Though he presented a strong front, she could see the signs of reluctance, of wariness, of tension. The way his back muscles refused to unwind, his exceedingly tense shoulders, the trembling of his hands, and the tired, vacant look in his eyes. All were signs that his will to fight had been broken.

"Boya."

"Kiara."

Kiara studied the young man some more. She wanted to cross her arms, but she only had one arm and it wouldn't have looked as cool. "How are you feeling?"

Kevin smiled, and it was the most transparent thing she'd ever seen. "I'm feeling better, thanks. Sorry about what happened yesterday. I know you must have gone through a lot of trouble setting up that lesson."

"I don't particularly care about the lesson plan," Kiara admitted. "What I want to know is what happened back there. I didn't push the other day because I knew you weren't in any shape to answer me, but now that you're apparently feeling better, I'd like you to tell me what the hell made you freak out so much."

Kevin remained silent. Kiara waited for him to answer, tapping her left foot against the dark blue matt.

"I… I don't really know what happened," Kevin said, looking away.

"Liar," Kiara accused. When Kevin looked back, mouth halfway open to deny her accusation, she continued. "Do not lie to me, boya. You think I don't know what you're going through? You think I don't understand what's happening to you? I wasn't born yesterday."

She watched Kevin, waiting to see if he would say something. It eventually became clear that he had no intention of speaking, or perhaps he simply wasn't capable of saying it out loud.

"I know that what happened at the convention bothers you." Kiara watched as Kevin flinched. Ah, a reaction. "Does it really bug you that much? Surely you knew that eventually you would be forced to kill? One cannot become a part of the yōkai world and expect their hands to remain clean. Even your mate has killed before."

"She didn't have any other choice," Kevin said, hands clenching into fists, knuckles turning white.

Kiara almost smirked. "And you're telling me that you did? In case you hadn't noticed, Kotohime and I had been defeated, and Lilian had received a terrible injury. Had you not done what you did, that woman would have killed me, Kotohime, and your mate. Now look me in the eye and tell me that you shouldn't have killed her."

When Kevin refused to look at her, Kiara clicked her tongue.

"Go home, boya," she said, ignoring the way his eyes bulged in astonishment. "It's clear to me that you lack resolve. In the world of yōkai, those who lack resolve never survive. I refuse to continue training you until you can show me your resolve."

Kiara didn't wait for Kevin to respond. She turned around and left.

After all, she still had paperwork to file.

***

Cassy was an unusual nekomata. While she shared many aspects with her kin—her curiosity, her playfulness, and her love of milk being just a few of those things, there was one thing about her that made her different from most nekomata.

She loved being in water.

Specifically, she loved taking hot showers.

Yes, there were few things that Cassy enjoyed more than taking a long, hot shower. The feel of water hitting her back, the heat loosening her tense muscles... she loved luxuriating under the hot spray of water.

She was lucky that she even had hot water, or water at all. Thanks to a deal she had cut with some contacts she'd made in the ghetto, she was able to have hot water, though she wasn't keen on the price. That said, she was fortunate in that the cost didn't involve giving her body to someone.

After turning off the water and wrapping a towel around her body, Cassy left the steaming room for the much colder studio room of her rundown apartment. She ignored the cold air as goosebumps prickled on her skin.

"Now there's a sight that I could get used to seeing every day," a voice said, making her nose wrinkle in disgust. She thought he was asleep. In hindsight, she should have expected otherwise. This man was a kitsune, and they loved their pranks. He'd probably been playing possum from the moment she'd woken up.

Seth Naraka was the man who'd been sent by Mistress Sarah to oversee the assassination. He sat on the couch, leaning back, his posture and demeanor displaying a casual arrogance that pissed her off. His eyes seeped with condescending amusement. The way he blatantly ogled her body, stripping her, devouring her, was a sickening feeling. It made her feel dirty. Tainted. She wanted to take a shower again.

Cassy did her best to ignore him.

She walked over to the dresser, feeling his eyes following her. After opening her drawer and reaching in, she pulled out the only article of clothes that she owned. It was her leather outfit.

I need another outfit, nya...

"Are you not going to talk to me?" he asked. She didn't speak. His supercilious chuckle made her grit her teeth. "You know that ignoring me is only going to make your situation worse, don't you?"

"I'm not ignoring you," Cassy lied. "I just don't want to talk to you while I'm naked, nya."

"Hmmm... that's too bad. I wouldn't mind having a conversation with you like this."

Pig.

Seth Naraka was well-known in her village for two things: His skills as a top-class assassin, and his lecherousness towards women. Many men in her village looked up to him, and many women were enamored with him.

She didn't know why. Sure, he was handsome, but he was also short, condescending, and had a god complex several miles wide. His arrogance knew no bounds, and unfortunately, no one had been able to put him in his place because he had the skills to back that arrogance up.

"Now don't be like that," Seth said behind her. Cassy stiffened as a pair of hands fell on her bare shoulders. She shuddered when those same hands began to rub up and down her arms. "You really shouldn't be so cold to me. I can make your life quite difficult, you know?"

"Let go of me, nya!" Cassy yanked his hands off of her and spun around, her yellow eyes narrowed in fury, and her mouth open to reveal sharp canines as she hissed. "Don't think for one second that just because I'm being forced to work with nyou, that it means I'm going to let nyou touch me! I'm nyot one of those floozies who'll whore herself out to nyou in the hopes that nyou'll favor them, nya!"

Despite her harsh words, Seth looked more amused than angry. "So you've always said, but we both know that it's only a matter of time before you fall for me. We're going to be working in close contact for this mission. You will eventually fall to my charms!"

A blush spread across Seth's face, and his eyes grew alight, shining with a disturbingly fervent ardor.

"Oh, yes. I can just imagine it all now. You and I, working side by side, our passions growing stronger with every passing second until it all boils over into a raunchy fuck-fest the likes of which this world has never seen!" Seth hugged himself and wiggled in place, moving in disturbing, boneless motions that an anthropomorphic body should not have been capable of. "It'll be amazing! It'll be glorious! I'll have you screaming out my name as your body, overcome with your desire for me, writhes about in ecstasy and—"

"Shut the fuck up!"

Crack!

"GRUGGBBLLLEE!"

Cassy glared at Seth, the fist that she had used to deck him in the face still extended. Steam wafted from her knuckles. Seth lay on the floor, his eyes glazed and his face caved in like someone had bashed it with a four-ton boulder.

"I would nyever stoop so low as to give myself over to a disgusting lech like nyou!"

Although his face was definitely far from pristine, Seth giggled. "Hehehe... you know you want the d—GYAAA!"

Seth squealed like a little girl after Cassy brutally stomped on his crotch as she made her way to the bathroom. She slammed the door shut and proceeded to get dressed, growling all the while. How dare that man paw at her like that?! Disgusting, filthy, perverted piece of crap! If he wasn't her superior, she would have killed him!

"Nya..." she sighed and leaned against the locked door. "I had been hoping that Mistress Sarah would send someone a little nicer." Then again, this was probably punishment for failing her latest assignment. "Nya... this sucks."

***

It was currently math class.

Lilian looked at Kevin from where she sat. The sound of pencils scratching against paper resounded all around her. She paid attention to none of that. Ms. Vis was giving a lecture about something math-related, but she ignored the pale woman in favor of her mate.

Kevin sat hunched over his seat, diligently taking notes. Nothing seemed out of place, but she could see the way his head would nod off, only to jerk back up a second later. His pencil would occasionally stop writing and droop, then it would snap back up, and he'd begin writing again. His shoulders would relax, and then tense, and then relax and tense again.

There were bags under his eyes.

It was Friday, the end of the week, and normally a day that she and everyone else would have been happy about. Not today. Instead of feeling joyous at the thought of the weekend, all she felt was worry. Her mate, the love of her life, was suffering, and she didn't know what to do. All week he'd been acting like nothing was wrong, feigning smiles and straining his voice to laugh.

She saw clean through it.

"Hey, Lilian," Lindsay whispered in her friend's ear, leaning over in her seat. They were near the back, so no one else was paying attention. "What's wrong with Kevin? He's been acting really depressed all week."

Lilian bit her lip. Should she tell Lindsay what was bothering Kevin? But she didn't really know herself. She had a guess, but she could be wrong. She didn't want to create a misunderstanding if her theory was incorrect.

"I don't really know," she said at last, shrugging her shoulders helplessly. "He's been like this for a while now."

Lindsay looked from Lilian to Kevin, and then back to her. "Do you think he's not getting enough sleep, maybe?"

"Maybe." That was definitely part of the problem. She knew that Kevin had been restless these last few days, but it was only a symptom, not the real issue. "But I think it's a little more complicated than that."

Iris leaned over from Lilian's other side. "I know what might help the stud," she said, making the two lean in to hear what she had to say. The devious vixen grinned. "Give him a good, hard fucking."

Lilian and Iris stared at Lindsay, who squawked, jerked backward as if scalded, fell off her seat, and then crashed face-first to the floor. Lindsay pushed herself up and rubbed her face, wincing. Everyone else had stopped what they were doing to stare at her.

"Ms. Diane, are you bothering Lilian?" Ms. Vis demanded with a stern frown.

Lindsay sat back on her seat, her nose red from where it had rubbed against the carpet. "Uh... no, Ms. Vis. I just dropped my pencil and fell when I went to pick it up."

"That's right," Lilian added in defense of her friend. "She didn't disturb me at all."

"Of course, Lilian darling, whatever you say!" Ms. Vis squealed. It was all kinds of freaky.

As the obsessive teacher turned back to her lecture, Iris whispered to her sister. "Is it just me or is Ms. Thinks-I'm-a-sparkly-vampire getting even more obsessed with you than usual?"

Lilian shuddered. "It's just you. It has to be just you."

She didn't want to think about Ms. Vis's odd obsession with her. She didn't know what had happened to make this woman have such an intense 180-degree reversal in regards to her, but the less she thought about it, the better, as far as she was concerned.

When the bell rang, everyone stood from their seats and began filing out. Lilian walked up to her mate as he finished putting away his notebook.

"Kevin?"

The young man stiffened. Lilian frowned as she moved in front of him. Kevin looked at her for a second, and then he turned his head—tried to turn his head. Lilian forced him to look at her by grabbing his face and turning it toward her. He held her gaze for a second, but then his eyes slowly shifted to the side.

Her frown deepened. "Kevin? Is everything okay?"

Her mate took a deep breath… and then he smiled. It was fake, so disgustingly fake that it made Lilian's heart clench.

"I'm fine…"

No, he wasn't. He was lying. She hated that he was lying to her. However, now wasn't the time to deal with this. They were at school, and this was something that they should talk about in private.

Putting on a smile that was every bit as fake as Kevin's, Lilian grabbed his hand. He flinched at her touch. "Come on. Let's head to our next class."

"Um, okay."

There was another thing that bothered Lilian. After Kevin had grown comfortable with their relationship, he had been the one to start initiating acts of physical intimacy between them, whether it was holding hands or kissing or even pleasuring her with oral sex. Now he didn't do any of those things.

It hadn't been so bad at first, but the more time that passed, the less intimate Kevin became. She didn't know what was wrong. He recoiled when she touched him, he refused to look her in the eyes, and he often crawled out of bed after she fell asleep and slept on the couch. Lilian was at her wits' end.

I'm going to get to the bottom of this.

"I really feel like I'm missing something here," Lindsay admitted as they left the classroom. "Did something happen between Lilian and Kevin that I don't know about?"

"Naw, nothing so dramatic," Iris said, waving her hand dismissively. "The stud's just got some hang-ups that he needs to get over."

Lindsay looked curious. "What kind of hang-ups?"

"Who knows?" Iris said with a shrug, earning herself a pout from the pixie-haired blonde.

Lindsay eventually split off from Lilian, Iris, and Kevin. Her next class was different than theirs.

The school was crowded as everyone wandered to their next class. Some people congregated together, chatting about whatever took their fancy as opposed to traveling to whatever class they attended. Others went to their lockers to grab their books. Kevin, Lilian, and Iris already had the necessary supplies and moved on their way.

Someone stepped in front of them before they could make it too far.

Chris Fleischer didn't look much different from the last time they'd seen him. He was skinnier, and he stood with a noticeable slouch, like his bones were no longer capable of supporting him. His hair had also grown out, showing that he'd not cut it in recent months. Sunken, bloodshot eyes with dark bags hanging underneath them glared at the trio with impotent malice.

Kevin instinctively moved to stand protectively in front of Lilian and Iris. The action seemed so natural that he didn't even seem to notice he'd done it.

"I've got a bone to pick with you, Swift," Chris's growl lacked the threatening demeanor that it used to have. No longer was it powerful and intimidating, but instead it was weak and, well, kind of pathetic.

While Kevin seemed oblivious to his own actions, Lilian had noticed them readily enough. His eyes, once lacking their usual vibrancy, became hard as diamonds. His posture became straighter, too, as if he'd just gained his second wind. It took her a moment to realize what had caused this change, but when she understood the reason for it, she allowed herself to smile.

Kevin, even now you're still protecting me.

Sure, she didn't necessarily need his protection. Kevin knew that she was capable of defending herself from the likes of Chris, but that he would put himself in harm's way for her even now warmed her heart.

Lilian's resolve hardened. She didn't know what was bothering Kevin, but she wouldn't let him face whatever it was alone.

"What did you want to talk to me about?" asked Kevin.

"I want to know why the fuck my sister is training you," Chris demanded. "You've been showing up at her gym every fucking day for the past five months. You might think I don't know, but I've seen you! I've fucking seen you. Why? What's so special about a pathetic little shit like you? Why would she bother training a waste of human excrement, huh?!"

Chris got up in Kevin's face and grabbed the front of his shirt.

"You think you're hot shit just because you've got my bitch of a sister teaching you? Well, guess what, Shitstain, you're nothing but a—ggrrrraaaahhhH!"

Even Lilian was shocked when, without warning, Kevin latched onto Chris's wrists and yanked them off of his shirt. He kicked Chris's legs out from underneath him, dropping the inu to the ground like a sack of stones. Kevin proceeded to roll the other boy onto his stomach with a kick and trap his arms behind his back, followed by pressing a single knee into Chris's lower vertebrae.

Even Kevin seemed surprised by his own actions. He stared at the boy underneath him, listened to the whimpers and grunts that were emitted as Chris's arms were forced to contort in ways that they were not meant to go.

Lilian had a front-row seat to her mate's eyes slowly widening, as if he was just now realizing what he'd done. His face shifted to an unhealthy shade of green and twisted into an expression of combined horror and disgust.

Kevin let Chris go and stood up, backing away from the other boy.

"Beloved…" Lilian reached out a hand despite knowing that she was too far away to touch him. She could do nothing as Kevin turned tail and ran off in the opposite direction of their class. She stood there for several seconds before, slowly, dejectedly, she brought her hand back down.

That look on Kevin's face had been startling. An expression filled with the horrifying realization of what he was doing. Lilian didn't know what that look was for, or why he had been wearing it, but she knew one thing for sure: She would need to speak with Kevin soon.

"Damn." Iris whistled. "That was pretty cool, but I was really hoping to see the stud put this stupid dog in his place." Lilian's lips squeezed into a thin line. Iris didn't seem to notice her glare until several seconds after she started. "What?"

"Can you not read the mood?!" Lilian shouted, her body twitching like she'd stuck her finger in an electric socket.

***

Kevin didn't pay attention to where he was running as he rushed across the campus. All he knew was that he needed to get away from Chris.

His mind reeled from what he had done, from the violence that he had displayed toward the inu. It was exactly like what had happened with Luna Mul. Sure, he hadn't killed Chris, but he still reacted without thinking, resorting to violence and causing someone else pain.

What kind of person am I turning into?

He turned a corner and bumped into somebody, causing him to stumble. He yelped. The other person grunted.

Kevin would have fallen to the ground, but he was saved from that fate by a hand latching onto his wrist.

"Whoa," the person he crashed into started, "take it easy, kiddo. What's the rush?"

Kevin looked up to see a man with long, messy red hair that ran all the way down his back and looked sort of like a lion's mane. Golden eyes peered at him from beneath dark bangs, and his grin revealed slightly sharper than average teeth.

He was also, Kevin noted almost self-consciously, extremely handsome. Strong jawline, attractive facial features, and a muscular physique. He was short, but that didn't seem to detract from his looks. Kevin felt horribly inadequate just looking at this man.

"I'm sorry," Kevin apologized, shaking his head. "But I'm in a bit of a hurry."

"No worries. Just be more careful."

Kevin nodded before rushing off again. He looked back to see the man that he'd bumped into watching him. For some reason, he was getting strange vibes from that guy.

I must be feeling more self-conscious than I thought.

***

Seth watched as the young boy who'd run into him disappeared around a corner. Kids were quite rude these days. Well, at least this one had apologized. He guessed that had to count for something.

Seconds after the boy vanished, two more people ran past him: a gorgeous young woman with red hair whose appearance was reminiscent of a princess, and another attractive female with black hair who oozed sex appeal from her very pores.

He already wanted them.

"Beloved! Please wait up!" the redhead shouted.

"Damn it," the raven-haired one swore. "I can't believe I'm being forced to work up a sweat like this. I hate getting sweaty unless it's from hot, raunchy sex. You're going to pay for this, Stud!"

"Oh, be quiet and just keep chasing after him!"

"Tch. Fine."

The two females eventually disappeared around the same corner as the boy. Seth stared at the spot where they'd vanished for a few seconds longer. Unbidden, a grin slowly spread across his face.

"That matched the picture I was given. So, that would make her my target, wouldn't it?" he asked of no one in particular. Licking his lips, Seth envisioned the young redhead in his mind once more. "She's quite beautiful. I wonder if I can add her to my collection after I've killed her?"

He continued walking along with seemingly no destination in mind. He wanted to get a feel for the school. Half the battle in an assassination was making sure that the assassin had all of the information they needed to flawlessly assassinate their target.

As he wandered, his mind went back to what he'd seen before that boy had crashed into him. It seemed his target and that young man had a problem with the inu boy. He didn't blame them. After all, dogs were the bane of yōkai. Nobody wanted to associate with a bunch of ugly, flea-ridden beasts.

"Hm… I wonder if I could fool that stupid mutt into doing my bidding?" he pondered before shrugging.

He could figure out the best way to use that inu later. With luck, maybe the inu would be killed off along with his target. He'd be able to rid the world of something hideous, and he wouldn't have to be responsible for killing such extravagant beauty with his own two hands.

It would be like killing two rabbits with one claw swipe.

***

Later that day, during lunch, Lilian went to the library with Christine, Iris, and Lindsay.

The library was a large building shaped like a cylinder. Dozens of shelves lined the inside, and there were several tables for people to sit at. The walls were made of glass, not bricks, so the people inside were given a clear view of the campus.

Lilian sat at one of several tables, a large stack of manga sitting on the table in front of her. She'd already grabbed one of the manga that she had selected and was going through it, skimming the pages, her narrowed eyes glaring at it as if she was attempting to derive all of its secrets through intense staring. So far, she wasn't having much luck.

She hadn't been able to catch up to Kevin after he ran out on her and Iris, and while she'd tried talking to him during gym, her mate had ignored her and everyone else completely. Lilian had later learned that Kevin had hidden inside of the weight room. She guessed he was trying to avoid people after what happened with Chris.

That was why, after their last two classes following gym, Lilian had proceeded to the library instead of traveling to lunch with Kevin. She longed to be with him, however, she also knew that if she wanted to help Kevin with his problems, then she needed to figure out the best method of confronting him. In other words, she needed to do some research.

So she sat in the library. She was quietly dissecting the manga that she'd chosen for research material, fingers idly flipping the pages, eyes scanning the content. Most regrettably, she had yet to find anything that could help her in this situation.

"I really don't mind lending a hand and everything," Lindsay commented from where she sat. The blonde stared at the stack of manga that Lilian had placed in front of her. Her right eyebrow erratically twitched as if she'd picked up a spasm. "But do you really think you're going to find anything in there to help you? Haven't we already been through this before? Manga can't help you in real life."

"I agree with Lindsay," Christine muttered, even as she turned a page in the manga that she was reading. "Manga has pretty artwork, and I'll even admit some of them have a good story, but I fail to see how this will help you solve real-life problems."

Lilian's cheeks swelled like balloons as she pouted at her friends. "You two don't know what you're talking about. Manga is filled with real-life problems. I've been reading this story about a straw hat-wearing pirate who's always getting into strange and dangerous situations—"

"And how does that possibly relate to real life?" Christine interrupted. Lilian's swelled-up cheeks turned red.

"I was getting to that," she muttered. "Just because the situations he finds himself in aren't realistic, that doesn't mean the lessons the story teaches aren't. This story is about protecting the people close to you even at the risk of your own life. It's all about friendship and Nakama."

"Friendship and Nakama mean the same thing, Lily-pad," Iris mumbled. She was sitting next to Lilian. Unlike the others, she was not reading through manga but was instead buffing her nails and winking at the boys that walked past their table.

She'd already caused several nosebleeds.

"W-whatever," a slightly embarrassed Lilian grumbled. "My point still stands."

"Again, I fail to see how this has anything to do with real life," Christine reiterated, scanning the contents of the page that she was on before flipping to the next page.

"You look like you're getting really into that manga, Frosty," Iris said. "Something you want to tell us?"

Christine's face turned blue as hoarfrost drifted off of her head like steam rising from a hot spring. "Sh-shut up! S-s-s-so I think this is a halfway decent story! So what?! Who cares?!"

While Lindsay just stared at her friend in surprise, Iris chuckled. "Why are you getting so defensive? I never said there was anything wrong with liking manga, did I? I'd never insult something that my Lily-pad loves so much."

"W-wh-whatever! Like I care what you think anyway! Hmph!"

Iris chuckled. "Really," she mumbled softly to herself, "this girl is almost as easy to tease as the stud."

"Mou…" Lilian glared at her friends and sister. "Why aren't you guys helping me? Stop talking and start researching!"

"What exactly are we supposed to be researching?" Lindsay fired back. "I don't know about these two, but I'm still confused."

"I need to find an appropriate way to confront Kevin." Lilian discarded the manga in her hand after realizing that it didn't have anything useful and grabbed another one. "I'm sure you all know by now that Kevin has been acting weird. He hasn't been himself, and even though he tries to act like nothing is wrong, I know that something is bothering him."

"And you want to find out what?" Lindsay asked for clarification.

"Exactly."

Christine and Lindsay shared a look. They looked back at Lilian, who had once again discarded the manga in her hand when she realized that it was about a musical prodigy who had a mental breakdown during a piano recital after his mother died. In the story, he met a girl, who was also a musician, and they ended up having a love/hate relationship that eventually culminated into a tragic tale of death. It was an incredible story, but she wouldn't find any useful information in it.

"Couldn't you just, you know, ask him what's wrong?" Christine asked.

Lilian put the manga back on the table and stared at her two friends. "You two clearly don't know how this works. You can't just ask someone what's wrong with them and expect them to answer, especially someone like Kevin."

"Someone like Kevin?" Christine glowered at Lilian as if she had just insulted her lover. "What's that supposed to mean?"

"She means that asking Kevin what's wrong won't fix things," Lindsay explained. "Kevin's never been the type to externalize his feelings… at least when he's not dealing with women. If there's one thing I've learned about him from our long years of friendship, it's that when he's hurt or sad, he'll suck it all in and pretend that nothing is wrong."

Lilian nodded in agreement. That was exactly how Kevin did things. He bottled his emotions up and refused to show them to others. When she asked him what was wrong, he'd say everything was fine. He'd been like that even when they first met. She loved him, but that aspect of his personality was annoying.

"Okay, so he doesn't like letting others know about his problems because he's like every other guy and likes to act macho or whatever," Christine said. "I still fail to see how looking through pages of comics—"

"Manga."

"—could possibly give us an idea on how to confront him about this," she finished, sending Lilian a somewhat scathing look for her interruption.

Lilian opened her mouth to answer, but before she could say anything, Iris spoke up. "While I don't really want to agree with the snow woman over there—" said "snow woman" glared at Iris "—I do agree that you're unlikely to learn anything from these manga. I mean, you might learn how to make the stud open up to you, but it will probably take hours of searching, and we don't really have that kind of time. Lunch will be ending in fifteen minutes, in case you haven't noticed."

"What should I do then?" Lilian asked, frustrated.

"Don't worry," Iris reassured her sister. "I've got an idea that's sure to get the stud to open up to you." Everyone stared at Iris, who stood up and smirked down at them. "You need to render him incapable of doing anything other than answering you. Don't give him a chance to run and don't let him put up a front. You need to hit him fast and hard."

"I hope you're not suggesting I use enchantments," Lilian deadpanned. "Because if you are…"

"No, no." Iris waved a hand in the air as a warding gesture. "I wouldn't dream of suggesting that you use enchantments on your mate."

"You used an enchantment on him before."

"She what?!" the shout came from both Christine and Lindsay.

"And it didn't work," Iris said. "He broke my enchantment, my strongest enchantment. Even if you were willing to use one on him, it wouldn't work. No offense, Lily, but I'm better at enchantments than you are."

Lilian conceded her sister's point, not really caring one way or the other. It was true anyway. While she excelled at illusions and they were both talented in their respective specialized power, Iris was better than her with enchantments. It made sense as, before they were sent to live in the United States, the matriarch had hired tutors for her twin to become a seductress.

Seductress wasn't really a title, of course, but it was what the matriarch had called it. Basically, a seductress was a person who went undercover and used her feminine wiles to become a member of high society in the human world. They used sex appeal and enchantments to enslave humans and gather valuable information.

Lilian believed that the matriarch had wanted to train Iris as a means of alienating her from the family. As a Void Kitsune, Iris was feared by most of their family members and a good deal of the people that the matriarch ruled over.

It was stupid. They were allowing their base fears of the Void to rule over them, ostracizing her sister because she was a Void Kitsune. Lilian hated how her sister had been treated by the people who served her clan.

"What's your idea?" Lilian asked Iris.

"Kukuku..." Letting out an extremely creepy chuckle that caused the hair on Lilian's arms to rise, Iris leaned over and whispered in her ear. Curious as to what was being said, Christine and Lindsay also leaned over to hear her words.

It wasn't long before bright blushes lit their faces.

"That's a good idea," Lilian admitted.

"No, it isn't!" The other two girls shouted.

"I know." Iris looked quite proud of herself. "My ideas are always great."

"No, they aren't!"

Christine and Lindsay made a wonderful tsukkomi duet.

***

Kevin was beginning to wonder if he was really cut out to be Lilian's mate. He'd been so sure of himself, so confident that he had made the right decision. Even after Jiāoào had abducted Lilian, Kevin had still been positive in his choice to become her mate.

Now he wasn't so sure.

It was after school. The weekend was almost upon him. This would have normally been cause for celebration, but right then, Kevin did not think he had anything to celebrate.

A week had passed since the comic convention that had changed his outlook on life, himself, and his decision. Looking at himself in the mirror, Kevin couldn't help but notice the physical changes that he'd undergone. His face was paler and gaunter. His eyes had sunken in, and dark bags hung underneath them. They were not truly noticeable unless one was looking, but they were visible if anyone looked closely enough.

He sighed and finished getting ready for bed.

Stepping into the hallway, Kevin immediately noticed the disquieting silence. Where was Kirihime as she hummed her gentle lullaby to Camellia so the woman would fall asleep? Where was Iris's laughter as she teased her sister about something? Where were Lilian's shouts as she chased after Iris for said teasing? It was like the apartment had been cast into another dimension, one in which noise didn't exist.

He crept into the bedroom, feeling unusually wary of his surroundings. Shutting the door behind him, listening as it softly clicked closed, Kevin turned around to walk further into the room.

He froze.

Lilian stood before him, her beauty enhanced to awe-inspiring levels as moonbeams broke through the window and shone on her figure. Silvery light caught her hair, turning the silken strands into ardent flames that captured and released moonlight in a manner that reminded him of a halo. She wore a sheer nightgown and nothing else. With the moon shining through the window causing the incredibly thin fabric of her gown to become semi-translucent, Kevin was able to see all of her.

Kevin tried to speak, but no words came out. His mind froze, leaving him incapable of muttering even monosyllables. He could do nothing, say nothing, as this vision of ephemeral loveliness slowly walked toward him with short, feminine steps. She stopped directly in front of him, seemingly basking in how she had rendered him all but speechless.

"Beloved…" Her lips parted to whisper that single word.

And then a hand went under his armpit while another grabbed his arm. Kevin had just enough time to realize that this was not how Lilian usually greeted him when she was dressed in sexy lingerie before the redhead lifted him up with monumental strength and tossed him over her shoulder.

Kevin screamed in shock as his back hit the bed. He scarcely had time to regain his bearings before Lilian was straddling his waist, holding his hands above his head, keeping him pinned.

"Lilian, what are you doing?" Kevin tried to get out from underneath her, but she must have been using reinforcement. He remained stuck.

"You've been avoiding me," she stated.

Kevin looked away. "N-no, I haven't."

"Maybe not physically," Lilian countered, "but you've been avoiding me in other ways. You're not talking to me like you used to. You always seem reluctant to hug me and kiss me. I even had to drag you into bed on Wednesday when you tried to sleep on the couch."

With each point that Lilian made to support her words, Kevin flinched. Had he really been that obvious? He supposed that, in hindsight, anyone who knew him would have been able to see through him. He should have tried to hide his feelings harder.

"Kevin, look at me, please." Lilian's pleading tone forced him to turn his head. With her eyes so close to his, they looked like two large emeralds sparkling as they reflected the light of the phantasmagoric night. "What's wrong? Why won't you talk to me? Why won't you let me help you?"

"I… I can't."

"Why not?" Lilian demanded, suddenly looking incredibly frustrated. "I've always been upfront and honest with you! I might be hiding some things from you, but I would tell you anything if you asked! When I was sad or hurt or confused, I'd tell you! Why can't you do the same with me?"

"Because I'm afraid you'll hate me!" Kevin shouted. Lilian recoiled as if physically struck.

He used her surprise to slip out from underneath her and attempt to make a getaway. He didn't get far, however, as Lilian was swift to recover, and she would not let him escape. Her two red tails shot out from behind her and wrapped around Kevin's body, one going around his waist and the other tightly constricting his legs. The twin appendages then grew to incredible lengths, slithering over his entire body and trapping him in what looked like furry bondage.

Kevin struggled against this new hold, despite knowing how pointless it was. A kitsune's power came from their tails; they were the strongest part of a kitsune's body. Their tails could be enhanced to strengths beyond what a human would ever be capable of producing. Still, he put up an admirable, if futile, struggle.

"Let go of me, Lilian!" Kevin demanded.

"How could you think I would ever hate you?" Lilian asked, her shoulders shaking. Within the sprinkling of moonlight, her canines glinted as she gritted her teeth. They looked longer than normal. "What makes you possibly think I could hate you? You're my mate!"

"I'm a monster!"

Once again, Lilian recoiled. However, this time, she prepared for it and didn't give Kevin room to escape. "You're not a monster. Do you think I would be mates with a monster? That I would love a monster? I wouldn't. You're not, nor will you ever be a monster. Why would you even think that? Is it because of what happened at Comic-Con? Because you killed that six-tails? Because if that's what this is about, then what about me? I've killed. Are you saying that I'm a monster, too?"

Kevin stopped struggling to stare at the girl holding him suspended in midair with her tails. His dishpan-sized eyes and gaping mouth revealed his surprise.

"N-no, of course not," he stuttered.

"Then what is it? If you're a monster for killing that woman, then I must also be a monster for killing that girl who worked as a maid for Jiāoào!"

"At least you regret killing her!" Kevin renewed his pointless struggling even as he shouted. "I remember how broken up you were about killing that girl, how much it hurt you! I remember holding you in my arms as you cried yourself to sleep, and I remember holding you even more when you'd wake up from a nightmare! You regret what you did! You never wanted to kill her!"

Kevin's eyes felt hot as if they were burning.

"But I don't! I don't regret killing that woman! I'm glad she's dead! If you put her in front of me and gave me a gun, I'd pump her full of holes all over again! I'm glad she's gone and I don't regret killing her at all!" His struggling grew weaker as the tears began to pour from his eyes, staining Lilian's fur coat. "What kind of person feels this way about someone they killed? How can I be anything but a monster when all I can think about is how I'm glad that she's no longer alive? How I'm glad that I killed her? I have to be a monster because there's no way someone who doesn't regret the lives he's taken could possibly be anything else!"

Lilian slowly lowered Kevin to the floor. As her tails were unwrapped from around his body, he sank to his knees. He looked down at the carpet, his bangs overshadowing his eyes as if he was afraid of letting Lilian look at him.

The sound of footsteps alerted him to Lilian's approach. A pair of beautiful and delicate bare feet appeared in his field of vision. Lilian knelt down. He gazed at her lovely thighs. Normally, the sight of her bare thighs and crotch would have aroused him. Right now, he couldn't feel anything, just a cold emptiness.

He stiffened when Lilian pulled him into a hug.

"Oh, Beloved," she breathed softly into his hair. He felt her pull him closer. Heat suffused his entire being as if Lilian's love for him was entering his body through their contact. "There is a difference between what happened to me and what happened to you, I won't deny that, but I think you're misunderstanding something. I don't regret killing that girl because I killed her, but because she was innocent, because she didn't deserve to die. That girl was a victim of circumstances beyond her control. She had been twisted by Jiāoào and turned into a pitiful creature who tried to kill me. My regret isn't that I killed, but that I killed someone who I feel like I should have helped."

Kevin said nothing. He didn't know what to say.

"Your circumstances were different," Lilian said, pausing when Kevin shuddered as if a cold chill had spread through his body. She pressed her lips to his forehead. "That woman attacked us. She sent her clansmen after us. She would have killed Kotohime and Kiara, and I nearly died at her hands. Had you not killed her, we would have died. You saved me. You saved us."

"Then why do I feel this way? Why do I feel so tainted? Why do I feel like I've become a monster?" Kevin asked in a voice so soft and small that Lilian felt her heart nearly break.

"Because you *do* regret what happened. You might not think you do, but I know that you do. You wouldn't feel this way if you didn't." Lilian paused and tried to collect her thoughts. "I think... I think you're just confused. That woman hurt Kotohime and Kiara. She hurt me. It's only natural that you wouldn't regret her death. At the same time, I think the idea of killing repulses you to the point that it makes you feel like some kind of monster. You hate that you killed someone, but not that it was her you killed."

Kevin lifted his head to stare at his mate. His eyes were so wide and vulnerable that Lilian almost cried for him. Had she ever seen him look so weak? No. Never. Kevin had never been weak—innocent, naive, and shy maybe, but never weak. Seeing this side of Kevin, seeing how much he was suffering, made Lilian's chest ache.

"I'm not a monster?" he asked.

"Of course not." Lilian pressed her forehead to his, bringing comfort to them both. "You are the farthest thing from a monster. You're a protector, Kevin. You saved me from that woman, you protected me from Chris. You are my protector and mate, just as I am yours."

Kevin stared at her for a moment longer before a tentative smile broke out on his face. It was tiny, but it was also genuine. Lilian felt a surge of relief at seeing it.

"Do you feel better now?" she asked.

"A little," Kevin admitted softly. "Thank you."

Lilian pulled Kevin closer and moved back until she was sitting on her butt and her upper back was resting against the bed. Kevin ended up on her lap. It was an odd form of reversal as, normally, Kevin would have been the one on bottom and she'd be sitting on his lap.

"You don't need to thank me," Lilian said, stroking his hair. "You're my mate. I love you, and I would do anything for you."

"I know." The smile on Kevin's face grew just a bit brighter. "Thank you. I love you, too."

Lilian's smile shifted. No longer merely happy, it now contained a hint of lust. "I'd much rather you show me how much you love me instead of just telling me."

Kevin bit his lip in a moment's indecision, but he quickly regained his bearings and smiled. "I can do that," he said, his voice a bare whisper.

Perhaps it was due to his own insecurities, but the kiss that Kevin initiated started off slow and tentative, almost like the first one they'd ever shared as a couple. Lilian's arms slid around Kevin's neck and sought to pull him close. As he felt the fullness of her body against his, Kevin became bolder.

He slipped his hands underneath Lilian's clothes—well, he tried to. He cursed when he remembered that she was wearing a nightgown, which was longer and harder to slip his hands underneath, but he settled for letting them roam across her back. Lilian's stifled gasp as his finger glided along her spine allowed him to deepen their kiss. The moans that she released reverberating inside of him and causing his body to become a furnace.

A pair of small, delicate hands slipped underneath Kevin's shirt. Lilian's hands were warm and felt like the softest silk. He'd always loved her hands, and remembering all of the things that Lilian had done to him with her hands caused more blood to rush to his lower regions. His dick could have probably cut adamantium.

Their kiss broke, but only for a second in order to take in some much-needed air. Then they were at it again.

Lilian stuck her tongue inside of Kevin's mouth and, in response, Kevin closed his mouth around her tongue and sucked on it. The lyrical moan that Lilian produced caressed his ears and drove him on.

Despite his disappointment at her nightgown being in the way, Kevin placed his hands on her chest. The nightgown was thin. Even though he'd placed his hands over her clothing, the fabric was so fine that he could feel her nipples harden beneath his fingers.

Lilian's breasts were large. They overflowed from his hands when cupped, and, like an oversized marshmallow, her boobs were softer than anything he'd ever felt. What's more, they were really sensitive. The slightest of touches seemed to elicit a response. Yet even though they were sensitive, Kevin had found multiple other places on his mate's body that gave him an even greater reaction. Some of those places were quite bizarre.

Kevin had every intention of taking their passion to the bed, and indeed, he was even prepared to pick Lilian up, lay her against the mattress, and straddle her to continue what they were doing.

"Hnnn!"

A loud moan interrupted them.

Kevin and Lilian both froze.

"That wasn't you, was it?" Kevin asked. Lilian shook her head. "Thought not."

Slowly, as if they were machines that needed a good oiling, Kevin and Lilian turned their heads to look at Iris.

Lilian's sexy twin sister sat against the wall. Her feet were planted firmly on the ground, her legs were spread lewdly and a hand rested between her thighs. Neither of them needed to be geniuses to know what she was doing. Iris blinked several times as if she was only now realizing the disquieting silence that surrounded her.

She looked at Kevin and Lilian.

"Why'd you two stop?" she moaned out in complaint, her left hand still busying itself between her legs. "It was just getting to the good part."

Iris's head was suddenly and swiftly implanted into the wall when Lilian smacked her right in the face with a youki-reinforced tail.

"Ouch," the raven-haired fox-girl muttered, her voice muffled by the wall that her head had become embedded in.

CHAPTER 5

The Date

THE NEXT DAY WAS THE START OF THEIR WEEKEND. Saturday had arrived, and with it, Kevin Swift found himself preparing for his date with Lilian. They hadn't really planned on what they would do for their date, but he would be with Lilian, so whatever they decided to do was bound to be fun.

He still had a lot on his mind, conflicted feelings over what had happened at the Comic-Con and Kiara's refusal to train him until he showed his "resolve" being at the forefront of them, but he did everything conceivably possible to push them to the back of his mind. Today wasn't about him. It was about Lilian.

He looked at himself in the mirror, checking to make sure nothing looked out of place. His blue jeans fit snugly and felt comfortable; the plain white T-shirt that he'd donned had a collared button-up charcoal shirt worn over it. The buttons were currently undone, allowing a dog tag necklace—a Christmas gift from Kiara—to be seen hanging around his neck.

Kevin absently tugged at his unruly blond hair. It had grown really long. He would need to have it cut soon.

Not seeing anything wrong with his looks, he exited the closet and entered his room. Lilian wasn't present. Voices from the living room drew his attention, and he wandered there to discover Lilian chatting with Iris and, surprisingly, Lindsay and Christine.

Huh, what are they doing here?

Lilian had chosen to dress up for their date. Gone was her usual green off-the-shoulder shirt, and in its place was a light pink crop top that complemented her hair. The shirt stretched across her chest, presenting a visually appealing image that he knew would attract attention from men everywhere. The black skirt that she wore, which looked like a spirited twirl would cause it to reveal more than Kevin felt comfortable with other men seeing, was just the icing on the cake. On her feet were her usual gladiator sandals.

"Kevin!" Lilian greeted upon seeing him. Kevin smiled as her already vibrant expression gained another level of brightness. Even if he still felt insecure, just seeing Lilian so happy and cheerful made him feel better. "Are you ready for our date?"

"Yep," Kevin said, walking up to Lilian's side and grabbing her hand. Then he turned to Christine and Lindsay, tilting his head slightly. "So, what exactly are you two doing here?"

"We show up to see how you're doing and that's all you have to say?" Lindsay asked, rolling her eyes. When Kevin raised an eyebrow in response to her words, she shrugged. "Since you and Lilian are going on a date, Iris called us up and asked if we wanted to hang out."

"It would be boring to spend all day on my own," Iris added. "So I thought I could hang out with Frosty and Dyke. They make good company."

"Shut up, skank!" Christine shouted. "By the gods, do I hate you! If it weren't for Lindsay pleading with me to come over, I would have never... eh?" The snow maiden blinked when she noticed that Lindsay was no longer standing beside her. "Lindsay? Where the hell did Lindsay go?"

"She's over there in the corner," Lilian said, pointing at Lindsay.

Kevin and the others looked over at the corner. The blonde high schooler was crouched, her face turned toward the wall. She appeared to be drawing circles on the carpet with her index finger. An aura of depression hovered over her, and a black miasma-like mist wafted off of her body as if it was a physical manifestation of her melancholy. She was sniffling.

"I can't believe she called me a dyke. Sure, I find the female form kind of attractive and everything, but it's not like I'm into girls." A pause. "At least I don't think I'm into girls." Another pause. "Then again, I do find girls to be more attractive than boys." One last pause. "Does that mean I really am into girls?"

After spending several seconds staring at her, Kevin, Lilian, Iris, and Christine decided to pretend that the last few seconds never happened. It was safer that way.

"Where are Kotohime, Kirihime, and Camellia?" Kevin asked.

"I think Kotohime went grocery shopping," Lilian said. "As for Mom and Kirihime..." she trailed off and shrugged. "Don't know. She's probably tripping over something."

***

"Ah-hahahaha! Ah-hahahaha! Look, Kirikiri! Look!"

Kirihime walked behind her mistress as she and Lady Camellia walked through a park near the Le Monte apartment complex. Her mistress had wanted to spend time outside today, and while a part of her felt like allowing this woman to go anywhere was permitting disaster to strike, she hadn't been able to find it in herself to deny the woman her desires.

Currently, her mistress was laughing and pointing at the number of kites soaring through the sky. There were an awful lot of them. She guessed it was because the weather was so pleasant.

"I see them," Kirihime said with a tender smile.

Her mistress's returning smile seemed brighter than any sun. "Hahahaha! They're so pretty!"

Lady Camellia, in her enthusiasm to follow the kites, did not see where she was walking and thus missed the steep hill naught but two steps in front of her. Kirihime saw it, however, and did her best to stop the woman before she could fall.

"Ah! W-wait! Lady Camellia, you need to be—"

"HAWA!"

"—careful…"

Kirihime winced as her mistress tumbled down the hill like a sack of flour. Her limbs flailed about. Her body bounced like a pair of beach balls. She was like a ragdoll.

"HAWAWAWAWAWAWA!!"

And she was yelling her head off.

Fortunately for Lady Camellia, the hill, while steep, wasn't very large. Her tumble was quite short. Unfortunately for her mistress, there were several people at the bottom.

Upon hearing her highly unusual shouts, these people turned around and, rather than do what most smart, logically thinking people would do and move out of the way, they chose to stand there like a bunch of idiots as Lady Camellia crashed right into them. The people shrieked as they were knocked over like bowling pins getting the smackdown after the Hulk decided to try his hand at bowling.

"M-Mistress Camellia!"

Kirihime ran down the hill to make sure her mistress was all right… and to apologize to the people that her mistress had bowled over, even if it was their fault.

They really should have moved out of the way.

***

"Very true." Kevin nodded, agreeing with Lilian's assessment.

Knowing Camellia as he did, that woman was probably running around somewhere, causing her maid no end of trouble with her childish antics. Knowing Kirihime, she was more than likely chasing after her mistress while trying to keep the woman from hurting herself, as well as inadvertently hurting others.

He only hoped that Kirihime could keep her "mistress" from falling breast-first into some poor boy. That much stimulation was too much for the male mind to handle. He knew this from experience.

"So, are we ready to go?" Lilian asked, and in response to her words, Kevin patted down his pants pockets. Wallet? Check. Cellphone? Check. Keys? They were right next to his cellphone. Check.

"Yep, we're good to go." Kevin and Lilian turned to Iris, Christine, and Lindsay—who'd recovered from her bout of depression with admirable swiftness—and raised their hands in farewell. "We'll see you guys later. Have fun doing… whatever it is you plan on doing."

"Oh, we will," Iris said. The expression on her face, which seemed to convey numerous dark and twisted secrets, made Kevin and Lilian feel uncomfortable around her.

"Right."

After exchanging a few more pleasantries, Kevin and Lilian left the apartment building. Iris, Christine, and Lindsay went over to the window and peered out to see the two hop on Kevin's bike and ride off.

Nodding to herself in satisfaction, Iris stepped back from the window and held a fist up to her face. "All right! Now that they're gone, it's time to finally put our plan into action. It's time to begin Operation Spy-On-That-Couple!"

Christine and Lindsay looked confused. They looked at each other, then at Iris.

"Um, why would we do something like that? Weren't we going to watch movies or something?" Lindsay asked, scratching at her cheek with her right index finger.

Iris looked at the girl like she'd said something stupid. "Whatever gave you that idea?"

"You did," Lindsay deadpanned. "When you told me that you wanted to know if Christine and I wanted to come over and watch movies with you."

"Did I say that?" Iris asked, smiling innocently as she pressed a finger to her lips. Of course, the term "innocent" could never have been applied to this vixen, and her smiles never looked remotely close to innocent.

"Yes, you did."

"Oh… well, what I meant to say was watch the stud and Lily-pad while they went on their date." Iris rapped her knuckles against her forehead as if to say that she'd made a mistake. "My bad."

"Somehow, I don't believe you," Lindsay said.

Christine face palmed. "And this is why I didn't want to come over here. I knew she'd pull something stupid like this. You see, Lindsay?"

"Okay, okay. So I shouldn't have given her the benefit of the doubt." Lindsay blushed. "So sue me."

"Maybe I will."

Iris just laughed. "Now, now, I know that both of you are interested in seeing what the stud and Lily-pad get up to on their dates. There's no need to deny it." Grinning, she held out her hand. "So, are you two in?"

Christine and Lindsay looked at each other as if they were holding a silent conversation. Iris would have made a comment about how they looked almost like a couple and should just start fucking, but that would have ruined the moment, so she remained silent and concocted ways to tease them later.

The silent conversation ended, and Christine and Lindsay placed their hands over Iris's.

"We're in," they said at the same time.

"Good." Iris gave the two a fanged smirk. "Then let's not waste any time."

***

Odd though it may have seemed, Kevin and Lilian hadn't gone on that many dates, despite having been a couple for several months.

While most couples felt like dating was the highlight of being a couple, and indeed, many magazines espoused that dating was what all couples needed to do to be a "true couple," Lilian and Kevin felt a little differently.

Dates were nice, certainly, but not a necessary proponent to enjoying a healthy relationship. Why spend money going out on a date when they could stay at home, snuggle under a warm blanket, and watch anime or read manga? There were also other things that they could do at home that they couldn't do in public.

Still, sometimes it was nice to go out and do the things that all couples did, even if their idea of a date was vastly different from normal people. Dinner and movie? Don't make them laugh.

The Metro Center Mall was the nearest shopping center. It had been a while since they'd been there. The last time they had visited this particular mall was when they'd gone shopping for winter clothes for Lilian. That was before Kotohime had arrived. It was also during that time that Kevin had finally confessed his feelings for Lindsay and been turned down. In some ways, it could almost have been said that this mall was the starting point for the way their relationship had progressed.

Being a Saturday, it was fairly busy. There must have been several hundred people wandering through the mall. Teenagers were hanging around stores and sitting in chairs. Parents were holding their children's hands as they wandered the halls. Several kids ran through the mall, laughing as they played a game of tag. It was a bustling den of vibrant activity.

It was a good thing, then, that their destination was not the mall itself, but rather, the bookstore on the northern side of North Metro Parkway, the street that encircled the mall like the moat of a castle.

The two already knew exactly where they wanted to go upon entering the store. They made a beeline for the manga section almost before the sliding doors had even opened.

There, the two of them tried to decide what manga they should buy.

Unfortunately, they both had very different opinions.

"Why do you want to get that?" Lilian said after seeing the manga that Kevin wanted to buy. Her mate frowned at her as he held out a manga volume for *Natsumo Shinobi*, the last one in the series. She ignored the look that he sent her, grabbed the volume to another manga, and held it out for him to see. "I think we should get the next volume showcasing the adventures of a certain straw hat pirate."

"Be careful with what you say," Kevin warned. "You don't want us getting sued for copyright, do you?"

"Aw, it's fine," Lilian dismissed his warning. "I doubt Eiichiro Oda would care if I talk about his manga. He makes millions of dollars each year, and it's not like we haven't made dozens of references already. What's one more?" Saying this, Lilian crossed her arms under her chest and pouted at him. "You're just saying that to avoid having to give me a reason why we should get *Natsumo Shinobi* instead of this epic work of fantasy and adventure. I think you just want to see Natsumo getting randomly stripped naked by her sensei."

"Who the hell do you think I am? Eric? Don't lump me in with that pervert." His cheeks turning just slightly red, Kevin furrowed his brows at her. "That's not why I like Natsumo Shinobi and you know it. I just think ninja are cooler than pirates. However, if you want a real reason, then how about because *Natsumo Shinobi* has actually ended while *One Piece* has over seventy-six volumes and there's still no end in sight. I'd prefer reading something that I know has a definite ending over something that I'm not sure will ever end."

"Ha! Ended? I don't think so!" Lilian grabbed another manga titled *The Adventures of Burrito*, which featured a blond-haired brat who looked like a male version of Natsumo. "You see this? This is the sequel to *Natsumo Shinobi*. This is the proof that *Natsumo Shinobi* hasn't ended."

"That crap isn't even worth mentioning." Kevin scowled at the manga in her hand as if it was horse manure. "That manga is just Shōnen Jump's attempt at milking more money from an already ended manga. I don't consider that garbage to be in the same league as *Natsumo Shinobi*."

"So you say, but *One Piece* is still better."

"Is not."

"Is too."

And thus, the great debate began.

***

As the pair argued over which manga they should get, several feet away, hidden behind a bookshelf, were three people dressed in large overcoats and even larger fedora hats that hung over their faces. They were also wearing sunglasses.

"What are they doing?" asked Christine, watching as the redhead and the blond waved their respective manga in front of each other. It would have been funny to watch, but she couldn't get over the weirdness of the whole situation. What the hell were they doing?

Lindsay bit her lip as she, too, watched the scene with a growing sense of "what the fuck am I looking at?"

"It looks like they're arguing," she said, "but…"

"They're probably arguing about which manga is better again." Iris rubbed her face. Honestly, those two… "It's the one thing they don't always seem to agree on, which manga is better: *One Piece* or *Natsumo Shinobi*."

Christine twitched. "So they're arguing over which manga is better?"

"Yep."

"… Are those two idiots?"

"… Do you really need to ask such an obvious question?"

***

It took several minutes of debate to decide which manga they would buy. They only had enough money for one volume today, since they planned on doing other activities and couldn't spend all of their money on manga.

After realizing that neither of them would give up on their stance, Lilian offered a compromise.

"How about this one?" she suggested, holding another manga volume before Kevin's eyes.

He looked at the front cover. It featured a blonde girl with boobs that might have even been bigger than Camellia's. She was dressed in a skimpy red outfit that only covered a portion of her breasts and crotch. Everything else was left bare.

"*Magika Swordsman and Summoner,*" Kevin read out loud, blinking. He looked over the manga to Lilian, frowning. "I've never heard of this one."

Lilian's eyes glowed brightly as she beamed at him. "It's really good! It's a fantasy series about a young man called Kazuki, who attends a school as the only male summoner. The artwork is gorgeous, and there's a lot of really nice fanservice."

"So, it's basically a harem manga," Kevin said.

"Mou, Beloved, this isn't just a harem manga." Lilian pouted. "This is a really good series about the trials and tribulations of the only male summoner in an all-girls school. It's based on a popular light novel series that hasn't been translated into English yet."

"It sounds like just another magical harem high school series to me."

"So what if it's just a magical harem series?" Lilian's eyes were like blazing flames as she passionately defended her manga of choice. "*Natsumo Shinobi* is just another shōnen series. Does that make it any less enjoyable? *JoJo's Bizarre Adventures* is the same as most shōnen series, but it's still really fun to read. What about *Fate/Stay Night?* It's based on an eroge. An eroge, Beloved! But it's still an excellent series! Just because a series shares similar themes with other manga, doesn't make it bad. You shouldn't—"

"All right. All right. I get your point," Kevin said abruptly, halting the girl before she could say anymore. "We'll get that one." Lilian's beaming smile caused him to smile and sigh at the same time. "Ha… if you kept going on like that, we might really have gotten sued for copyright."

The two traveled to the cash register at the front of the store, manga in hand. As they waited in line, Kevin observed the redhead with a curious gleam. Lilian seemed to notice the attention he was giving her. She looked at him and smiled innocently.

"Something wrong?"

"No." Kevin shook his head but kept his focus on Lilian. "I was just thinking about how you seem to know more about manga than I do, even though I've been reading it since I was in elementary school."

"Ah-hahaha!" Lilian's lyrical laughter was followed by a sheepish smile. "Kotohime introduced manga to me a couple of decades ago. Ever since she bought me my first manga, I've found the artwork and stories fascinating. Having never lived outside of my family's homes in Greece and Florida until I ran away, I've always wanted to see the outside world and go on an adventure. These manga let me go on even more adventures."

There was a twinkle in Lilian's eyes as she spoke as if she was imagining the many worlds that she could visit through reading manga.

"Traveling to new worlds, fighting evil, experiencing the powers of friendship, and gazing at the beautiful artwork, it's all so amazing."

Kevin grinned at his mate's enthusiasm. "Yeah, it is pretty cool. You know, considering how much you love manga, you should think of becoming a mangaka or something and make your own. I bet you'd be pretty good at it."

Lilian laughed and rubbed the back of her head. "I don't think I'm a good enough artist to create my own manga."

"You never know until you try, right? I bet you'd be amazing."

"Ufufufu, you're sweet, Beloved."

They reached the cash register and paid for their manga, volume one of *Magika Swordsman and Summoner*, and left the store.

They ignored the disgusted look that the clerk had given them when she saw what they were buying.

***

Unknown to the young couple, a trio of overcoat-clad females trailed after them, exiting the bookstore several seconds after they did.

The group of Iris, Christine, and Lindsay kept a suitable distance so as not to arouse suspicion... which made little sense because they were wearing long overcoats that reached down to their ankles and overgrown hats that covered most of their faces in shadow... plus they wore sunglasses. It was sort of like painting a big sign that screamed, *"Look at me! I'm a suspicious individual!"*

Everyone they passed stopped whatever they were doing to gawk at them. The girls, to their credit, were either very good at ignoring the stares or, the more plausible scenario, they weren't even paying attention.

At some point, the couple stopped.

Christine, Iris, and Lindsay hid behind a large column near a clothing shop and peeked their heads out from behind it to spy on Kevin and Lilian.

The young couple had made it to a small sitting area outside. Water spouted from an in-ground fountain several feet away on an elevated platform, and a fire crackled merrily inside of a large fireplace made of tan bricks and black metal.

The couple had chosen to sit on a cushy-looking leather couch. Kevin sat with his back against the chair, and Lilian was nestled between his legs, appearing awfully comfortable. The manga was open on her lap, and he had set his head on her left shoulder as they read together.

"Aw!" Lindsay cooed at the two. "Aren't they just adorable? Don't you think they look cute?"

"Disgustingly cute," Christina said with a twitch in her eye.

"You sound a little jealous," Iris commented, staring down at Christine with a twinkle in her eyes. "Don't tell me that even after all this time, you're still hung up on the stud?"

"W-wha—no! Of course not!" Christine exploded. The color of her cheeks had turned an icy blue. "What makes you possibly think that he and I—that I would still like him?! I don't! W-w-why would I possibly like an idiot like him?!"

"Your tsundere is showing again."

"SHUT UP!"

"Quiet down, you two," Lindsay hushed the pair to silence. "They'll notice us if we're too loud."

Christine huffed as Iris grinned. They went back to watching the couple, who continued to read their manga. It was actually kind of boring, watching two people who did nothing but flip pages in a book. Iris was used to this, of course, as, when the two were not doing homework, watching anime, or getting their freak on, this was usually what they did. However, Christine and Lindsay seemed put out by the pair's lack of activity.

They're probably going to be there for a while.

Iris sighed and prepared herself for a long wait.

She hoped something interesting would happen soon.

She needed something useful. Otherwise, all of her plans would go up in smoke.

***

"Hey, Kevin?"

Kevin's eyes flickered to Lilian for a moment before traveling back to the page. "Yes?"

Lilian finished reading, and then waited until Kevin tapped her stomach to let her know that he was done as well. She flipped the page.

"I was wondering, are you feeling better today? I mean, you seem to be doing better, but you were, well, you were really depressed yesterday about... um, what happened... back then..." She trailed off, not that Kevin couldn't see why; she was bringing up an awfully conflicting and emotional topic for him.

Smiling, he placed a kiss on her neck. "I'm feeling a lot better, thanks to you."

Lilian breathed a sigh of relief and relaxed deeper into his embrace. "I'm glad," she said, pausing for just a moment. "Does that mean you're going to start training with Kiara again soon? I know you stopped, but..."

"I'm not sure if Kiara will let me train with her anymore," Kevin admitted, scanning the page they were on. It looked like there were several girls whose breasts were even bigger than Camellia's in this manga. "She said that she won't train me until I can prove my resolve. The problem is that I don't really know what she means by that, or how I can prove my resolve to her. What am I supposed to do? Beat up a bunch of people in front of her to show my resolve? What does that even mean?"

"Well, resolve is just another word for commitment, right? Your determination to do something? I think she wants you to prove to her that you're determined to continue training with her, or maybe she wants you to prove that you're determined to remain involved in the yōkai world despite the… uglier aspects that come with it."

By uglier, Lilian obviously meant violence. The yōkai world was full of it. Kevin only had to look at his first meeting with Chris, a yōkai who wasn't as kind as Lilian, to see this.

Of course, the human world contained its dark elements as well, like the Sons and Daughters of Humanity and terrorists and stuff, but they didn't seem as prevalent in the everyday life for the average citizen. If anything, the Sons and Daughters of Humanity were more like a part of the yōkai world than the human one.

"My resolve, huh?" Kevin sighed as if thinking about how this whole situation exhausted him. His cheek came to rest against Lilian's, and he rubbed their cheeks together. "I'm not even sure if I can prove my resolve to myself, much less to Kiara."

"That's because you're confused," Lilian told him. "You just have to find your reason for wanting to stay in the yōkai world."

"My reason?"

"Yeah!" Lilian set their manga on the ground, moved out of his embrace, stood up, spun around, and placed her hands on her hips. She was grinning. "Your reason for staying in the yōkai world. It's like how Natsumo's reason for being a shinobi is to gain the recognition of her village, or how Luffy's reason for finding One Piece is because he feels like becoming the Pirate King represents the ultimate form of freedom, or how Natsu's reason for being a mage is to find his missing dragon father. Every shōnen hero has a reason to keep going, a reason to keep fighting." She pointed at him. "You need to find your reason to keep fighting, too."

"You do realize that we aren't characters in a shōnen manga, right?" Kevin asked.

"That's true. We're more like caricatures from a harem series."

"Don't call us caricatures! And don't mention harems!"

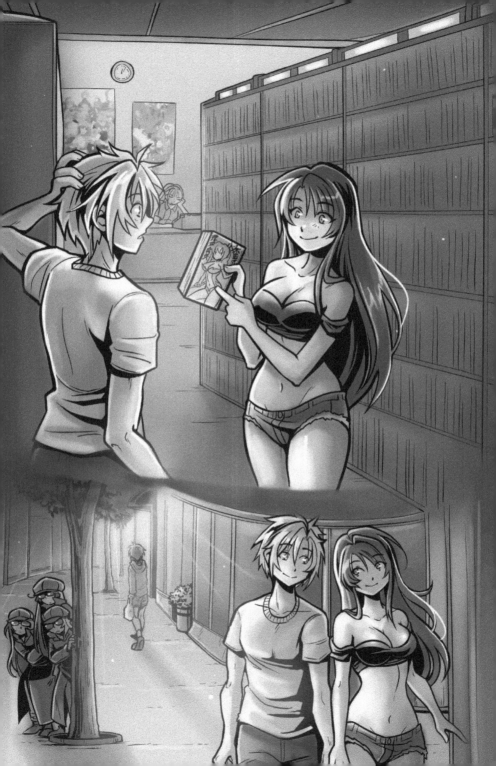

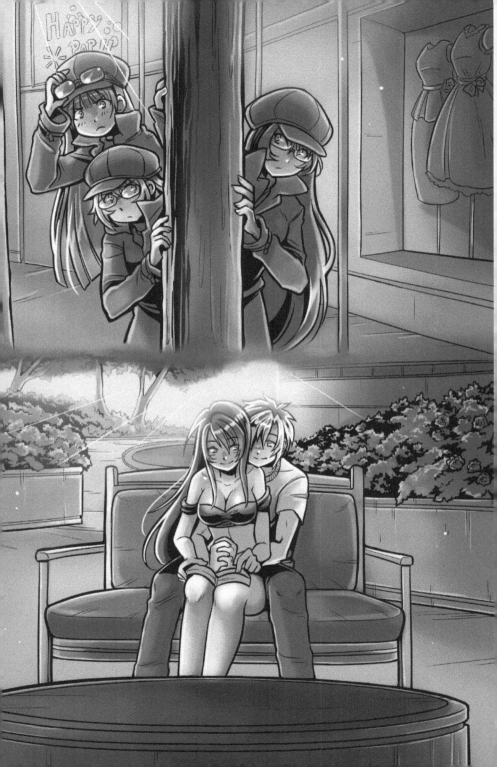

***

"What is she talking about?" Lindsay asked. "Ugh, I wish I could hear what they were saying."

Iris facepalmed. "No, you don't. She's giving a speech."

"A speech?" Christine and Lindsay asked at the same time.

"Yes…" Iris looked almost pained as if the idea of her sister giving speeches caused physical injury. "She likes giving speeches because it makes her feel like those heroes in shōnen manga."

"You're joking," Christine said. "Please, tell me you're joking?"

"Believe me, I wish I was." Iris sighed. "Lily-pad has been a manga fanatic since before even meeting the stud. She used to spend hours practicing her shōnen speeches in front of a mirror. I imagine that she's super excited to finally put all that practice to use."

To that, Christine and Lindsay had nothing to say.

***

Kevin sighed and leaned back in his seat. "Caricatures and harem themes aside, I'm not a hero from a shōnen manga."

"It doesn't matter if you're not a shōnen hero," Lilian declared. "Every choice you make and action you take determines the outcome of your life. Even if you're not the protagonist of a shōnen manga, you're still the main character to your own story."

It was something that children heard a lot. Movies, books, especially those aimed at a younger audience, often spoke about how "you are the hero of your own story." Most of these themes were done with the intent of empowering kids, of letting them feel like they mattered.

As people grew older, they tended to become disillusioned, but as someone who'd experienced a world so unlike the one that he was used to, Kevin could only concede Lilian's point with a nod. She was right, in a way. Even if his life wasn't like those heroes in shōnen manga, he still controlled his own life.

"And our life isn't exactly normal either," Lilian added. "You might not be a character in a shōnen manga, but you're hardly normal. You're my mate. You are in a relationship with a kitsune. You live with an entire family of kitsune, and let's not forget about all of the misadventures we've had since our meeting. You might not be living on the Grand Line, in the Elemental Nations, or Magnolia, but your life has been a lot like a shōnen manga."

"Don't remind me," Kevin groaned, his shoulders slumping. "Just thinking about some of the things that have happened to me since we've met makes me question my own sanity."

It really was pretty unbelievable when he thought about it. All of the things that he'd been through since meeting Lilian actually did resemble the sort of stories found in anime and manga.

There were differences, of course. Most of those people in anime and manga had superpowers of their own that allowed them to stand on par with their enemies—or at least train to get stronger. He had no superpowers, no special abilities. He was just a normal human. Aside from that small fact, his life was kind of similar to his favorite shōnen heroes.

It even had random acts of fanservice.

Go figure.

Just then, a loud, earth-shaking rumble filled the area. Everyone in the vicinity stopped what they were doing, turned, and stared.

"Was that your stomach?" Kevin asked incredulously.

Lilian's cheeks turned a lovely shade of pink. "W-well, all this speech giving has made me kinda hungry," she tried to defend her stomach, at the same time wrapping her arms around said stomach to keep people from looking at it.

"Let's get something to eat, then." Kevin stood up and, after picking up their manga and marking their place with a bookmark, he held out his free hand.

Grinning brightly, Lilian took his hand in hers. "Okay!"

***

Still wearing their overcoats, oversized hats, and sunglasses, Christine, Lindsay, and Iris followed the couple into a small bakery that sold sandwiches.

"It's so hot in these things," Iris complained as they sat at a table several feet away from the two that they were stalking... in broad daylight... while wearing ridiculous clothing...

It was enough to make Christine wonder how Lilian and Kevin hadn't noticed them yet.

"Stop complaining," Lindsay grumbled bitterly as she pulled at her own overcoat. "You think I like wearing this thing any more than you do? Newsflash, I don't. And you're the one who suggested we wear these anyway."

"Yeah, but you're used to sweating and stuff."

Lindsay rolled her eyes. "While I'm playing soccer, yeah, but not while I'm sitting at a table in a stuffy bathrobe. Why are we even wearing these things anyway? Don't you think we look kind of suspicious?"

"This is the only way we can hide our faces," Iris defended. "Unless we want to wear masks or something, but that would be just as, if not more, suspicious."

"Why are we following these two again?" Christine asked, having long since forgotten the reason. She was the only one among the trio who didn't complain about being in a sweaty overcoat. She actually liked the heat.

"This is for my research," Iris said seriously, and the solemnness in her tone made the other two look at her.

"Your research?" Christine asked, seemingly both fascinated and afraid.

"Hm!" Iris nodded her head, actually looking enthusiastic for once. "Very important research. You see, if there's one thing I've learned since coming here, it's that I won't be able to break up the stud and Lily-pad."

"Wait, wait, wait. Before you continue, can I ask something?" Upon receiving permission in the form of a nod, Lindsay asked the question that must have been bothering her for a while now. "Why do you call Kevin 'Stud'?"

"Oh, come on. Are you seriously asking me that?" Iris asked, not giving Lindsay a chance to answer before she continued. "You've seen him with his shirt off. I know you have, so you should know why I've given him that nickname."

At the mention of Kevin without a shirt, Christine's cheeks became extremely cold. She had seen Kevin sans upper-body clothing when they went to California. She wasn't sure if he'd always been that muscular, or if it was a recent change, but Kevin had an impressive physique. Lean muscles, six-pack abs, broad shoulders, a powerful chest, and defined arms. If Christine had been the drooling type, she would have considered him drool-worthy.

Over by the cash register, Kevin sneezed several times.

"Are you feeling okay, Beloved?"

"Yeah, I just had something tickling my nose."

"Someone could be talking about you."

"God, I hope not."

Back at the table, Lindsay stared at Iris for several seconds… and then she sighed.

"Oh… I guess I see your point," the blonde tomboy admitted.

"Right." Iris nodded. "So, any more stupid questions?" Lindsay shook her head. "Good."

"So… your research," Christine prompted Iris to continue, which she did, with glee.

"Like I was saying, the stud and Lily-pad can't be broken up. I've tried it before and have come to the conclusion that it's impossible. Besides, I actually kind of like the guy. He keeps life interesting, and he makes my Lily-pad happy, so it's cool."

"Kachoo!" Lilian let out a rather cute sneeze.

Kevin, who'd just picked up their order of food, looked at his mate in concern. "Bless you."

"Thanks." Lilian rubbed her nose. "Someone must be talking about me. I wonder who..."

"I don't care who they are so long as they're not talking about how they want to, uh..."

"Want to what?"

Kevin blushed. "You know..." When Lilian just looked at him, he leaned over and whispered in her ear, "... Do ecchi stuff."

Now Lilian was blushing as well. "Oh... I hope people aren't saying stuff like that about me either."

"Anyway," Iris continued heedlessly, "I've decided that if I can't have Lily-pad all to myself, then it would be better to share her with Kevin."

... Silence. Several crows cawed in the distance. Christine and Lindsay stared at the raven-haired vixen, realizing for perhaps the first time that this girl wasn't all there in the head.

"You plan on sharing Lilian?" Christine deadpanned.

"Hm-hm!" Iris nodded, looking quite proud of herself. "I'm magnanimous like that," she added.

"Sharing?"

"Yep."

"You plan on sharing Lilian?"

"I believe I have already stated that, yes, I plan on sharing Lily-pad." Iris crossed her arms and leaned back. "I personally think it's a great idea. I get to stay with Lily-pad, Lily-pad gets to stay with the stud, and the stud not only gets to stay with Lily-pad, but he also gets some two-girls-on-one-guy action. It's a win-win situation for everybody."

Christine didn't know what was worse: Iris's stupid idea, or the fact that said stupid idea was causing her to nosebleed.

"Are you thinking about it, nya?"

"W-w-wha—of course not! Why the hell would I want to share Kevin with anyone?!"

"I think it sounds fun."

"Shut up, you stupid cat!!"

"Nya-ha-ha!"

While Christine shoved tissue paper up her nostrils to keep from bleeding all over the table and her overcoat, Lindsay was crouched underneath the table. Her head was tucked between her knees, and her arms were wrapped around her legs. She was rocking back and forth, and there was a strange, black, mist-like substance emitting from her body.

"The hell is wrong with you?" Christine asked in a nasal voice due to the tissue paper in her nose.

"Iris keeps calling me a dyke and yet here she is, swooning over her own sister," Lindsay sniffled. "So not fair…"

It was at that moment, at that time, that Christine realized every single person she knew was certifiably insane.

She wanted to bang her head against the table.

***

Christine, Iris, and Lindsay eventually switched from sitting inside of the bakery to outside when Lilian and Kevin left after getting their food.

They sat several tables away, on the opposite end of the courtyard, watching as the redheaded fox-girl and her human mate talked and laughed about… something. They didn't know what. Not even Iris had hearing good enough to hear that far.

"They look like they're getting along well," Christine stated with a scowl. Iris noticed that despite saying otherwise, the pale-skinned girl was a lot more vested in Kevin and Lilian's date than she let on.

So I was right. She still loves the stud.

It was obvious, of course. The girl was a freaking yuki-onna. They were obsessive when it came to the people they loved, even more so than kitsune. Chances were good that this girl would love the stud for the rest of her life.

Maybe I should add her into my plans.

The more she thought about it, the better the idea sounded. Adding a tsun-loli into the mix could prove to make her sex life really interesting. Imagining a hot foursome with her, Lily-pad, the stud, and Frosty struck an erotic image in her mind that refused to leave.

I may have to alter my plans, but I'll wait to do that. First, I need to find a way to insert myself into their relationship.

Yes, Rome hadn't been built in a day, and neither had harems. If she wanted to have her own harem, then Iris would need to put some effort into this.

"Knowing those two, they're probably talking about anime or manga," Lindsay idly commented before going back to her drink, a mocha latte. Iris grabbed her own vanilla Frappuccino and took a sip. Its coolness did wonders for her throat.

They'd been forced to order drinks after the manager noticed them loafing around and said something to the effect of, *"If you're not going to buy something, then get the hell out of my store."* While Iris could have just enchanted the crotchety old woman, that would have required, at the very least, eye contact.

The eyes were the easiest place to channel youki into. This was due to how thin the film covering the eyes was. They didn't have much protection, and the cornea wasn't thick like skin, so it was easier for youki to travel through the eyes, all the way to the brain.

Unfortunately, Iris was wearing sunglasses. She also couldn't bring out her tails. That meant enchanting was out of the question.

"As much as I would love to deny your words, I honestly wouldn't be surprised if they were talking about the latest anime." Iris set her drink down and sighed. "I love my sister very much, but even I sometimes wonder about her obsession with Japanese cartoons."

Several meters away, sitting in their seats, Lilian and Kevin froze.

"Do you feel that, Kevin?"

"I did. I sense a disturbance in the animu. Someone is making fun of anime right this very second."

"And I have this strange urge to punch my sister for some reason."

"That's not very strange. Iris is always doing something to warrant you hitting her."

"Hmm... true."

"Well, you know, some of that anime stuff isn't too bad." Christine took a sip of her drink, black coffee, but then she paused. Suddenly. Abruptly. As if she had only now realized what she'd said, she looked over at Iris and Lindsay, who were giving her a pair of blank looks that made her feel awfully self-conscious. "W-what?"

"You like anime," Iris declared.

"Please don't tell me you're becoming one of those otaku people, too," Lindsay pleaded. "I've already lost Kevin to anime. I don't want to lose you as well."

"That doesn't sound dyke-ish at all."

Once more, Lindsay slipped under the table and began rocking back and forth while muttering to herself.

"I-I—shut up!" Christine hissed. She was grateful for her overcoat, hat, and sunglasses. It meant no one could see how blue her face was. "I am not turning into an otaku. I just... I wanted to see what it was all about and, well, some of the anime that I've watched aren't that bad."

"Hm, I guess I'll cut you some slack with this one," Iris said, even as she reached under the table, grabbed Lindsay by the back of her overcoat, and yanked the downtrodden girl into her seat. "I'll admit that I've watched a lot of anime with Lily-pad and the stud. Some of it can be pretty good, though I really only like the fanservice."

"Of course you do," Christine grumbled. "Why am I not surprised that the only anime you like are the ones with too much T and A?"

"Heh, because you love me?"

"Oh, shut up! I do not love you! There is absolutely no love between us!"

As Christine and Iris bickered, Lindsay took the time afforded her to recover, which was why she was the first to notice something. "Hey, you two, Lilian and Kevin are on the move."

Christine and Iris looked up to see that, indeed, Kevin and Lilian were already walking off hand in hand.

"So they are." Iris stood up. "Well, don't just sit there you two. Let's follow them."

The trio crept along behind the duo, following them from a distance. Several times they had to scramble to find cover, as there were a number of instances where either Kevin or Lilian would look back, but, for the most part, the pair appeared too engrossed in their conversation to pay attention to anything else.

They couldn't follow the two into any of the stores they went to. Most of the places they stopped at were small venues, tiny even. There was no place for even one of them to hide, much less all three of them. During these moments, the group of overcoat-wearing females would stand by a window, their faces nearly plastered to the glass as they stared in—much to the customer service rep or shopkeeper's chagrin. Several times they were even chased away by an irate manager.

It was beginning to get pretty late as Kevin and Lilian walked into another store. The sun had started to set, and the sky was becoming overcast with color.

Lindsay groaned as she leaned against the window, pressing her face into the glass and creating an imprint of her nose and left cheek. "So... tired... Iris, can we stop following them... please?"

"No way." Iris was pretty worn out, too, but there was no way she could stop now. "I haven't even learned anything new yet. I can't stop until I discover a way to seduce Lily-pad and the stud into letting me join them in bed."

"I'm not sure why you even think following them around like some kind of creeper is going to reveal something like that," Christine said. While Iris and Lindsay were sweating bullets, with their clothes practically caking to their skin, the yuki-onna seemed perfectly comfortable in her steaming hot overcoat. "Seriously, what kind of secret information are you expecting them to reveal here that you can't figure out at home?"

"I don't know. That's why I have to follow them," Iris determined, her eyes blazing like twin balls of fire. "I've tried everything I can think of to get in their good graces and nothing has worked."

Christine was afraid to ask, but she did anyway. "And what, exactly, have you tried?"

"I've snuck into bed with them after they fell asleep, tried to wash their backs while they were taking a shower, allowed them to see me naked, and attempted to bring both of them to multiple orgasms. That last one didn't work out so well," Iris admitted. "The stud complained to Lily-pad, and you know how protective she is of him."

The last time she'd tried pleasing the stud, Lilian had given her a tail smack so powerful that she had slammed headfirst into the ceiling. She swore there was still a lump on her head.

Christine's right eye began twitching violently. "Are you stupid?"

"Excuse me?"

"What makes you think any of that crap would work on them?"

"Oh, it works." Iris's eyes gleamed. "Lily-pad has never been resistant to my charms until the stud showed up, and the stud is definitely not immune to my seduction techniques. Believe me, I've seen it."

Christine blushed at the vixen's words, but she quickly shook her embarrassment off and replaced it with annoyance. "Even if that's the case, what you're doing now is never going to work. Did you ever think that maybe the reason you're not getting anywhere with them is that you're being so overbearing? I doubt Lilian and Kevin want you crowding around them like that. They're probably annoyed by the shit you pull and are just too nice to say anything about it."

"Tch, you clearly don't know what you're talking about." Iris crossed her arms under her chest, annoying Christine, who witnessed firsthand how the vixen's breasts were pushed together. Damn kitsune and their stupidly large tits. "My seduction techniques are flawless."

"Then how come you haven't managed to get in Kevin and Lilian's good graces yet?"

"I just haven't found the right technique that works on them," Iris said.

"Right. Sure, the right technique." Christine rolled her eyes. "I bet you couldn't seduce your way out of a wet paper bag."

"Oh, you wanna bet, huh?"

Iris's carmine eyes gained a brilliant luster as she stalked toward Christine, who suddenly found her body frozen in place. The snow maiden would have tried to move, but the moment she looked into Iris's eyes, she'd been ensnared, captured by those alluring, mysterious orbs.

The two-tailed kitsune walked toward her. Christine's pupils dilated as all of her focus was directed to her vision, which blotted out everything until all that was left was Iris; of the alluring sway of her hips, the enticing jiggle of her breasts, and the sensual nature of her eyes. Nothing except this impossibly sexy girl remained.

Iris stopped in front of Christine, reaching up and cupping the yuki-onna's face. Delicate fingers stroked intricate patterns along her cheeks. Christine knew that she should have done something, that she should have pushed this vixen away, but she couldn't. Her mind and body, it seemed, were bound by the strange charm that the other girl possessed.

Iris's condescending chuckle caused warm breath to wash over Christine's ear, making her shudder. Christine rubbed her thighs together, her butt cheeks clenching as unfathomably wonderful sensations shot through her groin.

"You see?" Iris said, her voice soft and gentle, the caressing lull of a dark and twisted lullaby that whispered sweet nothings in one's ear. "My techniques do work."

Then Iris stepped back.

And the strange spell that had held Christine vanished.

"E... enchantment," Christine muttered weakly, her cheeks blue and frosty. Her shoulders heaved as she gasped for air. She felt like a marathon runner who'd run without sleep for several days.

"Ha!" Iris barked. "Do you really think I'd stoop so low as to use an enchantment on you? Really? I might have used one on the stud when I was angry at him for stealing Lily-pad from me, but I don't use enchantments to capture my prey. I don't need to."

Christine covered her face with a hand. This girl hadn't used an enchantment on her? How shameful. She'd never felt so ashamed of herself in her life. How could she fall for another woman's allure?

And what did that say about her? She'd just been swayed by a woman! A woman had made her aroused! She felt disgusted with herself.

"What's this? Iris? Christine? What are you two doing here?" a voice asked.

Christine and Iris turned around. Heather Grant was standing before them, her hands on her hips and a grin on her face. She was wearing a pair of jean bell-bottoms, a light spaghetti strap shirt, and a pair of basic sandals. She looked a lot different when not wearing her coach outfit.

Christine found herself inexplicably drawn to the woman's breasts. While a part of this was undoubtedly due to envy, another part felt oddly drawn to them.

Then she realized she was ogling another woman's boobs and her face turned into an ice pop.

Damn that Iris!

Christine was straight. She knew that she was straight, but that damn vixen's previous actions were putting thoughts and ideas into her head.

I'm so going to smack her in the face for this! I'll eviscerate her!

"We're spying on the stud and Lily-pad's date," Iris said.

"Don't say that so proudly!" Christine embraced her role as the tsukkomi.

"Kevin and Lilian are on a date? Oh, my." Heather placed her hands on her cheeks and began to blush. "Young love is so romantic! And hot. I wonder how their date has been going so far? You know how teenagers are these days, don't you? Two young people go out together, enjoying the time they spend with each other, getting closer to each other until their passions overflow and they become brimming with lust before they start ripping each other's clothes off and... ah! That sounds like a great idea for a story!"

Christine and Iris were then witnesses to a blushing Heather as she pulled a notebook and pen from between her cleavage, crouched down, and began writing. Odd giggles emerged from her mouth, which reminded Christine of a perverted old man.

It was the most disturbing thing that Christine had ever seen. Iris didn't seem that bothered, however.

"So, what exactly are you doing here... Ms. Grant?" Was it wrong of Christine that the thought of calling Heather by such a proper and respectful title felt erroneous? Probably.

Heather heard the question and paused in her odd writing to stare at the two. She blinked once, twice, thrice.

"What am I doing here?" she parroted the question. "I'm training my apprentice, of course."

"Your... apprentice...?" Christine and Iris looked at each other, then back at Heather. Christine would be the one to speak up. "You still call that lecherous monkey your apprentice?"

"Of course I do," Heather said, sounding insulted that she would call Eric anything other than "apprentice." "I'm teaching him, aren't I? That makes him my apprentice, so the title of 'apprentice' is what I call him. It's only right," she finished, nodding to herself.

"So, what are you teaching him today?" asked an honestly curious Iris.

"How to grope women in public."

... Silence. Christine and Iris stared at the woman. A lot.

"How to grope women in public?" Christine repeated in a dull tone.

Was this woman really a teacher? Christine could only wonder how the hell that had happened... at least until she remembered that the principal of her school was Eric's dad. Then it all made sense.

"It's a very important skill for any pervert to have," Heather said in a very serious tone that was at complete odds with what she was talking about. "The ability to grope a woman in public without them being the wiser is something of an art form these days. I have worked hard to learn this skill."

Christine twitched. "You grope women in public?"

"That's pretty impressive," Iris said. Christine gawked at the other girl.

"Isn't it, though?" Heather looked awfully pleased to find someone who appreciated her stealth groping skills. Her smile stretched from ear to ear. "I learned how to do this from some of the H-games I've played. It takes incredible dexterity of the fingers and the ability to move around your prey unseen. It took me years of practice to truly master, but now I can proudly say that I can grope any female within my sights and they would never know it."

While Christine looked like she was just barely restraining herself from freezing the woman solid, Iris appeared thoughtful. "That does sound like an amazing skill. I'd love to learn it."

She could only imagine how useful such a skill like that would be. She could picture it now, using her legendary groping skills to assault her dear sister, coming up behind the redhead and grabbing handfuls of her darling Lily-pad's plentiful rear end, grasping and squeezing and caressing to her heart's content. And then... and then...

"Hee hee hee..."

Christine and Heather watched as Iris became a drooling, nosebleeding mass of flesh as her mind became filled with images of increasingly mature rating.

"Ugh, I can't believe I actually hang out with this girl," Christine muttered. "Why am I surrounded by perverts?"

"Speaking of perverts..." Heather pointed over to the glass window of the store that they stood in front of. "You may want to do something about Lindsay. She looks like she's lost an awful lot of blood."

Christine turned around to see what the woman meant. She began twitching when confronted by the sight of her tomboyish friend passed out cold, on the ground, her eyes swirling around inside of her eye sockets, with blood seeping out of her nose like a broken faucet.

"Beboop! Beboop!"

A pair of paramedics suddenly arrived on the scene. They were holding a stretcher between them, and the one in front was making siren-like sound effects. The two paramedics dressed in the white outfit of, well, paramedics, scooped up the nosebleeding girl and put her on the stretcher. Then they proceeded to rush out of the area.

"Beboop! Beboop! Beboop!"

They soon disappeared around a corner.

"What. The fuck. Was that?" Christine asked of no one in particular.

"Who knows," Heather said, shrugging.

"Maaaa...."

Just then, another strange sound penetrated their eardrums. The blonde human and the snow maiden cocked their heads to the side, listening. Even Iris snapped out of her hentai-induced fantasy upon hearing the strange noise.

"What is that?" she asked. "It sounds kind of like yelling."

"... ssssss..."

"I think it is yelling," Heather said.

"... teeeeEEERRRR!!!"

As the noise grew louder, the group turned to where the source was coming from.

Eric was running toward them, his arms pumping frantically, his legs taking great strides. Tears poured from his eyes in mass quantities, creating streamers that trailed behind him like odd, watery tentacles. Behind him, a horde of angry women chased after the boy. All of them were brandishing sharp and pointy objects, which they waved about furiously as they shouted death threats.

"Oh, dear," Heather said, sighing to herself. "It looks like my apprentice has failed to live up to my expectations once more."

Iris, too, stared at the young man as he ran from the horde of angry women. As she watched the mob grow ever closer, a devious idea took form in her mind.

Grabbing a small stick that happened to be lying on the ground, Iris reinforced her arm and threw it at the boy's legs.

"WWHYYY??!!"

Eric screamed as he fell to the ground. The volume of his screams increased as The Horde descended upon him. A large cloud of dust soon engulfed the area around Eric. Heather, Iris, and Christine could see nothing from within that cloud of dust except for the occasional leg or arm that stuck out. Eric's screams eventually began to peter off, growing softer and softer until they fell silent.

The cloud dispersed as the women, satisfied that they had taught the lecher a lesson, walked off in groups of two or three. Christine, Iris, and Heather stared at the lump of battered and beaten flesh that had once been known as Eric. Ever the curious one, Iris knelt down beside the young man and began poking him in the face, eliciting several whimpers and groans from the unconscious boy.

"Huh, he's still alive. I'm surprised."

"Of course," Heather declared proudly. "He's my apprentice. Even if he sucks at stealth, he's at least got the endurance and pain tolerance to withstand a beating from a horde of angry women."

Christine facepalmed, and, with her voice muffled, she said, "That's not something to be proud of."

Heather laughed as if all was right with the world. "By the way, weren't you guys spying on Kevin and Lilian? Because if so, I thought I'd tell you that they already left the store we're standing in front of."

"What?!" Iris stood up in shock. "When?"

"About fifteen minutes ago."

"And you didn't think to tell us this?!" Iris left Heather no time to answer as she grabbed Christine and began dragging her by the arm. "Come on, Frosty. We're leaving."

"Oi! Don't just grab me like this! I'm not some doll that you can drag off to wherever you please!"

"Quit complaining. We need to hurry."

Heather remained where she was as Iris dragged a reluctant and struggling Christine behind her. As the duo disappeared around a corner, she looked down at her groaning, moaning apprentice.

"We really need to work on your stealth skills some more."

Eric just moaned in response.

***

As the day wound to a close, Kevin and Lilian began their journey home.

Sitting on the small extension seat that her mate had added specifically for her, Lilian felt uplifted for the first time in a while. Her mate had been so depressed due to the events in California, so seeing him relaxed and happy again did her a world of good.

The sunset cast rays of light on Kevin as he pedaled down the road. Looking at his face revealed that the bags under his eyes had all but vanished, and the harsh shadows of a haggard face were gone, too. He looked so much better now than he had this past week.

"Today was really fun, wasn't it?" she asked, snuggling into his back. Inari-blessed did she love how warm he felt.

"Yeah, it was pretty fun," Kevin said, his voice just barely carrying over the rush of wind. "We should think about doing this more often."

"We really should," Lilian agreed.

She and Kevin had never seen much point in going out on dates since all of the things they liked to do could be done at home. Going out was often reserved for having fun with their friends. Still, she wouldn't deny that she'd had a blast. It had been so long since they'd done something, just the two of them, and she wanted to enjoy activities like what they had done today more often.

"Hey, Lilian?"

"Hmm?" Lilian cracked an eye open, having closed them at some point without realizing it. His warmth was making her sleepy.

"I just wanted to thank you for what you said, back at the mall. I'm still not really sure what my resolve is, or how I can show it to Kiara, but thanks to you, I think I'll be able to figure something out. You really are amazing."

Lilian felt heat encompass her chest. Her heart started to pump blood faster, and her cheeks began to feel warm.

She wondered if Kevin realized how much his words meant to her. He probably didn't, she reasoned, as he wasn't really the type to compliment her in order to invoke a reaction. If he was saying something complimentary, it was simply because that was what he believed. However, that made his compliments all the more meaningful to her.

Lilian's arms tightened around Kevin's waist.

"You're welcome," she said softly.

The rest of the ride was accompanied by the chirping of birds.

***

Ms. Vis pulled her little Toyota Corolla into its designated parking spot. She turned the vehicle off and stepped out, making sure to grab her small bag of groceries, and then walked toward her apartment.

Much like the residence that Ms. Swift and Lilian lived in, the complex that Ms. Vis rented out held the appearance of a standard, modern apartment complex. A series of almost identical structures lay sprawled out along several acres of land. The buildings, multi-storied constructs, were composed of a combination of brick, stucco, and red tiles. It was a nice place to live, cheap, and with a nice view of several acres of park.

She lived on the third floor.

After entering her apartment, the first thing that she did was put her groceries away. She didn't want them to spoil. After that, she made her way into the living room, where she planned on watching her favorite show—a talk show that involved a famous mathematician who lectured on how math could be applied in real-life situations.

She didn't even get halfway to her couch. A man with long red hair and golden eyes was sitting on it, lounging upon her furniture like an indulgent cat. It was hard to tell how long he'd been there, whether he'd been there since before she had arrived, or if he had somehow snuck in while she was in the kitchen. In the end, it didn't matter.

"W-who are you?" Ms. Vis stuttered, her heart rate quickening to the point where it hammered in her chest. "How did you get in here? Get out now before I call the cops!"

"Call the cops?" The man stood up, his eyes flashing and a fanged smile pulling at his lips. "How amusing. You think the cops will be able to do anything to me if you called them? They're nothing, just a group of pathetic monkeys who don't know their place. Not that I'd let you call them anyway."

Ms. Vis didn't know who this strange man was, or what he wanted, and she didn't rightly care. Some weird guy was standing in her apartment for unknown reasons. That was enough to make her rush for the phone.

She didn't get far. Quicker than Ms. Vis believed a human was capable of moving, the crimson-haired man appeared before her. He grabbed her by the wrist and lifted her off the ground.

"Unhand me, you brute!"

Ms. Vis kicked at the man, her heeled feet smacking against his legs and her free hand pounding on his chest. The man remained unbothered. His smile was wide, almost ear-splitting as if seeing her struggle was the greatest gift that she could have given him.

"Sorry," he said, not sounding sorry at all, "but I'm gonna have to use your body for a bit."

Had she not been frightened out of her mind, Ms. Vis would have asked what he meant by that. However, even if she hadn't been scared enough to release her bowels, she would have never gotten the chance to ask such a question.

Ms. Vis was forced onto the ground, on her knees. She stared up into the glowing golden eyes of her captor.

"Don't worry, though," he assured her. "I'll be sure to take good care of it for you."

As the man's eyes glowed with an ethereal molten color, her mind went blank and descended into darkness.

CHAPTER 6

Resolve

WITH HIS BACK TO THE EARLY MORNING SUN, casting him in shadow, Chris looked at the group of people that he had gathered together. They looked like regular people. Granted, the term normal was misleading. One of them was a weedy-looking kid, two looked like they spent all their time in a gym, and one of them held an appearance that all but screamed thug.

He had gathered these four for one purpose.

Revenge.

"You four know what you're supposed to do?" Chris asked.

"Of course we do," said one of them, the one in the middle. "You want us to rough up a couple of people for you. Heh. Never thought I'd see the day when you of all people would be asking us for help."

The spokesperson of the group was a large guy with thick, muscular arms, and a chest that reminded everyone who saw it of The Hulk. He wasn't the tallest person there, nor the bulkiest. That said, it was clear that the other three deferred to him. His black, liberty-spiked hair had several bells attached to them, similar to a certain Shinigami captain from a popular anime/manga series.

"You've grown weak since the last time I saw you." A grin twisted the man's face. "You used to be strong before—strong enough that you could have fought against some of our boys. Now?" He chuckled. "Now you can barely beat a human."

"Shut the fuck up!" Chris growled, baring his teeth. He didn't transform, though, having learned his lesson. Shifting to his inu form brought nothing but pain. "You wanna get fucking paid or not? 'Cause if you don't, then keep running your kami-damned mouth off and see what happens."

"It seems your temper hasn't improved," the man said, still chuckling as he held out his hands in a sign of nonaggression. "Anyway, take it easy. There's no need to get angry. I'm just surprised. After all, it's pretty odd for you to come to me for help after you turned down my offer to join our group."

Their group was a gang calling themselves the Yamata Alliance. Chris didn't know much about them, but he didn't particularly care to join others. Like his father before him, he was a lone wolf who needed help from no one—or that was how it used to be.

"Tch! Whatever," Chris grumbled, backing down. It was all he could do. Even if he wanted to put this punk ass in his place, he no longer possessed the strength needed to do it. "Do we have a fucking deal or not?"

"If you've got the money, we've got a deal."

At the mention of money, Chris grumbled and handed the man a thick wad of cash. "You get the first half now and the second half after dealing with that kitsune bitch and her human boy toy."

"That's fine." The burly man counted the cash, nodded, and then pocketed it. "My boys and I will handle those two, no problem." A dark grin spread across his face as he licked his lips. "They won't know what hit them."

***

Sitting in his usual spot near the front of the class, Kevin noticed almost right away that something was wrong with his tomboyish friend. Her face was pale, strange shadows cast stark lines on her face, and her cheekbones were hollow. She reminded him of a zombie… only without the desire to eat human flesh.

"Are you feeling okay, Lindsay? You're looking a little pale."

Lindsay froze halfway to her seat, and Kevin became a first-hand witness to the brilliant splash of color that appeared on the girl's cheeks.

Iris grinned. "The reason she's looking like a ghost is because she lost too much b—mppphhh!"

"Hahahaha!" Lindsay's laugh sounded awfully forced, strained even, as she clamped a hand over Iris's mouth to keep the two-tailed vixen from talking. "I'm just feeling a little under the weather because I didn't get much sleep last night."

"Have you been feeling restless or something?" Lilian asked, sitting on Kevin's right, looking at her friend while worrying her lower lip. "If you are, I know something that might help. Sometimes when Kevin is feeling restless after training, I'll give him a massage to help loosen his muscles and make him more relaxed. If you'd like, I can give you one during lunch to see if it helps."

Kevin couldn't be one hundred percent positive, because Lindsay's hands flew to her nose quicker than lightning, but he could have sworn that a small trickle of blood had escaped her nostrils. The fact that her face had become iridescent only made him more positive that Lindsay had just suffered a nosebleed.

Could she… he shook his head. *No, that's not possible. I must be imagining things.*

"Th-thank you for the offer, but I think I'll pass," Lindsay stuttered.

Lilian shrugged at her offer being rejected. She didn't seem too broken up.

Lindsay sat down, and, not long after she took to her desk, Ms. Vis walked in.

"Good morning, class."

Kevin thought there was something different about his teacher as she strolled into the room. He couldn't figure out what; she didn't appear any different. Her walk, her way of speaking, her mannerisms, nothing seemed out of place. However, there was an odd sort of presence about the woman now, an indefinable something that he knew she didn't have before.

Ms. Vis stopped in front of the classroom and turned to face the students. "All right, class, today we'll be—"

She stopped.

Her eyes locked with Kevin's.

"You!" She shouted, pointing an accusing finger. Kevin blinked stupidly, and then slowly raised his hand and pointed at himself. "Yes, you! What are you doing sitting in the front row?"

Okay, now Kevin knew that something was wrong with his math teacher. She had never really cared about him sitting in the front before, even when she'd been at his and Lilian's proverbial throats.

"Uh... because this is my seat?"

"No," Ms. Vis said, her head shaking emphatically. "No, no, no, no! That is not your seat! That will never be your seat! Don't you know how these things work? The main protagonist of every anime always sits in the back of the classroom near the window!"

It took Kevin a moment to register her words, but when he did, he started twitching as incredulity flooded his mind.

Did she really just say that?

"There is no way I'd ever allow myself to fall into that stereotype," he said blandly, his expression dry enough to make Arizona's deserts envious. "Don't lump me in with those god-awful protagonists of standard high school anime."

"What was that?" Ms. Vis seethed. "You dare to break such a long-standing tradition?!"

"You're damn right I do!" Kevin stood up and slammed his hands on the table. Sit in the back of the class like some kind of clichéd high school anime character? Who did this woman think she was talking to? "I'm not gonna become one of those anime romance clichés! I've already stepped on enough of those to last me a lifetime!"

As the two quarreled like a pair of children, the rest of the class watched them, their heads swiveling from left to right like they were watching a ping-pong match. Sitting at her desk, Iris offered Lilian a bag of popcorn, which she had pulled out of her bountiful cleavage. Lilian took a handful of popcorn and tossed it into her mouth. She munched on it while the bizarre fight came to a close.

"I don't care! You're going to sit your ass down in the back of the classroom next to the window like a good protagonist and you're going to like it!"

"I'm not going to sit in the back of the classroom! And here's a news flash for you, lady! This classroom has no windows!"

Ms. Vis's face became mottled red with rage. "That does it! Detention after class, Mr. Swift! De-ten-tion!"

***

Kevin was in a foul mood after Ms. Vis's class and all throughout his morning classes. How could that woman give him detention just because he refused to sit in the back of the class? She'd never cared about where he sat before, so why start now?

And what was up with her attitude? Kevin knew that Ms. Vis wasn't right in the head, but the way she'd been acting in class that day was even more unusual than, well, usual. Not only that, but to actually imply that he would allow himself to become even more like a harem protagonist than he already was, was an insult to his intelligence and dignity!

Sitting on the bleachers in the gymnasium, Kevin seethed in silence, even as his eyes panned over the expansive room to watch the other students.

They were playing dodgeball that day, girls versus boys. Kevin was kinda surprised they'd been made to play such a childish game—Coach Raide usually forced them to play more "serious" sports—but he figured the reason was due to their teacher that day. Coach Raide was absent, out sick apparently, so Heather—Ms. Grant—had been tasked with taking care of their physical education until Coach Raide was feeling better.

On a side note, Kevin believed that Coach Raide must have gotten ulcers from stress, or maybe he'd gotten a heat stroke because all of that hair he had acted as insulation.

Kevin had been knocked out of the game early, having received a powerful ball to the face for not paying attention. While he had no evidence to prove it, he was almost positive that Iris had been the one to throw that ball. When he'd looked at her with an accusing stare, she'd just turned away and whistled in a way that was far too innocent to be truly innocent.

Putting his mind off of Ms. Vis and her brand of crazy, Kevin turned his thoughts to another matter, one that had been causing him more problems than his freaky math teacher: How to show his resolve to Kiara.

He wasn't sure how to prove that he possessed the resolve to continue training. It wasn't as simple a matter as telling her, *"I'm ready to start training again."* He needed to show his resolve, but he didn't know how to go about accomplishing that. What was he supposed to do? Beat the crap out of a bunch of yōkai?

"You look like you've got something on your mind," a familiar voice said. He looked down. Heather Grant walked up the bleachers, sat down next to him, and leaned back in a casual manner that would have given Coach Raide fits. "You wanna talk about whatever is troubling you?"

Kevin debated the merits of telling Ms. Grant about his problem. He had never been all that close to the woman, but she had helped him quite a bit in the past few months, and he had been sparring with her before their trip to California. Also, although he didn't want to admit it, an added perspective may help him reach a conclusion that he wouldn't have found otherwise.

With nothing to lose, he told Ms. Grant about his problem. The assistant coach sat there, listening as he spoke, not saying a word. When he finished relating his issue to her, the woman leaned back against the bleachers.

"Kiara said all that, huh?" Ms. Grant rubbed her chin. "That definitely sounds like something she'd say. She's pretty big on things like commitment and resolve, especially when it comes to you."

"What do you mean?" Kevin expressed confusion by tilting his head and blinking.

"I mean that Kiara's sweet on you."

Kevin recoiled in shock, and a bit of horror, but mostly shock. Kiara was sweet on him? Really? That was just... he didn't even know what to say to that. The idea of Kiara liking him like, well, like *that* was kind of—no, it was really creepy.

His inner thoughts must have been reflected on his face because Ms. Grant was quick to amend her statement. "Not like that. I don't mean she wants to do the horizontal mambo with you or anything, just that you hold a special place in her heart." With a conspiratorial look on her face, the blonde woman leaned in and whispered, "Just between you and me, I'm pretty sure Kiara thinks of you as the brother she wishes Chris would be."

Kevin felt relief sweep through him. "Oh, thank god. For a moment I thought you meant—well, let's just say I'm very glad I'm wrong."

He was also touched. While he'd never really thought of Kiara as anything other than that really awesome instructor who was teaching him how to fight, he would admit that she was a pretty cool character, and he respected her a lot.

Kiara F. Kuyo was the owner of the largest chain of fitness centers in the United States. She was featured in almost every health and fitness magazine available. He saw her face at the freaking grocery store every time he looked at the magazine racks. She was one of the strongest people he knew, and, to top it all off, she had ripped her own arm off and thrown it at someone.

And, okay, yeah, ripping your own arm off and throwing it at someone was kind of gross, but it was also really cool. It took some serious grit to do something so insane.

"Heh, I can tell." Ms. Grant grinned at him. "Anyway, I'm pretty sure the reason Kiara is getting onto you about your resolve is that she cares about you more than she's willing to let on. The yōkai world is a dangerous place, as I'm sure you know. It's definitely not the kind of world you can enter and not expect to get your hands stained with blood. So far, you've been lucky. It's been almost six months since you entered this world, and you've only had to kill one person that entire time."

"Have you killed anyone before?" Kevin asked before he could stop himself. "I'm sorry! I shouldn't have asked something so personal. It's just that when you said that, it sounded like you were speaking from experience."

At the question, Ms. Grant's face became quite melancholic. Her smile, still in place, dimmed, shifting from cheerful to sad in seconds.

"It's all right. I understand your curiosity, and I don't mind answering that question." Ms. Grant paused as if gathering her thoughts. "Yes, I have killed before. Remember that while I might not be into the whole 'protect humanity from the yōkai menace' thing, I was still once a member of the Sons and Daughters of Humanity—and a captain to boot. You don't get to a position like that without taking lives. I myself have personally ended the lives of several yōkai, and the unit that I commanded before being relegated to Arizona was well-known for wiping out numerous yōkai clans."

"I see…" Kevin smiled sadly. "I guess I really have been lucky, then."

"Yep," Ms. Grant replied, acting cheerful once more. "I'd say you're luckier than any human who's entered the yōkai world has a right to be. So far, you've only faced off against small fry: two-tailed kitsune with a chip on their shoulder and the like. They're not that strong, and they're inherently cocky when fighting humans because we lack their supernatural powers. Defeating them without killing them isn't that hard, provided you know how."

Two-tailed kitsune were one of the weakest types of yōkai. They lacked the youki capacity to use more powerful techniques. Indeed, few were the two-tails who could use more than basic illusions.

Lilian and Iris were strong, but they had pedigree. Born to a prominent clan, their youki was naturally stronger than the average two-tails. More than that, both of them had a strong affinity for their element. A specialized technique required less youki from them than it would from the average two-tailed kitsune.

Kevin wouldn't deny that he was lucky. Sure, he'd gotten into some hairy situations, but none of the kitsune that he'd fought had been very strong. They were stronger than him, to be sure, but not strong enough that anyone other than a human would have had trouble dealing with them.

Ms. Grant studied him for a second before continuing where she'd left off. "But you're eventually gonna be forced into situations where your opponent is more powerful, where they won't underestimate you for being human, where you'll have to choose between killing them or getting killed by them." Ms. Grant put a hand on Kevin's shoulder. "I know that isn't something you wanna hear, but it is something that you need to hear. If you really are serious about being a part of this world, a part of Lilian's world, then you need to harden your heart, reaffirm your resolve, and continue to move forward. That's the only way humans like us will ever survive in a world where everybody else has supernatural powers."

Ms. Grant removed her hand from his shoulder and walked back down the bleachers. She blew her whistle and started yelling at some kids who were goofing off.

Kevin sat there, lost in thought.

The resolve to remain a part of Lilian's world, to fight against creatures that could kill him, to kill those creatures should it come to that. Could he really find that kind of resolve? Kevin didn't know.

That was why, for the rest of class, he sat there and stewed in silence.

***

Even after gym had ended and lunch began, Kevin was still thinking about his conversation with Ms. Grant. Even during the rest of his classes that day, his mind still churned in contemplation. He was even still thinking about it when he arrived at Ms. Vis's classroom to serve detention.

Lilian was not with him. She hadn't gotten detention, and while she'd offered to wait for him, he told her not to bother. He'd be home eventually. It wasn't like a few hours apart would kill them.

Almost before he knocked on the door to Ms. Vis's classroom, Kevin could tell that something was wrong. There was no indication that anything was out of place, nothing that warranted his sudden wariness. It was just a feeling. Some indefinable sensation was causing the hair on the back of his neck to tingle. Still, he knocked on the door all the same.

"Come in," the voice of his math teacher spoke from behind the door.

He opened the door and entered. The room was dark. Upon shutting the door, Kevin was cast within that darkness. A few candles arrayed around the room shed some light upon the class, burning, flickering, casting dark shadows that danced along the floor and walls and ceiling. Strange objects lay scattered around the floor, white and dark red—petals, Kevin realized. They were flower petals.

What the heck?

"I'm glad you could make it, Mr. Swift."

If Kevin had been given any indication of what he was about to see, he would have seriously considered running away screaming... or trying to gouge his eyes out with a rusty spork. Either one would have worked.

Ms. Vis lay sprawled on her desk, which had been cleared of everything, including her computer. She was on her side, facing him, her right hand used to pillow her head, and her left idly caressing her hips, fingers drawing circles on her bare skin. It was a position that reminded him of a *Playboy* cover model... or Iris. She took that position a lot, too.

Of course, thinking of Iris brought another point home—this woman, his teacher, was wearing negligée, a little black one-piece that barely covered her body and was partially translucent.

Kevin thought he was going to be sick.

"Wha-what the hell are you wearing?!" he shrieked.

"Do you like it?" Ms. Vis smirked. Kevin turned green. "I bought this a while ago but haven't had a chance to use it before now."

In one smooth, flowing motion that was far too graceful for someone like Ms. Vis to be capable of doing, the math teacher stood from her desk and began stalking over to Kevin.

He backed away from her. "W-what are you doing?"

"You've been an awfully bad boy, Mr. Swift." Dark eyes like smoldering flames burned in the low-lit room. A smirk that would have been tantalizing on someone like, say, Iris, just looked wrong on the face of his teacher. His stomach rebelled. He felt like he was going to throw up. "I've tried and tried and tried to make you see the error of your ways, but you just don't seem to want to listen. It is beginning to get... frustrating," she growled at the end, a guttural sound that didn't belong to a human.

Kevin pressed his back against the wall. He was unable to move further, and still, Ms. Vis stalked forward, pressing her hands on either side of his head and staring at him with eyes like black holes. Those eyes seemed to contain an unfathomable hunger that nothing could satiate.

"I have finally decided that to learn your lesson properly, a little... physical reinforcement is needed."

Kevin would have wondered about the veracity of her statement—what the hell was he supposed to be learning here anyway?—but his mind, horrified beyond measure, was a little too busy trying to keep from vomiting. Ms. Vis was not a terribly ugly woman, nor was she all that attractive. It was just that the sight of his teacher in skimpy clothing had caused his brain to short-circuit. Like an overheating computer, all of his internal components had been fried beyond recognition.

Ms. Vis seemed to notice his predicament. Her lips peeled back in a feral smile, revealing sharp canines that truly made her appearance similar to a vampire.

"Now then, Mr. Swift..."

Kevin shuddered as she closed the distance.

"For the next hour and a half..."

She breathed on him. It was horrendous.

"... You are—"

BANG!

"What the hell do nyou think nyou're doing to Master Kevin, nya!!"

The sound of the door slamming open was followed by loud shouting. Ms. Vis's startled face turned toward the source of the voice—and then she received a face full of boot.

Kevin remained frozen as the woman who, just seconds prior, looked like she was about to rape him, was sent flying. Ms. Vis's scream was abruptly silenced when she smacked against the wall with a harsh thud that rattled the room. Slowly, her body peeled off the wall like it had been stuck there with glue, clattering to the floor with a dull thump.

Standing before Kevin, looking absolutely livid, was a woman. Her black hair hung about her face and traveled down her back in several artistically intricate braids. Eyes like two yellow moons peered out from a face of incredible beauty, though that beauty was marred by anger at the moment. Then he noticed her clothes.

Who the heck wears so much leather? Isn't she burning up?

"I can't take my eyes off nyou for a single second, nya!" The woman hissed at the fallen teacher, who merely groaned in response. Kevin didn't even think Ms. Vis was conscious. "Nyou think nyou can just go off and do whatever nyou want because nyou're older than me?! Don't be foolish! As if I would let nyou lay a hand on Master Kevin, nya!"

Master Kevin...? The heck?

"Um, excuse me," Kevin said timidly. The aura that this woman was emitting frightened him, even if he would never admit it. "But... have we met somewhere before?" The dark-haired female peered at him, her head tilted curiously. "It's just that... you seem to know me..."

"Ah!" The woman gasped. Then her cheeks turned a brilliant crimson, visible even within the low lighting. "I-I... we met, but it was a really long time ago. I doubt you even remember me, nya." The way she said that and the forced laugh that she gave made Kevin feel kind of guilty.

"I'm sorry."

The woman's eyes widened as she began frantically waving her hands in front of her face. "No, no. There's no need to apologize, nya. It was a really long time ago, so it's okay, nya."

"W-well, if you say so…" Kevin felt awkward and guilty. This woman knew him when he didn't know her, and she called him "master." That took this situation to another level of awkward.

He also wondered what her relationship with Ms. Vis was, but he felt it would be inappropriate to ask.

"A-anyway." The woman coughed into her hand. "Why don't you head on home now, nya?" She glared at the still moaning woman lying on the floor. "I'll deal with hi—her."

Now that was an idea that Kevin could get behind. He didn't want to be in Ms. Vis's presence any longer.

"Okay." Kevin turned to leave, but on a whim, he stopped and looked back at the woman. "Um, would you mind giving me your name?"

The female's yellow eyes widened in surprise, but the look disappeared quickly to be replaced by a warm smile. "It's Cassy. Cassy Belladonna."

***

Cassy waited until the door slowly shut with a soft *click*. She proceeded to turn on the lights and snuff out the candles. Then she turned to look at "Ms. Vis," who had regained consciousness and was now climbing to her feet.

"What the hell was that about, nya?" she asked.

"Ms. Vis" smirked at her in a decidedly un-Ms. Vis fashion. "There's no need to get upset. I was just having a little bit of fun."

"Fun?" Cassy hissed. "You call nearly mentally scarring a young man fun, nya? You kitsune… all of you have a really sick sense of humor, nya. And don't think you can just lie to me. I don't know what you want with Master Kevin, but if you think for one second that I am going to allow you to harm a single hair on his head, nya, then you don't know me nearly as well as you think you do, nya."

"Ha..." Ms. Vis sighed, placing a hand on the back of her neck and cracking it several times. "I see you're still hung up on that boy, Inari only knows why. He doesn't look like anything special." His gaze became sharper than a katana. "Regardless, do not think you can order me around here. You forget who's in charge. It's not you, the failure who couldn't even accomplish a single mission. It's me."

Cassy bared her fangs in anger. Seth remained unconcerned.

"There is a reason why Sarah puts up with my antics. I have accomplished every single mission that I've ever been sent on with distinction. Never once have I failed, unlike you." His gaze, sharp enough to slice through steel, bore into her with intensity. "Do not think that you have any control over me or this mission. You are under my command. For all intents and purposes, you're nothing but a slave to my will. Remember that."

Cassy glared at her superior. She knew the real reason that Seth had gone after Master Kevin. He was close to Lilian. She'd seen the enchantment he'd been trying to weave over the boy. He'd been planning to use Kevin for his own purposes.

"And you remember this." Cassy pointed a finger at her superior. "I do not care if you're in charge of this mission or me. I will not allow you to harm Master Kevin, nya. Try casting an enchantment on him again, try using him like that again, nya, and I don't care if you are my superior, I will put you down faster than you can say 'Mistress Sarah.'"

"And once again the bleeding heart cries out." Seth was nothing if not amused. "You know that kindness is why you can't accomplish a single mission. You're too soft."

Cassy gritted her teeth. "I'd rather be soft and still retain my soul rather than turn into a disgusting monster who takes pleasure in the pain of others like you."

Seth shrugged Ms. Vis's shoulders. "And that is why you're a failure. You fail to realize that we are assassins. Compassion. Mercy. These words do not belong in our vocabulary. They will only hinder us. They'll keep us from being able to accomplish our goals and completing our missions. You'd best keep that in mind."

Did Seth think she didn't know that? Cassy was more aware of her own flaws than anyone. She had realized long ago that she lacked the heart of a cold-blooded killer. She knew that, but she didn't care. Her heart made her who she was, and if she had to sacrifice the ability to kill without mercy in exchange for retaining her morality, then that was fine with her.

"Still, for the sake of keeping things between us cordial, I shall hold off on doing anything to the boy... for now," Seth said. "However, whether or not that will continue to be the case is going to be largely dependent on the success of our mission. Should you fail, then I will not only use the boy as I please, but I'll also make sure you watch as I torture him to death and turn him into one of my puppets. Maybe seeing something you cherish taken away from you will make you understand why assassins aren't supposed to have any attachments."

Cassy stood, her clenched fists shaking with barely restrained rage. She wanted to rip Seth's face off but knew she couldn't. He was still her superior and, even if she would never admit this out loud, Seth frightened her. They may have had similar powers, but his were far more potent than her own.

That didn't stop her from wishing incredible bodily harm to his person.

"Now then," Seth said in Ms. Vis's voice and with her face. "You're going to head out and find that Lilian girl. I tricked some idiotic young pup with a grudge against her into paying a couple of thugs to deal with her. With luck, they'll kill her, but if they fail, I want you to finish the job. Go on now. You don't have all day."

Angry at her own helplessness and inability to fight against this man, Cassy could do nothing more than walk out of the door, heading in the direction that she knew Kevin's house was located.

***

Lilian and Iris rode the bus alone that day.

Staring out the window, watching as trees and cars and signs passed by in a blur, Lilian cursed Ms. Vis with all her heart. Who did that woman think she was? Giving Kevin detention for such a stupid reason as *"he wouldn't sit in the back of the class like an anime stereotype"* was the dumbest thing she'd ever heard. What kind of teacher did that?

Ms. Vis, apparently, though just why the woman seemed so set on punishing her mate for such a banal reason still eluded her.

"You know, I didn't think I'd be saying this, but it feels kinda odd to be on this bus without the stud around," Iris said, getting Lilian to look at her. "Don't you think it feels a little strange? Like there's something out of place or missing?"

After the initial hostilities between Kevin and Iris had ceased, the succubus of a kitsune had finally accepted Kevin as Lilian's mate. Of course, she still acted like a creepy siscon, but that was just a part of her character. Even though her personality caused a lot of trouble, Lilian didn't want Iris to change anything about herself.

"It does feel weird," Lilian agreed. "I've become so used to having Kevin always with me that not having him by my side makes me feel edgy."

"In that case, I suppose it'll be up to me to take the edge off." A grinning Iris threw an arm over Lilian's shoulder and drew her close. "I'm not the stud, but I'm sure I can make a pretty damn good replacement. Anything for my adorable Lily-pad."

"I wish you wouldn't say things like that," Lilian deadpanned, though she didn't deny her sister closeness either. She did, however, smack Iris when the girl got a little too frisky.

The bus soon came to halt at their stop. Lilian and Iris stepped off and began the walk home.

The bus had stopped at the crossroads of 17th Street and McDonald Road. The Le Monte apartment complex was about a fifteen minute walk at a sedate pace. While this area of Phoenix was mostly a residential district filled with apartment complexes, there were several office buildings, which Lilian and Iris cut through.

As they were walking, a strange prickling sensation crawled down Lilian's spine. She didn't know what it meant—not until a shimmering blue barrier appeared around them. It took the shape of a large dome, which encompassed the entire parking lot and all of the buildings.

Th-this is a barrier technique!

Barrier techniques were unique specialized skills that created barriers around objects. They were often used to protect people, but they could also be used to trap them too. Such was the case now. She and Iris were trapped, and the only way to escape from this barrier would be to defeat whoever had raised it.

Overpowering it was also an option, but neither she nor Iris possessed the necessary amount of youki to break a barrier that was powerful enough to cover an entire complex.

"Now what do we have here?" a voice spoke up. "A couple of little foxes all lost and alone, with nowhere to go, so far away from home."

Turning, the two girls found a group of people shimmering into existence like light particles coalescing into solid form. There were four of them, a weedy kid with beady eyes and large buck teeth, two hulking brutes that must have been part gorilla or something, and a man with spiky hair and dark eyes.

It was the man in the middle they paid attention to. Perhaps unsurprisingly, the first thing they noticed was how large he was. He wasn't just tall, but he was also big and bulky. He looked like one of those pro wrestlers in the WWF. He even dressed like one with his ripped black jeans, white muscle shirt, leather jacket, and combat boots. Lilian was reminded of those stereotypical bully characters that she always read about in shōnen manga with a high school setting.

He walked up to them, and Lilian and Iris both tensed when his hulking form blocked out the light.

"What do you want?" Lilian asked with a confidence she wasn't quite feeling.

The four were obviously yōkai, though what race they were remained unknown. She was confident in her illusions but having started training with Kotohime, Lilian knew that she lacked the battle instincts necessary to fight on par with yōkai who actually enjoyed combat—and these guys looked like they reveled in battle.

"I thought that would be obvious," the man said, his grinning face boring its way into her soul. "We've been asked by a certain individual to teach you a lesson, and while I'm loath to mar such pretty faces, money is money and so, we're gonna be teaching you what happens when you cross the wrong people."

***

Kevin Swift wondered what he should do for the next half hour. The late bus wouldn't be leaving until four, and it was currently three-thirty, which meant he had a bit of time to kill. Maybe he should go to the library and grab something to read? They had a small section dedicated to manga because of how popular it was becoming in North America. Maybe they would have something he hadn't read yet.

Before he could think about turning thoughts into action, a figure stood in his path. Kevin almost scowled when he saw who it was.

"Chris…"

"Swift."

Chris Fleischer had not been on Kevin's mind very much these days. While at one point, the boy in question had been the most frightening person in school, something akin to the high school boogeyman, these days he was a joke. Ever since Lilian destroyed his ability to use youki with her divine powers, he'd become the laughingstock of the school.

"What do you want?" Kevin asked.

Chris smirked. "I just wanted to see your face before it gets messed up."

That didn't sound ominous at all.

"What? What is that supposed to mean?"

Apparently all too happy to gloat, Chris said, "It means just what I said. I've got some people who are going to be taking care of you and that damn fox-whore of yours. In fact, I wouldn't be surprised if they've already ripped your precious little kitsune bitch limb from limb."

Something within Kevin's stomach tightened. An unpleasant ball had settled in his gut.

Chris was a fool and a gloater, as evidenced by what he was telling Kevin. It probably didn't even occur to the inu that Kevin might use this knowledge against him. As far as Chris was concerned, he had already won. Kevin could see it in the victorious glimmer contained within the other teen's eyes.

"Someone's attacking Lilian?"

"That's right!" Chris crowed. "You're both going to get it now! You thought I was strong? These guys are the fucking real deal! Each one of them is a powerful yōkai capable of tearing through steel and concrete like it's fucking paper! They're gonna murder your little cum bucket, and then they're going to—"

Chris did not get the chance to say anymore.

Because at that exact moment, the sole of Kevin's shoe slammed against his face.

As the former bully fell to the ground—the back of his head meeting concrete with a loud *crack!*—Kevin took off toward the parking lot. Lilian and Iris should have arrived home by now, but if they were being attacked, then they'd likely been ambushed after getting off the bus.

That meant it would take him thirty minutes of solid running to reach them.

Kevin pushed his body as hard as he could and sped out of the school gates. He would make it in twenty.

***

Christine was just leaving the library when she saw Kevin peel out of the school gate like a man possessed. She paused.

Are you thinking what I'm thinking, nya?

Yes.

She nodded, for once in agreement with her nekomata half.

Let's follow him! they thought at the same time.

***

From the moment the group of yōkai changed forms, the battle had begun. The group of four split up. Two of them went after Lilian while one went after Iris. The leader hung back, his arms crossed, and a fanged smirk adorning his now red-skinned face.

When Lilian initially thought that the two who were now trying to kill her looked like gorillas, she hadn't meant that in a literal sense. Of course, seeing them standing before her now, with fur sprouting from their bodies, crouched down on all fours and walking on their knuckles, Lilian knew these two were, indeed, gorilla yōkai.

Their bodies had easily grown to twice their original size. They loomed over her like Cthulhu over a city. Thick brow ridges protected their eyes and made their ugly, inhuman mugs look even more hideous.

One of them slammed their knuckles onto the ground. Concrete broke underneath the blow. That seemed to be the signal, as the two charged at Lilian faster than she would have believed possible, bounding toward her on all fours.

The one on the left reached her first. It roared while bringing down a massive fist to crush her like a human crushing an ant. The attack missed, or rather, Lilian simply wasn't there when it hit. The ground cracked underneath the powerful strike, but it went straight through Lilian as if she were a ghost...

... Or an illusion.

The world around the gorilla became distorted. Colors inverted. The world flipped upside down and reversed. White turned to black and shades became mute.

Kitsune Art: Inversion was a powerful illusory technique that screwed with a person's mind and messed up their brain's ability to render visual data properly. This resulted in a skewed sense of balance, damaged retina, and could even lead to insanity if the one who was trapped wasn't mentally strong enough to withstand having their perceptions twisted.

It would have worked. It should have worked. Unfortunately, Lilian hadn't realized something: Gorillas may look stupid, but they weren't. They were surprisingly intelligent and more than capable of thinking through a situation like this logically.

The gorilla yōkai that she'd trapped in her illusion closed his eyes. If his vision was impaired, then he just wouldn't use it. Instead, he sniffed Lilian out. His roar filled the air when he caught her scent. Cement was pulverized underneath his feet as he charged straight for Lilian, who, upon realizing that her illusion had failed, appeared within a shimmer of light.

"Do not think something like a simple illusion will work on me?!" The gorilla yōkai roared. "I'm not some simple-minded creature that will allow himself to be fooled by cheap parlor tricks!"

Lilian tensed and prepared to dodge her opponent's next move. However, with her attention turned toward the giant mass of muscle and fur charging at her, she'd completely forgotten about the other gorilla yōkai that had been there—not until a shadow suddenly loomed over her from behind.

"GYA!"

Lilian was sent flying when a large, hairy hand slammed into her with the force of a freight train.

***

"Lilian!" Iris shouted as her sister was smacked by a large hand.

Like a ragdoll that had been tossed by an angry child, Lilian slammed into the ground and rolled across the parking lot. Iris felt fear wash over her, overpowering her common sense. She'd never been so afraid in her life.

She turned around and tried to rush toward her sister, but the world around her suddenly changed. Lilian disappeared. The other yōkai vanished. Even the buildings, cars, and pavilions were gone as if they'd never existed in the first place.

What had once been a parking space between buildings had been replaced with sand. Everywhere she looked, there was nothing but sand. Large dunes that stretched out for miles, far beyond the event horizon, glowing dully in the light of the sunset.

Iris looked down to see that her feet were also covered in sand—no, not covered. She was getting pulled into the sand. Inch by inch, her body descended into the depths of countless shifting granules. Her calves soon disappeared, followed by her knees, then her thighs.

It took until her navel had nearly disappeared for Iris to get it together and flare her youki. The illusion shattered, and she was suddenly standing back in the parking lot, the sand gone, and her opponent standing several feet away. Over to her left, Lilian climbed shakily to her feet, blood dribbling down her mouth and her left hand holding her right shoulder.

Iris wanted to rush over to Lilian, but she couldn't do anything for her sister. Not right now. Not when she had her own opponent to deal with. All she could do was pray that Lilian would be able to hold on until she dealt with her own foe.

"Did you really think an illusion would work on me?" Iris asked, scoffing at her opponent. "I'm a kitsune. Illusions are in my blood. A yōkai like yourself would never be able to trap me within one for very long."

Her opponent was a rotund, bear-like animal, wearing a straw hat and carrying a bottle of sake in his left hand. Tan fur covered his body from head to toe. A large tail stuck out from behind his back, thick and flat, and his two squat legs kept him standing upright. Iris vaguely recognized this yōkai. He was a tanuki, a yōkai who was said to be the brother of kitsune.

She couldn't see the resemblance.

"That may be the case, but who said that my illusion was meant to trap you for long? I only needed you distracted and unable to act long enough to enact my plan."

"What?!"

That was when Iris noticed that her legs still felt like they were stuck in quicksand. A glance down revealed several thick strands of sand wrapped around her legs like a rope. They constricted around her tightly, the many grains rubbing her skin raw.

"Oh, shit!"

Iris was jerked off her feet and into the air. Gritting her teeth as wind sailed all around her, whistling loudly in her ear, she concentrated on producing a tiny black flame from the tip of her tails, which she slammed into the sand at least a meter from her own body so as not to be caught by her own attack.

The sand was erased from existence, consumed by the black fires of the Void. Unable to retain its cohesiveness due to the disruption, the rest of the sand broke apart, scattering and blowing away with the wind.

Glaring daggers at her enemy, Iris angled her descent so that she was going to land directly on top of the tanuki. Her tan-furred foe looked up and prepared to launch more sand her way, but Iris wasn't about to let this fat-ass of a yōkai pull it off.

"Kitsune Art: Rain of Oblivion."

From the tips of her tails, two black spheres burst into existence. The flames branched off, splitting and separating into more flames before moving off in different directions in a strange form of osmosis. By the time two seconds had passed, there were over one hundred tiny black flames hovering in the air.

"Now…"

Iris pointed a single finger at her opponent, her body still falling toward the earth as gravity pulled her down.

"You die…"

Like the furious rainstorms of the South American rain forests, the black flames descended upon the hapless tanuki with relentless tenacity.

* * *

There were very few times that Lilian cursed being born a kitsune. Back when she'd reached the age of a hundred and thirty and the matriarch decided to try marrying her off, she had cursed her fate. That had lasted for exactly twenty-three years until she met a young Kevin. She hadn't regretted being born kitsune after that… until now.

It was well-known among the yōkai world that kitsune, until they gained their fourth tail, were some of the weakest yōkai alive. A kitsune's body was just as weak as a human's, and because of their deficient youki capacity, no kitsune under four tails could use reinforcement to its fullest. That was why kitsune with three or two tails had to rely on illusions to get out of tricky situations.

It was also why most kitsune ran from a fight if the chance presented itself. They just weren't able to fight on par with other yōkai until they gained more tails and experience.

The number of tails a kitsune possessed equaled the amount of power they had, with each tail gained multiplying their power by the number of tails itself. A three-tails would have the strength of two two-tails, a four-tails would have the strength of nine three-tails, a five-tails would have the strength of sixteen four-tails, and so on.

Lilian, with only two tails worth of power, lacked the youki necessary for anything more than illusions, the less youki-intensive Celestial attacks, and short, precisely timed bursts of reinforcement.

It wasn't enough.

The two gorilla yōkai came at her from either side, trapping her in a pincer maneuver. One came in to swat her like a fly. The other tried to crush her beneath his fist.

The first attack went right through her, revealing that Lilian had used a very well-timed illusion to displace her own body and make it look like she'd been standing there. The real Lilian rolled across the ground, avoiding the crushing hammer blow and kipping back to her feet. She spun around, two spheres of light igniting on her tails, burning with the divine powers of a Celestial Kitsune.

"Celestial Art: Spheres of Light."

Her tails acted as a trebuchet. She slung them forward at maximum velocity and launched the spheres into the back of the nearest gorilla yōkai. The attacks struck the large mass of muscle right between the shoulder blades, causing him to stumble forward. His fur was singed, black, and created a distinct scent that wafted through the air.

Unfortunately, the attack didn't seem to have harmed him so much as angered him. The gorilla yōkai let loose with a roar and beat on his chest like Tarzan.

"Damn fox!"

Lilian reinforced her legs with youki, as much as she dared, and used her enhanced muscles to take several large leaps backward. She avoided one of the bull-rushing gorillas, allowing him to smash right into a car, crushing it like a tin can. The other also charged toward her, but she leaped into the air, clear over his head. Her intention was to land on his other side and attack from behind.

A large hand grabbed her shapely calf, showing that she'd misjudged the creature's reach.

"Take this!"

Screaming her head off, Lilian was sent hurtling toward the ground.

"AGH—GUH!"

Lilian nearly swallowed her tongue as her back slammed into the blacktop with enough force to form a crater. Pain the likes of which she hadn't felt since her fight with Kiara flooded her body. Her vision blurred. Darkness crowded around the edges. She wanted to curl up into a ball and weep until her body healed.

But she couldn't.

Because looming above her like a giant colossus was one of the gorilla yōkai, and his fist was descending toward her face at an incredible rate.

Lilian gritted her teeth as she launched two spheres of light at the furry supernatural being. The twin spheres of Celestial energy struck the yōkai right in the eyes, burning straight through his corneas.

"GRAAA!"

The fist continued to descend as the creature roared, but the pain knocked it off course. Lilian rolled along the ground, avoiding the blow and using her reinforced tails to leap out of the crater.

"IT BURNS! IT BURNS!"

The gorilla yōkai who'd had his eyes seared by divine powers stumbled around drunkenly, his hands covering his devastated corneas. Lilian hoped she'd blinded him for good. The amount of power that she had pumped into that attack should have been enough to destroy his eyeballs.

"DAMN YOU!"

Whether it worked or not soon became irrelevant when loud stomping alerted her to the other gorilla yōkai charging her from behind. She spun around…

… and was just in time to see her enemy right in front of her face. He plowed into her with the speed of a Gundam entering the atmosphere at terminal velocity.

Lilian's world became a torrent of agony.

**

The orbs of Void fire rained pandemonium on the hapless parking lot. Everywhere they struck was consumed by the insatiable sentient hunger that was the Void. Everything was erased from existence, right down to its very concept.

The Void is a most unusual thing. Unlike every other element, be they Celestial or otherwise, the Void had a limited form of sentience. It wasn't truly sentient, of course, but merely acted like it.

While not a living, sentient being, the Void hungered like one. It held one desire: To consume everything and bring the world closer to the final oblivion. In accordance with this fact, the Void had, if not true sentience, then at least the ability to determine what it should consume first.

Thus, when the orbs of hellish black flames descended upon the earth, the first thing they did was seek out the closest living organism. They sought to devour the tanuki.

"Aw, shit! Not good! Not good!"

Like a fox fleeing from a dog, the tanuki fled from the Void fire that rushed to consume him. As the flames of the Void doggedly tailed its foe, the blacktop it traveled over was consumed, leaving nothing but blackened earth still burning in hellish flames.

While Void fire is not sentient and therefore not capable of thinking tactically, it does have a sense, a desire to consume that which it seeks in the most expedient manner possible. It is not capable of thought, but it can sometimes behave as if it does.

Which explained why the tanuki suddenly found himself surrounded by black flames on all sides. The supernatural creature realized, at that moment, that he could not dodge the flames that even now rushed to consume him.

Iris watched in satisfaction as her Void fire crashed into the tanuki with the violence of a lion tearing apart an antelope. It had taken some work. She'd been forced to combine an illusion with standard Void fire, making the tanuki think that there was more Void fire than there actually was. Then she had used the illusion to guide the tanuki into her trap. Yes, it took a lot of effort, but it had been well worth it.

She turned away and prepared to help her sister, who was clearly outmatched by the two ferocious gorilla yōkai.

She was just about to run toward the redhead, only to stumble forward as blood splashed across the ground. Her mind exploded with agony as something penetrated her back, pierced all the way through her body, and jutted out of her right shoulder. Iris looked down, not quite able to believe what she was seeing.

Sticking out of her shoulder was a spear made entirely of sand.

"What is…?"

"Don't think this fight is over, kitsune," a voice said from behind her. It sent chills down her spine. "This battle is far from over."

With her legs wobbling precariously as they struggled to keep her standing, Iris turned around. The yōkai who she had thought she'd killed was walking out of the black Void flames. Her mind went numb with shock.

"No… no way… there's just… no way you could have survived that…"

The Void is known as the most destructive force in the world due to how it operates. The Void consumes everything it comes into contact with. It is the literal end of all things. Anything that touches the Void is erased; its very presence on this earth becoming nothing but a distant memory.

There should have been no way for this tanuki to survive.

And then she saw it.

The sand sloughing off his frame like molten slag as it was consumed by black flames.

He covered himself in a thick layer of sand, her pain-filled mind realized. *The top few layers of sand were consumed by the Void, allowing him to escape unharmed before the fire could reach his body.*

If she'd had more tails, at least three, she could have made the Void fire powerful enough to consume the tanuki, sand and all. Being only a two-tails with an incredible aptitude for her element meant that all she could do was use standard Void attacks that lacked the power to truly consume everything before the youki fueling it was consumed.

"You're a dangerous opponent," the tanuki said seriously. "I underestimated you because you've only got two tails. That won't happen again."

Sand gathered in the air like streamers blowing in the wind. They swirled around the tanuki, coalescing into a giant ball and hardening. Then, all at once, the sand burst forward and took shape. A streamlined muzzle filled with sharp, jagged teeth emerged from the giant sphere. The dragon head, one of the eastern variety, flew forward and clamped down on the nonplussed Iris's shoulder, biting through flesh, muscle, and bone with ease.

Iris's scream echoed across the parking lot turned battlefield.

***

The gorilla yōkai that had slammed into Lilian kept going well after ramming her like a speeding truck. He blasted straight into a building, the wall blowing inward as he continued running. Lilian's back screamed in pain as shards of broken brick carved bloody furrows into her skin.

Then, without warning, the gorilla yōkai stopped moving. However, Lilian, with nothing to halt her momentum, continued flying backward. She crashed into the wall on the opposite side of the room and broke through it. Brick fragments flew all around her. Pipes broke and slashed into her skin. Pain. Agony. It was all she knew.

Seconds later, she hit the ground outside, the impact jarring her right shoulder as she tumbled down a grassy slope.

Lilian gasped in breathless asphyxia. Everything hurt. Fire lanced down her back, her pain receptors had overloaded her body and cast her mind into an endless void where nothing existed except agony. Even her battle against Kiara hadn't made her feel this bad— probably because she'd been knocked unconscious quickly.

This... this pain...

Lilian had not realized that she could feel such pain. It hurt like nothing else had ever hurt before. Unfathomable agony held her mind in its ferocious, crushing grip, squeezing her with titan-like strength. Her vision blurred in and out of focus. She could barely even think, for the pain overwhelmed her ability for complex thought.

A shadow blocked out the sun. A dark muzzled face surrounded by fur met her fuzzy vision.

"And so the little kitsune's life ends here."

The gorilla yōkai raised his hand.

This... this is the end, isn't it? I'm gonna die here...

She didn't want to die. She didn't want this to be the end. There was still so much that she had to live for.

Beloved...

The image of her mate's smiling face filled Lilian's vision. Tears blurred her eyesight. She wanted to see her mate. She wanted to be with him, to hold him, to kiss him, to sleep with him—at least one last time.

...I'm sorry.

***

Everything was going according to plan. The thugs had attacked Lilian and her sister, separating them and taking them on simultaneously. As expected, the two kitsune were no match for the more powerful yōkai.

Cassy stood on the roof of the building that Lilian had been plowed straight through. She had a clear view of the young kitsune as she lay on the grass, the gorilla yōkai standing over her, his fist raised for the finishing blow. It looked like this was the end.

Relief swept through her. Lilian would die without Kevin being aware of what happened until it was too late. While Kevin would no doubt be sad for a while, she planned on staying in Arizona a bit longer than necessary to console him and hopefully start a relationship beyond that of a boy who'd taken in a stray.

All of those thoughts, dreams, and hopes were dashed when a familiar figure rushed out of the building carrying a long pole of twisted and sharp metal.

***

Lilian couldn't figure out what had happened. One second, the gorilla yōkai had been about to crush her like a Titan crushing a human. The next he was roaring in agony as he fell to a knee.

Snarling like a vicious beast, the gorilla yōkai turned to swat at something outside of her vision, but whatever it was had obviously evaded if the angry roar that the yōkai unleashed was any indication.

The gorilla yōkai stood back up, but he wobbled precariously. Without a clear view, Lilian couldn't tell what was happening, but it looked like the gorilla had been injured somewhere.

Surging forward, the gorilla yōkai disappeared from her line of sight. She wished to see what was happening, but her body refused to move. It just wouldn't respond to her mental commands. All she could do was lay there and listen as another earth-rending howl, this one of pain, rent the air, followed by a loud crash.

Seconds later, a figure appeared within her vision. Lilian nearly cried when she saw messy blond hair framing a handsome face and familiar light blue eyes.

"Beloved…"

***

Kevin knelt down next to Lilian, relief warring with worry and rage. He wanted to scoop the redhead into his arms but dared not to. She'd clearly suffered terrible injuries. Her body was broken, her arms bent at an awkward angle, her legs crushed. Bruises covered every inch of skin, spreading across her body like spilled ink soaking into a canvas. Who knew what sort of damage he would do if he moved her.

"I'm here," Kevin said. "Don't worry, Lilian, I'm here, and I'm gonna protect you."

"Kevin… you can't," Lilian gasped. Blood leaked from the corner of her mouth as she choked. "That's a gorilla yōkai. They're… known for their immense strength. He's too powerful for a human to fight…"

"Stop talking," Kevin admonished. "You keep talking and you're just going to injure yourself further. And it doesn't matter if that thing is a thousand times stronger than a human. I'm not leaving you to face this thing with the state you're in. I won't let you die."

Tears pricked at Lilian's eyes. Tears of joy? Maybe. Tears of sorrow? Possibly. Kevin had no way of knowing.

"… I don't want to lose you," Lilian whispered.

"And how do you think I feel? I don't want to lose you, either. I'd rather die than let you leave me."

"Beloved…"

Kevin stood up.

"However, I have no intention of dying either. Just sit back, focus on healing yourself. I'll deal with the ape." He smiled down at the redhead. Even beaten, battered, and covered in blood, Lilian remained ethereally beautiful to him. "I have a plan, so trust me, okay?"

The two stared at each other. Blue eyes into emerald green. For that single moment, nothing else existed. There were just two people, Lilian and Kevin, silently communicating in the way that only they could.

Lilian's breathing was ragged but even. Her wounds were severe but not life-threatening. Provided nothing else happened to her, she would survive.

Kevin intended to make sure that happened.

"Okay…" Lilian's soft, pained voice reached him. "I believe in you, Beloved."

"Thank you."

Kevin turned around to face the gorilla. He was getting back to his feet after Kevin had used a combination of his foe's own momentum and his speed to knock the yōkai down. The impression that the yōkai had left in the dewy grass was an exact mold of his body.

"A human?" The yōkai stared at him as if he couldn't believe what he was seeing. "You mean to tell me that a human is now fighting me? You may have gotten lucky with that last move, child of man, but that was merely because you caught me by surprise. Do you honestly think you can beat me now that I know you're here? Do not make me laugh. Your kind are even weaker than that kitsune you are trying to protect. You have neither the power nor the ability to kill a yōkai like me."

Throughout the yōkai's speech, Kevin found himself getting irritated. It boiled through him, this white-hot flame of anger and rage and annoyance, a conflagration that engulfed his soul in its fiery essence.

Anger tended to invoke shōnen-like speeches.

It was a protagonist thing.

"Just who the hell do you think I am, Furry?! Do you think you can look down on me because I'm a human?! I don't care if you have super special abilities that I don't! I don't care if you can crush a car like it was made of plastic! None of that matters to me! I might not have the strange powers of a yōkai, but that doesn't mean I'm weak! And I'll prove it to you when I break you for what you did to Lilian!"

That was right. This person, this yōkai, had hurt Lilian. It didn't matter to Kevin if this monster had the strength of a thousand men, for what he did to Lilian, Kevin would show no mercy.

"The yōkai world is a dangerous place. If you want to survive, then harden your heart and keep moving forward."

The words of Heather rang in his ears. He didn't want to kill. He didn't enjoy killing. The idea of taking a life was abhorrent to him. However, for Lilian, he would harden his heart and do whatever was necessary to protect her.

This was Kevin's love.

This was Kevin's resolve.

CHAPTER 7

Fighting Dirty

IRIS KNEW THE MOMENT she opened her eyes that she was not dead. A blue sky greeted her. Sparse clouds sprinkled the sky. She was lying on her back—or she assumed she was. She couldn't feel her back, or much of anything, really, so it was hard to tell.

"Are you finally awake?" a voice asked.

A face appeared above her seconds later, sharpening into focus. Familiar, icy blue eyes greeted Iris. They were set in a young-looking face that could have only been described as cute. Hair as black as raven feathers surrounded this face, contrasting with translucently pale skin.

"Hey, Frosty…" Iris muttered weakly.

Christine clicked her tongue. "Even though you're in such a sorry state, you still can't call me by my name. Do you know how annoying that is?"

"Heh… I can imagine." Iris gave the yuki-onna a weak smirk before she realized something. Christine was present, which meant she was here, with her, and not at school or home or wherever she went after school. "What are you doing here? And how did you know I was in trouble?"

"I thought that would be obvious." Christine's voice was laden with sarcasm. "I'm here to rescue your sorry ass. As for how I knew you were in trouble… I didn't. I saw Kevin running out of the school, looking frantic. I figured something happened and decided to follow him, though it took more effort than I thought it would." The snow maiden grimaced. "He's pretty fast for a human. Even skating, I could just barely keep up."

Skating was a term that yōkai with ice manipulation abilities liked to use. The basic idea was that they created a path made of ice and skated on it. This had the benefit of increasing their speed. Skilled "skaters" could even manipulate ice to fight three-dimensional battles by utilizing angles instead of simple linear movements.

"I guess all that track practice was good for something." Iris paused. "What happened to the tanuki?"

"If you're talking about that furred creature over there, then as you can plainly see, he's currently chilling out."

Iris groaned as she turned her head—why did such a simple movement hurt so much?—and saw what Christine was talking about. The tanuki was frozen in a large block of ice, his final expression, eyes bulging and mouth agape, was one of terror. Iris decided that it was a good look. It was fitting for someone she disliked after only their first meeting.

"Kotohime took care of one of those giant apes and is currently fighting the nama-something or other," Christine continued speaking.

"Kotohime is here, too? And you also said that the stud is here as well? Where is he?"

"Last I saw of him, Kevin went into that building." Christine pointed at something beyond Iris's sight.

"I can't see where you're pointing, you know," Iris muttered dryly.

Christine had the decency to at least look a little embarrassed. "Oh... right..."

***

Kotohime stared up and up and up, into the eyes of her foe.

"Oh, my. You are quite large, aren't you?"

Not that she had expected any less. The creature that she was in combat with was a namahage, after all.

Namahage were a type of oni, a demon yōkai with ogre qualities. Like all stories of yōkai, the tale of these supernal creatures originated in Japan... well technically, they originated from China. The legend went that Emperor Wu Han from China came to Japan, bringing with him five demonic ogres to the Oga area. These ogres established themselves at the two local high peaks, Honzan and Shinzan. There, they came down to the villages and stole crops and women.

The citizens of Oga made a wager with the demons. If the ogres could build a flight of stone steps, one thousand in all, from the village to the five shrine halls in a single night, then the villagers would supply them with a young woman every year. However, should they fail, then they would leave.

As luck would have it, the ogres were almost successful in completing the one thousand stone steps. Yet just as they were about to finish, one of the villagers mimicked the cry of a rooster. The ogres departed, then, believing that they had failed.

Of course, that was merely a legend perpetuated by humans and not real. The truth was that namahage was a breed of oni that lacked the brute strength of regular oni. However, in return for not having the brawn of a pure oni, they retained their sanity and ability to think rationally.

"You're the kitsune's bodyguard. I didn't expect to be facing you," the namahage said, his voice a deep, baritone growl.

Kotohime's placid smile hid all of her thoughts, though the killing intent that she released, the blood lust hidden beneath her calm veneer, betrayed her.

"You should have known that I would detect the use of youki so close to my residence. That you did not was a mistake on your part, one that I will not let you live to regret."

The namahage must have realized the hopelessness of his situation. A regular oni would have already attacked her, this one stood back and studied the situation. From his expression, the way his left foot shifted back, and the sweat trickling down his scalp, he'd come to the conclusion that he could not win.

It was a logical conclusion.

It was also correct.

The oni turned around to run away. Kotohime didn't let him.

"Ikken Hissatsu."

Kotohime shoved youki to the bottom of her feet. The ground cratered as she blasted forward like a ballistic missile. Her blade was out before the namahage could even turn around, a mere flicker of light that few people, be they human or otherwise, would have caught. There was a flash, a shutter, and then Kotohime was standing on the other side of the namahage.

Click.

Fully sheathing her blade, Kotohime ignored the gurgled scream of her opponent, who'd been sliced cleanly in half. She walked off, leaving behind the bloodied remains of her foe.

***

Even though Kevin couldn't claim to know everything about the various species of yōkai, he wasn't completely ignorant, either. While Kotohime had only taught him about kitsune, Kiara had taught him a lot about yōkai in general—usually while one of her disciples or Ms. Grant was beating the crap out of him.

Perhaps getting his ass periodically kicked somehow helped pound the information into his head. Then again, maybe that had done nothing but rattle his brain.

Either way, Kevin knew a lot about yōkai. More specifically, he knew a lot about the strengths and weaknesses of various yōkai races.

Gorilla yōkai were incredibly strong physically speaking, and they also had an amazing intellect. However, while they were impossibly strong and ridiculously smart, they weren't very fast— faster than humans, to be sure, but not faster than most yōkai. Their limbs were also long, which, while giving them incredible reach, didn't allow for them to fight in close. If someone could slip inside of their guard, then gorilla yōkai would have a hard time hitting their target.

Of course, even while staying within his opponent's guard, Kevin was having a bit of a problem. Namely, he couldn't injure this creature. The gorilla's hide was thick and tough, the mass of muscles covering the yōkai's body made damaging his foe with his purely human strength impossible. Every punch and kick he threw bounced off harmlessly, the yōkai merely laughing it off...

... Or at least, the yōkai would have been laughing it off, if Kevin wasn't proving to be such a troublesome opponent.

"Hold still!"

"Heck no! What kind of an idiot just stands still and lets his enemy attack him? If you want to hurt me, then you're going to have to work for it. Not that you actually can hurt me. You're too slow."

"Damn human! I'm going to kill you for your insolence!"

Thus far most of the fight had consisted of the gorilla swinging his large fists, and Kevin dodging each attack that came his way, moving in close, striking at his foe, and then retreating before the ape could wrap those thick arms around him and crush him like a grape.

While the gorilla was fast, faster than him, Kevin had an advantage: The gorilla's reach. That extra reach meant that the yōkai was telegraphing his attacks, making them easier to avoid. It was good practice, actually.

Kevin's unfinished style, which he'd been working on since his talk with Kiara during their trip to California, relied on predicting attacks.

Neither side had an advantage over the other. Kevin was too apt at dodging and the gorilla yōkai was too strong and too sturdy for any of Kevin's attacks to hurt. The only attacks from Kevin that had proven effective were his two opening moves. However, those wouldn't work anymore. There was no metal pole for him to stab the yōkai with, and the gorilla wasn't going to let himself be judo tossed again.

The gorilla yōkai must have realized his disadvantage. He jumped backward to get some distance. Then he clasped his hands together to form a giant fist that he raised above his head, which he brought down to try and smash Kevin into the ground.

The nimble Kevin proved too swift for such a slow attack. He swerved along the slick grass, dodging the fists as they slammed into the ground with concussive force, upchucking dirt and grass, leaving an impressive fist-shaped indent in the ground.

"Whoa, your aim is absolutely horrible, or maybe you're just too stupid to adapt to changes in combat. I guess all those stories about how gorillas are supposed to be really smart were just a lie, huh? You're actually pretty dumb."

"What was that?" the gorilla howled with anger. "You think you're more intelligent than I am? You, a lowly, insignificant worm of a human dare to insult my intellect?!"

Much like any other yōkai, gorilla yōkai had a lot of pride in their abilities—specifically, their intelligence was something they were quite proud of. With an IQ of over 200, they were some of the most insightful and perceptive yōkai in the world. Insulting their intelligence was like slapping them in the face with a dead fish. It was more vicious than a kick to the gonads.

"That's right. Everyone knows your kind are dumber than a sack of bricks. You gorilla yōkai are eleven branches from the stupidest key characters ever! Even Eric is smarter than you are!"

"That does it! I won't have you insulting my intelligence, you disgusting human! I'm going to demolish you!"

"I'd like to see you try!"

Kevin began moving backward, up the hill and toward the building he'd emerged from. In a battle against a yōkai whose strength exceeded anything a mere human like him could produce, fighting in an open space was detrimental to his health. He needed to entrap the yōkai, force the yōkai to fight on his terms. Maybe he would even find something inside that he could use against his opponent.

The ape followed, blinded by anger. Perhaps if he hadn't been so enraged, he would have realized what Kevin was doing, but that was exactly why Kevin had insulted him in the first place. He couldn't afford to let his opponent think clearly—not if he wanted to win.

He rushed for the gaping hole in the wall, which he assumed had been left by Lilian and the gorilla. His enemy tried to stop him, of course, but the wet grass made running more precarious for the large gorilla. Ducking low underneath a swipe, Kevin used the terrain to his advantage. He gripped the ground, fingers digging into the dirt, and slammed both of his heels into the gorilla's left shin. It didn't hurt the strong yōkai, but it did cause him to slip, fall onto his back, and roll down the hill.

Kevin used that moment to slip inside of the building before the gorilla recovered. He observed his new surroundings with a quick glance. It was an office building of some kind. There were cubicles situated in this section, and doors further on led to other parts of the building. There was also one section of the room that looked like a rhino had busted through it, with desks lying shattered and crushed, as if they'd been stepped on by a giant—or a gorilla yōkai.

He rushed into one of the cubicles, ducked down, and observed the hole through the reflection in the nearest glass window.

Loud stomping pounded against the ground as the gorilla yōkai blundered inside. He paused upon entering, a hand coming up to rest on the broken brick wall. A loud snort echoed around the room. His head turned left and right, dark orbs peering out from underneath his thick brow ridge.

"Do you really think you can hide from me, human?" the yōkai growled. "While my senses may not be as powerful as an inu's, I still have extraordinary perceptions. My auditory senses are particularly acute. We gorillas possess a unique genetic gift. It goes back to the time before we became the supernal beings that we are today, back when we were mere apes living in jungles."

Kevin used the glass window as a mirror to the world outside of his cubicle. He watched with bated breath as the gorilla yōkai stepped further into the room, the glass distorting the creature's legs, making them look stretched.

"The jungle is filled with dangers; elephant stampedes, angry hippopotami, poisonous snakes, hunters. Gorillas have developed the ability to pick out individual sounds with ease, despite our sense of hearing not being any better than a human's. For example, while my hearing is not good enough to hear your heartbeat, it is more than capable of picking out the sound of your breathing."

Kevin couldn't quite stifle his gasp. The gorilla roared in triumph and turned toward his cubicle.

"Found you!"

Without any recourse left to him, Kevin bolted from the cubicle just as the gorilla crashed into it. Chunks of plastic and twisted metal bars flew everywhere. The table upon which a computer sat was smashed to bits. The gorilla continued moving, crushing several more cubicles before he skidded to a stop.

Kevin's breath leaped into his throat when the gorilla turned to face him again. Despite the fear that was telling him to run away, he stood his ground. He couldn't afford to run. If he left now, who would protect Lilian?

"Do you take me for a fool, boy?" The gorilla asked. "Do you honestly think that I do not know what you are trying to do here? You think that by bringing me into this office building that you can control the pace of this battle. You believe that my large frame will be slowed down by the enclosed space and large objects in my way."

Kevin would have sworn if he was prone to such things. So the gorilla hadn't simply walked into his trap like he had assumed. The yōkai had come in willingly, knowing what Kevin was trying to do. That meant the yōkai wasn't concerned, that he believed that Kevin still wouldn't be able to defeat him.

The problem was that Kevin actually felt the yōkai was right. He hadn't found anything useful that he could use yet. The few twisted pieces of scrap metal lying around wouldn't penetrate the gorilla's flesh unless he had a running start and rammed it in as hard as he could like his initial attack. That was how thick this yōkai's skin was. Doing something like that would leave him vulnerable to attack, however, and that was something he wanted to avoid at all costs.

"Let me tell you right now that whatever plan you were cooking up, that is not the way this battle is going to go. Your plans. Are. Useless!"

With a resounding roar, the gorilla lifted up a large piece of warped metal and, using his immense strength, he straightened it. The yōkai did a few test swings. Each swing rent the air. He nodded before turning his attention back to Kevin.

"You're not the only one who can adapt to new situations," he said, lips peeling back into a feral grin.

Kevin realized, at that moment, that he might have made a huge mistake.

***

Lilian must have lost consciousness at one point because when she became aware of her surroundings again, something had changed. She was still lying on her back, though her head no longer rested on the grass. More importantly, the pain she'd expected to feel was gone. She was sore but not in agony. It was as if she'd simply strained her muscles from overuse. Her back also felt a little itchy.

Opening her eyes, Lilian was met with… a pair of boobs.

"I am pleased to see that you are awake, Lilian-sama," Kotohime's voice came to her from beyond the boobs. "Please accept my humblest apologies for not protecting you better. I was not aware that you were in danger until I felt the massive surge of youki coming from this direction. I failed you…"

"It's fine," Lilian muttered, even as she made a face. "Kotohime?"

"Yes, Lilian-sama?"

"I can't see your face."

"And I cannot see yours."

Despite not being able to see her face, Lilian could almost sense the amused smile that her maid was no doubt wearing.

As her mind kickstarted, Lilian eventually became more aware of her surroundings. She noticed that she was lying with her head on her maid's lap, which explained the boobs in her face. A tilt of her head to the right revealed that her sister was sitting next to her, looking a little worse for wear. Most of her clothing was gone, having been torn to shreds by something. Her right breast was bared, but her sister didn't seem to care that people could see her nipple.

She didn't appear injured, which was good. That meant she either hadn't been hurt or, more than likely, Kotohime had already healed her. Christine was also there, sitting a little ways away from Iris.

Lilian sat up, even though doing so took more effort than it should have.

"Please be careful, Lilian-sama," Kotohime said as she placed a hand on her back. "You should not strain yourself too much. I might have healed the damage done to you, but I cannot heal fatigue."

"I'm fine," Lilian said, smiling at her bodyguard. "Thank you for worrying about me."

Kotohime returned her smile. "You needn't thank me. This Kotohime will always watch over you."

Just then, a crash followed by a loud roar emanated from within the building nearest to them. Lilian recognized it as the building that the gorilla had rammed her through. Looking at that square structure and hearing that roar reminded her of something important.

"Kevin..."

She tried to stand, but a wave of dizziness forced her to sit down. It wouldn't have mattered anyway. Kotohime's hand on her shoulder firmly pushed her back onto the grass and held her in place.

"I apologize, Lilian-sama, but I cannot allow you to interfere in Kevin-sama's fight."

"B-but he's fighting against a gorilla yōkai!" Lilian argued. "That's not something a single human can take down on his own!"

She trusted her mate a great deal, but even she knew how improbable it was that he would be capable of defeating a creature like that. Even though she wanted to believe in him, she didn't want him fighting by himself. Lilian wanted to help him. If they fought together, then they might stand a chance.

"I'm with my sister," Iris added. "I've seen the stud in action, and he's got some moves, but he doesn't have a shot in hell of beating something like that overgrown ape."

Lilian turned to Christine. "I can't help him right now. I lack the strength, but you could. Why are you just sitting there?"

Having become the center of attention, Christine did the only thing she could think of. She scowled. "Don't look at me. Don't you think I already tried going in there to help Kevin, or have you not looked at me closely enough to realize that I can't FUCKING MOVE?!"

Lilian reared back as Christine shouted at the end, but she quickly realized what her friend meant upon closer inspection. Chains composed of hardened liquid were wrapped around her hands and legs, holding her in place. She recognized the technique: **Kitsune Art: Unbreakable Bindings of the Moon Goddess**. They could only be broken by someone with more youki than the one who created them, and Christine most certainly did not have more youki than Kotohime, who was this technique's creator.

She turned back to her maid, glaring at the woman as if doing so would make her catch fire. What she wouldn't give to have a Geass right about now. "Why aren't you going in there to help him?"

"Because Kevin-sama needs this fight more than anyone," Kotohime answered. "I have been watching him struggle since the end of spring break. Kevin-sama has finally realized what our world is really like and it's causing him to question his place in it. His resolve has been shaken by the unadulterated violence that was perpetrated on us in California, and of the fact that he was forced to kill someone in order to protect us."

Lilian's stomach clenched. Kotohime was being kind to not say it out loud, but they both knew the real reason that Kevin had killed.

It was because I had been injured. He was forced to kill someone because of me.

Kotohime continued. "Kevin-sama is an ordinary teenager. He possesses neither the power of a yōkai nor the mindset of a soldier. To top it off, he is extremely kind-hearted and giving."

Lilian knew that. She knew that better than anyone. After all, Kevin had accepted her into his home despite how she'd destroyed any semblance of normality his life might have had.

Kevin was the kind of boy who accepted others and didn't look down on people for being different. Never once had she heard him discriminate against someone for who or what they were. Despite freaking out on many occasions when he first learned about yōkai, Lilian had never seen him push someone away. She, Christine, Iris, her entire family, Kevin had accepted them all. He had even allowed her family to live with him despite how small his apartment was.

"For people like Kevin-sama, the act of killing is abhorrent. Even fighting is disturbing to him. However, he has accepted that he needs to be strong if he wants to remain by your side. To that end, he contacted Kiara and asked her to help him become stronger despite not being the kind of person who enjoys fighting."

Before spring break, Kevin had trained with Kiara almost every day for five months, and it was all because of Lilian, because he had accepted her, because he had agreed to become her mate. He wasn't naive enough to believe that the dangerous incidents they'd been involved in were singular events that wouldn't happen again. He knew they would. Thus he trained accordingly to protect himself and his friends from the supernatural forces they would no doubt find themselves at odds with.

"Right now, Kevin-sama is at a crossroad." Kotohime's dark gaze was as serious as Lilian had ever seen it. "He must be able to find the resolve to do whatever is necessary to not only survive but thrive in this violent world. That includes using every cheap, dirty, and dishonorable trick in the book to come out on top. More than that, Kevin-sama must find the resolve to kill if the situation calls for it."

Lilian's heart quaked at the words, as if she'd just been told that her entire life was a lie.

"If he cannot do that, then Kevin-sama will never be able to stand with you as an equal, much less be your mate," Kotohime concluded.

Silence descended upon them. Lilian didn't know what to say. She knew that Kotohime was right, but she didn't want to admit it. She wanted to have faith in Kevin, but she was worried for him. She didn't want him fighting alone. At the same time...

Kotohime is expressing her faith in Kevin.

She hadn't said it outright, but Kotohime's words had made it more than clear: She trusted Kevin. She had faith in him.

If she can show this much faith in Kevin, then I should be able to do the same.

Before now, Lilian had only placed her faith in Kevin when she felt it was a sure bet. She only believed in him when she truly thought he could win.

However, that kind of faith was half-assed. True faith wasn't about believing in someone only when it was convenient. It was knowing that the odds were stacked against you and believing in that ideal, that person, that something precious, regardless.

Lilian decided, right then, that she would place her faith in her mate, truly, and not the half-assed kind of faith that she'd shown up until now.

"That was a really deep speech," Iris said. "Did you practice that in front of a mirror—guag!"

Lilian and Christine became rooted to the spot when a long, black tail shot out from behind Kotohime and struck Iris across the face. The young vixen landed on her back, in a dazed heap. Kotohime, ever the elegant beauty, hid her mouth behind the sleeve of her kimono.

"Ufufufu, I have no idea what you mean by that, Iris-sama. I hope you were not implying that I practice shōnen manga speeches in from of the mirror like Lilian-sama does."

"Geh!" Lilian doubled over as if she'd been sucker-punched in the gut.

Why did everything always come back to her?

***

Kevin was beginning to wonder about his own sanity. Here he was, a human fighting against a creature of supernatural origins, in the middle of an office building not a mile from his house. There must have been something wrong with him.

The roar of his opponent caught his attention. His body moved without his brain telling it to, throwing him backward into a roll just in time to avoid getting crushed by a fist four times the size of his head. He skipped back to his feet as the gorilla yōkai charged at him again.

By this point in time, Kevin had already realized that he would never win this fight through conventional means. This wasn't an enemy that he could pummel into submission. This was a creature whose strength was on par with an inu, a creature of large, tightly packed muscles covered with an added layer of fat for protection. No amount of force that he could generate would damage something like that.

So he needed to improvise.

The office building was pretty much in shambles by this point. More than half of the cubicles had been destroyed, reduced to splinters and twisted steel frames. Much of the ground was covered in craters, from which a wide array of spider web cracks created fissures within the floor. The gorilla yōkai must have also hit a gas line or something, because an odd smell, something sulfuric and acetic, hung in the air.

Diving to the ground, Kevin avoided the swipe of the gorilla's large hand. This didn't stop the primate, though, and Kevin was forced to roll along the ground like a man on fire, lest he wish to be squashed by a palm that slammed into the concrete floor with the force of a pantheon of angry gods.

As he continued rolling, Kevin grabbed a handful of dust, leftover remnants of a destroyed table and pulverized concrete. He scrambled to his feet as the gorilla came at him with the intent to kill.

At the very last second, Kevin threw himself out of the way while also tossing the dust into the gorilla's face. The yōkai roared furiously as the dust irritated his eyes. The creature stumbled about, his enraged roar shaking the building to its foundations.

"Do you think this will be enough to stop me, human?! I don't need my eyes to kill you!"

"Tch!"

Kevin was aware of that, but he hoped that the creature's irritated eyes would distract it long enough for him to think up a plan. A glance around the room revealed... not much, honestly. There was a lot of debris, and he could probably use it as a means of distraction, but nothing that would provide a decisive victory.

Come on. Come on. There has to be something that I can—

Out of his peripheral vision, Kevin caught sight of a small wire that was hanging from the ceiling. It sparked and crackled with remnants of electricity.

It hit him like a Pikachu's thunderbolt.

Maybe the solution wasn't inside of the office, but behind the walls. All office buildings had a built-in sprinkler system along with electric cables running throughout their infrastructure. If he could set off the sprinkler system and find an active electrical cable, he could fry the gorilla before his foe smashed him like a bug getting hit by a flyswatter.

Another roar alerted him to his opponent's intent. The gorilla tried to body-slam Kevin, but he dove to the side and ran in the opposite direction. His large, furry foe crashed through another cubicle.

"Damn human!" The gorilla shouted, sounding quite angry. "Stop running around! Nothing you do will amount to anything! You can't win this, so why even bother trying?"

What kind of stupid question was that? His reason for fighting should have been obvious. Still, he deigned his opponent with an answer, if only because he felt like he needed to hear his own answer himself.

"Because I have something worth fighting for, a person who I want to stand beside. I don't care that she's a yōkai. I wouldn't care if she was an alien who randomly appeared in my bathtub. She and I might not be the same species, but I'm not willing to let her go just because I lack the supernatural abilities that you yōkai pride yourselves on."

It didn't matter if he was human and Lilian wasn't. It didn't matter if the world that she came from was filled with violence and death. She was important to him, the person who was closest to his heart. For her, he would become strong. For her, he would fight.

For her, I would kill.

Kevin glanced around. There was a fire alarm on the wall several feet away, and next to the alarm, a fire extinguisher.

He could use that.

The gorilla yōkai snorted. "Then you are a fool. Our world is not meant for humans to tread upon. You humans might be an arrogant and violent species, but you're also weak. You can't stand up to a threat like us unless it's with overwhelming numbers and superior technology, of which you possess neither. The only reason your species is even at the top of the food chain is because we yōkai lack the numbers and cohesiveness of a single nation. If all of the yōkai races combined, we would have crushed your kind long ago."

"Maybe so, but I don't really care about any of that. You can keep spouting crap about how humans are weak and pathetic. I'll take those words and shove them down your throat. I'll prove to you that it doesn't matter how weak a human is, because even someone weak like I am can still beat you into the ground!"

During his rant, Kevin had been inching closer to the fire alarm. The gorilla hadn't stopped him, likely because it was busy listening. That was another weak trait of gorillas. They would always let a person finish their sentences.

Without warning, he pulled on the alarm, causing sirens to begin blaring obnoxiously inside of the building. The gorilla covered his ears with his hands and roared. Kevin quickly smashed the glass panel protecting the fire hydrant with his elbow and pulled the device out.

He ran up to the gorilla, who hadn't noticed him yet due to the sudden noise blowing out his eardrums that the yōkai was so proud of, and, pointing the extinguisher at his foe, Kevin pressed the button that caused it to release the chemical compound stored inside.

The fire extinguisher was a halon extinguisher, the type that used compounds to break the chain of chemicals involved in a fire to stop combustion. Kevin didn't know this, of course. He'd never studied what went into fire extinguishers. All he knew was that most extinguishers, when shot in a person's face, tended to have adverse physical effects on said person.

While a gorilla yōkai was stronger than a human, and their hide was thick enough to withstand serious blunt force trauma, that didn't mean they didn't have a weakness.

Kevin sprayed the gorilla right in the face. The yōkai roared in pain. He reared back as the halon compounds blasted him. Not only did the compound get in his eyes, but it traveled down his throat when he accidentally inhaled it.

The creature began to cough and sputter. He flopped around onto his back, convulsing as he choked on the chemicals. Kevin expended the entire contents of the extinguisher before tossing it at the yōkai's head with as much force as he could muster. The extinguisher released a loud *kong!* as it bounced off of his foe's cranium.

Then he bolted, leaving the creature to suffer in agony. What he'd just done wasn't enough to defeat the yōkai. If he wanted a surefire win, then he needed to do something creative.

Like making this entire building go up in a blaze of glory.

Or something like that.

***

Alvis Anzo was a gorilla yōkai. His intelligence was beyond that of other primitive races, and his body had enough strength to halt speeding trains with his bare hands. Among the many yōkai races, gorilla yōkai were some of the strongest, most intelligent, and most able yōkai in the world.

Alvis Anzo was a gorilla yōkai, and he was not amused.

This entire fight had not gone the way he'd anticipated at all. Despite being stronger, more intelligent, and more powerful, that human child was giving him fits. From the very onset of their battle, the boy had fought using trickery and deception; he used the environment to keep Alvis from getting a clean hit, he tried enraging him and clouding his mind with insults, he threw fine granules into his eyes to blind and irritate him, and he caused the fire alarm to go off and damage his eardrums. That human brat had even blasted him in the face with the chemical compounds from a fire extinguisher, and now...

... the boy had set off the sprinkler system. Alvis glared up as his body became soaking wet, his thick fur matting to his skin. He could now add one more item to the list of things that had not gone right.

Observing his surroundings, and trying to ignore the way his fur clung to his body like it had been covered in gallons of oil, Alvis tried to find his annoying opponent. His foe wasn't in this area of the building anymore, that much he could already tell. He couldn't hear the boy's breathing.

This building was shaped like an L. It consisted of several large sections filled with cubicles, and a long hallway that ran through other sections. Within that hallway were numerous offices, which the boy could've used to hide.

Alvis would need to be careful.

Walking on feet and knuckles, he proceeded forward, glancing around carefully. His feet made squelching noises as he walked. The carpet was already soaked all the way through.

The hallway that he entered was long and straight, a narrow passage that he could barely squeeze through. He peered into the window of each office that he passed. No one was in them—at least he didn't think so. The boy could have hidden behind a desk, but he was almost positive that wasn't the case. He would have seen the boy's feet.

The hall eventually opened into another room, a reception area. A desk stood in the back of the room, containing a computer and a chair. Several seats were situated on either side of the wall near a glass door. On the opposite side was another hallway that led to the other side of the building.

His feet splashed against the wet tiles. There seemed to be more water in here, which, upon closer observation, he realized was because one of the water lines was broken. It looked like something had cracked the pipes located in the wall, from which large quantities of water spurted out.

A strange *bbzztt!* noise alerted him to movement. He panned over to where the sound originated from, thinking it might have been his enemy. It wasn't.

It was a cable.

A *sparking* cable that appeared to have been cut and was falling into the water.

Alvis's eyes widened.

The cable touched the wet tiled floor…

… and Alvis lit up like a New Year's fireworks display.

***

Kevin walked out through the large hole that he had entered. His hair was sopping wet, and his clothes were plastered to his skin. He was tired, sore, and could really use a nap. Actually, that sounded like a really good idea. When he got home, he was taking Lilian to bed…

… That sounded so wrong. No, actually, it sounded kind of right.

"Nggg…" Kevin pressed a hand to his face and groaned. "My mind is going down the gutter." He paused. "I blame Iris."

Kevin began walking across the small back parking lot that led to the grassy slope. Lilian, Iris, Christine, and Kotohime were all standing there. His heart felt light. They were waiting for him. His eyes locked onto Lilian, whose face lit up in a dazzling smile when she saw him. Unbidden, he began to smile as well. He took a single step forward—

—Right before a loud, ground-quaking roar nearly blew out his eardrums. That came from behind him!

Kevin barely had time to turn around before a large hand nearly four times the size of his head slammed into him with bone-breaking force. He experienced an odd moment of weightlessness. A scream sounded out from somewhere—at least, he thought it was a scream. His hearing was muffled as if someone had taken wax and shoved it into his ears.

The moment of weightlessness soon ended, and Kevin hit the pavement of the parking lot hard. His back exploded with agony. He would have screamed, but his breath had been stolen from him. His vision went black for a moment as something lodged itself in his back. Something wet trickled down from the impact point. Warm and sticky. Blood. His blood.

Gasping, Kevin reached underneath himself and pulled out a rock that had become embedded in his muscles. It was covered in red fluid, glinting like a Philosopher's Stone in the light.

A shadow blotted out the sun. Black skin stretched across an inhuman mug. Dark eyes glared down at him like he was the scum of the world. Thick brow ridges. A face surrounded in dark fur. It was the gorilla yōkai.

He looked like he had seen better days. His face was covered in scorch marks, and his hair was singed. Blood dribbled down his mouth, black and viscous, like coagulated human blood. The bloodshot eyes of someone who'd done way too many drugs—or been electrocuted by Inari-only-knew how many volts of electricity—glowered down at him in a vengeful rage.

"Did you really think something like that would be enough to do me in?!" The gorilla bellowed. Kevin screamed as something smashed his torso. It felt like an anvil had been dropped on him! "Your plan was a good one. It might have even worked on a lesser yōkai, but I am a gorilla, a yōkai of the primate race! A little bit of electricity is not going to be enough to stop me!"

Whatever had stomped on him left, but it was a short reprieve. Kevin cried out as the gorilla lifted him up and squeezed. He felt something crack. Several somethings. Breathing became difficult, and Kevin realized that the cracking was actually his ribs being ground into a fine powder. He fiercely gripped the rock in his hand, still slick with his blood, as if holding it was his only tenuous grip on his sanity.

"Beloved!" There was a scream.

"Stay back! Anyone moves any closer and the human is dead!"

Who was he talking to? Kevin wondered. Surely it wasn't him—ah, his friends were here. Christine and Iris and Kotohime and… Lilian. Lilian was also here. She was seeing this. She was watching as he was crushed by this creature.

"Let him go! Let him go, please!"

That was Lilian's voice. Kevin couldn't see her, and his hearing wasn't working quite right, but it sounded like she was crying.

She was crying for him…

Kevin gritted his teeth. His arms were pinned to his sides, but he wriggled his left arm out of the gorilla's grip. It was hard. It hurt. Everything hurt. But he didn't dare stop. He couldn't afford to.

"Hahaha! I think not! Do not take me for a fool. Right now, the only thing keeping that four-tails over there from slashing me to pieces with her katana is the boy. No, I think I'll be keeping him right here for a while yet."

"Then it seems we are at an impasse." That voice, smoother than silk and cooler than a yuki-onna's breath, it couldn't have been anyone but Kotohime. "A hostage is only valuable so long as they remain alive. Kill him and you will have nothing to hide behind, nothing to stop me from murdering you. However, you can't afford to let him go either, because you know that once you do, I will still murder you. This is a most vexing situation."

"And once again, you kitsune insult my intelligence. I am not ignorant of your kind, fox. I know that kitsune, despite using trickery and deceit to get their way, are also creatures of their word. Kitsune never break their promises, which is why you are going to promise not to harm me once I let the boy go."

"… Hey… aren't you forgetting about someone?" Kevin muttered tiredly, ignoring the way his lungs welled up with blood just by speaking.

The gorilla looked at him. "Oh? You're still conscious? This is a surprise. You must have an awfully high pain tolerance if you're capable of coherent speech. I'm almost impressed."

Kevin coughed up blood. "A compliment from you… doesn't really mean much to me… and I think you're… forgetting something…"

"Hmm?" The gorilla looked amused. It was hard to tell. His face was blurry, and Kevin was starting to see double, but he thought he saw the creature smiling. "And what have I forgotten?"

"That I'm not a kitsune."

With that, Kevin used the last ounce of strength he possessed and shoved the bloody, sharp rock straight into the gorilla's left eye.

The yōkai's shriek was an amalgamation of surprise, pain, and rage. He dropped Kevin to the ground, which Kevin hit with a meaty thud, and used his free hands to cover his now gouged-out eye.

"Beloved!"

As he stared up at the sky, listening to the cacophony of screams and cries, his last thought was inane, a completely pointless thought derived from a mind that could no longer think clearly.

The sky… it's really blue today…

CHAPTER 8

In Sickness and in Health

"SO, THAT YŌKAI GANG WASN'T ABLE TO KILL THE PNÉV̱MA GIRL, after all. Oh, well. It's not like I actually expected them to be capable of succeeding. Low-life dregs such as them lack the intelligence needed to deal with a competent opponent, and that Kotohime woman most definitely falls under that category."

Cassy stood before Seth, barely masking her disgust of the man. She'd just finished giving an oral briefing of what happened during the assassination attempt. Now she was standing there like an idiot while her "tutor" deliberated.

Seth sat on her couch, lounging back with his feet propped up on her table like he owned the place. He was still wearing the body of Ms. Vis.

He was also shamelessly naked. The pervert.

"The biggest problem will be that four-tails. Kotohime is a well-known warrior among kitsune, a swordswoman of incredible skill. She also has four tails. Even I am not confident in my chances of victory if I have to fight against her," Seth mused, absently fondling Ms. Vis's right breast and causing Cassy to wrinkle her nose and clench her fists. She knew that he was doing this to upset her, and he knew that it was working, judging by the hideous smirk plastered on his face.

I hate this man...

"Is she really that powerful, nya?" asked Cassy.

"It's not that she's powerful so much as she is highly skilled. Rumor has it that Kotohime is so skilled with a blade that she is capable of fighting on par with yōkai on the same level as the Four Saints."

"Nya. Surely those are just rumors, though."

"They are, but even rumors have a grain of truth to them. While I doubt she is capable of fighting on even grounds with someone like Davin Monstrang, Kuroneko, or even Orin, she may be a match for Sarah Phenex, provided she can get past Sarah's high-speed regeneration. However, with her river blood, she holds a distinct advantage over that woman."

Cassy remained silent. She didn't know if she believed Seth, but she wouldn't deny that Kotohime was a powerful foe. She'd seen the woman cut down the gang leader with nothing more than a sword. The four-tails had split the yōkai straight down the middle like it was nothing, and she hadn't used a single kitsune art, just swordsmanship.

Still, to speak about Mistress Sarah like that, does this man have no shame?

"Of a more interesting note is that boy you're so fond of. Defeating a gorilla yōkai is no small feat. Lesser yōkai can't even scar them. Even a nekomata with your talents would have trouble with a creature like that if you relied on nothing but your claws. The fact that he defeated one shows that he cannot be underestimated."

Seth observed Cassy with keen eyes, studying the way her hands clenched and her arms trembled. The lips belonging to Ms. Vis quirked in a way that the passionate math teacher would have never done. Then again, Ms. Vis would have never been lounging naked on someone's couch, either.

"I'll leave him to you when the time comes," Seth said, surprising Cassy. "Your job will be to keep him from interfering as I kill the Pnéyma girl."

Cassy's stare was hard as she searched Seth's—Ms. Vis's—face. There had to be some kind of catch here. Seth Naraka was not a kind man. He enjoyed wounding others, be it physically or mentally. The act of inflicting devastating pain was like an oenophile drinking a bottle of Domaine-Marey Mone.

"Of course, should he prove to be a problem, I expect you to kill him."

Ah, there it was.

"I won't kill Master, nya," Cassy spat.

Seth grinned. "Then keep him from interfering with my plan."

She glared at Seth, who remained on the couch, grinning like an arrogant fool. She hated this man. If she could, she would have ripped his face off. Seth was stronger than her, however, and so all she could do was concede.

"V-very well," Cassy said, her shoulders slumping. "I'll keep Master Kevin from coming near you as you kill Lilian."

"Excellent. I'm so pleased that you've come around to my way of thinking," Seth said, and his—or rather, Ms. Vis's—twisted lips made Cassy shudder.

Cassy fervently hoped that Lilian took this man down with her when she died.

***

Kevin woke up with a migraine. It felt like someone had used his head like a gong. His throat was also dry. Fortunately, he didn't feel any pain, which he presumed meant someone had healed him, probably Lilian or Kotohime.

He was in his bed, lying on his back. His mate was cuddled next to him. She was also naked. He could feel the fullness of her breasts pressing against him, two large fluffy pillows, soft and supple. Her nipples grazing his side were like an aphrodisiac. Kevin wasn't a pervert, but if anyone ever asked, he would gladly tell them that Lilian had the best sweater stuffers ever.

"No, I wouldn't," Kevin muttered to no one in particular.

Yes, you would.

"Shut up," Kevin groaned, then blinked. "Wait, who am I talking to?"

It was dark outside. A glance through the open window revealed that night had fallen. His room remained brightly lit, though, because the lights on the nightstand next to his bed provided soft illumination.

"I see that you're awake."

Kevin turned his head. She sat on the edge of the bed, near the foot, her back straight, hands placed in her lap, her demeanor every bit the proper Yamato Nadeshiko. Her kimono that evening depicted the night sky. He could see a large imprint of the moon, and thousands of little dots representing stars. Dark eyes framed by midnight strands of hair gazed at him with warm fondness.

"Kotohime..."

"Kevin-sama." Kotohime smiled at him. "I am pleased to see that you are in good health. Everyone was quite worried about you."

"I'm sorry for worrying you."

"It is fine. You are alive and whole, and that is what matters. Though you are also quite lucky. Your ribcage had been crushed. Were I not a River Kitsune, I dare say you would have died from those injuries. They were beyond even Lilian-sama's ability to heal."

So he'd been injured that badly? Well, he had been crushed by a gorilla yōkai. It only made sense that he had to suffer some major injuries.

"I was very impressed by your battle," Kotohime said suddenly, startling Kevin.

"H-huh?"

"The way you handled yourself was most impressive. Despite facing off against an overwhelming opponent, you didn't back down. You even managed to greatly injure him by coming up with an on-the-fly plan." Kotohime's smile was one of pride. "You fought magnificently."

Kevin blushed a bit, but then he remembered how the fight had ended, and his blush receded to be replaced by a grimace. "But I didn't defeat that yōkai…"

"True, but you are also a human. You have no supernatural powers and you had no weapons to fight with. Despite this, you still stood up to a creature many times your size, with powers beyond your ability to grasp, and you managed to wound him grievously. Even at the end, suffering what must have been incredible pain, you found the strength to act and took out one of his eyes, thereby forcing him to drop you and allowing me to deal with him accordingly."

"You killed him?"

"I did indeed. Does that bother you?"

Kevin remained silent for a moment. He felt Lilian's bare body shift, nearly groaning when her softer-than-silk leg caressed him. God, he was going to have the worst case of blue balls come the next morning.

"I still don't like the idea of killing," he admitted slowly. "I don't know if it's because I'm human, or if it's because the idea of killing just bothers me. This isn't the animal kingdom. It's not like we're living out in the savannas where we have to kill to survive. This isn't a matter of survival of the fittest. We're simply killing because the yōkai world is filled with violent yōkai who thoughtlessly kill each other."

"I wouldn't say we thoughtlessly kill each other," Kotohime muttered, her left eyebrow twitching. Then she sighed. "But I do understand what you are saying. Unfortunately, that is the way things are, the way they have been for thousands of years. Long before I or even the current Pnéyma matriarch were born, the world of yōkai has been in a state of constant war."

Kotohime paused. Whether this was to let Kevin absorb the information, or because she was lost in her own thoughts, he didn't know. She continued soon after anyway.

"It's not like the wars that you humans wage, where massive battles are fought and victory can be achieved within a few years. They still exist, battles being waged over the course of centuries. Clans fighting against clans. Different yōkai races constantly fighting for power and territory. Even we kitsune are embroiled in our own conflicts, though ours tend to be more subtle, relying on deceit and misdirection as opposed to straight-up battles." She paused again, and, almost as an afterthought, added, "Most of the time."

Kevin tried to imagine what she was saying, but it was hard. The idea of supernatural creatures battling each other for several centuries was unfathomable. Something like that wasn't a concept that a human like himself could truly comprehend.

Though it did remind him of this one manga he'd read. It was about a yōkai family living in modern-day Japan as a group of yakuza. What was that series called again? Nura-something? He couldn't remember.

"In either event," Kotohime continued, "I just wanted to let you know that I was very impressed with your fight against the gorilla yōkai. You didn't delude yourself into thinking you could win in a straight-up fight. You kept calm and used your head, your cunning, and the environment against him. Even if you didn't defeat him in the end, the fact that you survived against a creature like that is inspiring. I can tell you right now that most yōkai would not have survived against that gorilla unless they were particularly powerful."

"So I did good, then?"

"You did very well," Kotohime confirmed, standing up. "Now, then, I shall leave you to your rest. You should get some more sleep. I might have healed your wounds, but you're still going to be fatigued. A good night's rest will fix that."

Kevin knew that she was right. His entire body felt weighed down and weary, like led weights had been strapped to his arms and legs. Even his fingers refused to move, worn out and exhausted to the point that just getting them to twitch was a task in and of itself. He was just. That. Tired.

"Yeah… that sounds like a good idea." Kevin was about to go back to sleep, lulled by Lilian's warm body, when something occurred to him. "Kotohime, do you mind if I ask you something?"

Kotohime paused at the door. "Not at all. What do you wish to ask of me?"

"Why am I naked?"

"Ufufufu…" Hiding her smiling lips behind the sleeve of her kimono, all Kevin could see of the woman was her dark, mirthful eyes. "That was Lilian-sama's doing. I believe she wanted to be as close to you as possible and felt that your clothing was in the way."

"Hm…" Kevin thought about it, then slowly nodded. "That makes sense. Another question, if I may?"

"Of course."

"Why is Iris in my bed? And why is she naked?"

"That was two questions."

"Just answer them already."

Kotohime looked at Iris, who also lay cuddled up to Kevin on the opposite side of her sister. For a girl who seemed to be a major siscon, she appeared rather content holding him like he was an oversized teddy bear.

"Do you really need me to answer that question?"

"…"

"I thought not."

***

The next morning, Kevin woke up and took a shower.

Contrary to the belief of his friends, Kevin didn't always take a shower with Lilian—they would never get to school on time if he did. Most mornings he took a shower by himself, reserving joint showers for weekends.

After stepping out, drying off, and getting dressed, he made his way into the living room. The news played on TV. The news anchor was reporting about a couple of vandals who'd destroyed an office building not far from where he lived. When Kevin saw the building in question on the TV, he felt a small droplet of sweat run down his face. It was, in fact, the very same building that he, Lilian, Iris, Christine, and Kotohime had battled those yōkai in yesterday.

Just great. Now I'm a vandal.

The only silver lining he could see was that no one actually knew what happened, aside from them. The yōkai who had attacked them were all dead, from what he'd gathered during his conversation with Kotohime last night. It was a silver lining, he supposed, though not one that he was proud of.

Everyone was already in the kitchen when he entered. Camellia sat at the table, holding her chopsticks in a fist, showing that she still didn't know how to use them. Kirihime stood behind her, demure as always, a kind smile on her pretty face. Kotohime was positioned in front of the stove. Kevin could see something being baked in the oven, though he couldn't tell what.

"Morning, Beloved," Lilian greeted him with a smile from where she sat. Kevin smiled as well. He walked up behind her, leaned down, and gave her a good morning kiss.

"Hawa!" Camellia tried to stand up. "Camellia wants a kiss, too!"

"L-Lady Camellia, please don't joke about such things!"

"Hawa…"

Kevin ignored Camellia and Kirihime. It was just the poor maid trying to force Camellia back in her seat. Nothing new there.

"How are you feeling?" Lilian asked as Kevin sat down next to her.

248

"I feel fine. Nothing seems to be broken at least." Kevin rotated his shoulders, testing them. "I'm a little stiff, but that's to be expected."

"Indeed it is," Kotohime said as she walked up to the table, a tray in hand. "I can heal many types of damage: blunt force trauma, broken bones, and lacerations. However, not even a River Kitsune can heal fatigue and overused muscles. Those will only heal with time."

She set the tray down on the table. While everyone else began putting food onto their plates, Kevin stared at the breakfast like it was some kind of alien tentacle monster.

"That's not Japanese cuisine."

"Ufufufu, I thought I'd make something different today." When Kevin looked at Kotohime, she presented him with a beautiful smile. "Think of it as my way of saying 'I'm proud of you.'"

Kevin felt warmth, both in the chest and the face. Great. Now he was blushing.

"Th-thank you," he mumbled.

Kotohime raised the sleeve of her kimono to her mouth. "Ufufufu... you're most welcome, Kevin-sama."

"Iris isn't awake yet, is she?" Lilian asked as she began eating Kotohime's French toast.

"Last I saw her, she was still asleep," Kevin said, standing up. "I'll go wake her. Save some French toast for me."

"M'kay," Lilian mumbled around a mouthful of food.

Upon entering his room, Kevin discovered that Iris was indeed still sleeping. He walked up to the bed and, for a moment, simply observed the girl as she slumbered. It was almost ridiculous, the way these fox-girls could make even the most mundane of activities look like a piece of art.

Iris lay on her side. Her gorgeous legs were on full display, milky thighs and gently sloping calves that ended in a pair of small, cute feet and erotic toes that begged to be sucked on. Her hips were partially covered by the blanket, allowing her to keep a semblance of modesty while teasing him with the tantalizing shape of her amazing figure. Her breasts were completely uncovered, as she had slept naked last night and the blanket wasn't covering her chest. Her arms were pushing her notorious bosoms together. It made them seem even larger than they actually were.

A work of art indeed.

Iris looked so much more peaceful asleep than she did during the day. With her eyes closed, thick lashes concealing her carnelian gaze from the world, and her pink mouth partially opened, the condescending expression that she normally possessed when awake was absent.

Shaking his head and silently cursing his teenage hormones, Kevin lightly shook the girl awake and called her name. It took some time, but she eventually woke up, her eyes fluttering open as she sat up in bed.

Kevin's eyes nearly popped out of his head as she stretched her arms in the air, her bare bosom jiggling enticingly. From the devious curvature of her lips, Kevin knew that Iris knew that he was looking at her.

Her arms came down, and she leaned back on them, her crimson eyes shimmering as they locked onto Kevin.

"Mornin', Stud. How'd you sleep?"

"Fine." Kevin tore his eyes away from Iris's breasts. "And you?"

"Never better."

"Right. Well, you should get up now. Breakfast is on the table."

"Right. Breakfast."

Iris swung her legs over the edge of the bed, then lowered herself to the carpeted floor. She stood up and took a step forward, and then she stumbled after seemingly losing her balance.

Kevin's eyes widened even as he moved forward to break her fall. Rather than tumble to the floor, she landed against his chest. Kevin stiffened when he felt the fullness of Iris's body press into him. She placed her hands on his chest and looked up, appearing just as surprised as him.

"You okay?" he asked.

"Yes, I'm fine," Iris said, blinking. The look of astonishment disappeared and was replaced by amusement. "Huhuhu... thanks for catching my fall, Stud. I guess that makes you my hero."

For some reason, Kevin did not like the sound of that. "Uh..."

"And you know what they say," Iris continued, leaning up on her tiptoes. "Heroes deserve a reward."

Kevin panicked. He tried to pull out of her grasp upon realizing her devious intentions, but Iris kept a firm grip around him. Instead of jerking himself out of her grip, he sent them both tumbling to the floor. Now, instead of a naked fox-girl hugging him, it was a naked fox-girl straddling his waist.

"Come on, Stud. Accept your reward like a good boy."

She leaned down. Her lips were pursed ever so slightly. Kevin shuddered as her bum rubbed against his erection. This was a worst-case scenario situation if he'd ever heard of one.

"W-wait, Iris! We can't do this!"

"Huhuhu... and why not?"

"B-because I'm dating Lilian! I refuse to cheat on her! Now get off!"

"A kiss isn't cheating."

"Says you!"

"And even if it was, don't worry so much. I won't tell anyone. Besides, it's not like Lilian will care."

"I care! I'm caring so much right now!"

Kevin put up an admirable struggle, kicking and bucking like a bronco. But Iris remained steadfast and refused to get off, even going so far as to use her tails to hogtie him. She'd also reinforced her limbs, though he noticed how hard they were shaking, as if she needed to concentrate harder than normal.

That would have been the end of it, but Lilian chose that moment to enter the room. "Hey, Kevin. Is Iris awake yet? We need to… get… ready… for… eh?"

Lilian stared at the panicking Kevin and grinning Iris.

"L-Lilian! This is not what it looks like!"

"What are you talking about, Stud? This is so what it looks like."

"You're not helping here!"

As Lilian continued staring at Kevin and Iris, her face slowly turned red. It wasn't long before her cheeks could have outshone the sun. Delicate hands clenched themselves into white-knuckled fists, and her body shook with emotion. Her two tails, which had been hidden, extended from beneath her skirt and writhed in agitation.

"You see that! Now Lilian's mad! Get off me, Iris!"

"She's got no reason to be mad. I promise I'm not trying to steal you. I'll give you back after I… huhuhu… reward you."

"I don't want your reward, dang it! Get off of me! Lilian! Help!"

Kevin's words caused something inside of Lilian to snap. Without warning, one of her tails extended to incredible lengths and flew toward the downed pair at speeds neither of them could comprehend.

Several seconds later, Iris crashed into the wall, denting it.

"Ow…" she muttered as her body slowly peeled off of the wall and fell to the floor with a dull thud.

***

It was official: Lilian was mad.

Kevin didn't know if she was mad at him or mad at Iris, though he hoped it was Iris. He hadn't actually done anything wrong. Sure, the situation had looked bad, but it wasn't like he'd been trying to kiss Iris. It was the other way around! He shouldn't have been blamed for that, should he?

Then again, shōnen protagonists often tended to get the short end of the stick. He only had to look at some of the most prominent examples to know the truth of this statement. Rito Yuuki, Tsukune Aono, Bell Cranel, Touma Kamijou... yes, harem protags had it hard, especially because most of them were stupid. Kevin was lucky in that he was at least aware of the strange harem-esque circumstances surrounding his life.

It was almost enough to make him feel like someone was out to get him.

But surely that couldn't be it, could it?

His cell phone vibrated, knocking Kevin out of his thoughts and causing him to nearly jump out of his seat.

"Is there a problem, Mr. Swift?" Ms. Vis asked, looking quite displeased at having her class interrupted by the young man who refused to follow long-standing anime tradition.

"No, ma'am," Kevin said. "No problem."

"I see. In that case, please try not to disrupt my class again with your unusually loud antics."

Kevin's cheeks gained heat as several of his peers snickered. When Ms. Vis went back to her lecture, he pulled out his cellphone. He had a text message from Lindsay. It read: *Is something going on between you and Lilian? She seems kind of upset. You didn't do anything to hurt her, did you?*

With his cheeks swelling in annoyance at how Lindsay's first thought was that he'd done something wrong, Kevin furiously typed his response: *Of course not. Why would you even think that? You know I would never do anything to upset Lilian.*

He received a reply a few seconds later: *Really? You didn't do anything? Or you don't think you did anything? There's a difference between the two, you know.*

Kevin frowned, calming his mind enough to think about how to respond. Finally, he typed: *There was something that happened between Iris and me this morning, but it's not like I did anything to her. Iris was just being her usual self, and Lilian walked in during a compromising moment when I tried to wake Iris up.*

I see. Yeah, that makes more sense. You might be a guy, but you're not the type to cheat on your girlfriend.

What's that supposed to mean?

Nothing.

Kevin frowned at the screen, which he hid on his lap underneath the desk. *So... do you have any ideas on what I should do? I don't want Lilian to remain mad at me.*

Clear the air during PE. Just let her know what happened. I'm sure she'll forgive you.

You make it sound like I did something wrong.

Kev, you'll learn that when you're in a relationship with a woman, it's always the man's fault whenever something goes wrong.

Kevin's right eyebrow began twitching. He was about to reply when a clattering noise caused him to stop.

He, along with everyone else, turned to Iris, who'd dropped the pencil that she had been writing with. Her wide, round eyes stared at her hand like it was something foreign. The entire hand was shaking. Her fingers were twitching. It was almost like they were undergoing random muscle spasms.

"Is there a problem, Ms. Pnévma?"

Iris shook her head. "No, sorry, Teach. I think I just got writer's cramp or something."

"Very well. See to it that it doesn't happen again."

Ms. Vis went back to the board, grumbling about how people kept interrupting her lectures. Kevin stared at Iris as she bent down to pick up her pencil. On her way back up, she noticed him staring and grinned, causing him to look away and turn his gaze to a pouting

Lilian, whose brows were furrowed as though she was in deep contemplation. She didn't even seem to notice his stare.

"Hmph!" she huffed.

Kevin sighed and scratched his head. How was he supposed to clear the air with her when she still seemed so upset?

His phone vibrated again.

Digging yourself into a bigger hole?

Kevin twitched.

Shut up.

***

Kevin was glad that PE was on the track field that day. Coach Raide apparently wanted to check everyone's times for the one-mile run. While most people groaned and complained, he was actually quite thrilled, especially as he'd managed to cut his time from a 5.32-minute mile to a 4.35-minute mile.

Kiara's training had more advantages than just learning how to fight, it seemed.

However, he had another reason for being glad that they were checking mile times: Boys and girls weren't separated. They all did this together, which meant he would have a chance to speak with Lilian.

He sat on the bleachers with his friends. Alex and Andrew had just finished their one mile a few seconds ago, getting a 5.43 time for their troubles. They did the four hundred-meter relay and weren't good at longer distances. While Kevin also did the hundred-meter dash, he'd been increasing his endurance by riding his bike with Lilian on the back and training with Kiara every day for the past five months. Eric had gotten a 4.53—an impressive feat, to be sure.

"Ugh, why do I always feel like you're leaving us in the dust these days?" Alex asked, giving Kevin a look that used to make him feel like he'd stuck his finger in an outlet. "Seriously, man, what's happening to you? I know we've joked about this before, but you're so different now. I sometimes feel like I'm looking at a completely different person."

Kevin scratched the back of his neck, wondering if he should feel embarrassed or pleased. "I don't feel any different, but if I have changed, then I guess it's because I needed to change."

Andrew perked up from where he lay sprawled on a metal bench. "What do you mean?"

"You all know that Lilian and the other people living with me are kitsune."

"You mean the women living with you," Alex corrected.

"Hot women," Andrew added.

"Hot women I'd love to fuck," Eric said unnecessarily.

Alex and Andrew pointed at Eric. "What he said."

Kevin facepalmed. Were his friends always this perverted?

"Whatever. In any case, you know they're not human. They're kitsune. Yōkai. They live in a world completely different from our own. You three already saw some of what happens in that world when we went to California."

"You mean that massive showdown during the con?" Andrew asked.

"Yes, that. The battle we got caught up in wasn't an isolated incident. It also wasn't the first time I'd been forced into a conflict against a yōkai."

Kevin remembered that first week he'd met Lilian. Chris had nearly killed him. He also remembered when Kiara had demolished Lilian in battle. Then there was the time he'd been kidnapped by the Sons and Daughters of Humanity, and after that, Lilian had been kidnapped and he'd fought against a two-tailed kitsune. Those were four separate occasions in which he and Lilian had been forced into battle.

"So wait, you're saying that you've had to deal with crap like that before?" Alex's eyes were bulging from his sockets and his mouth hung agape. Beside him, Andrew appeared just as flabbergasted. "How come you never told us about this?"

"I knew," Eric said, only to get punched in the face by both Alex and Andrew. "Ouch! The hell was that for?!"

"For being an idiot!" the fraternal twins shouted.

"What was I supposed to say?" asked Kevin. "Should have said something like 'Oh, by the way, my girlfriend is a yōkai, I've almost been killed by several other yōkai, and I was kidnapped by an anti-yōkai faction who may or may not be affiliated with the government'? Could you have seen that conversation going over well? Because I can't."

"Okay, I see your point," Alex admitted. "But it still would have been nice to know about all this stuff sooner. You know, like after we learned about yōkai?"

Kevin waved off his words. "All of that's in the past. There was no point in bringing it up anymore. I only brought it up now because I was trying to make a point."

"And what is that point?"

"That if I want to be able to stay with Lilian, I need to be stronger. I can't keep being a weak, under-confident teenager with girl problems. I have to become someone who can take care of himself—no..." Kevin shook his head. "I need to become someone who can stand by Lilian's side as an equal. To do that, I need to become strong enough to fight on par with yōkai, which means becoming as physically fit as a human is capable of."

Alex and Andrew looked at each other. Eric rubbed his cheeks, which had swelled to the size of tennis balls. He was muttering about violent friends.

"Do you really think you can become as strong as a yōkai, though?" Andrew sounded skeptical. "Not to burst your bubble or anything, but aren't yōkai, like, these super-powerful creatures with strange abilities? How can you hope to match that?"

"I can't, not with just physical strength." Kevin's eyes strayed to the track field. Lilian had just finished her mile and was walking toward the fountain. "But if I can combine my physical abilities with the ability to wield various types of weapons, I'm hoping to at least be able to match them." He stood up. "Now, if you'll excuse me, I need to speak with someone."

He left his friends on the bleachers and wandered over to Lilian, who was sipping from the fountain. She was leaning over while wearing the really short, light blue gym shorts of their school. Kevin's eyes traveled the expanse of her mile-long legs. The shapeliness of her calves, the supple muscles of her thighs, and dear god, that small, perfect little bubble butt! It was way too much! By all eight million Shinto gods, did everything these kitsune do have to be so sexy?

Kevin shook his head. What was he thinking? Of course, everything they did was sexy. They were kitsune for crying out loud!

"Lilian?"

Kevin stopped several feet from the redhead, who straightened and turned around.

"Kevin."

He winced at the tone. It wasn't cold, but it sounded distracted as if she wasn't interested in talking to him. That wasn't a good sign.

"Listen, Lilian, I, uh…" Oh, dang it. Why was this so hard? "I just… w-well, I wanted to apologize for, um, this morning… and stuff…" When all Lilian did was blink, Kevin hastened to continue. "What I mean is I know it looked bad and stuff… back there, you know, with Iris and me. B-but I swear that nothing happened! I would never cheat on you! You've gotta believe me!"

Lilian stared at him for several seconds longer. It wasn't until she began scratching her head that he realized Lilian was confused. "What are you talking about?"

"Eh? A-aren't you mad at me?"

Lilian furrowed her brows. "Why would I be mad at you?"

"B-because of this morning," Kevin said. "You haven't spoken to me since this morning when you caught Iris trying to kiss me. I thought you were mad at me."

The way Lilian's mouth formed a pretty "O" of surprise made Kevin feel stupid. The expression only lasted for a moment, and then she rubbed her forehead and sighed. "I'm not mad at you."

Kevin was nonplussed. "You're not?"

"No… I'm just frustrated."

"At what?"

"At Iris." Lilian's cheeks swelled as she pouted. It was adorable. "My sister is constantly teasing you and me, even though I keep telling her not to. She doesn't seem to understand that I've made up my mind and decided to have a normal human relationship with you. Even though I've told her this dozens of times, she keeps trying and trying and it really pisses me off!"

Lilian proceeded to stomp on the ground like a child having a tantrum. Even while having a childish fit, she was still impossibly cute. He didn't know how someone so freaking sexy could be so blindingly winsome.

"Beloved?"

Kevin blinked and snapped back to reality. He was going to blame his distracted state on hormones.

"Yes?"

Lilian walked up to him, her hands behind her back. When she reached him, she brought her hands forward and placed them on his chest.

"I'm sorry. I didn't mean to make you think that I was upset with you. Will you forgive me?"

"Of course!" Kevin exclaimed. "You know I could never be upset at you… well, not anymore at least. What I mean is that we're dating now, you know? I mean, you're my mate. What kind of boyfriend—no, what kind of mate would I be if I got upset because of a misunderstanding?"

Lilian giggled as Kevin continued to babble. He stopped when she walked into his personal space and pulled him into a hug.

"Lilian?"

"Never change, Beloved," Lilian said, resting her chin on his shoulder.

"Uh... okay..."

What was with this change of atmosphere? What was Lilian talking about? Never change. Why would he change? He didn't get it, but he guessed it didn't matter.

Kevin returned her hug, taking more pleasure from such a simple action than he had anything else today. There was something amazing about holding his girlfriend-slash-mate. Maybe it was because of the way her thin waist seemed to fit within his arms, or perhaps it was how her arms wrapped around him, with her hands resting against his shoulder blades, clutching the fabric of his shirt— or maybe it was just her boobs. The way they felt pressed against his chest was pretty amazing. He'd said it before, but few things in this world could match the pure amazingness of her bust.

Ugh, pervy thoughts. Kevin grimaced. By the gods of anime and manga, his mind was beginning to sound like Eric!

"Kevin," Lilian mumbled, nuzzling her nose against his neck.

"Yes?" Kevin asked.

"You smell."

Kevin twitched. "Gee, thanks. That's just what I want my mate to tell me after a heartfelt apology."

Lilian giggled as she pulled her head back to look at him.

"Sorry, Beloved. Here, let me make it up to you," she said, leaning up on her tiptoes. As Lilian's eyes fluttered closed, Kevin leaned down and slowly closed his own eyes.

There were times when Kevin wondered if kissing Lilian would ever lose its novelty, like if he would ever think of kissing her as "just another kiss." Then they would kiss and he could only wonder at how he could ever think such blasphemous thoughts. The feel of her lips as they caressed his and the heavenly flame that was her tongue in his mouth was beyond compare. Nothing could top kisses from Lilian.

Wanting to get more of that feeling, Kevin pushed Lilian against the wall and ground his pelvis into hers. Lilian's muffled moan reverberated through his mouth. The sound of her voice, even hampered, was more than he could withstand.

His hands moved down to grasp her tight buttocks.

"Hn!"

Lilian gasped. With her lips now parted, he pushed his tongue into her mouth. She welcomed the intrusion, closing her mouth around his tongue and sucking on it. If he hadn't already been stiffer than a pair of nipples being hit by winter's chill, this would have certainly done the trick.

He rubbed his body against hers, continuing to grind through his clothing. Lilian helped by wrapping her legs around his waist.

Thanks to their gym clothes, the action felt rough and kind of coarse against his skin, and a small part of him was beginning to regret how they were wearing clothing. Even more than that, Kevin was actually getting kind of tired of foreplay... well, not tired per se. He actually loved doing the so-called "ecchi stuff" with Lilian, but he wouldn't deny that he wanted more.

Maybe he should think about repealing his "no sex" policy. Kevin honestly didn't know how much more of this he could take.

"Holy shit!" a voice said off to his left.

The words were like a bucket of ice-cold water being dumped all over him. He and Lilian broke apart—or at least stopped kissing. Their heads turned in synchronization.

They were no longer alone.

Alex, Andrew, Eric, and Heather stood before them, along with several other students. While their blonde assistant coach was grinning from ear to ear, his three friends were crying, as in, really crying, like their eyes had become dams that finally broke and let out the floodgates. The others who'd decided to stare were the girls in their class. They were blushing, giggling, and looked about ready to suffer a nose—oh, wait. One of them had already passed out from a nosebleed.

And girls said that only men were perverts.

"That was the hottest thing I've ever seen," Eric declared. "I think I just found some new fap material for my databanks. Don't stop now, My Lord. It looked like you two were just getting to the good part."

It wasn't until Eric spoke that Kevin noticed the phone in his soon-to-be-dead friend's hand. It was pointed at them, obviously recording what he and Lilian had done.

Rage engulfed him.

"Come on now, My Lord. Keep going! Grind your man bits into that sexy piece of ass's little girl spot, until she's— GYYYAAAA!"

Eric's words were halted and replaced with a squeal as something hard smacked him in the gonads. The young man covered his crotch as he fell to the ground and curled up in the fetal position. Alex and Andrew both winced and covered their own man-bits.

"Get bent, Eric!" Kevin shouted, the hand that had thrown the rock still extended. Dang that pervert! Ruin his and Lilian's moment, would he? Who did he think he was?!

"While I don't want to say anything for fear of sounding like my idiot of an apprentice," Heather started, her grin widening. She looked like the cat that got the cream. "I have to agree with him on one thing. That was pretty hot. You two must have been practicing a lot at home."

Kevin found his face turning into a furnace of shame. Lilian, despite being fairly shameless when it came to acts of intimacy, also blushed rather heavily.

This moment probably would have lasted for some time, with Kevin and Lilian expressing mutual embarrassment with burning red faces, were it not for another girl running up to the group, her eyes wide and frantic.

"Ms. Grant, come quick! Something horrible has happened!"

"Something horrible? What happened?" asked Heather.

"Iris has collapsed!"

***

Kevin and Lilian stood in the hallway outside of the hospital room that Iris resided in.

After finding out that Iris had collapsed, they'd called Kiara, who'd in turn made arrangements for an ambulance to pick them up. Iris had been unconscious as the paramedics loaded her onto a stretcher. Her face had been flushed red, and she'd been covered in sweat, much like a person who had the flu.

Both of them were worried, incredibly so. Yōkai rarely suffered from illnesses. Of those illnesses that they could contract, five were fatal, and the other two tended to be crippling.

"Relax, you two," Kiara said from where she leaned against the wall. Unlike the other two, she looked cool as a cucumber. "I know you're worried, and you have every right to be, but getting all bent out of shape and losing your cool isn't going to help anyone, least of all your sister."

"That's easy for you to say," Lilian snapped. "It's not your sister who's currently in the hospital."

"Yeah, you got me there." Kiara ran her only remaining hand through her hair. "However, my point still stands. You need to remain calm. Otherwise, you won't be able to help your sister when the time comes. Besides, I have my personal physician looking over her. He's an expert on yōkai physiology and an amazing healer. If your sister is sick, provided her illness isn't too far along, he'll expedite it quicker than you can say kami."

Lilian relaxed just a bit, the tenseness in her shoulders loosened, and her abnormally straight back slouched in relief. She stopped pacing back and forth across the hall and sighed. It sounded like her sister was in good hands.

Just then, the door to Iris's room opened, and out stepped a wizened old man in a lab coat. He held a clipboard in his hand and wore a pair of rimless glasses. Kevin thought he looked like an old hermit trying to play doctor.

"How's my sister?" Lilian didn't give the man much time to exit before she was on him with the zealousness of a child who wanted candy. She stared at him with her big, imploring eyes, a silent demand to know about her sister's status gleaming within them.

"Your sister is just fine," the doctor said, his wrinkled mouth twisting into a semblance of a smile.

Lilian's sigh of relief sounded several decibels louder in the nearly empty hall. Kevin felt relieved as well, though he didn't express it like she did.

"So you cured her sickness, then?" he asked, coming to stand beside his mate and grabbing her hand.

"Oh, she wasn't sick," the doctor informed them. "What Iris has is a very unique case of Void poisoning."

"Void..." Kevin started.

"Poisoning?" Lilian finished his question.

"Yes, Void poisoning is what happens when immature Void users go over the limits of their own abilities. The Void is a very dark power, and it carries a terrible price for those who use it. Iris called upon more of the Void than she could control. The Void infected her body in turn, causing her to collapse and take on the symptoms of being ill. It's a relatively rare thing to have happen, as most Void users know the limits of their power before this becomes a problem. That said, hers is a very mild case and isn't terminal. She will recover with a few days of bed rest, though she'll be weak in the meantime and continue to exhibit flu-like symptoms."

"I-I see." Lilian held her free hand up to her chest, clenching the fabric of her shirt. Her grip on Kevin's hand also tightened. "That's good."

The doctor smiled. "Iris is conscious at the moment and can be moved from this hospital if you desire. I suggest you take her home and allow her to rest there. It's much easier for a patient to recover in places that he or she is familiar with."

* * *

After receiving the all-clear from Kiara's physician that they could take Iris home, the group was quick to get the raven-haired beauty a wheelchair and move her to the car. She and Lilian sat in the back. Iris rested her head on Lilian's shoulder, while his mate idly played with her sister's hair. Kevin sat in the front with Kiara, who kept her single remaining hand on the steering wheel.

"Kiara?" Kevin said as he looked at her out of his peripheral vision.

Kiara kept her eyes on the road as she drove. "Hm?"

"I just wanted to tell you that I've found my resolve. I'm ready to begin training again."

"Is that so?" Kevin could see her gazing at him in the mirror, piercing him with her keen, feral eyes, which seemed to see far more than eyes should. "I heard about your fight with the gorilla yōkai. Gorillas are a powerful race, incredibly dangerous to face unless you've got the power to match. Kotohime gave me a glowing review of your battle."

Kevin wanted to bask in the praise. It felt good to know that Kotohime had been so proud of him that she'd told Kiara.

His teacher's next words stopped him in his tracks, though. "But, do you think you can kill if it becomes necessary?"

Kevin didn't say anything at first. A part of him wanted to shout out something like *"Of course I can kill!"* or *"I'll kill if it means protecting the people I love"*—something cool like that—but he didn't. While a part of him wanted to say those things, another part hesitated.

"Honestly, I still don't want to kill anybody," Kevin admitted. He stared down at the hands on his lap, weak hands, the hands of a human. "I dislike the idea of killing. It's one thing to see it in cartoons, on TV, and in video games, but killing in real life? It's horrifying. I can't imagine why anyone would want to kill someone else in the first place."

He knew why people killed from an objective standpoint: Greed, revenge, black emotions that stained the soul. While some people claimed they killed to protect, that was just a lie, a cover-up. Governments all over the world spoke of killing to protect the people, but many of those governments started the very wars they claimed were for the protection of the people. Starting a war to protect someone, killing to protect someone, it was a contradiction unto itself, as far as he was concerned.

Greed. Malice. The desire to obtain more than you already have by taking it from others.

He only needed to look at his own government to know what the world was really about. The wars against the Native Americans to drive them out of their homes and force them to travel across the country in search of new land. While many people claimed that the civil war had been about the abolishment of slavery, the truth was that slavery had merely been the spark needed to start the war. The true reason had been economic superiority.

He wasn't confirming nor denying that the civil war had to happen, nor was he condoning slavery. The act of enslaving another was just as abominable as the act of killing. It didn't change the fact that the freedom of slavery was not the first and foremost reason for the civil war. It was greed. The greed of the north pitted against that of the south.

Kevin didn't know what wars yōkai had fought. He had read a lot of manga and watched many an anime, quite a few of which featured yōkai, but it wasn't like he'd studied up on their history. He imagined they fought for the same reasons, though: greed, malice, revenge, and negative emotions that corrupted the hearts and minds of people.

He still didn't understand it. People could explain the concept of the need to kill endlessly, and he still wouldn't understand it. He couldn't comprehend how people, human or yōkai, could ever want to kill another sentient creature. They didn't do it for food. They did it because they could, because the other person had something they wanted, or even out of the simple desire to prove their own dominance. It disgusted him.

However…

"I don't want to kill, and I'm going to continue trying not to, but that doesn't mean I'm just going to let people who try to kill me and my family do whatever they want," Kevin declared. Lilian looked up at him, and even Iris was startled awake by his voice. "If someone comes at me, then I'll kick their ass until they're down. If someone tries to hurt my family, I'll beat the crap out of them until they decide that trying to hurt my friends is a bad idea… and if it becomes necessary, if it becomes a matter between taking a life and saving the life of myself or someone I love, then yes, I will kill. But I refuse to allow myself to become like everybody else. Killing people is easy. Anyone can take a gun and pull the trigger. How much harder is it to pull the finger back and let someone live?"

Kevin narrowed his eyes, glaring his defiance at Kiara through the mirror.

"That's my answer."

Silence pervaded the expensive sports car. Kevin noticed that Lilian and Iris were staring at him with the same expression that he was sure they'd have if someone told them that Inari was coming to earth to get wasted. Lilian's cheeks were quite red, and Iris sensually licked her lips when she noticed his eyes on her.

Gulp.

As for Kiara...

"Pfft! Hahahahahahahaha!"

Kevin's cheeks became beacons of heat as his instructor laughed at him. He tried ducking his head into his shirt, and when that didn't work, he crossed his arms and tried to play off his embarrassment. "I don't see what's so funny."

Kiara's laughter petered off into light chuckles. "You're a really good kid, you know that? Most people would've called you an idiot if they ever heard you say something like that. The idea of fighting but not killing is ludicrous. You'd be the laughingstock of all yōkai if anyone other than maybe Kotohime heard you say that."

Kevin scratched the back of his head. He didn't really know how to take her words. Was she insulting him?

"But I don't really care about that." Kiara grinned fiercely. "You've got guts, determination, and the resolve to create your own path regardless of what awaits you. I like that, so I'll keep helping you get stronger, provided you make me a promise that no matter what happens, you always stay true to the path you've chosen."

Kevin contemplated his teacher for a moment before giving her a confident grin. "It's a promise."

"Good."

In the back of the car, Iris whispered to her sister. "Are you sure letting him train with that dog is a good idea?"

"No," Lilian said. "But it's what Beloved wants to do."

"Hn. Well, that speech was pretty cool, but if he keeps sticking around the mutt, he's going start smelling bad."

"You know that I can hear everything you two just said, right?" Kiara asked.

Iris and Lilian *eeped!* at the same time.

***

Kiara pulled to a stop in front of the Swift residence, and, as the doors lifted like a set of wings, Kevin stepped out of the red

Giugiaro. He turned back around to help Lilian get Iris out. Lilian unbuckled her sister's seatbelt and then scooted her over so Kevin could scoop Iris into his arms. Iris had fallen asleep again, and her lolling head rested against his shoulder.

"She's really burning up," Kevin commented as Lilian stepped out. "I hadn't realized she was so hot. It feels like her body's on fire."

"That's just a symptom of Void poisoning," Kiara said from within the car. "Anyway, be sure to have her get plenty of bed rest. I'll see you kids later."

The doors closed and Kiara drove off. Kevin and Lilian watched the car until it disappeared around the corner. As the stupidly expensive vehicle vanished, Kevin had to wonder about the number of cars that woman had. Seriously, first a Lamborghini, and now this?

"Let's get Iris inside," Kevin said, with Lilian nodding in agreement.

"Right."

They made it up the stairs and Lilian used her key to open the door. Kevin preceded her and entered, expecting to find a frantic Kirihime chasing after a naked Camellia and Kotohime doing some housecleaning. Instead, he discovered that the apartment was empty.

"I wonder where everyone went off to," Kevin commented. It felt odd not having people running around, creating shenanigans these days. This silence was disquieting.

"I don't know where Kotohime is, but Kirihime and Mom are probably out playing or something," Lilian said. "That, or Kirihime's just trying to keep Mom out of trouble. You know how she is."

Kevin felt some sweat coalesce on his head. "Hahaha... ha... yeah..." He shook his head and got back on track. "Anyway, could you get a bowl full of cool water and some rags for me? I'll put Iris to bed."

"Okay."

While Lilian went to grab a bowl and a rag, Kevin walked into their bedroom. He placed Iris on the bed. Then he took off her running shoes—she was still wearing her gym clothes—followed by her socks, which he set on the floor. After that, he took a step back to observe the beautiful kitsune.

Her face had become flushed, her cheeks a vibrant red. Sweat covered her forehead, face, neck, and much of her body. Her clothes were sticking almost erotically to her skin. His eyebrow twitched a bit when he noticed that, even when feverish, the two-tailed vixen still looked ridiculously sexy. It was like being a study in sex appeal had become such a habit for her that she oozed sexuality from her pores even when not trying to. It was disturbing, especially because Kevin was almost positive it meant that there was something wrong with him for thinking this way.

A hand latched onto his wrist, gripping him in a weak hold. Iris had woken up, and she was staring at him with half-lidded eyes. She was also giving him a surprisingly genuine smile, no condescension or her usual holier-than-thou attitude could be found anywhere on her face.

"Hey, Stud. Thanks for taking care of me."

"It's no problem," Kevin said. "We're family... sorta, so it's only right that I take care of you when you're like this."

"Heh, I guess."

Lilian came in a few seconds later, carrying a bowl filled with water and a towel soaking in it. "Here's the bowl and towel you wanted, Beloved. Where do you want me to set it?"

"Just set it over here by the bed," Kevin instructed, patting the nightstand.

Lilian did as told and set the bowl on the nightstand, then she sat down on the bed's edge, the comforter depressing to accommodate her weight. She took her sister's hand in her own, squeezing it with sisterly tenderness.

"How are you feeling, Iris?"

"Like I'm about to vomit," Iris admitted. "I've never felt so weak before. Tch. Inari's saggy scrotum, this is why I hate being a Void user. The drawbacks of using this power really blow."

Kevin grabbed the towel from the bowl and wrung it out until it was just damp. He sat next to Lilian and wiped the sweat from Iris's face and forehead, eliciting a sigh of relief from the bedridden kitsune. After wiping the sweat away, Kevin grabbed and wrung out another towel before folding it and placing it on her forehead.

"That feels so nice," Iris murmured.

"I imagine so. Anyway, since you have a fever, the best thing to do is to get as much rest as possible and try to keep sweat off. You're also going to want to eat light meals like chicken noodle soup. Speaking of which." Kevin stood up. "I know for a fact that we don't have any ingredients for soup, so I'm going to head over to the grocery store. Lilian, you'll be in charge of taking care of Iris."

"Don't worry, Beloved." Lilian gave him a cheesy thumbs-up. "I'll be sure to look after my sister."

"Right. I shouldn't be gone for long."

Iris and Lilian followed Kevin with their eyes as he left the room.

"You know something," Iris started, her voice weak and exhausted. "Even though I was really upset after finding out that you had a mate, I can see why you like him."

"Um, Kevin's the best!" Lilian's enthusiastic agreement, complete with a brilliant smile and head bobbing, earned a chuckle from Iris.

"And you're sure you're not willing to share—gya!" Iris glared at her sister. "You just pinched my boob!"

"Ufufufu, I have no clue what you're talking about." Iris grumbled a bit as Lilian flashed her an innocent smile. "Now, then, please be quiet and let me take care of you like a good sister, okay?"

"Tch, you've been spending way too much time with Kotohime."

"Now that isn't a very nice thing to say."

***

Kotohime stood in front of a plain square building with gray walls and a flat roof.

The newspaper distribution center that was Davin Monstrang's base of operations held an underwhelming appearance that made her frown. A man of his stature should have a more ostentatious place to receive guests, but she also knew that these were her thoughts as a kitsune. Despite being a rather unorthodox member of her race, there were some habits that even she couldn't break. Her desire to impress others was one of them.

Steadying herself, Kotohime entered the distribution center, walked up to Davin's office, knocked on the door, and waited for a response.

"Come in," a voice grunted.

The office looked just as it had the last time she'd been there, a spartan room bereft of everything but the bare essentials. The white walls lacked any sort of decoration, not even a picture so much as hung from them. It also lacked furniture, with only a desk, a chair, and a filing cabinet situated against a wall. This place felt lifeless.

Sitting behind his desk was Davin Monstrang, a large, beefy man with dark eyes and little hair. Thick brow ridges that lacked eyebrows hid rhomboidal eyes like a visor. He wore a Hawaiian collared shirt that day while his expansive gut and large chest strained against the buttons, which seemed ready to snap.

"Davin-dono," Kotohime greeted courteously, clasping her hands in front of her and bowing. "I am pleased to see that you are doing well."

Davin shifted, his chair creaking as though it was ready to snap. "Kotohime, I haven't seen you for a while, not since you requested my permission to live here with your charge and her family."

Due to Davin's position, she had only met with him on a few occasions. The first time was when she had first arrived in Arizona, and the second was when she'd asked for his permission to allow Camellia and the others to live in this state. It was only appropriate, after all. Davin Monstrang was one of the Four Saints, and Arizona was his territory.

"Indeed it has."

"How is the brat doing?" Davin asked. Kotohime almost smiled. Davin tried to act uncaring and aloof, but she could tell that he had a soft spot for Kevin.

"Kevin-sama has been well. He is growing stronger by the day, though he will eventually reach the peak of human limitations. Still, Kiara has a plan to help Kevin overcome such physical boundaries. I doubt it will allow him to fight on par with stronger yōkai, but against lesser yōkai and maybe even those whose powers are slightly above average, he should be able to defeat them in time."

They both knew what Kotohime was speaking of when she mentioned Kiara's plan. Guns. Human weapons. They were the single biggest reason that yōkai had, for the first time in centuries, come together in order to create a code of laws that all yōkai must obey regardless of race.

With the knowledge and ability to use a variety of weaponry, Kevin would be able to match the powers of certain yōkai races. He would never become strong enough to fight on par with someone like Davin or even Kotohime, and he would certainly never wield the ability to slay a nine-tails or one of the other great entities whose powers were on par with a god's. Then again, he also didn't need that much power.

After all, the chances of a Kyūbi coming personally to kill him were so slim as to be nonexistent.

Davin-dono grunted. "That's good to hear, but you didn't come here to tell me about the brat, did you? You wish to know about the yōkai who attacked your charge, right?"

Kotohime smiled politely. "Indeed."

"In that case, take a seat. This explanation will be a bit long."

While Kotohime normally preferred standing or sitting seiza, one did not decline the suggestion of a saint. She sat down and placed the sheathed katana in her lap, back straight and posture proper.

"You are aware that there are many yōkai within the United States," Davin said, speaking in his low, grunting tone. "To be precise, we have calculated that there are somewhere over five hundred and fifty-two thousand yōkai living here."

"That… is a lot of yōkai, yes."

There weren't that many yōkai in the world. Compared to humanity, which made up 6.5 billion people, yōkai only made up, at most, 1.5 million, maybe a little more. Even as far back as the first century, humans had outnumbered yōkai one thousand to one. These days, those numbers had skyrocketed. That so many yōkai had gathered in one country astonished her. If Davin wanted to, he could have probably waged war against the humans with that many yōkai.

Before the production of guns and weapons of mass destruction, it was the population difference and wars between races that kept yōkai from outright subjugating humans. Now yōkai had been forced to integrate themselves into the human society, lest they be discovered and destroyed.

She didn't consider this a bad thing, and many yōkai agreed with her, though the great yōkai clans, such as the Tengu Clan who lived in Russia and the Oni Clan of Shuten Doji, likely did not.

"It is. This is just a rough estimate, but it's accurate enough. We have a means of ensuring that we know when a yōkai enters and leaves this country, though the system itself is still full of glitches and ineffective when it comes to unprecedented variables, such as entering the country through illegal means."

Kotohime would have normally said "I see" or something to that effect, but she knew what was required of her and remained silent, allowing the man to continue.

"The four that you and the others fought are part of a rogue faction of yōkai who have entered the country illegally." Davin Monstrang placed his monstrous hands on the desk, palms flat. "We have reason to believe they are part of a larger group, though we have no way of knowing for sure. If they are part of a greater organization, then they were merely low-level grunts."

"What makes you believe that they were part of a larger group?"

"Because for a yōkai to enter the United States through illegal means requires them to have a yōkai on the inside who is willing to help them. While our screening process can't account for all variables, when a yōkai enters legally, there is no way we wouldn't know about it."

Yōkai entering the country had to register themselves so they could be entered into a database. This was done to help the people charged with maintaining yōkai secrecy do their job.

The system had been set up by the Four Saints, and it was being maintained by Kuroneko. Even Kotohime, Lilian, and the other members of her family were registered.

"Does that mean there are criminal yōkai elements within the United States?"

Davin tapped a meaty finger on his desk. The sound, a staccato and off-time rhythm, made Kotohime twitch.

She didn't want to admit it, but being in Davin's presence was always a nerve-wracking experience. His power was understated. He kept it carefully concealed. However, it still leaked out. While most people would never feel it, she could sense his overwhelming aura, and it made her nervous.

"There are criminal elements within every country. It is impossible to rid a place of crime unless someone abolished the laws that made crime illegal, and then we'd just have a bunch of criminals running around, doing whatever they wanted without fear of justice. Already we know of at least two large criminal syndicates within the country. The Morello Crime Family and the Cardinelli Gang. However, while they both have power enough that they can exist without us being able to do anything, we do not believe they are the ones who helped the four you killed."

"And why is that?"

"Because of their differences in philosophy. Morello and Cardinelli believe in using humans to further their own goals. The yōkai you killed were all believers of yōkai supremacy and the complete subjugation of humanity to yōkai rule. Neither of those groups would have allowed yōkai like that into the United States."

"That makes sense." Kotohime felt depressed by this knowledge. "I don't suppose you would know why those yōkai attacked Lilian and Iris, then, would you? If they do indeed espouse the concepts of human subjugation, then why go after two yōkai?"

"Because you live alongside a human." Davin shrugged. "That's certainly one reason they might have gone after your charges, though I suspect they were also paid."

Kotohime blinked. "Paid?"

"Yes, paid."

"By whom?"

Davin's smile caused Kotohime's insides to feel squeamish. It wasn't malicious, but his larger-than-average canines, which reminded her of dragon fangs, gleamed with an unnerving light. She never wanted to see that smile directed at her again.

"By someone who hates your charge and the brat, of course."

***

Kevin Swift walked through the produce department. Fresh vegetables sat on racks. Overhead misters kept the produce fresh, or as fresh as could be. He scanned the items with a keen eye, checking the freshness of the produce, comparing prices between organic and nonorganic, and just making sure that he was getting the most out of his ingredients.

Iris had a preference for tomatoes, so he planned on making a cream of tomato soup for her. Tomato soup was chock-full of vitamin C, which he believed would help her recover, even if she wasn't actually sick. He gave a brief thought to making a grilled cheese sandwich as well but shoved the notion aside. Grilled cheese might be too heavy for her, and he didn't want to exacerbate the problem.

He already had several tomatoes, so after grabbing some extra seasonings for the soup, Kevin was about to head over to the cash register.

Before he could leave, he caught sight of a familiar raven-haired figure. Curly locks of hair fell about her face. Yellow eyes peered out from between her bangs. She had a small nose and full lips, reminding Kevin of a cover model. She was standing near the meat section, her gaze longing. Also...

Why the heck is she wearing so much leather?

Leather pants, leather shirt, everything that she wore was leather. It was also really skimpy.

"Hey!" Kevin called out as he walked up to the woman, who turned upon hearing him, revealing her startled yellow eyes. "You're the one who rescued me from Ms. Vis the other day. Cassy, right?"

"N-Nya, Master Kevin?!" The woman squeaked.

Kevin looked at her oddly. "This is the second time you've called me 'Master'..."

"Nya!" Cassy covered her mouth with her hands. "I-I mean, Kevin, nya! Kevin! What are you doing here?"

Kevin decided right then and there to ignore the woman's odd manner of speech. It was actually very easy. He'd ignored stranger things for the sake of keeping his sanity intact.

"I'm just doing a bit of shopping." He held up his basket filled with tomatoes and seasonings. "Iris has come down with the, uh, flu, so I plan on making something that won't upset her stomach."

"Oh, hahaha, nya, I see."

"Right. So, what are you doing here?"

"Oh, me? I'm just trying to find something to eat," Cassy admitted sheepishly. She glanced longingly at the fresh fish sitting in the display case. If he didn't know any better, he would have said that she was drooling.

Her stomach rumbled.

"Um, do you not have enough money to buy food?"

At the mention of money, Cassy slumped to the ground, a black cloud of depression hovering over as she drew circles on the checkered tile. "I-it's not that I don't have any money, per se... I just..."

Kevin sighed as the woman trailed off. "Would you like me to buy some fish for you?"

Cassy looked up, her eyes large and teary, her head tilting with the inquisitiveness of a cat. "Nya? You would do that for me?"

Under the force of her gaze, Kevin's will, which had already been pretty weak, to begin with, crumbled.

"Sure." He smiled in resignation. "Grab whatever you want and follow me."

His wallet was already crying, but seeing the jubilant look on Cassy's face made it hard to complain.

***

Lilian watched as the bowl filled with cold water, shutting off the tap once it was full. She placed the rags in the bowl and then picked it up. The soft thudding of her feet as she carried it to her bedroom echoed along the silent hallway.

Iris was still in bed. Her cheeks were still flushed, and her body still dripped with sweat. She was breathing heavily as well, the kind of harsh breathing that reminded Lilian of Kevin immediately after he finished a hundred-meter dash at full speed.

"Lilian…" Iris mumbled.

"Are you feeling any better?" Lilian asked as she sat down and set the bowl on the nightstand. She did exactly as Kevin had done, wringing out a towel and using it to wipe the sweat off Iris's forehead, face, and neck, and then taking another one, folding it, and placing it on Iris's head.

"I've been better," Iris said, sighing as the cold towel touched her forehead, which was still burning like a furnace on full blast. "Thanks for doing this. I really do have the best sister ever."

Lilian felt her cheeks warm just a bit at the praise. It was such a rare thing to hear from her sister. Iris wasn't one for giving praise.

"You're welcome."

Lilian set the towel she'd used to wipe the sweat back into the bowl. She was about to get up and see if maybe adding some ice cubes would help keep the water cool, but then Iris suddenly shot up and vomited all over her own lap.

"Kya!"

With a girlish shriek, Lilian leaped into the air, landing on the floor several feet away. Iris continued to cough and hack as bile spewed from her mouth like a broken faucet shooting water. Getting over her shock, Lilian sat near the head of the bed and moved Iris's hair away from her face. She kept this up until her sister stopped regurgitating.

"Inari's left testicle, I hate this," the raven-haired vixen mumbled disgustedly. "I feel so weak."

Lilian felt sympathy for her sister. It couldn't have been pleasant, getting sick and bedridden like a human with the flu. She wished she could do more for Iris.

Lilian helped her sister lay back down, noticing the grimace that was plastered on Iris's face, no doubt from the aftertaste. Lilian had never vomited before. Judging from the nose-curdling smell, however, she knew that it couldn't have tasted pleasant.

"Here, let me clean these sheets and get some new ones for you."

"Thanks, Lily."

"Anytime."

Lilian pulled the comforter off the bed and bundled it into a ball, which she tossed into the washing machine before turning it on. She also remembered to use the pods that Kevin had spoken of before they'd started dating. After that, she found another comforter and re-entered the room to find Iris trying to reach for the bowl with little success.

"Iris, you shouldn't strain yourself so much." Lilian set the comforter on the floor and walked up to her sister. "If you need something, all you have to do is ask me."

"Really?" Iris turned hopeful eyes on her sister.

"Of course."

"Anything?"

Completely missing the emphasis her sister put on the word "anything," Lilian nodded as she smiled compassionately at her sister. "Of course. You're my sister, and you're bedridden. If there is anything I can do to help, just ask."

"Will you give me a sponge bath?"

… Silence. Several crickets began chirping most annoyingly.

"W-what?" Lilian asked, trying not to blush. "I-I'm sorry, but I don't think I heard you right. Could you repeat that, please?"

"I know you heard what I said." Iris gave her sister a pleading look complete with large, carmine eyes. She looked like a cute, fluffy animal, or one of those chibi anime characters. "Please? I feel disgusting, and I have sweat and vomit all over me, but I don't have the strength to clean myself."

Lilian tried to resist her sister's expression but found her will crumbling faster than Kevin when she used to use that look on him. Was this what her mate felt every time she used this technique? If so, then she really needed to apologize when he returned.

"Ha... all right, all right, fine, just... stop looking at me like that."

Lilian turned her head so that she wouldn't have to see Iris's expression, thereby missing the grin and victory sign that her sister held up.

The first step toward giving Iris a sponge bath was stripping her clothes off. This proved to be a tad difficult because Iris couldn't move much on her own. Lilian had to place a hand behind her back and lift her into a sitting position, which caused Iris to slouch over as if all of her strength had been exhausted.

"Can you raise your arms?"

Iris managed to lift her arms, but they shook as she did. In the end, Lilian was forced to hold them up with her tails. She then grabbed the hem of Iris's gym shirt and slowly raised it. She gulped as inch after inch of her sister's pale, silky skin revealed itself to her. Even though it was covered in sweat, even though it looked pallid, her sister's skin was quite possibly the loveliest thing she'd ever seen.

Come on, Lilian! It's just Iris! There's no need to be so nervous.

Lilian didn't know why, but with each inch of skin that was revealed, Lilian felt herself becoming increasingly excited. Her palms became sweaty, and her face felt hot as the shirt traveled over Iris's breasts. Much like Lilian, her sister didn't wear a bra, and when the shirt moved past her chest, her breasts popped free of their confines with a flamboyant bounce.

Lilian closed her eyes, thinking that maybe if she didn't look, it would allow her to control her breathing, which had become heavy in the last few seconds. She slid the shirt over Iris's head and up her arms until they were past her hands. Without anything keeping her up, Iris fell back onto the bed while Lilian discarded the sweaty, vomit-covered shirt.

"My shorts, too, Lily."

"U-unn… right."

Moving to the foot of the bed, Lilian got a good look at her sister's shorts. They were covered in puke, stained, and disgusting. Her acute nose wrinkled at the smell coming off of them. She could see why Iris wanted to get clean now.

Grabbing the hem of her sister's blue gym shorts, Lilian proceeded to slowly pull them off. Iris tried to help by lifting her hips, but she couldn't get them very far above the bed. An inch was about all that she was capable of.

Despite this, Lilian was able to slide the shorts down across her sister's lovely hips, beautiful thighs, and shapely calves, before pulling them over Iris's small feet.

She discarded the shorts, tossing them in the dirty hamper. Then she turned back around. Her breath was stolen from her.

Kitsune are naturally drawn toward beauty in all its forms. While each kitsune has their own perceptions of what they feel is beautiful—for example, Lilian thought Kevin was dashingly handsome—there are some things in this world that can be deemed as "universally beautiful."

Iris's nude body was one of those things.

Lilian couldn't help but feel a mixed sense of awe, envy, and lust as she stared at Iris. She didn't know what bothered her more: The fact that her sister looked so unbelievably sexy despite having flu-like symptoms, or the fact that Lilian felt drawn to her sister in a rather unsisterly way.

Laying on the bed, the cheeks of Iris's flushed and sweaty face held a vibrant glow, and her half-lidded eyes and dark red, partially opened mouth appeared to almost be teasing Lilian as if saying, *"Come get some if you dare."* Her bosoms jiggled enticingly with each labored breath she took. Lilian found her eyes drawn towards a droplet of sweat that meandered a slow trail down her sister's right breast. She watched, her mouth dry, as the drop trickled down the side and dripped onto the bed. Iris's flat stomach and shapely hips flexed and squirmed as her legs moved, and a small thatch of midnight black hair hung just above the v of her crotch.

"I know I'm sexy, Lily-pad, but if you could stop looking at me and hurry up with that sponge bath, I would be much obliged."

"Eep!" Lilian squeaked like a mouse. She shook her head and tried to set her mind straight.

Damn it, Lilian! What's wrong with you?! This is Iris! Didn't you already break off all sexual relations with her? That's right. You did. You need to think about something else, like Kevin! Yes, think about your beloved, Lilian. That's it, think about Kevin. Think about Kevin. Kevin in a bathing suit—no, Kevin in a speedo.

Within her mind, Lilian conjured an image of Kevin in nothing but a small speedo, his muscular arms and torso on full display, his strong runner legs unveiled before her eyes, and the bulge of his crotch completely visible.

Unfortunately for Lilian, doing this turned out to be a mistake. Her mind, already fixated on Iris, suddenly conjured an image of her nude sister rubbing herself against Kevin in provocative ways, using her mate like he was a pole and she an expert pole dancer.

Lilian's hands flew to her nose to keep it from bleeding. This was not good. This was so not good.

"Lily... the sponge bath?"

"R-right!" Lilian's squeaky voice came out several octaves higher than she would have liked.

Lilian tried to remain calm as she grabbed a wet rag. Leaning over her sister, her breathing stilted, she wiped off Iris's thighs, which was where her sister had vomited. Fortunately, the acrid scent helped calm her nerves. After that, she took the bowl away and filled it with warm, soapy water, and grabbed a sponge from underneath the cabinet. She discarded the towel that she'd used to wipe Iris's thighs.

Returning to the bedroom, she set the bowl back down, and, grabbing a soapy sponge, Lilian decided to start at the bottom.

She sat at the end of the bed, lifted Iris's right foot, and began cleaning it off. Her face felt hot as she slowly dragged the warm, wet sponge over the sole and arch of her sister's foot, cleansing it of the sweat that had accumulated from the day's events and flu-like symptoms. When she got to Iris's toes, she moved the sponge between each toe.

Iris had lovely feet. Her skin was soft, smooth to the touch. Delicate arches traced a curve along the bottom of her feet. Her long toes were practically begging to be sucked on. Lilian did not have a foot fetish—though if Kevin ever asked it of her, she would be more than willing to let him suck on her toes and vice versa—but as she stared at her sister's feet, she wondered if maybe she was beginning to spontaneously develop one.

"A-ahn! Lily, that… feels really good!"

It didn't help that Iris's feet were apparently quite sensitive.

Lilian's body felt like it had been thrown into the sun. Her sister's moan, combined with the unusual act of cleaning her sister's feet, made Lilian hotter and bothered than she was willing to admit. Her face blazed like an inferno and she was sure that, were she to look into a mirror, it would have been luminescent.

After cleaning both of Iris's feet, Lilian began to move up. She licked her dry lips as she wiped the sweat from Iris's ankles, which were every bit as sexy as her feet. Lilian moved the sponge up Iris's shapely calves next. Their curvature was a perfect blend of toned

and soft. It was hard on Lilian's vivid imagination. Her mind played tricks on her, making her picture what would happen if she leaned down and kissed her way up those calves instead of cleaning them. That Iris had done something similar to her—the kissing, not the cleaning—only made her mind run that much wilder.

When she got to cleaning Iris's inner thighs, her face began to steam. Matters weren't helped when Iris spread her legs to reveal herself in all her glory. Lilian was forced to pinch her nose with her free hand while cleaning the area between Iris's thighs, lest more carnelian fluid came out.

"A-ah!—oh! Lily... your hands—ahn! They feel amazing!"

She's enjoying this! Lilian's mind screamed at her. *My sister is totally getting off on this!*

Inari-blessed, this was so not cool. Her sister's hot, naked body squirmed as she wiped the vixen down, and the moans that Iris released caused Lilian's own body to feel like a video game console that had melted from overheating. So. Not. Cool.

What made it worse was that Lilian could feel herself responding to Iris's siren call and the incredible sensuality of her hands tenderly caressing her sister's bare skin. She licked her dry lips, watching the muscles in Iris's stomach twitch and flex as the sponge roved over pale flesh. Iris's tummy was perfectly flat, without an inch of flab. Lilian had to close her eyes as a sudden urge to lick the sweat off Iris's stomach came over her.

Kitsune are very sexual creatures. Because they were, at their base, foxes, kitsune don't hold the same taboos that humans do. They mimic human behavior, but they are not human.

Like all kitsune, Lilian was curious about and craved the pleasure and intimacy that came from sex. Back when they were younger, Iris had been the person that she was closest to and therefore the one who she experimented with. Being in this situation, giving her sister a sponge bath and listening to the vixen moan, the two decades' worth of erotic encounters that they shared all came back to her.

Matters only became more exacerbated when Lilian reached her sister's breasts. They were like two proud hills stretched across unblemished skin and capped with light pink nipples. Small droplets of sweat formed on them as Iris continued to exhibit her flu-like symptoms. Rather than detract, these symptoms only seemed to enhance Iris's already impressive sex appeal.

The moans and sighs that her fellow two-tails released as she wiped down her sister's breasts caused her own breathing to pick up. Lilian's chest felt tight as if something had been lodged in her chest, constricting the flow of air. It caused her once regulated breathing to increase until she was panting.

Lilian was glad when the moment ended. By this point, she felt like she was sweatier and more flushed than her sister.

I'm almost done... I... surely I can hold out for just a little longer.

Wanting to do something less stimulating, Lilian gently took Iris's hands and soothingly rubbed them down, gliding from the tips of Iris's slender fingers all the way down the vixen's arm. Iris still exuded wanton moans of lust, but Lilian did her best to ignore those, even if her own face felt similar to someone who'd stuck their head in a raging bonfire.

Oddly enough, it was when Lilian began wiping down Iris's armpits that she became truly mortified. Cleaning someone's armpits didn't sound all that sexy. They were armpits. There wasn't anything about them that could be sexy. But, when Lilian took the sponge and wiped them down, Lilian could no longer deny that she was aroused.

Iris was laying with her hands above her head. With her flushed skin, breasts jiggling, and her smooth armpits on display, she looked like someone out of a pervert's wet dream.

Lilian didn't understand how it was possible to feel sexually aroused by such a sight, but she couldn't deny that she was, indeed, turned on. Her body was on fire. Her mind was clouded. Her panties had grown damp.

She soon came to the startling conclusion that there was something seriously wrong with her.

"Ha… ha…" Iris's breathing was deep and heavy. Her face was a dark scarlet that, when combined with the smile on her lips and her half-lidded succubus eyes, made Lilian feel like she was drowning in a pool of ecstasy. "Lily… that was… ha… amazing…"

"I'm glad someone enjoyed it," Lilian muttered. She tried to make it sound bitter, but with how aroused she was, it sounded more sensual than she'd intended.

"Can… can you clean my back, too? It's… ha… it's all sticky and gross…"

Lilian felt trepidation at the request, but she ended up helping her sister anyway. She moved behind Iris, sitting with her fraternal twin tucked between her legs, and began to tenderly scrub her sister's back after dunking the sponge in warm water again.

The sponge glided over her smooth back, tracing delicate trails between her slender shoulders. Iris's shoulder blades created a small crevice through which the sponge could move. The muscles in her back, supple and smooth, twitched as Lilian lathered them in warm soapy suds.

Iris continued to moan and whimper. She released a string of alluring tones designed to provoke and tease, a liberal siren's call that triggered a response from Lilian, whose desire skyrocketed. There was a fire in her belly, and it hadn't come from eating flames. It didn't help that her sister had started to massage her thighs.

"Lilian…" A shudder ran through her body at the sound of her sister's pleading tone. Iris turned her head, lips pursed in sultry temptation, eyes hooded with arousal. "Kiss me…"

By this point in time, Lilian was so worked up that Iris could have asked her anything and she probably would have done it. Her mind was caught in a haze of lust. Her body had grown into a bonfire. The heat between her legs had spread out to encompass the rest of her body. Already, her head was leaning toward Iris, her eyes fluttering closed, mind silent, body ready to give in to temptation.

Then the door opened.

"Uh…"

And a voice spoke up, dropping several thousand gallons of metaphorical ice water on Lilian's head.

She turned her head slowly, almost afraid of what she'd find. Standing in the doorway with a *"staring down the barrel of a Gundam"* expression, Kevin gazed at the two sisters who sat together provocatively, a bowl of warm soup in his hands.

"Beloved…" Lilian felt numb.

"S-sorry," Kevin stuttered, his face becoming a flame. "I-I'll leave you two alone."

"W-wait!" Lilian's mind jolted awake with a start. She shouted at Kevin, even going so far as to extend a hand toward him. "This isn't what it looks like!"

The door slammed shut. Anguish washed over Lilian, stronger than a riptide and more powerful than a hurricane. Her mate had just seen her… and with Iris! How could this have happened? Hadn't she decided to have a normal human relationship with Kevin? It felt like she'd just broken the promise that she had made to herself.

"Oh, dear," Iris said, sounding almost disappointed, though Lilian couldn't say if it was because Kevin had walked out or because his interruption shattered the hold that Iris had over her. "And I was going to ask if he wanted to join us, too."

Lilian twitched.

"I hate you…" Her shoulders slumped in dejection. "I really, really hate you right now."

"Now don't say that." Iris's eyes glimmered in a teasing manner. "Because you know that I love you."

***

Despite having a metaphorical bucket of snow dumped on her via Kevin's arrival, Lilian still felt aroused by what happened between her and Iris. That said, she couldn't do anything about it. She was too embarrassed to face Kevin, and there was no way she'd restart what happened with Iris.

She ended up taking a very cold shower.

After her shower, she discovered that Kevin had gone into their bedroom and given Iris her soup. He hadn't stayed for long, apparently leaving moments after delivering it, much to Iris's silent amusement.

"It's almost cute how he's still so innocent even after everything that you two have done," Iris said before she opened her mouth and let Lilian feed her.

Iris was sitting against the headboard. Several pillows were propped up behind her, apparently having been fluffed by Kevin before he ran out. She couldn't move much. Indeed, even keeping her head raised made Iris shaky. It made being mad at her difficult.

"I can't believe you'd try to take advantage of your weakened state like that," Lilian mumbled.

"To get in your pants, I'll take any advantage I can get."

Lilian sighed. She wanted to be angry, wanted to tell her sister off, but she couldn't. It wasn't just that Iris was sick. Her body still remembered being aroused, the deluge of pleasurable sensations that had been caused by what they'd done. It was hard to be mad when her thoughts were focused on those feelings.

Either way, Lilian didn't stay long. She fed Iris her soup, and then set the bowl on the nightstand before traveling out of the room in search of Kevin. She needed to clear the air between them somehow. She needed to let him know that what happened between her and Iris didn't mean anything, that she still had every intention of being in a normal human relationship with him.

She found Kevin in the living room, cleaning. He didn't clean anymore these days, as Kotohime and Kirihime had taken over that duty, which meant he was cleaning to keep busy. From the blush on his face, he was clearly not successful.

"K-Kevin," Lilian stuttered. Kevin stiffened, making her hesitate for a moment. "L-listen, I just want you to know that what happened between Iris and me... it wasn't what it looked like. She asked me to give her a sponge bath because she was too weak to clean herself, so I..." Lilian trailed off.

She didn't even know where she was going with this anyway. Honestly, how could she say that what happened was just a sponge bath when she'd been ready to give her sister some serious tongue to tongue resuscitation?

"I'm not upset or anything," Kevin said, snapping Lilian out of her fugue and making her stare at him in surprise.

"You're not?"

"No... it's not like you cheated on me with another man, and I'm perfectly aware of Iris's talents at temptation. Besides I... w-well, it's not like what happened was gross or anything..."

Did Kevin mean what she thought he meant? She studied his face, noting the inflammation of his cheeks. They were a brighter shade of red than she'd seen in a while. He hadn't blushed this hard since their first two weeks of living together.

"So do you... does that mean you like this sort of thing...?"

"Ah... ah..." Kevin tried to hide his blush by not facing her, but she could see the redness spread from his cheeks to the rest of his face through the window's reflection. It was even beginning to travel down his neck. "W-well, I am a guy, so..."

"O-oh..."

Lilian looked away, her own cheeks aflame. Maybe it was because of what happened, but she was actually seriously considering what it would be like to let Iris occasionally join her and Kevin when they were intimate. The images those thoughts invoked, which increased in rating until they were no longer borderline but straight-up hentai, caused enough blood to rush to her head that it felt like her red-furred fox ears were emitting steam.

It was at this exact moment, as both Kevin and Lilian's faces became increasingly red as their mutual embarrassment reached a peak, that Kirihime walked in through the front door, carrying a soundly sleeping Camellia piggyback.

"Oro?" Kirihime looked at the two youngsters in curiosity, seemingly noticing how their cheeks looked permanently stained with color. "I wonder what happened with those two."

"Hawa-hawa-hawa... zzz..." Camellia had nothing to say on the matter.

She was, after all, still asleep.

***

Chris Fleischer paced back and forth across the floor of his living room, growling like a rabid dog.

Those fools that he'd paid to take care of the fox-whore and her toy had failed. He couldn't believe he'd wasted the last of his allowance on them. Now he was back to square one.

His snarling face a rictus of anger, Chris tried to decide on his next course of action. He wouldn't rest until he'd had his revenge. The thought of not making that bitch and her toy suffer made it impossible to even sleep these days. He needed them to suffer, needed them to feel the same pain he had felt ever since his battle with that red-haired whore. He wouldn't accept anything less than her complete and utter humiliation. He wanted to break her, to make her undergo such unspeakable horrors that by the time he was finished, she'd be begging for death. The question was how? How could he accomplish this?

The loud explosion of his door shattering caused Chris to shout in terror. Wood chips flew everywhere, hitting the floors and walls in addition to striking his body. Chris covered his arms with his face to keep from getting anything in his eyes. When the remnants of his door stopped bouncing off his skin, he looked at the person who stood in the doorway and snarled.

"What the fuck, Kiara?! Who the hell breaks down a man's fucking door?!"

His older sister walked into the room with a look on her face that Chris had never seen before. It wasn't the angry look she'd often give him when he refused to listen to her, or even the mask of hatred she had whenever he brought up their father. Those looks made him quake, but they did not instill the sense of absolute terror that the expression she wore right now inspired.

"K-Kiara... what are you doing?"

Chris backed away from the woman as she stalked forward, her youki flaring wildly. The air became stifled, choking, like someone had dunked his head underwater and then heated it until the liquid became boiling hot. His face—his entire body even, broke out into a sweat. His breathing became ragged gasps. There was an indescribable sensation pushing down on him, forcing him to his knees. If Chris knew his physics, he would have described it as a several hundredfold increase in the Earth's gravitational pull.

"I hear you hired some thugs to beat up Kevin and his mate." Kiara's tone sounded oddly conversational as if she hadn't noticed the feeling of DOOM emanating from her body. "You know, Chris, you are my brother, and as my brother, I love you very much. I support you and help you because you are my brother. That said, I despise you as a person and, if given the choice between my brother and my current pupil, you should know that I will choose my pupil."

Chris wanted to say something. He wanted to shout, *"So what?!"* or *"Do you think I give a fuck?!"* but he couldn't. The overwhelmingly murderous feeling radiating from Kiara had him biting his tongue. All he could do was stare at the floor, unable to even lift his head.

"Back in the old days, long before you were even born, inu who disobeyed their parents were sent to the pits. You probably don't know what that is, so let me explain it for you. The pits are the place where disobedient dogs are forced to fight each other until they've been thoroughly torn apart, barely alive and scarred beyond recognition. It was a very harsh method of punishment, one that I don't agree with doing."

Loud cracking echoed around the room as Kiara used her thumb to crack her knuckles. One. By. One.

"However, you have crossed a line today. While I'm not so cruel as to find a pit and throw you into it, I do think some punishment is required as recompense for what you've done. Your revenge against Lilian and Kevin should have ended after I thoroughly defeated her. That you continue attempting to inflict harm is a sign that I have been too soft on you. So, I'm going to punish you. For the next two hours, you are going to do squats underneath a fire while holding onto forty-pound lead weights. If your arms sag, the countdown will start over again. If your legs sag, the countdown will start over again. If you speak out of turn, the countdown will start over again."

Kiara's eyes held no pity as she stared down at her brother.

"You brought this on yourself, Chris."

For the next six hours, until night had fallen, the complex would play host to the howls and whimpers of one Chris Fleischer. A rumor would eventually spread that the complex was haunted, causing over seventy-five percent of the residents to move out.

It was a bad day to be Chris Fleischer.

CHAPTER 9

Guns, Guts, and Genjutsu

CASSY TOOK A DEEP BREATH AS SHE WAITED AT A PARK.

It was early morning, and she was dressed in a brand-new outfit: Black spandex jogging shorts, a black sports bra, and white sneakers. They'd cost her all of the money that she currently had, but she felt it was money well spent.

The morning air was mild. Summer was coming. It wouldn't be long before the days became hot again, even at this early hour.

As she watched the trees blowing in the wind, a person riding a bike entered her view. It was Kevin, out for his Sunday morning newspaper run.

Okay, Cassy. It's time to do this.

Before Kevin could spot her, she began jogging in the same general direction but ahead of him. She didn't look back. She kept staring straight ahead, even as she strained her ears to listen.

"Cassy?"

This is it.

"Ma—Kevin," Cassy quickly corrected. "What are you doing out so early in the morning?"

Kevin slowed his pedaling and pulled his bike alongside her. "I'm just delivering the morning newspaper. Are you going for a jog?"

"Oh, um, yes." Cassy nodded quickly, then winced. Was she being too enthusiastic? "I like jogging... you know, because it keeps me in shape."

It was almost amazing, the way Kevin's eyes lit up like fog lights at midnight. "Jogging is truly a really great way to keep in shape. Actually, I'm on the track and field team with my friends, so I do a lot of running too. I've been training a lot. I've even gotten so fast that I finally beat my rival at the hundred-meter dash and..."

Conversation flowed easily once Kevin started talking. Cassy was grateful. She'd been worried that he would be suspicious of her, but it seemed like paranoia wasn't in his vocabulary. He spoke with her as if they were old friends.

Cassy had rarely been happier.

***

The air was crisp and refreshing, as Kevin had expected. It was still spring, even though March was coming to a close. He imagined it would be getting hot soon.

Kevin stared at the building that Kiara had driven him to. C2 Tactical looked as imposing as ever, with its impressive height, gleaming windows, and monolithic columns. Standing in front of the building that he had run away from, Kevin couldn't help but remember the overwhelming feeling of vertigo that holding a gun had given him.

It was the weekend after his battle with the gorilla yōkai. Iris had overcome her Void poisoning and was back in full form. She and Lilian were out doing something together. He didn't know what, but he hoped they were having fun.

Just as Kiara had asked, he'd met her at Mad Dawg Fitness after his newspaper run, and then she'd driven him back to this place. Kiara wanted him to learn about guns. She said that, for a human to match a yōkai, he needed to use weapons that could harm a yōkai. He agreed with her, even if he didn't like it.

"Are you ready for this, boya?" Kiara asked, standing next to him, her single arm on her hip as she gazed at him out of the corner of her eye.

Kevin took a deep breath, then nodded. "Yes."

"Good."

They entered the gun store/tactical shooting range. Jeffrey was waiting for them behind the counter.

"Well, if it ain't Kiara and her disciple!" he crowed joyfully. Kevin clicked his tongue, annoyed by how excited this man sounded. "So, are ya finally ready to learn how to wield a gun, boyo? Not gonna run out on me this time, are ye?"

"Of course not, and I have a name, you know," Kevin muttered, trying to shake off his unease. Being around all these guns made him jittery.

Kiara chuckled and placed her hand on his shoulder. "Don't worry. The kid's ready to learn this time. He was just dealing with some… personal issues the last time we came in."

"Alrighty. Well, if yer ready, then why don't we head on into the tactical range and get started?"

The shooting range looked the same as last time, a large open room shaped like a rectangle. A wall blocked off one side while the other was sectioned off by stations, and beyond that was the range itself, where the targets were set.

A target had already been set up, a very human-looking target. It stood on two legs, had the shape of a man, and centered around certain areas of its body—namely the joints—were several bullseyes. Kiara had clearly informed Jeffrey of his desire to learn how to fight using nonlethal means.

"Now I don't know how much ye remember about shooting a gun, but I'll give ye a basic review on the one ye'll be learning to use today." He held up a black 9mm handgun. "This here is a Beretta 92A1, a reliable and easy-to-use tactical handgun. It's accurate, safe, dependable, and it has some added features that make it one of the best home defense or personal protection weapons on the market today. One of the key features that make this gun so great is that it's got a Picatinny rail situated in the front of the trigger guard, right here, see? This allows ye to add a wide variety of tactical accessories…"

Kevin listened intently as the man continued giving him a rundown of the weapon he'd be using. It was different from the last one that Jeffrey had tried to show him. Was there a reason for that?

When the man finished speaking, he lowered the weapon and said, "Now then, let's head on over to the tactical range and I'll show ye how to shoot this sucker."

There were apparently two ways to fire a handgun, according to Jeffrey. The first stance that Kevin was shown had a person standing with their legs shoulder-width apart, and the leg of their dominant hand acting as a brace behind them. The dominant hand was then fully extended while the weak arm was bent slightly and used to keep the shooting hand steady. The second stance was known as the isosceles stance due to how the feet, knees, hips, and shoulders were fully squared to the target and both arms were fully extended.

Kevin was then told to try holding the gun using both stances. If he was honest, he didn't like either stance as they limited his mobility, and if he was going to fight yōkai, he couldn't afford to stand in one place. He didn't say this, though, as he doubted the other man realized why he was learning to shoot a gun.

"I'm pretty comfortable with both stances," Kevin said. "Though I think I'll stick with the first stance you showed me."

"If that's how ye want it," Jeffrey said with a shrug. "I personally prefer the isosceles stance meself, but everyone is different. Now then, let's see how much ye remember. Load the gun, take aim, and try to shoot the target."

Kevin stared at the gun in his hand. His breathing tried to pick up, but he forced it to remain steady. Acting with slow, meticulous care, he did as instructed, loading the ammo magazine into the empty slot, taking up his stance, and aiming at the target.

He aimed for the left kneecap, figuring that the best way to take out a yōkai would be to inhibit their ability to move. Unfortunately, he wasn't prepared for the amount of kick the gun had, and his hand was jerked way off course. The bullet didn't even come close to grazing his target.

"Gya-hahaha!" Jeffrey slapped his hand against his knee, ignoring the glare that Kevin sent his way. Even Kiara was snickering at him! "Be careful of the recoil, brat! It might have little kick, but it's still enough to knock off the aim of a newbie like you!"

"Whatever," Kevin grumbled, looking over at Kiara. "How long are we staying here?"

"At least another hour," Kiara answered. "After that, we'll head back to my gym to do some exercises and light sparring."

"Good."

That would give him plenty of time to get better at shooting this stupid thing. By the time he was finished here, Jeffrey would be stunned speechless!

Stupid old man. Kevin scowled as he lined up his next shot. *I'll show him.*

His next shot missed.

"Gya-hahahahaha!"

"Stop laughing!"

***

Kotohime rushed at Lilian with speeds that the young redhead could scarcely keep up with. The katana-wielding femme appeared in front of Lilian before she could prepare a defense, her still-sheathed blade already lashing out to strike her in the head.

It didn't. Like a ghost, Lilian's body vanished, dispersing into particles of light, and the real Lilian appeared right next to her illusory copy. Her fists were tucked into her torso, but only for a moment. Then they lashed out with youki-fueled strength.

Kotohime remained calm as she twirled about, allowing the double thrust to miss her by a wide margin. Some ridiculously fancy footwork brought her into Lilian's guard, where she struck at the girl with her katana again, this time thrusting the sheathed weapon into Lilian's throat.

This Lilian did not disappear. She gagged as the attack hit her, hands rising to her throat as she stumbled backward and fell to the ground. Kotohime's eyes narrowed. Though the girl before her acted like she'd been hit, the swordswoman had not felt any resistance to her attack, which meant…

She sped away from the spot that she was standing on just in time to avoid getting blasted in the back by a sphere of light. The tiny golden orb struck the ground instead, creating a perfect circle of burnt grass.

"That was an impressive use of a double-layered illusion," Kotohime complimented. "The first illusion that I dispelled hid the second illusion, which was the one that fooled my senses into thinking you were standing right in front of me. An excellent job, Lilian-sama."

Several feet away, Lilian shimmered into existence. She was sweating a lot, and her breathing was heavy. That was the price one paid for using so much youki. Lilian might have had a stronger affinity for her Celestial element than most, but she was still just a two-tails.

"It still wasn't enough to fool you," Lilian rasped.

"True enough. However, I have more experience than you do, and as a kitsune, I am well-versed in illusions, even I if prefer not to use them. Now then." Kotohime set herself in a wide stance, feet spread, knees bent, and her katana raised near her head with the tip of her sheathed blade pointing at Lilian. "Shall we continue?"

Lilian nodded and the battle started anew.

Over on the sidelines, Iris sat with Christine and Lindsay, a blanket laid out underneath them. The trio watched the sparring match being undertaken by Lilian and Kotohime, though it may have been more accurate to say they were watching Kotohime toy with Lilian like a cat playing with a mouse before swallowing it whole—only less violent and not nearly as savage.

"I'm not really into the whole yōkai battle thing like the guys are," Lindsay started as she followed the battle, her eyes wide, "but I've gotta admit, it looks pretty cool."

"Speaking of guys, where's Kevin?" Christine asked. "Shouldn't he be here? I figured he'd want to watch his girlfriend sparring and stuff."

"The stud is hanging out with the dog today," Iris muttered, enunciating the word dog as one would a curse. "I think he mentioned something about finding a way to match the power of yōkai somehow, but I have no clue what he meant by that."

"He's training pretty hard, too, isn't he?" said Lindsay, biting her thumb. "From what I understand, he's been training with Kiara ever since he and Lilian became a couple... I think. I'm not really privy to everything that goes on in Kevin's life these days, though, so I could be wrong."

Lindsay's eyes dimmed as she thought about how far apart she and Kevin had drifted. Before he met Lilian, they'd moved apart because of his strange inability to speak with women. After Lilian had arrived, that distance remained because he had begun falling for the redhead. When he and Lilian finally started dating, he only seemed to move farther and farther away, as he began getting more involved in the world that his mate was a part of.

She knew it was wrong to blame Lilian for this—it was her fault for not accepting his half-hearted confession—but part of her wondered what would have happened if Lilian hadn't come into the picture. Would she and Kevin be dating now? What about if she had accepted his confession back then? Would they have been happy? She didn't know, and that depressed her.

Christine took one look at Lindsay... and then cuffed her on the back of the head.

"Owch!" Holding her head where she'd been smacked, Lindsay sent Christine a tear-filled look. "What was that for?"

"For being an idiot," Christine answered. "You were thinking that you and Kevin aren't as good of friends as you used to be, right? That he stopped being your friend because he's entered a different world? Newsflash Lindsay, you're a part of that world, too. Did you forget about the fact that you also know about yōkai? Just the act of knowing means you've already become a part of our world, which means you're a part of Kevin's world. He's trusting you with this knowledge. That more than anything shows how important you are to him."

Lindsay looked hopeful. "You think so?"

Christine rolled her eyes. "Of course I do. I wouldn't have said it if I didn't."

"Yeah, I guess." Lindsay sniffed a bit before smiling at Christine. "Thanks, Christy."

"Whatever."

Iris looked back and forth between the two, her dark eyes gleaming with amusement. "Ah, young love is such a beautiful thing."

While Lindsay's face became a mild shade of red, Christine gave the more amusing reaction.

"Y-y-y-y-young—WHAT THE HELL ARE YOU SAYING?!"

"Oh? Do you deny being in love with Lindsay? I thought that was the whole reason you spend so much time cheering her up."

After mastering her humiliated blush, Christine scowled at Iris. "That's not the reason why I was trying to cheer her up, you wench! I'm just trying to be nice to a friend! In case you haven't noticed,

Lindsay is a girl, and I'm not into girls! The only person I like is—
"

"Kevin?" Iris supplied helpfully.

"Right. Kevin—wait! No, I mean I don't like anyone!"

"Really? I could have sworn you just said—"

"Shut up! I didn't say anything! Idiot! Fox-wench!"

"Huhuhu…" Iris chuckled. "If you say so. Well, whether you decide to follow your lesbian instincts or keep chasing after the stud is up to you. I don't care what you do."

"Uuuuu! Shut up! Shut up, shut up, shut up!"

While Christine's tsundere protocols activated, leading to her standing up and stomping on the ground like a child having a tantrum, Lindsay curled her knees up to her chest. There was a gloomy aura surrounding her. Like smoke, black miasma wafted off of her body.

"She said she doesn't love me? Am I really that unattractive?" The girl perked up a second later as a panting Christine came down from her tsundere-induced high. "Oh, yeah, I forgot to ask, how goes your attempts at seducing Lilian and Kevin?"

While Christine gave her a look that all but asked if she was crazy, Iris's face split into a mile-wide grin. "Huhuhu, it's going quite well, thank you. I really have to thank myself for overusing my Void powers. The whole sickness thing really helped bring Lily-pad and me closer together."

As Christine and Lindsay watched her zone out, Iris recalled what happened between her and Lilian.

Just remembering the way her sister had washed her body sent chills down her spine. Lilian had been so tender at first, but once things had heated up, she had clearly lost her composure. Iris was sure that she and Lilian would have given into their passion if Kevin hadn't interrupted them.

"Just you wait." Iris stood up and held a fist to her face, her eyes burning with lustful passion. "It won't be long now. Very soon,

Lilian will fall for my charms, and the stud will fall for me shortly after that. Yes, it's only a matter of time before Lilian, the stud, and I begin our journey of debauchery! Uhuhuhuhuhu!"

Christine and Lindsay stared at the girl, who continued laughing like a loon, heedless of the looks she was getting.

"Christine, this girl scares me." Lindsay hid behind her gothic friend.

"I don't blame you," Christine admitted. "She freaks me out too."

Still unaware of how badly she was freaking out her friends, Iris continued laughing.

"Heeheeheeeheehee!"

It was damn creepy.

***

Kevin did improve his aim as the hour wore on. By the time the hour was up, he could hit his target seven out of ten times with a reasonable degree of accuracy. It wasn't perfect, but Jeffrey had told him that he'd improved faster than anyone he'd ever seen.

After he practiced shooting, Kiara had bought him a gun. It wasn't a large gun. Actually, it was pretty tiny, like, Noisy Cricket tiny.

The Bond Arms Texas Defender Derringer Handgun was a single shot, .375 magnum. It had a single barrel and only one shot before it needed to be reloaded. That said, it was more powerful than a 9mm. Even a gorilla yōkai would die if they were shot in the face with this.

The gun had felt abnormally heavy in his hand when Kiara handed it to him.

They had returned to the gym after practicing at the tactical shooting range. Several hours after exercising with Kiara and getting his butt kicked by Heather, a freshly showered and dressed Kevin joined up with Lilian, Iris, Christine, and Lindsay, and then the five of them met up with their friends at the mall.

It was crowded that day, though this didn't surprise him with it being Sunday and everything. Despite the crowd, they were able to easily glide past everyone.

This was probably due to who was with them. Christine, Lilian, Lindsay, and Iris were all gorgeous. Having so many pretty girls in one place must have been intimidating to many of the guys who were wandering around.

As they walked through the mall, Kevin thought about what had happened when he and Kiara returned to Mad Dawg Fitness. Heather had been waiting for them upon their return. She had not been pleased when she discovered that Kiara had taken him to a tactical shooting range.

"I can't believe you took him to a shooting range without me! I can't believe you decided to let someone else teach him how to handle a gun! I'm two thousand times better than any old coot with a funny accent could ever be. Plus, I'm cuter, too!"

Those had been her words, complete with a childishly pouting face and her hands on her hips. He swore that lady was one of the most unusual people he'd ever met. She was a self-proclaimed pervert and writer of smut, had taken on Eric as an apprentice in the ways of perversion, and she apparently wanted to be the one who taught him, Kevin, how to shoot a gun. The fact that she'd been making dirty gun jokes had only made the whole situation more surreal.

Kiara had been ready with her counterargument, however.

"I decided not to have you teach Kevin because I know you, and I know that you would end up throwing him into the deep end by trying to teach him advanced techniques before he's ready. While

I'm all for teaching someone using the trial by fire method, I'm not willing to risk my disciple's safety. Shooting a gun isn't the same thing as learning martial arts."

Heather had pouted a bit, but she'd been forced to concede. Kiara had then added the ringer.

"Besides, if you spent too much time teaching the boy a how to shoot a gun, you'll end up neglecting your apprentice, and we wouldn't want that now, would we?"

Yes, apparently teaching Eric the art of peeping and public groping meant more to Heather than teaching him how to shoot a gun. That woman was so weird.

"Ah-ha! Take that, zombies!"

Kevin snorted in amusement as he and Lilian continued playing *House of Haunted Horrors*. It was something of a pastime for them—zombie killing, that is. Whenever they came to the arcade, this was their go-to game.

While Kevin had taken a relaxed stance and casually blasted heads off, Lilian was firing like a madwoman on crack. It always amused him to see how enthusiastic his mate was when she played video games. That part of her personality, the part that put her all into everything she did, was something that he loved about her.

"Ne, Lilian. How's your training with Kotohime going?"

His question caught Lilian off guard, causing the redhead to get hit by a zombie with a chainsaw, dropping the number of hearts that she had to two. His mate got back in the game quickly, though, and she fired off several rounds at its head. Blood splattered against the screen as the zombie's head exploded.

"It's going fine, I guess." Her left cheek swelled as if she was on the verge of pouting. "I still can't beat her—not that I actually think I'll be able to. She's got way more experience than I do at fighting. I don't really like fighting." The last zombie died from their combined gunfire, making way for a cutscene, which allowed Lilian a moment to cast him a smile. "I'd rather live in peace with you."

Kevin returned her smile. "Yeah, me too."

They continued playing, but while Kevin used his skills as an ace arcade shooter, his mind was a million miles away.

Neither he nor Lilian wanted to have anything to do with the yōkai world. All they wanted was to live in peace. Unfortunate circumstances and the origins of Lilian's birth forced them to remain forever with one foot in that world, however, and there wasn't much that they could do about it. Being a yōkai herself, Lilian would always be a part of that world, never mind the fact that she came from one of the three strongest kitsune clans in existence—and she was an heiress of that clan to boot.

Kevin sometimes wondered about what his life would have been like if he'd never met Lilian. Would he still be that boy whose shyness around girls kept him from speaking to Lindsay, forcing him to pine after her from a distance? Would he have ever worked up the courage to ask her out on a date? He knew now that she had actually liked him, so he imagined that, if he had ever plucked his courage from whatever hole it had been hiding under, they would have started dating. But that left him with another question.

Would I have been happy?

It was always on his mind. Would he have been happy dating Lindsay? Thinking on it now, he wasn't so sure. While he and Lindsay were both athletic and had been friends long before he'd ever been stricken with that horrendous case of Cannot Talk to Girls, they were also very different. Lindsay enjoyed doing, well, girly things. Outside of soccer, she enjoyed gossiping with friends and talking about the latest celebrity scandal.

On the other hand, Kevin enjoyed watching anime, reading manga, and playing video games. These days, he could also add intense physical training with Kiara and sparring with Heather or the three stooges—his nickname for Kiara's underlings—to the list. He was on the fence about shooting guns. He still didn't like them.

Oddly enough, the one girly thing that Lindsay didn't like—clothes shopping—was the one thing that Kevin actually did enjoy doing. With a fashionista for a mom, it was only natural that he'd know a lot about fashion. He bought and read all of the magazines that his mom was featured in. It was his way to show support for what she was doing.

In some ways, Lilian was Lindsay's polar opposite. Oh, Lilian was certainly girly. She was chatty, enjoyed gossiping, and loved shopping for cute clothes, but she enjoyed talking about things that most of the girls that he knew didn't like.

Lilian didn't care about the latest gossip or what celebrity was involved in which scandal. None of that mattered to her. She loved anime, manga, and video games just as much, if not more, than he did. She'd even begun learning how to draw recently as he'd seen a *How to Draw Manga Characters* book on his shelf that he knew hadn't been there before.

In the end, Kevin often conceded that his reasons for liking Lindsay had been due to many factors. They were both athletic. They'd been friends for a long time. She was the only girl who he'd ever spoken with. She was also super cute. While none of those were bad reasons to like someone, they were kind of shallow.

He would also admit, if only to himself, that a part of him had wanted to date Lindsay because he felt like she would have been a safe bet. They were already friends, so asking her out would have been easier. Lindsay had been his security blanket. He actually felt guilty for thinking that way. What kind of friend uses someone like that?

He and Lilian continued clearing several more stages of the game, getting all the way to the boss, before a voice that neither of them wanted to hear sounded out through the throng of people.

"Hola, my beautiful senorita... and Sweeft."

"Do you make it a point to bother us while we're having fun?" Kevin asked while Lilian wrinkled her nose.

"Great, it's the pompadour boy."

"Ugh! My dulce la flor, such harsh words you use." Juan grabbed at his chest, feigning someone having a heart attack. "Must you always speak to me so severamente? Why can't you whisper to me tiernamente?"

"How about because I don't like you? And stop using internet translations when you speak! I can't understand those!"

"Such coldness from my two favorite people. And here I was, wishing to see if you were okay because I'd heard you got into a fight with a group of yōkai."

Lilian narrowed her eyes. "Were you responsible for sending those yōkai after me?"

"My preciosa flor, I am wounded." Juan held a hand to his heart. "How could you ever think that I, your valiant caballero, would send such violent and ill-bred fiends after you? No, no, I merely found out about it after the fact and wished to see if you were well."

"For some reason, I don't believe you," was Lilian's retort.

"What do you want, Juan?" Kevin asked, already sick of seeing this boy's face. "If you're simply here to bother us, then you can leave."

Juan chuckled condescendingly. "If that is your wish, though I also wanted to tell you both to be cautious. Odd things are afoot in school, so you'd best be on your guard. Farewell, hermosa flor, Kevin Sweeft."

"I really don't like that guy," Lilian said, glaring at the half-yōkai's back.

"I'm not much of a fan of him either," Kevin said, though he did have to wonder about Juan's words. Was something happening at school? He hoped not. They had dealt with enough trouble to last several lifetimes.

***

After their encounter with Juan, Kevin and Lilian met up with their friends.

When they had first arrived at the arcade, they had split off into groups and gone their separate ways. Everyone had different tastes in games. Most games were also single or two-player. There wasn't much point in sticking together. They had promised to meet up at the pizza parlor located inside of the arcade at twelve.

Upon arriving, the pair was met with an interesting sight.

"GOD DAMN PERVERT!"

"GYA!!"

"ALL OF YOU LECHS DESERVE TO DIE!"

"MOMMY!"

Kevin resisted the strong urge to facepalm. He turned away from the sight of the violent beatdown and looked at Alex and Andrew. "Care to explain what happened here? I think I can already guess, but I'd like to hear it from someone."

"OH, GOD! HAVE MERCY, PLEASE!"

"I HAVE NO MERCY FOR PERVERTS!"

"AAAIIIIEEEEE!!!"

"Eric tried to grope Christine again..." Alex started, wincing as the sound of someone's face being stomped on by a heel echoed around them.

"... And he actually succeeded this time," Andrew finished, right before a particularly loud and almost feminine squeal erupted from the boy on the floor. Both of the twins brought their hands to their crotches as if they felt the phantom pain of having their balls stomped on.

"I see..." Kevin said.

Then it was just as he suspected and Eric had—

"Wait." Kevin studied the two more closely. "You say he succeeded?"

"Yep." Alex nodded, his own expression somewhat slack—dazed even, as if he couldn't believe what he'd seen. "Shoved his hand right into Christine's long, frilly dress and squeezed a handful of her ass."

"GOD DAMN IT! WHY! WON'T! YOU! DIE!?"

"UGYAAAA!"

"As you can see, she isn't too happy about that."

"Right..."

Talk about understatement of the century. He'd rarely ever seen Christine look so pissed. It wasn't even that she was losing control of her powers, evidenced by how hoarfrost was creeping along the carpet. The violence that she was displaying was much more savage than her normal tsundere violence.

"What about Lindsay?" asked Lilian, pointing at something. "Why does she look so depressed? She looks like someone murdered her favorite pet fox."

Kevin looked at Lindsay, who was hiding underneath a table, her knees drawn to her chest as she rocked back and forth. An aura of gloom seemed to be emitting from her body in waves, dark black clouds of streamer-like vapor that poured off her body. The girl appeared absolutely despondent.

"I can't believe he managed to touch her... even I haven't been able to touch her yet... sob..."

She was also mumbling something really stupid under her breath.

"And that girl says she isn't a dyke," Iris said with a grin. She was standing next to the table that Lindsay was curled up under. Her expression reminded Kevin of the Cheshire Cat from *Alice in Wonderland.*

Kevin wondered if a facepalm would have been enough to adequately express his feelings. Something incredibly stupid had happened while he and Lilian were killing zombies. He didn't think a simple facepalm would do the trick.

"DIE, DIE, DIE, DIE!"

"GGGGUUUUUUOOOOOEEEEEEE!"

Yes, he decided as Eric's screams turned into high-pitched, pig-like squeals, a simple facepalm definitely wouldn't be enough to express how stupid this situation was.

**

It took a while, but Kevin eventually convinced Christine to stop emasculating Eric via stomping on his crotch. Once the girl had calmed down, Lindsay had crawled out from underneath the table, Iris had stopped poking fun at Lindsay and then disappeared somewhere, and the group sat down to order some food. During the time where they waited for their order to arrive, Kevin told the group that he was learning to shoot.

"What? You're really learning how to use a gun?" asked a befuddled Alex. His eyes were about the size of a pizza. Kevin had never seen them so wide.

"Yep," Kevin replied in his best "I don't give a damn" tone of voice.

"So not fair. First, you get a super-hot kitsune girlfriend. Then you find out that she's got a super-hot sister. Then you start learning martial arts from Kiara F. Kuyo, and now you're being taught how to shoot guns. Why does all the cool stuff happen to you?"

"You forgot the fact that I've already had to fight against several yōkai, was nearly killed each time, was stabbed in the stomach with a water spear when we went to Comic-Con, and just recently had my entire ribcage crushed by a gorilla."

A waitress arrived and set their pizza on the table. They'd bought two: Pepperoni and cheese. Everyone served themselves, grabbing a slice or two and putting it on their plate.

"Okay, point," Alex conceded.

"It still doesn't change the fact that you've had a lot of awesome stuff happen to you," Andrew grumbled before taking a bite of his pizza.

"Who cares about any of that," Eric said, turning to Kevin. "No offense to you, My Lord. Your awesomeness knows no bounds, but learning to shoot a gun isn't that cool." Proudly pointing at himself with his thumb, Eric grinned a lecherous grin. "I'm learning how to grope women in public—DOOF!"

"Can it, pervert!" Christine shouted right after smashing Eric's face into the table—and his pizza. "No one wants to hear about the lecherous crap you're getting up to."

"Oh, my Gothic Hottie." Eric cried. "You are so cruel—guag!"

"Don't call me that!"

"Hey, did you guys see where my sister went off to?" Lilian asked, ignoring the way Christine shoved Eric's face into his pizza and tried to make him choke by inhaling cheese through his nose. "I could have sworn she was here just a second ago…"

"Yahoo!" As if summoned by her name being called, Iris appeared behind Lilian and Kevin and draped herself across the two. "You called?"

Being so close to Iris brought memories of their sexual encounter to Lilian's mind, which promptly caused her face to turn red. "N-n-no, I didn't. I just wanted to know where you were."

"You're blushing," Iris said in a sing-song voice. There was a smirk that oozed superiority and amusement adorning her ruby red lips. "Could it be that you're thinking about—"

"All right, that's enough out of you!" Lilian declared, shoving a pizza into her sister's mouth, and making her gag at the unexpected intrusion.

"So rough," Iris moaned around the pizza. "I like that."

While Lilian groaned and tried to hide her face in her hands, Kevin sighed. "Sit down and eat your pizza, Iris."

"Huhuhu, sure thing, Stud." Winking at the blond boy, Iris forced him to scoot over in the booth so she could sit down on the end.

"So, you're really learning how to use guns?" Lindsay asked, restarting their earlier conversation.

"Um, yeah…" Kevin squirmed in his seat just a bit. He didn't know why, but for some reason, the look that Lindsay was giving him caused something inside of his gut to squirm most unpleasantly. "Is something wrong?"

"No." Lindsay shook her head, the blonde bangs of her pixie-cut swaying. "Nothing's wrong. I guess I'm just now realizing how much you've changed. I could never have imagined you learning to shoot guns before."

"Ah-ha! Ahahahaha!" Kevin rubbed the back of his head with something of a sheepish expression in play. "I-I don't think I've really changed all that much. I mean, it's not like I've stopped being me, you know?"

Lindsay chuckled, seemingly pleased to see he could still blush like that. "Yeah, I guess."

"Oh, that reminds me." Kevin turned to Lilian. "You never told me what you're learning with Kotohime?"

Lilian looked surprised, though Kevin didn't know why. Did she really think he wouldn't have been interested in what she was learning?

"Oh, I'm just learning how to fight more effectively, I guess," she said. "Most of my fights have been me trying to overwhelm my enemies with specialized attacks, but because I'm only a two-tails, I don't have that much youki to spare, and using Celestial techniques consumes a lot of youki. Kotohime is trying to get me into the habit of using more illusions to fool my opponent's senses and hit them with a surprise attack. It's a lot harder than it sounds."

"That's just because you lack the mindset to fight properly," Iris said, which earned her a rather irksome look from Lilian.

"What do you mean?" Kevin asked. Lilian opened her mouth to say something, but her sister beat her to the punch.

"It's because Lilian doesn't act like a kitsune."

"Ugh." Lilian doubled over as an arrow appeared seemingly out of nowhere and shot her in the back.

"She lacks the ability to properly use deception to fool her opponents."

"Urk." Another arrow materialized and pierced Lilian's spine.

"She also fights at full power right off the bat, which means she's usually out of youki before her enemy is beaten."

"Gurk." One more projectile for good measure. Lilian fell onto the table, groaning as three arrows poked out of her back. Oddly enough, there was no blood, and the arrows didn't appear to have hurt her.

Like a good boyfriend, Kevin gently pulled out the arrows that had randomly appeared out of nowhere to spear Lilian's body. Meanwhile, the redhead lay on the table, groaning in discomfort as her fraternal twin blatantly told everyone about her inefficiencies.

"Truth be told, Lily-pad tends to act more like a human with a slightly devious side than a kitsune. I think the only time I've ever seen her act with any deception and cunning was back when she used to prank those men that Granny would have her meet at the marriage arrangement meetings."

"Marriage arrangement meetings?" Christine and Lindsay said simultaneously. They looked at each other before looking back at Lilian. Lindsay continued speaking. "You mean your grandmother tried to arrange a marriage with a bunch of random men for you?"

"Uh-huh." Lilian nodded, then furrowed her brows, and then tilted her head as if she was confused. "Didn't I tell you that?"

"Um, I don't think so." Lindsay scratched the side of her head, her face scrunching up, eyes narrowing thoughtfully. "I can't remember you ever mentioning it before."

"Huh, maybe I just told Kevin, then," Lilian mumbled before shaking her head. "To make a long story short, our matriarch set up marriage meetings in order to marry me off to another kitsune clan, but I didn't like that idea very much, so I would prank the people she sent to me. That's actually how we ended up in the United States. I caused so much trouble that the matriarch sent us out of the country."

"Really? I never knew that." Lindsay turned to Christine. "Did you know that?"

"Nope," Christine said, right before she took a chunk out of her pizza.

Throughout the entire conversation, one Eric Corromperre had been getting progressively more annoyed. Why were they talking about this garbage when they could talk about something more interesting? Like the new technique that he had learned?

Standing up and slamming his hands into the table, Eric glared at the lot of them. "If you think crap like that is awesome, just wait until you see my new groping technique. I'm sure it'll blow your— woah! Ack! Guh!"

With deceptive swiftness, Christine kicked Eric's legs out from under him, causing the young man to slam face-first into the table, knocking him unconscious. Everyone there was silent as Eric crumpled to the floor in a heap.

"No one cares about your perverted techniques, bastard!" Christine shouted, shaking her fist at the now unconscious pervert.

Alex leaned over and whispered into his brother's ear. "Damn, she's scary."

"For once, you and I are in agreement. That girl is frightening."

"I heard that!"

"Meep!"

"Whatever. I don't really care about being subtle when I fight." Continuing along with the previous vein before they'd been interrupted by Eric, Lilian started speaking again. "I'd much rather use super awesome moves that are cool and flashy. They're so much more fun than simple illusions and misdirection. If anything, I'd want to pull out a technique similar to what Monkey D. Luffy uses." Her eyes widened. "And maybe I can! I can use the extension and reinforcement techniques to make my tails super long and hard. Then I can smack people with them. I've done it to Iris enough times."

"Oi!" Iris twitched at Lilian mentioning all the times she'd been tail-whipped.

"I can call it something like 'Gomu-Gomu no Tail Extension.'"

"Actually, I don't think you can," Kevin said. "Copyright issues, you understand."

And just like that, Lilian deflated like a balloon. "Way to take the wind out of my sails, Beloved."

Kevin placed a hand on her thigh and rubbed it underneath the table. "Sorry, but I don't want you getting in trouble for stealing someone else's technique."

"It wouldn't be stealing," Lilian mumbled. "I'd just say I was inspired by Eiichiro Oda's writing."

"Would you even be able to use a technique like that?" Kevin inquired curiously. "I mean, you've mentioned before that enhancement is one of the most youki-intensive techniques. That's why you can only reinforce yourself for short bursts instead of sustaining it over a long period of time."

It was something that he'd first learned from Lilian back when his biggest issue was her desire to walk around the apartment naked. The enhancement technique was the act of strengthening the body by shoving youki into one or more parts of the body. It was a very inefficient method. The technique generally cost more youki than it was worth, and by the time most kitsune had enough youki to use it properly, they had already learned more efficient means of fighting.

Extension was an easier form of enhancement compared to enhancing the body since their tails were where all of a kitsune's power came from, but it still cost a lot of youki depending on how far the kitsune in question wished to extend their tails and how durable they wanted their tails to be.

"Ugh." Lilian grimaced as she realized that her mate was correct. She crossed her arms and pouted at him. "You're crushing all my dreams today."

"I'm sorry, Lilian. It was never my intention to crush your dreams like this," Kevin said earnestly, his eyes glimmering like the light of an unknown star. "Is there any way I can make it up to you?"

"Well…" Lilian thought about it for around a second. "A hug would be nice."

"I can do that… Lilian."

"Kevin."

"Lilian!"

"Kevin!"

Everyone stared at the two as they began hugging. Their faces were blank except for the twitching in their eyes.

"I feel like Kevin's doing this just to taunt me," Alex muttered, glaring at Kevin like he wanted the boy to catch fire.

"I know how you feel." Andrew was also glaring. "And it's working."

Lindsay sighed at her two friends before turning a slightly teasing gaze on the girl who normally tormented her. "Aren't you going to join them?"

"Shut up," Iris mumbled, staring bitterly at the couple engrossed in their hug. Why was she imagining the two surrounded by a beach filled with crashing waves and a sunset?

While everyone else stared at the human/kitsune couple in consternation, Christine slammed her face down on the table.

Because when a facepalm didn't cut it, a faceplant got the job done.

***

Christine returned to her empty apartment just as the sun was setting. She was tired, but it was a good kind of tiredness, the kind that came from spending time with people she cared about.

She locked the front door, slipped out of her shoes, and wandered into her one-bedroom, one-bathroom apartment. There were no real decorations in her apartment. Christine had never been one for decor—and it wasn't like she ever had anyone over. Outside of a couch, a television with a stand, and a table, her living room/kitchen contained nothing. No posters, no paintings, nothing.

Ignoring the utter lack of anything resembling life in her apartment, Christine wandered into her bedroom, walked over to her king-sized bed complete with canopy—the only part of her house that was decorated—and flopped face down on the bed. It wasn't long until she once more revisited the day so long ago that had changed her life forever, the day that she met the boy who would become the most important existence in her life.

Consequently, it happened to be the same boy who had rejected her.

Life sucked sometimes.

***

The weather that day was freezing. I had expected it. The small village that I lived in was always cold, though I had been hoping it would be a bit warmer because the sun was almost always out now. It was also summer, but I guess it was too much to expect that summer meant warm in Alaska.

I sat by the window, watching the snow fall outside, ignoring the other kids as they played together. I remember trying to play with them once, but none of them wanted to play with me because I was weird, because I had strange powers that they didn't. They were scared of me, so when they weren't making fun of me, they did their best to ignore me.

Most of the children were orphans like I was. The place where I lived was a combination of a daycare center and an orphanage. Children who didn't have parents lived there, while children who did came there during the day so their parents could work. Our village was tiny. I guess they couldn't afford to separate the daycare from the orphanage.

That day someone I had never seen before entered the daycare. It was a young woman with shoulder-length brown hair and brown eyes. She wore a large overcoat, thick brown gloves, and sturdy boots. Holding her hand was a little boy around my age. His hair was blond and messy, and several bangs hid his blue eyes. He looked around the room, his large, thick jacket creating squeaking sounds as he moved.

His eyes locked with mine. He tilted his head as I looked away. A few seconds later, I looked back when I heard who I guessed was his mom speak.

"I have a lot of work to do today, so I need you to be a good boy and stay here. No running off on your own today, got it?"

"Kay!"

The mother just sighed and stood up. She ruffled the boy's hair, which he didn't seem to like, and then walked outside into the freezing cold weather.

The matron and caretaker smiled down at the boy. "Why don't you go and make some friends with the other kids here?" she suggested.

The boy looked at her before grinning widely. "Kay!"

I stopped paying attention after that. That boy would probably get together with the other boys and do whatever it was boys did, like play Cops and Robbers or something. I just hoped they didn't decide to "play" with me. The last time they did that, they pulled my hair and it had really hurt.

To my surprise, the boy did not play with the other boys. While I looked out the window, watching the snow fall and wishing I was somewhere warmer, someone tapped on my shoulder. Was it the boys coming to make fun of me? No, if it was, they would have started off by yanking on my hair.

That meant it was probably the girls. They were more vicious than the boys. Girls would pretend to be my friend, and then they would do something awful like shove glue up my nose or tear off my clothes and throw me outside. I feared them more than I feared anyone else.

I whirled around, my heart hammering in my chest.

"Please don't hurt—" I started to say, only to stop when I saw who was standing in front of me.

It was the boy. He wore the same big grin that I saw him wearing when he first entered. I was taken aback. This was the first time anyone had grinned at me so cheerfully.

"Hi!" The boy greeted me with a happiness that made me shy away.

"W-what do you want?" I tried not to stutter, but I was frightened of this boy. I was scared of everyone, but this boy, for some reason, was particularly unnerving. I didn't know why, but his smile made something weird flutter in my chest. I think I felt this way because of what would happen once he learned about me.

I was always being made fun of. Everyone, all the time, constantly made fun of me. This boy was new, so he didn't know about my powers, but once he learned about them, he would make fun of me just like everyone else. That was how it had always been. That thought made my chest ache and my desire to hide almost overpowering.

"Do you want to play with me?" he asked.

I was so shocked by the question that I lost my balance and fell to the floor. I yelped as I crashed into the ground. My butt really hurt. As I rubbed my sore bottom, a hand suddenly entered my field of vision.

"Are you all right?" the boy asked.

"I'm fine—eek!" My words were cut off by a shriek as the boy grabbed my hands and pulled me up. Then he began dusting me off, though I swatted his hands away, feeling my face grow colder than it already was. "W-what are you doing?"

The boy looked at me with this strange expression, like I had just asked him a really stupid question. "Uh, because you fell? I wanted to make sure your clothes didn't get dirty and stuff."

"W-well don't do that!" I told him. I could feel my heart pounding in my chest. Why was it beating so fast? "P-please go away. I don't want to play with anybody."

"Eh? Why not?"

"B-because everyone I try to play with just makes fun of me. You're going to be the same as everyone else. I know it."

"Why would anyone make fun of you? That sounds mean."

"Yeah? Well, people are mean."

"I'm not mean."

Christine frowned at the boy, who had yet to leave. "Why do you even want to play with me anyway?"

"Hmm... I don't know," the boy admitted before grinning. "But I've decided that I want to play with you, so that's what I'm going to do."

Then the boy grabbed my hand and started dragging me over to the toy box.

"What—hey! You can't just drag me like this! Let go!"

"Hahaha! Come on! Let's play something fun!"

"I don't wanna play something fun! I want you to let go!"

"Oh, by the way, my name is Kevin. What's yours?"

The boy turned around, walking backward while still pulling me along. He stared at me with his big blue eyes, and my cheeks became really cold. It felt like they were being hit by shards of ice. I didn't like this feeling, but at the same time, I didn't think it was an unpleasant feeling. It was strange. I didn't understand. My heart was beating really fast, too.

"Uh... it's Christine," I muttered. I wanted to hide in my coat. "Christine Fraust."

"Nice to meet you, Christy! Now, let's have some fun!"

The rest of the day, Kevin and I played games, and Kevin even stuck up for me when several other kids tried to tell him that he shouldn't play with me.

He only stayed there for one day. Apparently, his mom had come because she was some kind of writer or something. Even though I only saw him that one day, I would always remember my first friend, the boy with blond hair, blue eyes, and a big grin.

From that first meeting, my heart had been stolen.

***

Yuki-onna, otherwise known as snow maidens, are a type of yōkai often found in the most inhospitable regions of the world, places where sleet and snow are a constant, and where more humans die from hypothermia than anywhere else. They love the cold, and why shouldn't they? Their very powers are derived from the ice and snow that they so covet.

Christine hated the cold. Despite having the blood of a yuki-onna, she despised the cold more than anything. Perhaps it was the nekomata in her. Cat yōkai loved warm weather and possessed powers over fire, or so she'd been told. She'd never met another nekomata before, and she couldn't control fire, so it wasn't like she could confirm or deny what Orin had taught her.

Either way, it didn't change the fact that she hated the cold, despite wielding the power to control ice. It made her different than other yuki-onna.

Another fact that made her different was her enjoyment of scalding hot showers. She always took her showers at the hottest setting, where steam rose all around her, and the fierce droplets raining down on her back scorched her skin. It was her biggest guilty pleasure.

After turning off the water, Christine stepped out and walked over to the mirror, running a hand over the surface to defog it.

She stared at her reflection. Her skin was so pale as to be nearly translucent. Long, dark hair trailed all the way down to her butt, sticking to her skin because it was still soaking wet. Icy blue eyes stared back at her.

She looked down, toward her chest. Christine could feel the frown twisting her face. Raising her hands to cup her breasts, she grimaced at how small they were. Even though she was sixteen years old, she wasn't even a B cup.

"Is the reason Kevin chose Lilian over me because of her breasts?" she wondered out loud mere seconds before realizing what she'd said. She promptly blushed. "Why the hell am I even thinking about that idiot?! Damn it, Christine! Get a hold of yourself!"

Nya... a yawn sounded out in her head. *What are nyou nyelling about at this early hour, nya?*

Nothing. Go back to sleep.

Marching into her room, she began getting dressed, trying to put thoughts of Kevin out of her mind. Yet the thoughts persisted, much to her annoyance. How pathetic was it that she still retained feelings for him several months after he shot her down? Why did she still feel this way?

Christine cursed her race. She cursed the blood that made her feel this way. If she'd never been born a yuki-onna, if she'd been born a full-blooded nekomata, her love for Kevin would have evaporated by now... maybe.

With a sigh, Christine finished getting dressed and made preparations to start her day.

***

It was the beginning of April. The air was a bit too chilly for her taste, but Arizona was still the warmest state in the United States, though she really hoped the temperature would rise again. 96 to 106 degree weather would have been ideal.

School had ended some time ago, and Christine had gone to work at her job. She worked at Cold Stone Creamery, an ice cream parlor. Why she ever thought that working at a place that sold something with the word "ice" in it was a good idea, she'd never know. Still, the pay was good. She made ninety-four dollars for fifteen hours of work a week, and she really did need the money.

While her benefactor paid for her living expenses, he didn't pay for anything else. If she wanted to have spending money, then she needed to earn it herself.

She'd only had this job for a few months, having found employment two weeks before Christmas. Her original reason for getting this job was to buy gifts for her friends, something that she hadn't needed to do since moving to Arizona due to a distinct lack of them. Now that she'd befriended Kevin, Lilian, and Lindsay— and Iris, too, she guessed—she had several friends who she wanted to buy presents for.

After Christmas, she decided to continue working. With Lindsay and the others always inviting her to go places, Christine found herself in need of more spending money. She didn't regret this need, as the reason for it was because she had friends who wanted to spend time with her, but it still meant she needed stable employment.

The Cold Stone Creamery uniform consisted of a black collared shirt, a black apron, and a visor with the Cold Stone logo on it. She also wore black pants and tennis shoes.

This particular style of dress was not something that she enjoyed wearing. She had a preference for lolita-style clothing. For the sake of her job, she put up with the horrendous outfit.

Because she went to high school, Christine had a fixed schedule. She worked Mondays and Wednesdays from three p.m. to eight p.m., and Saturdays from eight a.m. to one p.m. They were good shifts that didn't interfere with her daily life. Her manager was a nice person, even if the old codger enjoyed poking fun at her a little too much.

The parlor wasn't too full that day, but there were more people than she was used to. With it being halfway through spring, more people were beginning to enjoy the cool delights offered by ice cream parlors like this one. Her manager had said that when summer hit, there would be even more customers.

She didn't get it. Why would anyone want to have ice cream during the summer? That negated the whole point of enjoying Arizona's heat.

"Ha… the men's restroom is all clean," a voice said off to her left. "Man, that was not fun. You'd think parents would be more responsible and not let their kids take a dump all over the floor."

The person standing before her was a coworker, Alan Baker, a tall boy who towered over her like a giant. He had dark hair and dark eyes. His skin was lightly tanned from spending a lot of time in the sun. He was a soccer player for the men's varsity team at their school, which she only knew thanks to Lindsay.

"Most parents don't really seem to care about their children these days," Christine said with a shrug. Hers sure didn't. Her mom had abandoned her after she'd been born, and she didn't even know who her dad was. What kind of parents did that to their children?

"Yeah, I guess." Alan leaned against the display case and crossed his arms over his chest.

"You'd better not let the manager catch you like that. I doubt even being his grandson would save you from getting fired."

"Aw, it'll be all right. We don't have that many customers right now."

"Whatever." Christine sighed and got back to work, wiping down the counter and making sure everything looked nice and sparkly. Even as she worked, however, she could feel Alan's eyes on her.

"Hey, Christine, I was wondering if you wanted to do something this Saturday? I promise it'll be fun."

Christine resisted a groan. Alan was a nice enough guy, and he was handsome. She knew that several girls had a crush on him, but she wasn't one of those girls.

"Um, that's really nice of you to offer, but I've already got plans this weekend."

Saturday after work she would be hanging out with Lindsay, Lilian, and Iris for a "girl's night" kind of thing over at Kevin's apartment. Kevin wouldn't be there. He would be spending the night with Alex, Andrew, and Eric.

"Okay, then what about this Sunday?"

Alan was persistent, Christine would give him that. He'd been asking her out on dates ever since she started working there. Part of her thought she should just accept his offer. If she did, maybe it would help her get over Kevin, but another part of her, a much stronger part, was repulsed by the idea.

Despite being rejected, Christine didn't want to give up on Kevin.

Curse my yuki-onna blood.

Don't blame nyour blood on this. Just admit it. Nyou love him.

Shut up!

Ignoring her "inner kitty," she tried to give the much taller figure a smile. Seeing how she wasn't one for smiling, it probably didn't come out right, but hey, at least she tried.

"I'm sorry, Alan. My entire weekend is pretty much booked."

All of her weekends were like this. Saturdays, she either spent time with Lindsay, or in the group that she, Lindsay, Lilian, and Iris had formed. Sometimes Lindsay's soccer friends would join them. Christine had gotten to know Jessica and a few of the other girls, though she didn't like any of them. Sundays were spent with the larger group, meaning Kevin and the other boys would join them. They would usually go to the mall, or travel to Dave and Busters, or watch a movie, or even head to Kevin's place and hang out there. Christine would admit, if only to herself, that she greatly enjoyed the times she spent with everyone.

Alan clicked his tongue and ran a hand through his hair. "You always say that."

"Sorry," she apologized, even though she wasn't all that sorry. She didn't know why, but his pushy attitude grated on her.

A jingle going off alerted them to more customers entering. Christine put on her best smile and greeted the group that walked up to the register.

Or at least, she would have.

If she hadn't known the people standing before her.

"Christine?" Blue eyes gawked at her.

"K-K-Kevin?!" she squeaked, her face turning into an icy flame. "W-w-what are you doing here?"

The trio that walked into the ice cream parlor was none other than Kevin, Lilian, and Iris. Christine felt mortified that some of her friends were seeing her while she was working. No one knew that she had a job. She wasn't sure why she hid this information—Kevin had a job, after all—but she did, because for some reason, the thought of everyone finding out embarrassed her.

That day, Kevin had chosen to don a dark shirt that stretched across his torso, revealing the muscles he'd gained through his intense training with Kiara. Christine would never admit it out loud, but Kevin had some of the sexiest arms she'd ever seen. They weren't large, but they were sculpted and defined, like those Greek statues she'd seen in museums. Just thinking about his defined arms and pectorals made her cheeks feel cold.

"Um, we're here to get ice cream," Kevin said, sounding as befuddled as he looked. "I thought it would be a nice treat since it's getting warmer." He tilted his head. "I didn't know you worked here, though."

Christine could've cursed. This was just her luck. She should have known that this would happen eventually. It was like she was permanently unlucky.

It looks like nyou're in a pinch.

Shut up, cat!

Nya-ha-ha-ha!

Christine withheld her grimace as her other half's laughter faded into the background of her mind. "I, um, I've only been working here for a few months…"

"Really? I had no idea."

That's because you've never been here before now, Christine thought sarcastically. She didn't say this, though, because she was still embarrassed.

Out of the corner of her eyes, she caught Alan staring at Lilian and Iris, his cheeks aflame. And was that drool running down his mouth? And why the hell was his nose bleeding? She wrinkled her nose.

Fucking pig.

Nya, I agree. It's a good thing nyou didn't accept his offer for a date.

Christine didn't say anything, but she agreed with her counterpart.

"So, wait," Lilian started, also appearing bemused. "You're working at an ice cream store, but you hate the cold? How does that work?"

"Ah…" Christine felt like hiding in her shirt. By the gods, this was so mortifying. "I-it was the first place that offered to hire me, so…"

"Oh, I see." Lilian nodded her head in a sage-like manner, arms crossed under her chest. Christine felt a bit of breast envy when Lilian's two mountainous mammaries were pushed together. Why couldn't she have breasts like that? "It's pretty cool that you have a job."

"R-really?"

"Um!" Lilian smiled. "I actually thought about getting a job, too, but that would mean I have less time to spend with Kevin."

Unspoken was the *"it would also mean letting Iris be alone with Kevin"* that Christine knew they were both thinking.

She didn't really understand Lilian's twin sister. The raven-haired wench was a prolific and self-proclaimed siscon, who wanted to do perverted things to Lilian. She had even hatched a plan to score with her own sister by seducing both Kevin and Lilian, all to convince them to join her in a twisted three-way relationship.

Christine didn't get it. Why would anyone want to get it on with their sibling? Then again, Iris was a kitsune. They were a strange breed.

"That's too bad." Speak of the devil, Iris just had to open her mouth. "I'd love to see what you look like in a uniform. You'd be the sexiest employee ever."

Lilian and Christine scowled when Iris draped herself over Kevin, who seemed unsure of whether he should be annoyed or uncomfortable by the proximity.

"What do you think, Stud? Would you like to see Lily-pad in a sexy worker's outfit?"

"I don't think there are any work uniforms that could be considered sexy unless she worked at Hooters or a gentleman's club, and I wouldn't want Lilian to work at a place where a bunch of dirty old men could ogle her."

"Hmm. Good point," Iris conceded.

"Still..." Christine shot ramrod straight when Kevin's eyes landed on her. "... I have to admit, you look really cute in that uniform."

Christine's eyes widened. Fuck, her cheeks were turning icy again. "Y-you think so?"

"Yeah." Showing his pearly whites with a grin, Kevin gave her a thumbs-up. Christine thought she saw light gleaming off his teeth. It even made an odd *ping!* sound. "It definitely suits you!"

Tsundere protocols: activated.

"D-d-d-d-don't think that makes me happy, idiot! G-g-getting a compliment from you doesn't make me happy at all!"

Kevin scratched the back of his neck, smiling sheepishly. "Yeah, I guess it wouldn't."

Realizing that she was overreacting again, Christine coughed into her hand. "A-anyway, are you guys going to order something, or are you just going to stand there?"

After her prompting, the trio ordered some ice cream. Iris got chocolate ice cream in a chocolate-covered cone, while Kevin and Lilian ordered a large cone bowl of cheesecake-flavored ice cream with cookie dough. While Christine made their orders, she thought about the blond teen standing naught but five feet away.

The problem with Kevin, she reflected, was that he was too honest for his own good and not smart enough to keep his mouth shut. If he thought something looked good on someone, he would tell them. That was just how he was. Oddly enough, this tendency only extended to people he knew and was mostly clothes-related.

She blamed this habit on his mom. He seemed to have inherited Ms. Swift's sense of fashion and outspoken demeanor when it came to fashion.

While she made the ice cream, Alan chose that moment to snap out of his stupor and start a confrontation.

"So you're Kevin Swift," he said. "I've heard a lot about you, but this is the first time I've seen you in person. I'm surprised you're so short."

Christine gritted her teeth as her coworker decided to get into a male pissing contest with her friend. Fortunately, Kevin didn't seem to realize what Alan was doing, or if he did, he was choosing to play it cool.

"I guess I am a little on the small side," Kevin admitted, "At least compared to you. I always thought my height was pretty average."

Alan frowned at the smaller teen. "How do you know Christine?"

"Uh… because we're friends? Didn't you know that? I mean, Christine and I sit together at lunch every day, we go out on weekends, and sometimes we hang out after school."

As Kevin began listing off all of the things they did together, conveniently neglecting to mention that all of these activities were done with a large group of people, Christine felt more and more like crawling into a hole somewhere. She wanted to die. The way he said it made it sound like they did all those things on their own, just the two of them, like they were dating or something!

What is this idiot saying?

Alan also seemed to take it this way rather than the way it was meant to be taken. The frown on his face grew into a scowl, and his right eye gained a violent twitch.

"Oh, is that so?" Alan said through a spiteful smile. "You spend an awful lot of time around Christine. Aren't you dating that girl over there?" He pointed to Lilian. "Don't you think you should spend more time with her and less time with a girl you aren't even dating?"

Kevin appeared genuinely confused. Christine felt like facepalming. He clearly didn't realize that his words had been completely misinterpreted. She knew that Kevin wasn't dense or stupid, but he really should start thinking about the way he worded things.

Knowing that she needed to resolve this confrontation before it became a conflict—she didn't want Kevin beating the utter living crap out of Alan because her idiot of a coworker tried to start a fight—Christine quickly made their ice cream.

"Here you guys go. Enjoy."

Kevin, Lilian, and Iris grabbed their ice cream and left after some not-so-subtle prodding from Christine. However, they didn't leave before Kevin said, "By the way, you're going to Lindsay's game this Friday, right?"

"Um, yes," Christine said. That was right. Lindsay had a soccer game this Friday. She'd almost forgotten.

"In that case, we'll see you there."

As her three friends left the parlor, Christine's thoughts turned, once again, to Kevin. He'd gone through a lot of changes since they had been reunited in that arcade all those months ago. She would have said that he was growing into a more confident person, a better person, but the things she originally liked about him, like his kindness and ability to accept others regardless of whether they were yōkai or human, remained unchanged.

Perhaps that was why it still hurt every time she saw him with Lilian, because she knew those changes had nothing to do with her, but with the redhead who'd stolen his heart.

***

The sun had gone down by the time Christine returned home. While she normally didn't mind work, her coworker had been insufferable after Kevin had arrived. Jealousy. Alan was jealous of her friend. It made sense. Kevin wasn't oblivious to the fact that a lot of men were jealous of him; he just ignored it.

Of course, given that Kevin and she weren't dating, or, indeed, that Alan had a thing for her, he probably didn't know why her coworker was jealous of him. That said, he likely didn't care either.

Making her way into her bedroom, Christine fell face-first onto the bed. She didn't bother eating dinner that night. She wasn't hungry. Instead, she drifted off into a fitful sleep filled with blue eyes and blond hair.

CHAPTER 10

A Seemingly Normal Day

DESPITE HAVING TO DEAL WITH THAT BASTARD SETH, Cassy would admit that she'd been having a very good time these past three weeks. Her "superior" didn't have any outstanding orders for her, so she'd been free to do what she wanted, and what she wanted to do was spend time with Master Kevin.

Cassy still remembered the first time that she and Master Kevin had held a true conversation. It was when she'd been shopping—or trying to—and Master Kevin had been kind enough to buy her some fish, which she lacked the funds to buy herself. After that day, she had made it a point to meet up with him whenever she could. She always made it look like their meeting was just a coincidence. Master Kevin never suspected a thing, simply accepting her words at face value and talking to her like they were old friends.

She did feel guilty about lying to him, but it wasn't like she had any other choice. Master Kevin couldn't know who she was. Even if he knew about yōkai, their village had a strict policy on not revealing who and what they were to outsiders. Secrecy was paramount.

While she would have normally told him about her being a nekomata anyway, the fact that she'd been ordered to kill his girlfriend forced her not to. There was no need to arouse unnecessary suspicion upon herself.

Skipping into her apartment, Cassy had the largest smile on her face. She had met up with Master Kevin again this morning by pretending to be a jogger, which she did every Sunday. It had been a lot of fun. He'd rode the bike slowly, and they'd spoken about their hobbies. She'd learned a lot more about him, which was always a good thing in her book.

She did have to wonder about his weird obsession with Japanese pop culture. She couldn't remember if he'd had the same obsession when he was younger. Were all teenage boys like that?

"Did you have fun with your human friend?"

Cassy stiffened, hands clenching. She slowly turned around to face Seth, still wearing the body of Ms. Vis, smirking at her from his place on the couch.

"I did, actually. Not that it's any of your business, nya."

"Such an insolent girl." Seth sighed, pushing himself to his feet. As always, he chose to walk around the apartment completely naked, which disturbed Cassy a great deal. "Well, I suppose it doesn't matter. Tomorrow is our last day here anyway. I've already set everything up so we can kill the Pnéyma girl without interference from her bodyguard. I've even set up a little surprise for her friends in case they try to rescue her. Can I count on you to take care of the boy?"

"Of course," Cassy replied, insulted that he would even ask. "There's no way I'll let you lay a hand on Master Kevin, nya."

Seth's diabolical chuckle sounded wrong with Ms. Vis's voice. "Is that so? In that case, you had better not fail me. If the Swift boy ends up interfering while I'm killing the Pnéyma girl, then I will end him."

Cassy hissed. "Nya! I'll kill nyou if nyou even touch him!"

"Now, now." Seth wagged a chastising finger at her. "You had better be more careful with your words. What you just said could be considered treason. Were I not as compassionate as I am, I could have you executed."

Cassy gritted her teeth. Compassionate her ass. This man didn't know the meaning of the word. He was doing this to torture her. He knew that she hated the idea of fighting Master Kevin, just as he knew that it was the only way Master Kevin could live. Seth and Master Kevin could not be allowed to fight. The young man she'd become fond of would meet his end if that were to happen.

Even if she had to knock Master Kevin out cold, she would not let him fight against Seth.

On that day, the sun shone brightly, and the birds chirped lovely songs.

***

Kevin wondered if there was something wrong with him. As he lay in bed, staring up at the ceiling and feeling two soft, feminine, and half-naked bodies snuggling with him, he figured there must have been something wrong with him.

I should be freaking out right now…

Looking to his left revealed Lilian, his girlfriend and mate, her head resting on his shoulder, long red hair fanned out and haloed by the light that filtered in through the window. Lilian's hair reminded him of a wildfire. A glance to the left showed Iris, who was also using one of his shoulders as a pillow and had wrapped herself around him like a koala bear. Her sleeping face looked peaceful, yet somehow seductive as well. Unlike Lilian, who wore one of his shirts, Iris wore a nighty that was the same midnight black as her hair.

Yes, there was definitely something wrong with this situation.

Thinking back on it, he probably shouldn't have even been comfortable sleeping with Lilian. How many boys his age slept with their girlfriend? Well, there were probably a lot, but they didn't sleep with their girlfriend on a daily basis. He wondered, was his lack of surprise at his situation because Lilian was a kitsune? Did that balance things out? He didn't know, but thinking like that gave him a headache, so he decided to stop.

Extricating himself from the bed with careful use of the famed replacement technique, which involved swapping his body out with a pillow, Kevin turned just for a second to look at the two. It was probably a mistake—no, it was definitely a mistake. Just looking at Lilian and Iris as they lay wrapped around each other in a mess of tangled limbs, their faces inches away from each other as if they were about to kiss, was enough to make him rock hard.

Morning wood had nothing on this.

"Ugh, I really hope these thoughts aren't Eric's influence," Kevin mumbled, pressing a palm to his face as he made his way to the restroom.

Self-gratification was not something that Kevin did often. In truth, he didn't know a whole lot about masturbation since no one had ever taught him about it. His school was notoriously bad regarding its sex education program, and his mom had always been uncomfortable talking about the subject. Still, with a raging hard-on that could have been used in a fencing tournament, he was left with little recourse.

After relieving himself over the toilet, Kevin took a quick shower, and then returned to his bedroom to get dressed. He was interrupted seconds after putting on his boxers by a wolf whistle.

"Nice show, Stud. Can I expect a striptease like this every time I wake up?"

"Iris." Kevin hid his embarrassment with irritation. "I thought you were still asleep."

Kevin turned around. Iris was wide awake and gazing at him from over her sister's shoulder. It appeared that she had turned Lilian over, and she was now spooning her sister. The covers had been peeled away as well, revealing that Iris was gently stroking Lilian's flat stomach, which twitched under her touch.

I don't know what's worse: The fact that I'm annoyed or the fact that I'm aroused again.

"I actually woke up a few minutes before you did."

"Then why didn't you get out of bed?"

"Didn't feel like it."

Iris and Kevin stared at each other for a moment. Kevin looked away first. "Okay. I walked into that one."

"That you did." Iris nodded with sage-like wisdom. "But at least you realize that, which means you're learning."

"Whatever," Kevin mumbled. "Anyway, could you not watch me while I'm getting dressed?"

"And deprive myself of a good show?" Iris grinned at him. "I think not."

"Tch!"

Kevin dressed quickly after that, pulling up his black jeans and donning a white T-shirt, along with a pair of socks. After a second, he also grabbed his single-shot pistol, which was hidden in the bottom drawer of his dresser, and slid it into his back pocket.

Kiara had told him to keep it on him at all times, even when he went to school. Though he was loath to carry a weapon around, Kevin understood the precaution. There was no telling when he might run into a hostile yōkai—he'd already run into several at school. He needed to be ready at all times.

"Could you wake up Lilian?" Kevin asked. He'd normally do it himself, but he didn't want Iris watching him smooch her sister awake. That would be annoying—and embarrassing, but mostly annoying, especially because, knowing Iris, the vixen would probably catcall or do something even more humiliating.

"Huhuhu, sure thing. Just leave it to me, Stud."

A bad premonition suddenly came over him. Maybe he shouldn't have asked her to wake Lilian up, after all. The smile on her face was disturbing. Ah, well. It was too late to back out now.

"Right."

339

After leaving the room, Kevin traveled down the hallway, where he bumped into Kirihime, who appeared to have exited from the master bedroom where Camellia resided.

"Oh, Lord Kevin," Kirihime greeted with a demure curtsy. "Good morning."

"Morning, Kirihime," Kevin greeted the kind and polite woman with a smile. "Camellia's still asleep?"

"Yes, I think she's worn out from last night," Kirihime admitted, blushing just a bit.

Kevin found his own cheeks heating up. Last night Camellia had somehow found his mother's secret stash of alcohol, which not even Kevin had known existed. What happened after that was... well, the less said about that incident, the better.

"Ah-ha, w-well, at least it means you'll get some time to relax," he said.

Kirihime nodded. "Y-yes."

Making their way into the kitchen, the two were greeted by Kotohime. She was standing by the stove. A wonderful scent that tantalized Kevin's nose wafted around the room.

Kevin often wondered how early she got up to cook them breakfast every morning. He rose fairly early as well, but somehow, the kimono-clad femme fatale was always up before him.

He also wondered about her clothing. He'd never seen her entire wardrobe before, but she seemed to have several hundred different kimonos. This morning she wore a light tan kimono with the image of a savanna stamped on the back, a dead tree in the middle of a desert with the dying sun shining light through its branches, presenting a truly melancholic yet beautiful scene.

"Good morning, Kevin-sama, Kirihime." Kotohime presented them with a wondrous smile. "I take it Iris-sama and Lilian-sama have not woken up yet?"

"Well, Iris is awake, but I don't know about—"

"KYA!" a familiar cry rang throughout the house.

Kevin deadpanned. "Never mind. Lilian is awake, too."

Seconds later, Iris and Lilian burst out of the hallway.

"Iris! Get back here!"

"Huhuhu, if you want me, you'll have to catch me!"

"Oh, I'll catch you all right. I'll catch you and make you regret ever being caught!"

"Oh, my. That sounds so violent. I love it when my Lily-pad enjoys playing rough with me."

"Don't say it like that! You make it sound dirty!"

Kevin, Kirihime, and Kotohime watched silently as Lilian chased Iris around the living room. Lilian lunged at her sister, tackling the raven-haired succubus and sending them both tumbling to the ground. While lying on the ground, Lilian tried to wrestle with the laughing Iris, who seemed to enjoy herself far more than he thought was natural.

"It's like watching two squirrels bickering over who ate the last acorn," Kevin remarked. He wondered if it was wrong that he thought watching two half-naked vixens roll around on the floor was hot. Stupid hormones.

"Indeed." Kotohime nodded.

"I wonder what Lady Iris did to make Lady Lilian so angry at her?" Kirihime asked.

Hearing her name being called, Lilian looked up from where she lay, straddling Iris's waist. Her eyes zeroed in on Kevin, who realized the danger that he was in a second too late.

"Beloved!"

"Wait, Lili—oof!"

The world spun for a brief moment, and then, without warning, all of the air left Kevin's lungs as his back slammed into the ground. Gasping, Kevin looked up with bleary eyes. The vision blurring in front of him soon sharpened. Red hair. Green eyes. They hovered over him. It made him realize that Lilian was straddling him now.

"How could you let Iris wake me up like that, Beloved? How could you?"

"Ugh," Kevin groaned. Dang, Lilian knew how to tackle people. He was seeing stars! "I don't even know what Iris did to wake you up."

"Urk!" Lilian made strange choking noises. Her face became suffused with a shade of red so vibrant Kevin feared the house would catch fire. "I-I'd rather not talk about it. Anyway, you should have woken me up instead of her. Why didn't you wake me up?"

"I didn't realize it was that important."

"Not that important?" Lilian stared at Kevin like he'd said the damning words. "Beloved, the good morning kiss is a most sacred ritual between couples."

"R-really?" This was his first time hearing about this ritual.

"Of course!" Lilian's nod was emphatic. "It is a time-honored ritual that must be adhered to."

"I thought the time-honored way of waking someone up was a blowjob," Iris commented as she walked into the kitchen and sat down at the table.

Lilian glared at her. "Quiet, you!"

"Un, well, if it's that important I could kiss you right now," Kevin offered.

"That goes without saying." Lilian's pout as she spoke was adorable. "You have to make it up to me. Because you didn't wake me up, Iris was the one who gave me my morning kiss—eep!"

Kevin's eyes widened as Lilian's hands shot to her mouth. Out of the corner of his eye, he saw Iris grinning like a loon, her smile the utter definition of satisfaction… at least, until she saw what they were having for breakfast. The smile faded and a grimace replaced it.

"Ugh, Japanese cuisine again?"

"Oh, dear. Is that dissatisfaction I hear? Is there a problem with my breakfast, Iris-sama?" Kotohime asked with the dazzling smile of a monster.

It was almost amusing, the way Iris's face went paler than a ghost. She raised one trembling hand, which she placed behind her head, rubbing the back of her neck, a sheepish grin laced with primal terror etched onto her face.

"Ah… ah-ahahaha! W-what I meant was that I'm so happy we're having another traditional Japanese breakfast."

Kotohime's smile shifted, becoming tender and kind, like a loving mother as she watched her child play in a sandbox. "I'm glad you think so."

"Ha…" Iris sighed. At the same time, Kevin was still staring at his mate, stunned into silence by the most recent shocking news.

"Oh, wow. I had no idea that's what happened. Though now that I think about it, I probably should have expected this. Yuri moments between you and Iris seem to be happening with disturbingly increasing frequency. Maybe we should—mph!"

Lilian's tongue didn't allow him to say anymore.

"L-Lady Lilian!" Kirihime's stuttered shout came at the same time as Kotohime's, "Oh, my."

Iris just chuckled.

"Huhuhu…"

Like that.

***

Lilian couldn't believe that her morning kiss had been stolen by Iris. Just thinking about it made her skin flush.

As much as she loved Kevin, Iris knew her best. Her likes and dislikes, the places to touch her that made her body sing, she knew everything.

It wasn't so surprising. She and Iris had known each other forever. They'd been born together, raised together, and become kitsune together. They had comforted each other when they were hurt, supported each other when something went wrong. When Iris became curious about sex, Lilian had volunteered herself for experimentation. In her mind, it was only natural. Until Kevin had come along, Iris was the person that she'd relied on.

Lilian had always admired how Iris never put up with their relative's badmouthing, how she was more than willing to pick fights with others, how she could speak her mind without reserve. Until Kevin had come along and set her straight, Lilian had never been like that.

Class had started several minutes ago. It was math. Ms. Vis was lecturing them on basic calculus.

Lilian looked up from where she was taking notes and studied her mate. Kevin sat in front of her, diligently jotting down in his notebook. She looked to her left, and then frowned when she noticed that Lindsay was doing nothing. Her friend was just staring blankly at the wall.

Is something up?

Leaning over, she carefully tapped on her friend's shoulder. Lindsay blinked once, looked at her, then blinked again. Her lips twisted into a facsimile of a smile.

"Something up, Lilian?"

"Are you feeling okay? You look kinda tired."

Lindsay tilted her head quizzically. "Tired?"

"Yeah, you've been staring at the wall since class started." Lilian's worry for her friend deepened when Lindsay simply continued blinking at her. "Actually, you've been really out of it since we met up this morning. Is everything all right?"

"Of course. Everything's great. Why wouldn't it be?"

Something was definitely up. Lindsay was giving her a full-blown, ear-to-ear smile, but it was different from her normal smiles. Lindsay's smiles were normally bright and optimistic. This one looked like it was trying too hard to be that, but it wasn't quite hitting the mark.

As her friend went back to staring at the wall, Lilian leaned over to her sister. "Ne, Iris, is it just me, or is Lindsay acting a little weird today?"

"Hmm?" Iris looked at her sister. "Sorry, did you say something? I was too busy staring at your rack to pay attention."

"I-Iris!" Lilian hissed quietly as she covered her breasts with her arms. "Don't say things like that in public! In fact, don't say those things at all!"

"Huhuhu," Iris's quiet chuckle caused Lilian's cheeks to heat up like boiling water. "Sorry, I couldn't help myself. You're just too easy, Lily-pad."

"Mou... I'm being serious here."

"So was I." When Lilian continued pouting at Iris, her fraternal twin's lips twitched. "All right, all right, no more teasing. I got it. So, you were saying something about Lindsay?"

Lilian nodded and got back on track. "Yes, Lindsay is acting kind of weird, don't you think?"

"Hm..."

Iris observed the tomboy, who was still staring at the wall with a blank expression. She hummed as if contemplating the girl like one might a puzzle.

"Hey, Dyke? Dykie? Raging lesbo with the hots for Frosty?"

Lindsay didn't respond. She didn't even blink.

Lilian twitched. "Iris, do you have to be so rude?"

Iris shrugged and leaned back in her seat. "What? I was just checking to see if she'd respond to insults, and it looks like you're right. Something is definitely wrong. Whenever I say something like that to her, she always gets really depressed."

Lilian bit her lip and looked at her friend again. "Maybe she's tired?" Lilian suggested, even though she didn't believe her own words.

"Excuse me," a voice interrupted them. They turned to Ms. Vis, who glared at them with a stern frown of disapproval. "Why are you talking in my class, Ms. Pnéyma? Do you enjoy disrupting the learning process of your peers? Or perhaps you think you can teach this class better than I can?"

Lilian's eyes widened. "That isn't it. I was just talking to Iris about—"

"I do not care what you were talking about," Ms. Vis cut her off. "All that matters is that you are disrupting my class and impeding the other students' learning process. If you do not want to have a good education, that is fine, but you shouldn't ruin it for others. I am afraid I'm going to have to give you detention."

Detention? She was getting detention? Lilian didn't know how to take that. For the last several months, Ms. Vis had treated Lilian like she was the woman's childhood crush. The math teacher had been abnormally kind to her, to the point that it was creepy. What had changed? Why was she getting in trouble now, of all times?

"Now hold on a second," Kevin said, standing up in his seat before Iris could. "Don't you think you're going a little too far? There are plenty of students who occasionally speak out in class, yet I don't see you punishing them."

Ms. Vis's smile was positively carnivorous. "And who, Mr. Swift, do you see speaking out in class? Are you sure you're not just imagining things?"

"Of course not. I know for a fact that Jannice—"

"Do you see Jannice speaking out right now?"

Kevin blinked. "W-well, no, but—"

"Exactly. She is not speaking out right now. Neither is anyone else, for that matter. The only people who have spoken out in class today are Ms. Pnéyma and now you. Now please sit down, Mr. Swift, or I shall have you written up and sent to the principal's office for talking back to a teacher."

Kevin clenched his hands until his knuckles turned white, but he reluctantly sat down. As Ms. Vis resumed her lecture, he sent Lilian an apologetic smile, but she simply responded with her own smile and a shake of her head, telling him not to worry.

Class finished in unusual silence.

***

"Can you believe that bitch? How dare she make my Lily-pad suffer in detention! I was talking as well, but she didn't give me detention! How is that even fair?"

Kevin, Lilian, and Christine listened to Iris as she ranted about the math teacher. It was lunchtime, and the group was sitting outside, underneath the shaded patio, on a long stone table. With them were Lindsay, Alex, Andrew, and Eric, which was a surprise.

Their lecherous friend did not eat lunch with them often anymore, busy as he was spending time learning to peep from Heather. It made Kevin wary of what he was doing with them now.

"You're the only person in the entire world who could possibly be unhappy about not getting detention," Kevin said as he ate from his bento box.

Eating beside him, Lilian nodded in agreement. "Beloved, can I have some of your pork cutlets?"

"Hm? Oh, sure."

"Thank you!"

Kevin grabbed a pork cutlet with his chopsticks and held it up for Lilian. His mate leaned over and took the food into her mouth, humming in delight. It was anyone's guess if she was excited because of the food or because Kevin was feeding her.

"And what about you?" Iris asked. "Aren't you the least bit bothered about Lily-pad getting detention?"

"Here, Beloved. Try some of my calamari."

Lilian fed Kevin a piece of calamari, her bright eyes and vibrant smile making Christine shift in her seat. If the young couple noticed how uncomfortable their friend was, then they did an exemplary job of ignoring it. None of the others acted like they were bothered. It was strange. Alex and Andrew would normally make wisecracks about how lovey-dovey the two acted.

After he swallowed the food in his mouth, he addressed Iris. "Of course I am, but there isn't much I can do about that. Ms. Vis is a teacher. If she wants to give detention, that's her right. I don't agree with her giving Lilian detention, but I also know better than to fight her over it."

"Speaking of Ms. Vis, don't you think she was acting kind of strange today?" Lilian asked, poking at her calamari.

"How so?" asked Christine.

"Well, Ms. Vis is normally really, uh, concerned about my well-being for some reason. You know how she's always asking me if I'm all right in class and if I need anything and stuff?"

"I'm not in your class." Christine shrugged. "But go on."

"Well, she didn't act nice or concerned at all today. She didn't ask me if I was doing all right, or if I needed any help on my math work. Even more strange is that she gave me detention. I haven't had detention with her since my first day of school."

"Now that you mention it, that is a little odd," Kevin said before shrugging. "But then, Ms. Vis has always been off her rocker. Remember how she originally hated you? Then there was that time she got upset with me for not sitting in the back of the classroom by the window, never mind the fact that our class doesn't have a single window. That woman's got more than just a few screws loose."

"Makes you wonder why someone like that is even teaching here," Iris said, getting several nods in return.

"Speaking of acting strange today," Christine started, leaning into the other four. "Do any of you guys know what's wrong with the other students? Some of the kids in my classes have been acting really odd, like they're in some kind of trance. All they do is stare at the wall. Even Lindsay and Eric are acting like that."

Kevin, Lilian, and Iris looked at their friends. The fact that Eric was even present and not trying to peek at the freshman girls while they changed was odd enough. That he was eating at a snail's pace while staring at the table creeped them out. Then there was Alex and Andrew, who weren't fighting each other like usual, followed by the abnormally silent and unresponsive Lindsay. Yeah, their friends were acting odd, but none of them knew why.

"We kinda thought you would know what's wrong with Lindsay," Lilian admitted.

"Yeah, because you and Lindsay are yuri for each other," Iris added.

"Y-y-y-y-YURI?!" Christine's face burst into color. However, this wasn't the embarrassed, tsundere expression that they were used to seeing. Christine looked legitimately mad. "Why would you think something like that?! I'm not yuri for Lindsay! I like Kev—I mean, I like boys! BOYS!"

"Does that mean you still like the stud?"

"Th-th-that's—grr! Shut up! Shut up, shut up, shut up! Boobzilla!"

Lilian and Kevin remained silent as Iris wound the poor yuki-onna up worse than a toy soldier. They tried to ignore the freezing chill that caused their skin to break out into goosebumps. Christine was losing control of her powers and causing frosty vapor to appear in the air.

"You know, if this ever gets an anime, I think Rei Kugimiya should be Christine's seiyuu," Lilian said.

Rie Kugimiya was a famous Japanese voice actress and singer, born in 1979, who had played in several prominent anime roles, including Nagi from *Hayate no Gotoku*, Louise Francoise from *Louise the Zero*, Shana from *Shakugan no Shana*, and Taiga from *Toradora*. Due to a good few of her roles being for tsundere characters, she was given the nickname "Queen of Tsundere" by her fans.

Kevin's stupefied face at her exclamation expressed his confusion better than words ever could. "What's this about a seiyuu?"

Lilian gave Kevin a blank stare. When it became clear that he didn't know what she was talking about, her shoulders slumped.

"... Never mind."

***

School ended. Most of the students were already leaving. Kevin had said that he was going to stay after class and wait for her detention to end. As for Iris, well, she decided to follow Lilian and suffer detention with her.

"You really don't have to come to detention with me, you know."

"What are you talking about? Of course, I do. You only got detention because I was talking to you."

Lilian really didn't know what to think about her sister coming to serve detention with her. It wasn't like Iris had been the one to get detention, though it did feel nice to know that her sister would stick up for her like this.

Not that either of them had any intention of serving. Oh, no. Why serve detention when they could just cast an enchantment on their teacher and make the woman think they had served detention? Yes, that sounded like a much better idea to Lilian, and it was the reason for her confusion toward Iris's actions. There wasn't much need for her fraternal twin to join her when she just planned on enchanting her way out.

"Ha... well, if you really want to follow me, I guess I can't stop you."

"That's right," Iris declared, sounding quite proud of herself. She walked alongside her sister, her hands laced together behind the back of her head. The grin on her face was a mile wide and showed off her perfect ivory teeth. "There's no way I would let my cute

350

sister be alone with that creepy old hag. Besides, would you rather I stay with you, or hang out with the stud without any adult supervision?"

From the moment Iris mentioned spending alone time with Kevin, Lilian's overactive imagination painted a vivid image of her mate and sister lying naked together in a tangle of sheets, their bodies writhing in the throes of ecstasy, as Iris's siren call echoed out for all to hear.

She immediately covered her nose to stem the tide of blood that threatened to escape. Damn her sister! She was thinking all of these lecherous thoughts because of her!

"Ho?" Most unfortunately for Lilian, Iris immediately noticed her nasal problem and sent her a seductive, narrow-eyed grin. "Are you thinking about what the stud and I could get up to on our own?"

"N-no! Of course not!" Lilian wasn't a very convincing liar. "Shut up!"

Lilian couldn't give in to temptation. She couldn't. No, she wouldn't. For the sake of their somewhat normal lives, she wouldn't let Iris tempt her.

I need to be strong for Beloved.

"Now, now, there is no need to get upset," Iris soothed her sister's worries—or she tried to. She wasn't very successful. "While I admit that the stud is a fine male specimen, you know that I would never betray you, my darling Lily-pad."

Upon saying this, Iris stuck her index finger inside of her mouth, moaning as she coated it in saliva. Then she removed the finger and placed the delicate digit against her backside. She made a strange hissing sound.

"The only way Kevin is getting some of this is if it's during a hot, raunchy threesome between you, me, and him."

"You shouldn't say things like that," Lilian mumbled lowly.

Did her sister honestly have to keep acting like this? Lilian was aware that human taboos meant nothing to a kitsune, that incest and other acts of debauchery happened all the time among her race, and that no kitsune worth their weight in anime would bat an eyelash if a pair of siblings got freaky in the sheets. She knew that. She accepted that. She'd even partaken in that before.

But it didn't matter. Kevin was a human, and he wanted a human relationship. For accepting her, for being her mate, she had promised herself that she would give Kevin a normal relationship. It was a promise that she wasn't willing to break.

Seconds later, they arrived at Ms. Vis's classroom, and Lilian knocked on the door. There was no answer. She knocked again, louder this time. She still received no answer.

"Hello?" Lilian called, knocking some more. "Ms. Vis? It's Lilian! Are you in there?"

"Maybe she's sucking off the gym teacher or something?" Iris suggested.

"Ew." Lilian shuddered. "Please don't say something so disgusting in my presence again. That's just gross."

"Huhuhu, I'm just messing with you, Lily-pad. I doubt even that hairy old fart would let someone like Ms. Vis give him head."

Lilian took a deep breath and pinched the bridge of her nose. She loved Iris, but her sister seriously creeped her out sometimes.

Since she hadn't received an answer, Lilian opened the door and entered the classroom. She didn't feel like standing outside, and Ms. Vis was the one who had ordered her to show up. If she showed up and her teacher was gone, then it was no one's fault but Ms. Vis's if she decided to leave.

The classroom was disturbingly empty. Not a soul could be seen. Despite this, or maybe because of it, Lilian felt tense, like a coiled spring ready to snap.

The door slammed closed, startling Iris and Lilian, who spun around.

They were shocked by what they saw.

"Ms. Vis!"

The stern math teacher hung from the door, her wrists tied above her head. She was still alive; Lilian could see her shoulders and chest rise and fall, but she looked weak. Her cheeks were hollowed out, and her skin appeared more pallid than normal. Eyes like soulless husks gazed at nothing and drool leaked from her open mouth.

"Welcome, Ms. Pnévma, to your detention," a voice spoke up, male, older, and reeking with a sense of superiority. "Though I do not remember inviting the other Ms. Pnévma to our little punishment session. Ah, well. It matters not either way. It just means more entertainment for me."

Whirling around, Lilian found herself staring into the face of a handsome man with red hair that was long and untamed, traveling all the way down to his back like a lion's mane. Golden eyes glinted from beneath his bangs. They contained a cold amusement that sent chills down Lilian's spine. He was short, almost as short as Christine, but that didn't make him any less intimidating.

His black business suit stretched across his physique, showing off a muscular build not dissimilar to that of a swimmer—lithe, like whipcord. He wasn't wearing shoes, revealing sharp claw-like nails on his toes.

The air around them became thick, heavy, as something that neither she nor Iris could define descended upon them, causing their bodies to shake like leaves trapped in a tornado. Lilian's breathing began to grow labored. Her pulse started to race. Every fiber in her body screamed at her, telling her to run, that the person before her was dangerous.

"Who are you?" Iris asked, stepping protectively in front of her sister.

"Who am I?" The man chuckled and then, unfurling like a poisonous flower, three fluffy red fox tails emerged from behind his back. "I, my dear, am Seth Naraka, and I will be adding the two of you to my collection."

***

Kevin perused the library, unsure of what he was looking for, or if he was even looking for anything. He'd first thought to find books on proper gun maintenance, but he soon realized that a school library wouldn't have anything on guns. After that, he just sort of wandered the aisles, his fingers trailing across the spines of books.

Lilian was serving detention, and Iris had gone with her. Kevin had thought about doing the same, but he had decided not to in the end. He would instead wait in the library until Lilian's detention was over, and then pick them up so they could head home on the late bus.

The library had a lot of books in all manner of genres. Fiction. Science Fiction. Nonfiction. Historical. Romance. Fantasy. They even had a section dedicated to manga. It was a truly impressive collection, especially when he took the time to consider how this was a school library.

Of course, they don't have any manga in the harem or ecchi variety.

Iris had complained a lot when she discovered that. It was the only genre that she liked. The only genre. Kevin remembered her dragging him and Lilian to the principal's office to try and convince the man that they should carry more risqué manga.

The principal was all for it. It's a good thing the vice principal was around to put a stop to that before Iris could continue.

Kevin wasn't a big fan of harem manga. He'd read the ones that Lilian suggested, like that *Magika Swordsman and Summoner* one, but his life too closely mirrored something out of a harem manga for him to be comfortable reading them. Iris had made fun of him when he said as much.

Deciding that what he needed right now was a good manga to pass the time with, Kevin traveled into the manga section, where he discovered a surprise waiting for him.

"Christine?"

Wearing her unmistakable gothic lolita outfit and with her equally unmistakable short stature, Christine was easy to pick out amongst a crowd—provided the crowd didn't stand over four feet ten inches. The girl in question had several manga volumes in hand, all of which he recognized as the shōjo variety.

At the sound of her name being called, Christine spun around with a mouse-like squeak. She almost dropped her books.

"K-Kevin?" she said, surprised, right before surprise turned into anger. "W-what the hell?! Don't sneak up on me like that, jerk!"

Already used to her personality by now, and knowing that she wasn't being rude on purpose, Kevin ignored her insult. "What are you doing here? I thought you'd have gone home by now, or gone to Lindsay's place."

Kevin had noticed that Christine and Lindsay hung out a lot. When they weren't doing something with everyone else, or when Lindsay didn't have soccer practice, the two of them were together. He guessed that was why Iris made fun of them.

"And do what? There's no one waiting for me at home," Christine retorted, then sighed. "And I actually did have plans to spend the night at Lindsay's, but she canceled at the last second, something about having unfinished work that she needed to stay at school for."

"Really?" Kevin was surprised. Lindsay rarely ever stayed at school because of "unfinished work." He didn't even know what that meant. "Well, she doesn't have soccer practice, so I don't know what she could be doing."

"Me neither." Christine bit her lip. "Though I wonder if it has to do with how she's been acting lately. She's been really absentminded for the past week like she's not all there."

"I noticed that," Kevin agreed. All of their friends had been acting strangely. He tried not to think about that, though, because doing so made him feel uneasy. "Speaking of Lindsay, I really have to ask, are you and she... well, you know?"

From the clouded expression on Christine's face, which reminded him of a wrinkled kinrath pup, Kevin inferred that she didn't know what he was talking about—at least for the first second. Then her face turned a unique shade of blue.

"W-w—of course not! How could you even think that?!"

Kevin ignored the strange feeling wiggling inside of his stomach and shrugged. "It's not that I think you and she are, um, together. It's just that Iris kept on making fun of you, and you two are really close, so…"

Christine's expression went flat. "So you thought that Lindsay and I were a couple?"

His face heating up, Kevin looked away and nodded.

She groaned. "I can't believe you would think that. Iris I can understand. She's always trying to get a reaction out of me, but at least she doesn't actually mean it. You sounded like you were seriously asking me that."

"Sorry."

"Whatever. Just forget about it."

He and Christine moved over to a table and sat down. Kevin set the manga that he'd chosen, a good old-fashioned shōnen called *Yu Yu Hakusho*, on the table. Christine set her manga in her lap.

"I want you to know right now that Lindsay is just a friend," Christine said suddenly. "I'm not into girls."

"I understand. Sorry for asking something so stupid."

"As long as you understand."

Silence engulfed them. Kevin tried to pay attention to his manga, but for whatever reason, he felt uncomfortable. Was it because Lilian wasn't with him? Because he was with Christine instead?

It was strange, but when he and Lilian read together, they rarely spoke, engrossed as they were in the story. Being with

357

Christine instead of Lilian, Kevin felt a strange urge to engage in conversation. It was weird.

"I didn't know you were into shōjo manga."

"W-what? You mean this?" Christine let out a strained laugh. "I'm not really into manga or anything. I just started reading a few to see what they were all about. That's all."

"Is that so…?"

"Yes, the only reason I'm reading these manga things is that you and Lilian kept talking about them. No other reason."

"Hmm…"

"W-what?" Christine blushed. "What are you smiling for? Wipe that stupid smile off your face!"

Kevin chuckled, just a bit. "Sorry, I'm not smiling because I'm amused or anything. I'm just glad to see that you're giving manga a shot. Lindsay never gave the stuff that I enjoyed watching or reading a chance. I'm pretty sure that when we all get together and watch anime, she falls asleep."

"She does," Christine admitted. "I'm the one whose shoulder she's drooling on when she falls asleep."

"So what do you think about those?" Kevin gestured toward the manga in her hands.

"Th-they're alright," she admitted, looking down as if she didn't want him to see how blue her blush was. "The stories are decent, and the artwork is really pretty… b-but it's, like, they're not anything special."

Kevin knew that she wasn't being entirely honest. Those manga in her hand were third and fourth volumes, meaning she had already read the previous ones. He didn't call her out on it, though, because he didn't feel like teasing her. That was more Iris's forte anyway.

Just then, a loud explosion blasted across the campus and caused the windows to rattle. He and Christine snapped their heads up and looked in the direction of the nearest window. Smoke was rising from one of the school buildings.

Kevin's eyes widened. "That's where Ms. Vis's classroom is!"

"Let's go!" Christine said.

He and Christine rushed toward the library exit, but they found their way blocked by the head librarian. The normally mousy woman wrapped in a gray skirt and a white-collared shirt stared at them with dead eyes, eyes that contained nothing, eyes that were nothing.

"Ms. Leerge? What are you doing?"

The woman stared at them for a second longer, then, without warning, she lunged at Kevin. Surprised, Kevin reacted on instinct. He fell backward, grabbing onto the woman's outstretched wrists, his feet going straight to her gut as he used the muscles in his legs to lift her off of the ground and toss her behind him. The woman crashed face-first into the floor. He thought she would stay there, but she slowly climbed back to her feet.

Not wanting to stick around, Kevin grabbed Christine's hand and raced out of the door and down the hall. He burst through the double-door exits and rushed onto the campus grounds—only to find himself and Christine surrounded.

"What the heck?!" Kevin shouted. "These are all students from my math class!"

Indeed, everyone in Kevin's class was surrounding them, and even quite a few who weren't in his class were present. They all looked at him and Christine with the same dead eyes as the librarian. What the heck was going on here?

The first one to lunge at Kevin was mercilessly put down when he slammed into the boy with a swift uppercut palm strike. With his legs having been bent to increase his power, Kevin's attack packed a lot of punch. The hapless student was thrown into the air before landing on the ground with a harsh thud. He didn't get back up.

"They've been hypnotized," Christine said in shocked realization. "All of them have been hypnotized by some kind of enchantment!"

The look that Kevin sent her was filled with equal amounts of shock and anger. Was this what Juan had warned him about? "You mean a kitsune did this?"

"Or another yōkai capable of using enchantments." Christine warily eyed the people around them as she answered. Several came at her, but they were all met with small pellets of ice that pelted them, showering their faces and bodies until they fell back underneath the onslaught. "Kitsune don't have a monopoly on enchantments. They're simply the best at using them."

Two more people lunged at Kevin, but through the use of some fancy footwork, he slipped around their attempts and retaliated. The one to his left found a fist planted into their side, a powerful punch that knocked the wind right out of their sails. As the person, a young man, fell to his knees and coughed, Kevin knocked him out with a deft kick to the face.

At the same time, he tripped up the other person by latching onto her arm and swinging her into a group that had been trying to sneak up on them from behind. The people were sent to the ground like bowling pins after a strike.

"So what you're basically telling me is that we have no clue who or what we're up against." Kevin clicked his tongue. "That's just great."

"Seems that way." A ball of ice formed in front of Christine and was then launched right into someone's chest, knocking the person back and causing him to bowl over several other people. "Fortunately, enchantments like these are easy to break—all you have to do is knock them out."

"That's all well and good, but I don't think we have the time for that right now. That explosion came from Ms. Vis's classroom, which means whoever enchanted these people is currently fighting Lilian and Iris. I have to get over there."

Even as he spoke, Kevin wove his way through several attacks, knocking people's legs out from underneath them with swift kicks to the shins. He ducked underneath a punch. His hair swayed as a gust of wind flew over him. Straightening up, he swiftly knocked his attacker unconscious with a head-butt.

"In that case, just leave this to me!" Christine commanded as she sent a blast of freezing cold air at some unfortunate girl. The poor lass was shrouded with frost, which coated her entire body and sapped her strength. She collapsed to the ground seconds later.

"Are you sure?" Kevin spared her a glance after knocking someone out by whacking them in the temple. He hoped they didn't suffer brain damage, but he couldn't afford to go easy on them.

"Don't start acting like some kind of clichéd hero by worrying about everyone," Christine admonished. "You want to rescue Lilian, right? Then this is the only way to reach her in time! Whoever she's facing must be incredibly powerful to subjugate so many people, which means Lilian and the wench are going to need help."

"And even now you call Iris a wench..."

"Oh, stuff it and just go!"

"All right. Thanks, Christine! And be careful! I don't want to see anyone I care about getting hurt, all right?"

Christine saw Kevin run off out of her peripheral vision, knocking out several people with some impressive punches and kicks. She couldn't pay much more attention to him, though, because their ambushers were now enfolded around her.

"Okay," Christine muttered darkly, creating several dozen golf ball-sized pellets that hovered in the air around her. Now that Kevin was gone, she could cut loose without fear of inadvertently hurting him. "I'm warning you all right now that this is going to hurt you a lot more than it hurts me, so you'd better be prepared to wake up with a serious headache!"

***

"Celestial Art: Barrier that Protects the Princess!"

In desperation, Lilian wove a barrier in front of her and Iris. Barely a second later, a large beam of energy slammed into it. The air seemed to scream as she fell to her knees, or maybe that was Iris. Blood trickled down her ears as the earth shook. Cracks appeared along the surface of her shield.

Gritting her teeth, Lilian tried to maintain her barrier, pouring as much youki into it as she dared. The world around them was crumbling. Fragments fell from the ceiling. The ground cracked and dented. Walls broke apart as they were devastated by the aftereffects of the silvery energy beam, which shrieked as if outraged that it couldn't reach its target.

And then it was over. The beam dissipated, and Lilian's barrier shattered.

"L-Lily-pad!" Iris shouted, kneeling down next to her and placing a hand on her shoulder. "A-are you okay?"

"Yeah... I'm fine... how about you?"

"I'm not dead. I suppose that's something."

The room had been destroyed. There was almost nothing left. It reminded Lilian of those decrepit buildings from *Call of Duty*. Seth was nowhere to be seen.

"Let's get out of here," Iris suggested.

"Good idea," Lilian said.

Standing up, Lilian and her sister walked out of the now-ruined building. The campus, or at least the area around them, was empty. Not a soul was in sight. Above them, the shimmering form of a white dome revealed that they were trapped within some kind of barrier, though Lilian couldn't determine which kind. It didn't really matter in the end.

"It looks like we're in trouble," Iris said.

"You think?" Lilian snarked.

"My, oh my. I was sure an attack of that caliber would've killed you, but it looks like you two are stronger than I gave either of you credit for."

Lilian's eyes widened as she looked up. Seth was standing on the roof of a building, though he quickly hopped down. His hands were at his sides, relaxed, and there was a smile on his face.

That feeling, the bloodlust and desire to kill that this man exuded, still lingered in the air, a malignant sensation that tried to fill her with dread. She fought it, though, using the training that she had received from Kotohime to counter such techniques.

Killing intent was the physical manifestation of someone's desire to cause another person harm. To fight it, Lilian created a protective barrier of youki around her body. The feeling lessened.

Standing tall, Lilian moved protectively in front of Iris, whose eyes widened.

"Lily-pad…"

"Why are you here?! What do you want from us?!" Lilian demanded.

Seth chuckled. "Didn't I tell you? I'm here to add you two to my collection."

His tails curled over his shoulder, the tips roaring with strange white flames—no, they weren't flames. A closer examination revealed faces within the flickering fires, tormented faces, and the roaring was, in fact, the cries of agony that those faces howled to the world.

"Those are the Souls of the Damned," Lilian mumbled, her body stiffening in shock. "You're a Spirit Kitsune!"

"Indeed I am. It's so nice of you to finally realize that." Seth's lips twisted into a sickening grin. "Though just knowing what I am isn't going to save you. Now then, why don't you two play with me for a bit? I would like to be entertained before I turn the both of you into my puppets."

363

***

"Spirit Art: Spirit Wave."

The damned souls coalesced in front of Seth before they surged forward at incredible speeds, creating a giant wave that engulfed Lilian and Iris, smothering them.

Or so Seth was led to believe.

"Tch."

Seth clicked his tongue when, upon his wave dispersing with an agonized wail, nothing remained. hellfire that he'd created. His technique didn't burn things to ash. It disconnected a person's spirit from their body. There should have been two soulless corpses lying on the ground.

"Celestial Art: Divine Spears that Strike the Earth."

Looking up, Seth saw hundreds—no, thousands of light spears descending upon his position. It was like a wave of death sent by the gods themselves to smite him.

Seth moved before the first projectile hit. It sank into the ground before dispersing into particles of divine energy. Two more spears flew down. Seth hopped backward, but this time, the spears turned at the last second and shot at him. They followed him, tracking him of their own accord as if they were heat-seeking missiles.

More and more spears fell. Some came one at a time, others descended in twos, threes, and even fours. Seth was forced to constantly move backward and zigzag across the ground. Even reinforcing his body just barely kept him ahead of the attacks.

It wasn't until one came close enough to singe his skin but didn't that he realized what was happening.

"An illusion? How quaint."

With a flare of youki, the illusion shattered. The spears that hovered above him disappeared. All that remained was an empty schoolyard.

Seth narrowed his eyes. "I should have realized your attack was just an illusion. You're a two-tails, so you lack the power required for an actual attack of that level." Silence met him. "Let me guess, your plan was to hem me in with those illusory attacks, and then strike me from behind while I was too busy dodging the fakes. Not a bad strategy. Too bad I'm also a kitsune."

Still no answer.

"Tch! Do you really think you can hide from me?!"

Whirling around, Seth's tails shot forward, extending to well beyond their original length, heading straight for a set of nearby lockers.

"Extension: Spirit Art: Soul Stealer."

The tails struck the lockers with force, but nothing was destroyed. The tails passed right through the lockers like a ghost and came out the other side. Lilian and Iris, who'd been using it as their hiding place, burst out from behind the lockers, racing in opposite directions.

"Oh, no you don't! **Spirit Art: Hellfire.**"

As if it was emerging from the very depths of hell, dark purple flames erupted from the ground and raced forward. The flames branched off, splitting like a fork and traveling in two different directions: one toward Lilian and the other toward Iris. It didn't take long for the hellish fire to overrun them, sweeping over them like a tidal wave of darkness.

There was no way they could have survived that. Hellfire destroyed everything that it touched, consuming even their bones and dragging their souls to the underworld. Seth frowned. He'd been hoping to add them to his collection.

The feeling of something latching onto his legs caused him to look down. Wrapped around his calves were several chains composed entirely out of light.

"What the—"

"Celestial Art: Underground Chambers Prison."

"Void Art: Fires of Oblivion."

Seth looked up in time to see a wall of flames even blacker than his own rush across the ground. It was dark. Malevolence pulsed from it. He could practically feel the fire's hunger, its desire to consume everything, from where he stood.

Void fire. The flames of a Void Kitsune.

He tried to move, to escape, but the chains were impossible to escape from. He was unable to do anything but struggle as the flames blazed toward him, consuming the pavement and leaving nothing but black gravel in its wake.

The fires of the Void swept over him, not even giving him time to yell as his body was consumed by the flames. His screams of pain echoed throughout the school until even those screams became nothing more than incoherent gurgles.

***

Several feet away, two forms shimmered into existence, revealing themselves to be Lilian and Iris. They watched as the three-tailed kitsune was consumed by the Void.

"It looks like we've beaten him," Lilian said as she stared at the burning body.

"I'm surprised by how weak he was," Iris agreed.

"Weak, am I?" a voice asked. "Do you really think I'm so weak that I'd allow myself to be killed by a pair of two-tails?"

Lilian and Iris gasped when the man they'd set on fire—or so they thought—disappeared like a ghost. That same man then emerged from Ms. Vis's partially destroyed classroom and dashed at them quicker than they believed possible.

He chose Lilian as his target, deeming her the weaker link. His left hand, coated in misty ectoplasm, or spirit matter, lashed out with a palm strike that Lilian avoided by spinning around and moving backward, taking her out of Seth's strike range.

"Extension."

Her two tails extended to beyond their normal length, their tips engulfed in the divine energy of a Celestial Kitsune.

"Celestial Art: Flare."

The divine energy leaped from Lilian's tails and took the shape of two spheres, which shot across the distance separating her from Seth like bullets.

The three-tailed kitsune dove out of the way. The first sphere struck the ground that he'd been standing on a second later, going off in a brilliant blaze of light like a supernova. The sphere expanded, retaining its perfectly spherical shape as it grew to encompass a two-foot radius. Seconds later, the second sphere struck the ground and the same thing happened. When the spheres disappeared, they left a perfectly smooth dome-shaped crater in their wake.

Seth landed on the ground several feet away and whistled at the destruction caused by Lilian's technique. Sure, they weren't large craters, but the fact that they were created by a two-tails said a lot about the girl's potential.

"Oh, boy. Would you look at that? It's almost a shame I've gotta kill you. So much potential wasted."

"As if I'd let you kill my Lily-pad," Iris shouted.

"Void Art: The Eye of Oblivion."

The world around Seth vanished. Darkness engulfed everything. Looking around revealed nothing, for this was a world in which nothing existed.

"An illusion?"

As the words were spoken, the world became engulfed in hellish flames. Void fire surrounded him on all sides. There was no heat being emitted, for Void fire was not hot. It was not a fire that burned, but one that consumed.

High above his position, a slit appeared within the tapestry of reality. It opened, parting to reveal a blood-red eye surrounded by infinite darkness. From the eye a flame emerged, descending upon

Seth like the torrential downpour of a fierce storm. Seth watched the fires set on consuming him loom ever closer.

He sighed, flared his youki, and shattered the illusion before it could make him believe he'd been consumed by the Void. Seth was once again standing outside, with school buildings surrounding him and pavement under his feet.

"Celestial Art: Orbs of an Evanescent Realm."

"Hmm? What this?"

Half a dozen spheres composed of light appeared before Seth, surrounding him. Each sphere hovered about two feet away from each other, forming a circle around him. The spheres were still for but a moment before shooting at him with speeds that made them appear as mere blurs.

Seth remained still, not even moving when the spheres reached him. The orbs of light energy phased right through him as if he wasn't there. His body flickered once, twice, and then it vanished.

"An illusion!" Lilian shouted.

"Don't act so surprised," a voice said behind her. "You should have known that I'd never let someone hit me with an attack like that, just as you should have realized that you were only attacking an illusion. Really, what kind of kitsune are you?"

Lilian turned her head to glare at Seth, who stood directly behind her. The three-tails grinned as his hand, once more covered in ectoplasm, shot straight for her back.

"Lilian!" Iris screamed when she saw what was happening.

"Spirit Art: Soul Steal—eh?"

Seth blinked when his hand traveled through Lilian's body. While that was supposed to happen when he used this technique, there should have been some resistance as he fought to penetrate the thin layer of youki that surrounded her. He also should have grabbed her soul, which he couldn't feel in his grasp. That meant...

Lilian vanished and a long, hard tail smacked him flush in the face. The attack lifted him off the ground and sent him sailing through the air.

"Iris, now!"

"Right! **Void Art: Void Fire.**"

Iris launched a blast of Void fire at Seth's falling form. The red-haired man clicked his tongue as he spun about in midair, righting himself so that his feet were oriented toward the ground.

"Extension."

His tails raced down, spearing the earth and acting as anchors before rapidly retracting and pulling him down, allowing him to avoid the Void fire, which continued racing through the sky until it ran out of youki and dissipated.

As Seth landed on the ground, he was attacked by Lilian, who came in close to attack him with hand-to-hand techniques—or so he thought. When his hand phased through the redhead's body like it wasn't there, he realized it was just an illusion.

"Celestial Art: Sphere of Light."

Seth moved to the side, avoiding the light sphere that tried to strike him from behind. The sphere continued traveling on, smacking against a wall and detonating, leaving a small black scorch mark.

"You're quite talented," Seth said, grinning as he sent off a crescent wave of damned souls at Lilian. His grin widened when the attack phased through her. "I've never met a two-tails with as much talent for the kitsune arts as you."

Lilian stood several yards from Seth, having reappeared from within another illusion, her eyes narrowed in clear annoyance at the failure of her last attack. "Being complimented by you doesn't make me very happy. There is only one person in this entire world whose compliments mean anything to me, and you aren't him."

"Hm hm hm." Seth's stifled chuckles, though quiet, were heard clearly by Lilian, whose fur bristled. "You're talking about your mate, aren't you? That human boy, Kevin Swift. It really is too bad you'll never see him again, even if you did manage to defeat me."

Lilian felt alarmed by his words. Standing by her side, Iris jolted upright as if she'd been struck by lightning. "What do you mean by that?"

"Only that I've sent one of my subordinates after him," Seth said. "An incredibly talented yōkai who's actually stronger than I am, though she doesn't have the talent for killing that I do. It doesn't matter, though. Even if she can't kill other yōkai to save her life, killing one measly human won't be a problem for someone like her."

As Seth drank in her expression like it was a fine wine, Lilian felt fear course through her body. Her mate was in danger!

"Beloved!"

Lilian tried to run off and find her mate, but Seth blocked her path, appearing before her and then splitting apart like a cell going through osmosis. Each figure wavered around her like a ghost. Each face wore a ghastly grin that raised Lilian's hackles. Over to her left, her sister was in the same situation as her, surrounded by ghostly figures that wavered like candles flickering in a breeze.

"I'm sorry, but there's no way I'm going to let you leave. Neither you nor your sister is going anywhere. You're both mine."

Seth didn't give Lilian time to retort before the copies lunged.

***

Sweat poured down Christine's face as she finished knocking out all of the enchanted students.

She'd never been forced to use her powers so extensively before. She had rarely ever used her powers period. Yet in the past few minutes, she'd had to incapacitate upwards of a hundred students and even a few teachers. It was insane! How many people could this yōkai have under his or her thrall?

Standing in front of the library building, surrounded by a pile of bodies, Christine caught her second wind. She didn't know what was going on, if that was all of the people who'd been enchanted, or if there were more waiting in the wings. She hoped that wasn't the case. She was tired. She needed to rest.

Too bad she wasn't going to get any respite.

Rushing out from behind the walls were several people that she'd recognize anywhere: Alex, Andrew, and Eric, who were all holding the same zombie-esque appearance she'd seen them wearing during lunch. They charged at her, but Christine wasn't in the mood for playing games. Three balls of ice formed in front of her. Those same three balls of ice struck the trio right in the cranium, knocking them out cold.

"Ha… idiots," she muttered in disgust.

The sound of something clicking alerted her to the danger that she was in seconds before the sound of a thunderclap went off. Christine had just enough time to throw herself to the ground. She bit back a yelp as her elbows smacked against the concrete. She rolled along the pavement as more gunshots rang out, then scrambled to her feet after the gun clicked empty.

Christine had planned to turn around, confront the person shooting at her, and beat them with an ice club.

She never got the chance.

A set of arms wrapped around her body, pinning her arms to her sides. Christine struggled, but she couldn't break out of this person's hold. She turned her head and received the shock of her life.

"Lindsay?!"

Her friend stood behind her, pinning her in place. Lindsay's eyes stared at her with the same blank look that she had seen on everyone else.

The sound of a gun cocking alerted her to the fact that she was still in danger. She looked away from her friend to where the noise had come from.

Heather was standing a few feet away. There was some kind of handgun in her grasp. She also wore an empty expression on her face.

A single gunshot rang out, echoing across the school.

***

Kevin ran across the campus, cursing, or as close to cursing as Kevin got.

Why did Ms. Vis's classroom have to be on the other side of the school? Couldn't they have put it just a little closer to the library? Now he had to run all the way across the large campus, and while he excelled at running, he was more of a sprinter than a long-distance runner.

The school was practically empty, or at least the area that he was running through was. It was probably because all of the people who stayed after, those who had been enchanted, had congregated around Christine's location. He was worried about his friend, but he also had faith that she'd be all right. He'd only seen her ice abilities in action once, against Kiara's three goons, but they'd left an impression. If anyone could stop those people, it would be her.

He arrived at the shaded patio, the place where he and his friends ate lunch, which meant he was about halfway there.

Someone was standing in his way.

Kevin skidded to a stop, his heart thudding in his chest. She was decked out in black leather pants, a leather shirt, and leather boots. Her raven-colored hair was tied into a ponytail and her yellow eyes were shining like moons. Two tails waved behind her, and a pair of cat ears twitched incessantly on her head. Cassy stood before him in all her glory.

"Cassy…"

"I won't let you go past this point, nya," Cassy said, her eyes gleaming.

CHAPTER 11

A Reason to Never Give Up

THE BATTLE HAD NOT BEEN going as well as Lilian had hoped it would. While it seemed like she and Iris were holding their own at first, it soon became clear that Seth had been toying with them since the beginning. Every attack they sent his way had been defeated with ease. Every illusion they put him under didn't work or only worked long enough to let them avoid being outright annihilated. Worse still, she and her sister were running out of youki.

"What's the matter? Are you done already?" Seth asked, grinning from ear to ear. He was obviously enjoying this fight way too much. "Surely you two aren't finished. And here I was hoping fighting two on one would be a challenge."

"You're a sadist, you know that?" Iris said through clenched teeth. "Who the hell enjoys beating on a bunch of girls so much?"

Standing behind Seth, Iris had definitely seen better days. A good portion of her clothing was ripped, including her shirt, which looked like it had been slashed apart by a set of claws. The entire lower half was missing, exposing her flat tummy and the underside of her breasts. She was bleeding from a wound on her stomach.

Not that Lilian was in much better shape. Her torso was bruised, blood dripping down her left thigh from where she'd been stabbed by flying debris. Body aching. Lungs burning. Lilian had expended a lot more youki than her sister. In terms of who was more physically damaged, Iris was the victor, but in terms of who was in worse shape, that award belonged to Lilian.

Iris glanced at Lilian, a statement in her eyes. *"Buy me some time,"* it seemed to say. Lilian nodded her head.

I need to keep Seth busy.

"Why are you doing this? If you're so strong, how come you haven't killed us yet?" Lilian asked.

"Heh… for you to say that shows you clearly don't understand the joys of crushing your victims." Seth spread his arms wide. "Not that I blame you. Few people are able to comprehend how enthralling it is to watch the hope fade from the eyes of people before you kill them, of the crushing weight that comes from knowing, beyond a shadow of a doubt, that they are going to die by my hands." The man shuddered with almost orgasmic bliss. "Even the people in my village don't seem to understand the pleasure that I derive from snuffing the lives out of my enemies."

This man was insane. However, after listening to his words, the two sisters picked up something curious about them.

"What do you mean your village?" asked Lilian.

"Oops, did I mention my village? Must have been a slip of the tongue."

Lilian wasn't fooled for a second. This man was arrogant and loved bragging, but he wasn't stupid. A man like him wouldn't have a "slip of the tongue."

"But yes, that is correct. I come from a small village here in the United States, you see. We're a tiny place in an undisclosed location that I certainly won't be giving you directions to. All you need to know is that we're sort of like a village of mercenaries. We get hired by various people to do jobs for them, and we're the best at getting the job done."

"You mean you're assassins." Lilian narrowed her eyes. "I've heard of you people. You're part of a group of yōkai who kill others for money. A hidden village."

"Hidden village" was a term used for a group of "villages" where yōkai assassins were raised. They took jobs from humans and yōkai alike. No job was too dirty, no task too unclean, so long as the pay was good.

The leaders who were in charge of these villages kept their locations a secret, even from each other. According to Kotohime, this was done as a safety precaution. Even if one of the villages was discovered and dismantled, the others would still be safe.

"I'm surprised you know even that much about us. Then again, you are the granddaughter of Delphine Pnévma. I suppose it's only natural that someone like her would make sure her heirs are well-informed about the dangers in this world."

Lilian gritted her teeth in anger. "I've got a newsflash for you, jerk. The matriarch didn't tell me a single thing about you or anyone else! Everything I know I learned from Kotohime!"

She tried not to look at Iris for fear of tipping Seth off to what her sister was doing. Darkness gathered around Iris's tails. Lilian didn't know how long it would take for Iris to finish, but she needed to keep Seth occupied for a little while longer.

"Ah, yes, the famed Blood Moon Princess. I should have guessed that she would be the one to teach you about us. I hear she was offered a position among our ranks once. Isn't she your bodyguard these days?" The smirk on Seth's face bugged the crap out of Lilian. She wanted to wipe it off with a spirit bomb to the face. "I wonder where she is now. Too bad she's not here to save you, eh?"

Rather than grow flustered, Lilian gave Seth a grin. "I don't need Kotohime to save me. You've already lost."

"Eh?"

"Void Art: The All-Consuming Flame."

While Lilian kept Seth talking, Iris had gathered as much Void fire as she could and compressed it into a tiny sphere about the size of a baseball. Hovering above the tips of her tails, which had curled around her body like some kind of strange pseudopodia, the tiny orb crackled with repressed energy, flames leaping from its surface like the hungry tentacles of an abominable horror from the abyss.

Sweat poured down Iris's forehead. She gritted her teeth. Then, when she'd gathered as much youki as she dared, she launched the attack at Seth.

The sphere blasted forward at speeds that he had no hope of dodging.

Too bad he didn't need to dodge.

Lilian's eyes widened when the flame passed right through him as if he wasn't even there.

"Another illusion!"

She couldn't believe it. When had he replaced himself with an illusory image? Lilian wasn't given time to think about it as a voice echoed out all around her.

"Spirit Art: Damned Souls, Cursed Guardians."

The earth around them was rent asunder, cracking and splitting apart like something out of a video game. From within the many crevices created, white mist poured out. Ghoulish shrieks emerged from the depths, haunting voices that cursed the living, that demanded revenge, that desired death. Lilian trembled as feelings of hatred, of jealousy, of rage, swept over her like a deluge.

"Lily-pad!" Iris rushed to her side, hopping over chasms with reinforced limbs.

"Watch out, Iris!"

A gunshot rang out. It missed Iris by mere inches, shooting through her fluttering hair instead of her head. Iris landed on the ground and raised a hand to her hair, her eyes bulging from their sockets like a demented chibi figurine.

"What the... he almost shot me!"

"You need to be more careful," Lilian admonished—right before the earth shook violently. "Something's coming."

Indeed. Crawling out from the abysmal splits that rent the schoolyard were several skeletal figures, decked out in the tattered uniforms of Confederate soldiers. They rose bearing muskets, with hats on their heads and empty eye sockets that gleamed red.

"Now then, my eternal warriors!" Seth's voice rang out clearly enough for Lilian and Iris to hear, but not to determine his location. "Kill them. However, be sure not to damage them too badly. I still want to add them to my collection."

As the undead skeletons took aim with outdated muskets, Iris and Lilian stood back-to-back.

"So," Iris started, warily eying their new bony enemies. "Got any ideas?"

"..."

"You don't have any, do you?"

"... I'm sure I'll think of something," Lilian said as the skeletons placed their bony fingers on the triggers. "... I hope."

"That doesn't inspire much confidence."

"Hawa..."

* * *

Kevin stared at the woman that he had met a few weeks ago at the grocery store. She wore the same clothes that he'd first met her in. However, that was the only thing about her that remained unchanged. Her expression, her countenance, everything about her contained a sobriety that made him hesitate.

There was also the cat tail that jutted out from her tailbone, splitting in half to look like two cat tails, and the cat ears that twitched on her head. She was a yōkai, a nekomata, to be exact.

"Cassy, what are you doing here?" His body felt tense, coiled, like a loaded spring. The hairs on his arms and neck were tingling. "Why are you here? Are you working for whoever is fighting Lilian right now?"

When all Cassy did was look away, Kevin felt his gut clench as he realized something. All those times that Cassy had shown up while he did his Sunday newspaper run, they hadn't been coincidental meetings. She'd been watching him, spying on him, learning his secrets, and he'd let her. He'd allowed himself to grow complacent around her.

"Why are you doing this?" Kevin asked, his voice a low growl. "Why are you working for whoever's trying to kill Lilian? Tell me why, Cassy!"

Cassy flinched, but she quickly mastered herself and presented him with a scowl. "You wanna know why I'm here? Fine! I'll tell you! I'm here because right now the person I'm being forced to work under is about to kill your girlfriend, and I'm going to make sure you don't get in his way!"

Kevin clenched his fists and gritted his teeth. He'd figured that much, but hearing her say it still hurt. While he wasn't close to this woman, they'd gotten along pretty well whenever they met up. He'd kind of thought of her as a big sister, all teasing and playful, but also kind of helpless, just like a real good-for-nothing yet well-meaning big sister.

I need to stop watching anime.

"Fine then," Kevin gritted out. "If you're going to stand in my way, then I'm just going to move you!"

"Don't think it will be that easy." Cassy's feet slid across the pavement. Her center of gravity lowered, fists rising in a basic karate stance. "In case you haven't noticed, I'm a yōkai, a nekomata. Fighting me isn't going to be like fighting a two-tails."

Kevin slid into his own stance. He felt the small gun in his back pocket shift. Should he use it? No. Cassy said that she was working under someone, and that someone was fighting Lilian and Iris. If he used the single bullet that his gun had now, then he would be useless against whoever they were fighting. He had to deal with Cassy without using his sole firearm.

"You think so, huh? Then listen up because I'm only going to say this once." Kevin's eyes narrowed into a fierce glare. "I don't care if you're human or yōkai. It doesn't matter to me. Nothing is going to stop me from reaching Lilian and Iris. I might be a human, but that doesn't mean I'm not without any tricks up my sleeve. Underestimate me and you're going to be in for a world of hurt!"

Kevin spoke with enough confidence that anyone who knew him would have thought he was being serious.

However, Kevin knew the truth.

He was in a lot of trouble.

***

A shield of ice sprung up in front of Christine. The bullet ricocheted off it. Heather didn't frown, but she did reload her gun and open fire again.

Christine winced as more bullets tried to penetrate her shield. They wouldn't break through it so long as she continued pumping youki into it, but that was also dependent on her not running out of youki before Heather ran out of bullets.

"Lindsay, what are you doing? Let me go!"

Even though Christine implored her friend, Lindsay didn't let go. If anything, her grip tightened, and Christine couldn't break out of it. She was a yuki-onna. They were known for their powers over ice, not their physical prowess. They were no stronger than a human—weaker in some cases. Lindsay, with her athletic abilities, was far stronger than Christine.

"Why are you doing this, Lindsay? Let me go! You need to snap out of it!"

Several more bullets clanged off her ice shield, chipping away at it. Because she was connected to her ice, Christine felt each piece that was blasted away by Heather's bullets. She repaired the damaged areas, but it took up a lot of her youki—certainly more than it would have for a pureblood yuki-onna. Christine, with her half yuki-onna/half-nekomata status, needed to use a lot more energy to create something as complex as an ice shield.

"Please, Lindsay, you have to let me go! She'll kill us both if you keep me trapped like this!"

More gunfire. More ice fell away. Cracks appeared on the surface of her shield like a black widow's intricate web.

"Lindsay, you need to snap out of it! Please! You're my friend and I don't want to lose you like this! Don't let the bastard control you!"

But Lindsay didn't let go. She gripped Christine all the more tightly, burying her face nose-first in Christine's back. Christine started to struggle some more, but then she stopped when she noticed something that tore at her heart.

Lindsay's body was shaking. Christine's back was getting wet. Lindsay was crying. Even though someone was controlling her, she still seemed at least subconsciously aware of what she was doing, and she was crying because she couldn't do anything about it. She was crying because some bastard was making her fight against one of her friends, and she could only do what she was commanded.

Because she's human and the dickweed controlling her is a yōkai.

Fire flooded her veins. The thought enraged Christine. Who gave someone the right to cast an enchantment on her friend? What right did he or she have to steal her friend's freedom? Who was the prick that would be tasting her boot when she escaped from this troublesome predicament?

Heather's gunfire continued.

The ice dome shattered into thousands of crystalline fragments.

The remaining fragments, along with the bullets released from Heather's gun, melted as flames of the purest white burst from the ground and formed a circle around Christine and Lindsay, who

Christine rendered unconscious with a strike to the temple. It hurt to injure her friend, but it hurt even more to see her being controlled.

A tail popped out from underneath her lolita dress. Cat ears protruded from within her hair. Her canines became longer while her nails lengthened and turned into claws.

N-nya! Christine, what are nyou doing?!

I'm protecting my friend. What's it look like I'm doing?

Nya, nya, nya! Nyou can't do that! Nyou haven't learned how to control nyour powers. Also, nyour body is still that of a yuki-onna! If nyou use our power, it will—

That's fine. I don't care.

Her nekomata half fell silent. Christine, sweat pouring from her body, caking her outfit to her skin, glared daggers at the still-enchanted Heather.

"I don't know who this bastard thinks he is, but he had better pray to whatever god he worships that Kevin finishes him off before I get to him because if I find him, I'm going to shove my foot so far up his ass it's going to come out of his throat!"

The flames began to gather, swirling around Christine as she crouched on the ground, holding Lindsay close. The fires then morphed, gaining coherency and form.

Standing on four legs as it towered Christine and Lindsay, as if protecting them from all threats, was a giant cat made of bright white flames.

***

Kevin backpedaled away from Cassy as she swiped at him with her claws. Her right hand made a slashing motion from left to right. Kevin halted his backward movement by placing his left foot behind him, bracing his body as he ducked down and avoided the swipe. Air rustled his hair. Her attack had nearly taken his head off! Gritting his teeth, he came back up, pushing himself into a rising punch that smashed into Cassy's jaw.

"Iron Human Fist!"

At least, he would have smashed into Cassy's jaw, if the nekomata hadn't jumped back, avoiding the strike entirely.

She stared at him incredulously as he set himself in another stance. "Did you actually name your punch 'Iron Human Fist'? Seriously? What kind of name is that?"

Despite the situation, Kevin's cheeks gained a brilliant heat as if Cassy had shot him in the face with hellfire. "Ah... well, I'm not very good at naming things, so I thought I'd take the name of an attack in a manga I read and just changed some of the words. You know, to avoid copyright issues and stuff."

"Um, what?"

"Never mind that! I've still got to rescue Lilian and Iris, and you're not going to stop me!"

Kevin rushed forward, meeting Cassy in a blur of fists and feet. It became immediately apparent to him that his opponent's style was much more refined than his own. While his style was still sloppy and full of holes, Cassy's was graceful and agile, like a cat. Her fists came in swifter than lightning, trying to pick him apart with swift jabs that wove around his guard as if her fists were water flowing around a rock. Kevin blocked them as best he could, but she proved to be much faster than him.

Dang. Picking a fight with a yōkai really was a pain. Maybe he should have tried something else? It was too bad there wasn't anything there that he could use against her.

As another fist slipped around his guard and stung his face, Kevin realized that he really did need to think of another way to defeat this woman. She may not have had the strength of a gorilla yōkai, but she was still more skilled than him. She was also stronger, faster, and more experienced—a bad combination if there ever was one.

A glance around revealed that he was right next to a classroom. The door was probably locked, but it still had a window. Without a second thought, Kevin ducked under another punch, spun around, and then ran straight for the window. He leaped, crashing into it and causing it to shatter like, well, glass.

"Ow!!"

Kevin winced as he crouched on the ground, pulling out several glass shards that jutted from his skin. They weren't very deep, but they still hurt.

"How come all the movies and anime I've seen make jumping through windows look so easy? Why did that hurt so much?"

A shadow leaped in through the window. It was Cassy. She landed on her feet several meters away, standing on top of a desk, which she crouched upon much like a cat.

"I can't believe you just jumped through a window like that, nya. When did you get so reckless?"

"Oh, stuff it," Kevin grumbled as he finished pulling the small glass fragments out of his arms. The wounds bled a little, but he determined that they wouldn't hamper his fighting ability. "I'm a human fighting a yōkai. I took a calculated risk and thought jumping through a window into a classroom would let me deal with you better."

"Was it really a calculated risk?"

"... No, it was spur of the moment," Kevin admitted sheepishly. "But that doesn't mean it wasn't a good idea."

"I suppose, nya." Cassy observed all of the desks that cluttered the room. "You probably assumed that all of these desks and other objects would hamper my mobility, didn't you? That would normally be a solid plan, but you're forgetting something important, nya."

"Oh, yeah? What's that?"

"I'm a nekomata. A cat yōkai. We're the most agile race in the entire world. Avoiding stationary objects is a simple matter for us. If anything, you're the one who's going to find their movements hampered in this room."

"Well, shoot." Kevin scratched the back of his neck. "I really didn't think this through, did I?"

"No," Cassy agreed. "No, you did not."

***

The fire cat leaped at Heather with a ferocious pounce, forcing the woman to dodge. When it landed, flames burst from its feet, scorching the ground.

The construct wouldn't last long. Christine had never used her nekomata powers before. Chances were good that her flames would only last for a few more seconds.

A few seconds was all she needed.

As gunshots went off, striking the fire cat to no effect, Christine used the distraction presented to escape. With Lindsay being carried by her via piggyback, she scampered away, not caring which direction she ran so long as it wasn't near Heather. While she'd managed to avoid human casualties through luck, that wouldn't last if the fight continued around all those unconscious people.

Thinking back on it, she probably shouldn't have taken Lindsay with her, but it was too late to change her mind now.

Her breathing had already grown ragged after barely a minute of running. Sweat formed on her brow. She wasn't an athlete. Running around while carrying Lindsay while also wearing a lolita dress was hard.

Fortunately, the gymnasium was close by.

Entering the large gymnasium, Christine rushed through the halls at random. It didn't matter where she went. She merely needed to disappear so she could think about her next course of action.

As she ran, Christine thought about her situation. She had an enchanted Heather chasing after her with a gun, an unconscious Lindsay on her back, and she was running low on youki. Things definitely weren't looking good. Why did she agree to stick around and fight again? Oh, right. Lilian and Iris were in trouble. Curse her bleeding heart.

A gunshot went off, echoing in the hall. Sparks exploded against the tiles near her left foot. Christine cursed. She'd been hoping for more time.

As more bullets flowed around her, Christine ducked through the nearest door and found herself in the back room of the theater. With barely any light to illuminate her path, she ran through the backstage, avoiding the various props. The door burst open just as she ducked around a corner and into a hallway filled with more doors. Choosing the first one available, she ducked in and closed the door before locking it.

Christine did her best to regain control of her breathing as she walked further into the room. Her feet sank into the soft carpet. Mirrors and stools stood off to one side, while a table sat on the other. This place looked like a dressing room. Still...

How the heck can our school afford something like this?

She knew that a school with a theater club had to have a changing room, but this was a little too nice, a little too luxurious. It must have cost a fortune. Could a school afford to spend their money so frivolously like this?

It was while she was thinking these thoughts that Christine noticed it, the camera that was situated in the left-most corner of the room.

That was when she realized that Eric's father, the principal, had probably made this room to get a free peep show.

A second later, several tiny needles of ice penetrated the camera, which burst into sparks and smoke.

"Damn pervert," Christine grumbled before walking further into the room.

A couch sat in the back, against the wall, which was where she set Lindsay. The girl fell over, unable to stay upright, so Christine tried to straighten her friend's limbs. Then she stood up and walked back to the door, grabbing a foldout chair along the way and pressing her back against the wall.

She tried to slow down her breathing and calm her rapidly beating heart as she strained her ears to listen through the door. She could hear footsteps, softly at first but growing louder—Heather, no doubt. The footsteps increased in volume at the same time that her heartbeat seemed to increase in speed.

And then the footsteps stopped. Christine found breathing impossible. Did Heather know where she was hiding? She waited, her heart hammering in her chest. She wished she could see what was happening on the other side.

The footsteps started up again, and Christine thought she might die of relief. Opening the door as slowly and quietly as possible, she slipped outside. Heather was walking further down the hall. Her back was turned.

Moving as stealthily as possible, Christine crept closer to the woman. She raised the chair over her head, preparing to bash the woman and knock her out cold. That was the plan anyway.

Unfortunately, Heather didn't seem to be very cooperative.

Quicker than Christine believed possible, the woman spun around and kicked her in the stomach. The chair clattered to the floor as her hands went to her gut, which felt like a jackhammer had slammed into it. Bile rose to her throat. She forced it down as she stumbled backward.

How could a human be this strong? Had Heather strapped one-hundred-pound weights to her legs to increase her strength?

The woman aimed her gun, but a ball of ice struck her hand and knocked the gun away, causing it to fly into the darkness and clatter to the floor somewhere out of their sight. This didn't deter Heather. She rushed in before Christine could create more ice.

A strike to the face caused Christine to stumble back. Raising her hand to her stinging left cheek, Christine tried to gather her powers and smack the assistant PE coach with a golf ball-sized ice cube.

Heather dodged, ducking low and pushing off the ground with her legs to come at Christine before she could do anything else. A hand slammed into Christine's jaw. Her vision went white. She could've sworn she felt something break just then.

I never realized humans could hit so hard!

This would have been so much easier if Heather wasn't a victim in all this. If she was another yōkai or an evil human, Christine wouldn't have had to play it so safe. It was bad luck that she was fighting someone familiar, someone that she didn't want to hurt.

Yuki-onna were not fighters. They were neither good at it nor did they enjoy it. Most of them preferred a peaceful life.

Christine was no different in that regard, and it showed as Heather continued to pummel her with punches and kicks that felt like tiny mallets smacking her with concussive force.

Blood and spittle flew from her mouth as a fist planted itself in her gut. Her head snapped back when a knee broke her nose. Her vision became blurry and disoriented as two palms were thrust into her chest, knocking the wind from her lungs. Everything turned into a dizzying display of blurred lines and silhouettes.

A kick smashed into her with enough force to lift her off her feet. Christine opened her mouth to scream, but then her back smashed into something hard and unyielding, and she felt like she'd swallowed her tongue. That something shattered underneath her.

Christine heard a scream, though it took her a second to realize that she was the one screaming. Her body twitched with micro-spasms. Her back hurt. She'd never felt pain like this. Her vision was blurry and darkness crowded around the edges. Gritting her teeth, she tried to force herself to remain conscious. She'd be killed if she didn't.

A shadow loomed over her. Heather's fuzzy face swam into view. She was holding the gun again, which was pointed right at her.

So this is it, huh?

Christine closed her eyes and sighed. She knew that she should have been frightened, but at that moment, all she could think about were her friends. Was Lindsay okay and waking up right now? How were Alex, Andrew, and Eric doing? She really hoped that Eric had a huge migraine from her ice sphere, the damn pervert. Of all the people she thought about, the most important was...

Did Kevin manage to save Lilian and Iris?

It was pathetic. She was staring down the barrel of a gun, awaiting death, and all she could think about was Kevin. Heather's finger went to the trigger. Christine watched the finger begin to squeeze it as if in slow motio—

BAM!

Christine blinked as a loud noise echoed all around her. Heather blinked several times as if she was confused. Then her eyes rolled up into the back of her head, and the woman crumpled to the floor, revealing a conscious Lindsay standing behind her, a bent folding chair in her grip.

"Lindsay?"

"Are you all right, Christine?"

Christine needed a second to think up a response. "Um, yes?"

"That's good." Lindsay breathed a sigh of relief. "I'm glad you're safe."

"Me too," Christine mumbled.

"By the way..." Lindsay started again, scratching at her cheek with an index finger. "You wouldn't happen to know what's going on, would you? Because the last thing I remember was going to the bathroom and then waking up on a couch. Where are we? Why are we here? Why was Heather pointing a gun at you?"

Christine stared at Lindsay with a sense of incredulity, then looked down at Heather, who was sporting a rather prominent bump on her head. She glanced at Lindsay. Then Heather. Lindsay one more time… and then she began laughing.

Lindsay pouted. "I fail to see what's so funny about this!"

"I-I'm sorry," Christine said between chuckles. "I didn't mean t-to—to laugh or anything. You're right, this situation isn't very funny, but for some reason, I-I can't stop laughing…"

Lindsay's pout reached new levels. Several large veins also popped out on her forehead, as if to convey her annoyance. However, she still held out her hand to help Christine up.

"Come on. Let's get you somewhere so I can check for injuries. Then you can tell me all about what's happening and why I have a headache."

"Okay."

After a few more chuckles, Christine and Lindsay walked back to the changing room.

As her pixie-haired friend bade her sit down and began checking for injuries, Christine's mind went toward her other friends.

I hope those three are all right.

***

Kevin was not all right. He was not all right at all. From the moment he'd decided that jumping into a classroom was a good idea, he'd been on the defensive.

Cassy was an incredibly agile fighter. She didn't just weave through the desks. She used the desks as springboards, leaping from one to another, or jumping from one to the ceiling and then launching herself at him from above like an avenging angel. He'd been forced to use every unorthodox method he knew to avoid getting hit.

In short, the battle really wasn't going as planned.

Something that Kevin took specific notice of about Cassy was her speed. She was quick, to be sure, but she didn't move as fast as he thought she would. She also didn't hit as hard. While she'd gotten plenty of strikes in and all of them stung, none of them were debilitating. Her strength was about what he imagined a really strong human would have.

"Nya!"

Like a cat leaping from the dining room table, Cassy sprung at him from the ceiling. Kevin hit the floor, shoulder-rolling away and skipping back up. He then had to block a series of bicycle kicks as Cassy leaped at him from a desk.

His forearms stung as they were assaulted by numerous swift attacks. Each strike thudded against his arm like baseballs being thrown by a star pitcher. He managed to block the worst of it, but one of them got through and clipped his ear. He hissed. The nekomata landed back on the ground and came at him with a straight-on frontal assault.

Cassy swiped at him. Kevin spun around. The attack whooshed against his clothes, which tore across his chest. He felt his pectorals being exposed to the mild air.

Moving backward, Kevin avoided numerous punches while blocking those that he couldn't. Several still made it through, pummeling his chest, arms, and face. However, while each attack stung, they didn't hurt.

A fist whizzed by his ear as he tilted his head at an angle. Cassy retracted her hand, which had nearly clawed him across the face, and immediately launched a series of high and mid kicks. He was forced to raise his arms to block. Each successive strike thudded against his forearms, stinging like dozens of mutant wasps. Kevin gritted his teeth and rode the attacks out, constantly backing away.

There has to be something around here that I can use.

Kevin couldn't afford to take his eyes off his opponent, for doing so would be all but asking her to defeat him. He rapidly glanced around the room. He moved around, forcing Cassy to turn with him so he could study the room's layout while keeping his eyes on her as well. Several bruises formed on his skin from continuously getting hit. It wasn't until Kevin started to worry for his health that he located something that could help him.

The fire extinguisher.

If it worked once before...

Changing his plans, Kevin continued retreating, but this time, he moved toward the extinguisher. If Cassy knew about his intentions, she didn't let on. Her attacks came in with the same speed as before, and they still lacked the punch that he would have expected. Soon, Kevin's back was pressed against the wall.

"You're a persistent fighter, nya," Cassy said. Her breathing was a lot heavier than he imagined it should have been.

"That's because I can't afford to give up," Kevin said.

"Tch! In that case, I'll make nyou give up, nya!"

As Cassy sprang at him again, Kevin grabbed the fire extinguisher and used it to block the nekomata's latest attack. The loud ringing of Cassy's fist meeting the metal extinguisher filled the air, followed quickly by the cat woman's pained howl.

"NYA!!"

Kevin didn't waste this opportunity and quickly shot the woman in the face with the extinguisher's contents. Cassy stumbled back, her hands going to her eyes and rubbing at them as she hacked and coughed. He used her distracted state to sneak away. He left the classroom, closed the door behind him, and ran toward Ms. Vis's classroom again.

He didn't know how much time had elapsed during his fight, but surely Lilian and Iris were still in trouble. He needed to—

W-what?

Kevin's eyes widened as his legs ceased to function and he tumbled to the ground. Pain flooded him as his face smacked hard concrete. Groaning, he pushed the pain aside and tried to move, to get up. However, his body wouldn't obey him. When he attempted to move his left arm, his right index finger twitched. When he tried moving his right arm, his left leg would twitch. No matter what he did, his body refused to respond like it was supposed to.

"What's going on?"

Footsteps reached his ears.

"I scrambled your body's nervous system," Cassy said. A pair of bare feet with leather straps wrapped around the arches appeared in his field of vision. "You didn't think all those baby punches I gave you were for no reason, did you? Each time I hit you, I aimed for a specific nerve in your body and injected a small portion of my youki into them. All of the commands and signals that your brain gives out are sent throughout the body using the nerves. By injecting my youki into them, I've scrambled them so they won't respond to you like they should. I'm sure you've noticed this."

Kevin indeed noticed this. Each time he tried to move a part of his body, a different limb would move as opposed to the one he wanted. He hadn't realized that such a thing was possible outside of shōnen manga.

"Stay here and wait for Seth to deal with your girlfriend and her sister," Cassy continued. "After that, I'll take care of you just like you did for me. I'll make sure you're never hurt like this again."

Kevin gritted his teeth. "D-do you really think I'm just going to give up...?"

"You're in no position to say something like that. I've already beaten you."

"No, you haven't..."

Kevin tried moving his left leg. His right arm twitched.

"I-I refuse to lose here..."

He tried to move the big toe on his right foot. His left index finger moved instead.

"I won't let myself be beaten..."

"W-what are you doing?!"

I think I've got this...

If he could find out which parts of his body the corresponding signals were being sent to, then he should be able to move like normal. It would be hard, but he'd already figured out one thing: The signals were being sent to their opposing limb. Right and left. Foot and hand. Toes and fingers. So long as he kept this in mind...

I can do this.

Slowly, he moved his feet. His hands pressed against the ground instead, palms flat. With a grunt of effort, he pushed himself up.

"Not by you or anyone else..."

"Impossible! How are you getting up?! You shouldn't even be able to move!"

"Heh, who the hell do you think I am?" With his legs shaking, Kevin rose to his feet. His back was hunched, but his head was tilted up to look at the shocked Cassy. "I told you, didn't I? It doesn't matter to me if you're a yōkai or whatever. Nothing is going to stop me from getting to Lilian and Iris. Not you or anyone else. Don't underestimate me just because I'm a human."

Cassy's eyes were bulging. They were so wide Kevin wondered how they hadn't popped from her sockets.

"Y-you... I can't believe this..."

Kevin slowly slid back into a combat stance, a narrow one designed for fleet-footed movement. His legs wobbled as he accidentally sent the wrong signal to his brain. Still, he worked it out and faced Cassy with his dominant foot forward, his right hand extended and forming a fist, and his left hand a few inches from his cheek.

"So go ahead and scramble my nerves as much as you want. It won't change a thing! I'm still going to beat you!"

Cassy didn't seem to know what she should do. After a moment's hesitation, her face hardened and became firm. She slowly slid into her stance, her eyes never leaving his.

A wind blew through the small section of the school. Several leaves floated past them. Cassy waited until the leaves flew by, and then she attacked.

Kevin didn't know if he was being an idiot for not giving up. He probably was. What he was doing, fighting someone so far beyond him in skill, strength, and ability, was stupid.

Even so, he refused to stop.

Hang on, Lilian, Iris.

***

Lilian barely had time to perform a technique. She bent the light around them, distorting her and her sister's bodies to make it look like they were still standing. Then she grabbed Iris by the arm and yanked her to the ground.

Guns blazed. A sound like roaring thunder resounded across the campus. The bullets hit nothing but air as the forms of Lilian and Iris dispersed like holograms.

Despite having avoided the initial barrage, the situation was not looking good. Lilian was running low on youki, and she was sure that her sister was in the same predicament. On the other hand, Seth looked as fresh as ever.

It didn't help that they were fighting off several skeleton warriors that had been summoned from the Sanzu River. The skeletons were weak. A good Celestial or Void attack would have destroyed them, but neither could afford to use their kitsune techniques carelessly anymore. That left them with hand-to-hand combat.

Unfortunately, neither she nor Iris was very good at martial arts. They'd not trained much, and although Lilian was being trained by Kotohime, three weeks of training couldn't increase her abilities by a wide enough margin to make a difference.

"I'm impressed," Seth complimented the two as they continued fighting. "You managed to avoid the initial barrage by tricking my warriors with an illusion that bent the light around you to make them think you were standing when you were really lying on the ground. Very impressive. But it's all over now. You two are nearly out of youki. Pretty soon you'll be completely empty. Why don't you just give up and become my dolls?"

"Shut up, you old coot!"

"Not a chance!"

Lilian and Iris shouted at the same time. Another skeleton lined up a shot but found its gun being knocked out of its grasp when Lilian struck it with one of her tails. The other tail rose and knocked its head off its body.

It was a good thing these warriors were so weak, though that meant little when they just got right back up and continued attacking. She was getting tired. Her ragged breathing sounded harsh to her ears. Her heart was going to burst out of her chest if she didn't do something soon.

Seth laughed at them. "Hahaha! Struggle as much as you want, girls! It won't change the outcome of this battle! You two are hopelessly outmatched!"

"Tch, I hate to admit it, but the man's got a point," Iris said to Lilian. "I'm running on empty here, so unless you've got some trick up your sleeve, we're screwed."

"I do have something that might get us out of this situation," Lilian huffed. "It's a long shot, but I don't really see what choice we have. Think you can buy me a little time?"

"I guess it depends on the amount of time you need."

"At least a minute."

"Ugh, that's a tall order, but I'll do my best."

"If you two are done trying to plan your way out of this hopeless situation, let's get this party started again. I'm curious to see what you two have up your sleeves," Seth said, snapping his fingers.

The warriors attacked. Those without guns surged forward while those with guns took aim. Since there were more than a dozen of them, it meant they had a lot of opponents to deal with.

Iris gritted her teeth as she wove an illusion around herself and Lilian, replacing their images with those of other skeletons and putting their own image on a pair of enemies—the ones that were charging at them.

The muskets suddenly swiveled, aiming at the surging enemies and firing. This didn't do much, for even though the skeletons' bones broke and split apart, more just crawled out from the abyss. However, Iris didn't stop. She continued weaving illusions, creating anarchy amongst the skeletons' ranks, causing them to constantly attack each other rather than her and her sister.

Void Kitsune, and Void users in general, were an interesting bunch. Most illusions didn't work on spirits since they were essentially ectoplasmic matter that had been forced onto this plane of existence. Even Lilian was only capable of fooling them by bending light. However, because of the Void's very nature, Void users could manipulate spirits by erasing the youki that had summoned them and supplanting it with their own youki.

While Iris sowed confusion and disorder, Lilian concentrated on the ball of light that hovered equidistant between her hands. Her tails had encircled the appendages and were constantly emitting light particles that gathered into the tiny sphere of energy, which hummed with a vibrancy, unlike anything she'd ever produced.

Just a few more seconds.

"Lily-pad..." Iris was panting, and her cheeks were growing flushed as her skin started to glisten with sweat. "I... I don't have much youki left... whatever you plan on doing... you had better do it now..."

"Don't worry. I'm done."

"Celestial Art: Divine Wave."

Lilian clapped her hands together and the light contained between her palms was released. It shot out in a ring of energy that passed through everything, yet seemingly harmed nothing. However, as the divine youki passed through the skeletons, all of them collapsed, clattering into a pile of bones, their forms unable to hold together as the energy used to revive them was purified.

Upon her technique's completion, Lilian collapsed to the ground, on her hands and knees, exhausted beyond comprehension. Her vision blurred before snapping into focus, and she started to teeter before righting herself. Inari-blessed, she was tired. At that moment, all she wanted to do was cuddle up beside Kevin and sleep.

Slow clapping caught her attention. Lifting her head took more effort than it should've. Seth walked towards her, his slow, mocking claps echoing across the school grounds.

"Bravo. Bravo. You two have done an extraordinary job. Truly. I don't think I've ever seen such a magnificent show being put on, and to think it came from a pair of two-tails. However, this is the end for you. You two are out of youki, which means it's my turn."

"Spirit Art: Soul Stealer."

Unlike last time he had used this technique, where his tails had struck nothing, this time they slammed into both Iris and Lilian, passing through their chests. From that moment on, all either of them knew was pain.

Their screams echoed across the empty school.

***

Something was wrong.

From the very onset of this battle, Cassy knew that she had it in the bag. She was faster than Master Kevin, stronger than Master Kevin, was a better fighter than Master Kevin, and had more experience than Master Kevin. He'd done well for a human, but the only reason he'd lasted this long was that she couldn't bring herself to truly hurt him.

That was what she had thought at first. Now she wasn't so sure.

The battle had taken a sudden turn. She didn't know how. She didn't know when. She just knew that somehow, Master Kevin had taken control of the battle's flow. Every time she attacked, he avoided it and countered. He used a minimalistic style that she hadn't seen before. His moves remained sloppy and unrefined—no, they were even worse than before, as he left his defense full of holes that were easy to exploit. In spite of this, he'd somehow managed to dodge every strike thrown his way with the minimum amount of effort.

And his reaction times were so fast! It was like he could see her every attack before she even made it. Every time she threw a punch or a kick, he was already in motion, moving to counter her attacks at the same time that she attacked like he could see into the future. But that shouldn't be possible! No one was capable of seeing into the future. Not yōkai and certainly not humans.

How is he doing this?!

She thrust her left hand out in a quick jab at Master Kevin's face. He avoided it, tilting his body ever so slightly to the side, allowing her fist to brush past his face, rustling his hair. At the same time, his hand came up and gently brushed her attack aside.

Realizing that she'd been thwarted, Cassy sought another opening. She found one near his torso and lashed out with a lightning-quick strike that should have taken the wind right out of his sails.

Master Kevin began to twist and bend, contorting around her attack. His right hand came up. His palm touched her wrist, pushing her arm wide at the same time that he took a single step forward. Then his left hand extended in a swift palm strike that caught her in the chest, forcing her to stumble back.

She stamped on the ground, left foot behind her, halting her backward momentum, leg bending to absorb the impact, which she then used to push herself forward. She took exactly two quick steps toward Master Kevin. Then she twisted her body and lashed out with a straight kick aimed at an opening on his left.

Once again, Master Kevin moved at the exact same time as her—no, he was moving even before her. Two steps to the right. He raised his arm. Her kick passed between his arm and torso, and then his arm moved back in just as quickly, trapping her leg under his armpit.

"What?!"

Before Cassy knew what was happening, he'd pulled her forward and slammed into her with a vicious head-butt that knocked her back. Blood welled up in her nose. Pain stung her eyes, which had crossed. Cassy ignored it. She recovered quickly and threw a straight jab at his chest, but Master Kevin lowered his body and tilted to the left. Her fist grazed his shoulder. He came back up, his left hand pushing her arm up toward the sky, right hand striking her in the face. Once again, it all happened simultaneously.

This time Cassy came in with a high kick aimed at his face, wanting to knock him out swiftly. She only realized her mistake a second later, when Master Kevin lowered himself all the way to the ground and kicked her leg out from underneath her. The world spun for a second, and then Cassy was on her back, staring into a pair of hooded blue eyes, and feeling the barrel of a gun pressed firmly under her chin.

"I don't understand, nya," she muttered. "How did you beat me?"

Breathing heavily, and with sweat dripping down his face, Master Kevin stared into the eyes with an unwavering gaze. "I realized after my fight with a two-tailed kitsune back at the Comic-Con that I couldn't continue fighting the way I have been. I was fighting the same way I would against a regular human. That was

my mistake. You people aren't human. You're yōkai. I knew that if I wanted to win against yōkai in combat, then I needed to learn how to fight smart, not just fight using my strength and my mouth."

"Fight... smart?"

"That's right."

Cassy didn't understand, but she realized that Kevin wasn't going to tell her anything. He had no reason to.

"I see." She closed her eyes and sighed. "Go ahead, nya. Finish it."

"No."

"Nya?" Cassy opened her eyes as Master Kevin stood up and backed away from her.

He looked down at her with a gaze that she couldn't fathom. "I won't kill someone when I don't have to. I refuse to do that. I won't become some kind of monster because I was willing to take the easy way out."

Ba-dump.

Cassy stared at the boy as her heartbeat increased. Master Kevin stood over her, his shoulders straight and his gaze firm, resolute in ways that she'd never seen from anyone, much less a human.

"And besides," Master Kevin added. "There's no way I could kill you."

"Nya?" Cassy tilted her head. "I don't understand."

"You're the cat I took with me to Comic-Con, aren't you?" Master Kevin asked, and Cassy felt her cheeks become warm. "And if I'm correct, then you're also the same cat that I took care of all those years ago back when I was a child."

Cassy looked away. "When did you realize that?"

"During this fight, actually," he said. "I noticed during our fight that you never went all out. You never used your full strength or speed, and you never used those hellfire attacks that Lilian told me about. I wondered why at first, but it wasn't until you said you would take care of me that I realized who you were."

Cassy couldn't believe it. He'd figured out who she was just from that?

"It took me a while," Master Kevin continued sheepishly. "I'm still coming to terms with the fact that yōkai have disguised themselves as humans. For some reason, the idea that a yōkai would disguise herself as an animal never occurred to me."

This boy...

She had seriously underestimated Master Kevin. Thinking on it, even though he lit a fire in her loins, she hadn't thought much of him as a person. He was only human, after all. It was only now that she realized her mistake.

"Anyway, you can stay here or leave. I don't really care so long as you don't try to stop me anymore," Master Kevin said.

"I don't think I could stop you no matter how hard I tried, nya." She could still fight, of course, but it was becoming clear to her that short of killing him, nothing would stop Master Kevin from rescuing Lilian—and that would have defeated the purpose of fighting him. "Just tell me one thing, nya. Why do you care about Lilian so much? What makes her so special, nya?"

When Master Kevin's face shifted, lips quirking in a tender smile and eyes growing warm, Cassy realized that Master Kevin would never belong to her—unless she was willing to share, which she wasn't. Cassy was not the sharing type.

"Because she changed me. Because she helped me. Because she made me into a better person. Because she makes me want to be a better person. Because I can understand her better than anyone else, just as she understands me. Because when I'm with her, every day feels bright and new and exciting. I could give you a thousand reasons and it still wouldn't be enough to tell you why she's so important to me."

"I see," Cassy said, smiling sadly. "She's one lucky girl."

Master Kevin shook his head. "I'm the lucky one. Anyway, you can do whatever you want from here on out. Leave, stay, whatever, but this is where we part ways."

Cassy watched as Master Kevin ran off. While her body was still in good shape, she felt defeated in ways that she'd never imagined possible.

"Maybe that vixen was right," she muttered, remembering the conversation that she'd had with Lilian during her attempted assassination in Los Angeles.

Cassy looked at the clear, blue sky. Such a strange thing, that sky. It contradicted her stormy emotions, which felt like a downpour of self-recriminations, so perfectly.

"Maybe it was my own hesitation that led to her taking the place in Master Kevin's heart that I wanted for myself."

It was something to think about, at least.

That thought didn't console her very much.

***

Lilian stared dully at the sky. Everything hurt. She could scarcely remember the last time she'd felt this much pain. The memory of what she'd suffered when that gorilla had beaten her was a pittance compared to this.

She looked down at the tail that had phased through her body, squeezing her spirit with a crushing grip, and then at the man who was responsible.

"Oh, my. You two are still awake?" Seth chuckled, his dark grin filling her vision. "You're awfully resilient. And here I thought you'd be unconscious by now. That would have made this so much easier on you. I'm still not used to ripping souls from bodies, you see. It's a terribly difficult technique that requires more youki than most three-tails have. However, I've learned that if someone is rendered unconscious, the process becomes simpler. Now you two will need to suffer some more because of your own stubbornness."

Lying next to her, Iris gritted her bloodstained teeth. "F-fuck you, old ma—aa-aahhh!!"

"Iris!" Lilian screamed as her sister writhed. She turned her angry, hate-filled gaze onto Seth. "Stop it! Stop hurting her!"

But Seth didn't stop, and Lilian soon found herself writhing along with her sister. Her body screamed, her vision blurred, her mouth opened in a silent scream as her tongue lolled out. A thousand hot fire pokers were stabbing her from the inside out.

She didn't know how long the torture lasted. It could have been seconds, or it could have been hours. All she knew was that when the hurting stopped, Lilian couldn't feel much of anything. Her entire body felt numb.

"Hmm... still holding onto your consciousness. I must say, you two show some incredible resistance. I wonder if this is because of your Void and Celestial natures. Kuku. Adding you to my collection will be my greatest joy."

"Y-your collection?" Lilian's lips somehow moved to form the words.

"Oh, yes. I have a wonderful collection of all the fascinating people I've killed. You haven't seen them because I haven't had a chance to bring them out yet, but that's okay. You'll become well-acquainted with them soon enough. Now, I do believe it is about time I continued."

Despite her entire body feeling numb, Lilian somehow still felt pain. It was because Seth wasn't attacking her body, but her spirit, and her body suffered alongside it because the two were connected.

Fire flooded her nerves. Her body writhed along the ground like a worm digging in the dirt. She tasted copper on her tongue, which had swelled, nearly doubling in size.

This couldn't be the end, could it? Hadn't she sworn to herself that she would become stronger? Strong enough that she could remain by Kevin's side? How come she was still so weak? Or was this merely the vast difference between a kitsune with two tails and one with three? Was the gap just that large?

Because her mind was overcome with pain, it took Lilian several seconds to realize that the pain had inexplicably stopped, and all she felt now were its aftereffects.

It took another second to realize that Seth's tail no longer held its icy grip on her soul.

Another to realize that Seth was howling in pain, gripping his left knee, from which massive quantities of blood leaked through his fingers like a river of wine.

And one more to realize that she and Iris were no longer alone.

"Get-your-grubby-tails-off-my-girlfriend-and-Iris-kick!"

There was a loud, familiar shout that came from behind her— right before a pair of shoes flew over her shoulder and smashed into Seth's face, which seemed to distort at the point of impact. A body followed the feet. After planting his shoes into the three-tailed yōkai, the figure used Seth's face as a springboard to move into a corkscrewing leap. He landed on his feet between her and Seth.

Seth was sent crashing to the ground several yards away.

Standing tall, with his back to her, Kevin turned his head and looked at her with worry clear in his eyes.

"B-Beloved?"

"Are you all right?" he asked, keeping one eye on her and the other on Seth.

"Uh, um, yes," Lilian muttered. That wasn't exactly true, but she would live. There was no need to worry Kevin unnecessarily.

"Good. Iris, what about you?"

"Ugh, I think something broke in here." Iris somehow managed to raise a shaky hand and give him a thumbs-up. Unlike Lilian, who lay on her back, Iris was actually unsteadily climbing to her feet. "But I should live. Thanks for the save, Stud."

"I'm glad to hear that," Kevin said, his worried frown morphing into a grin. "I'm sorry for being a little late, but you know how it is. The hero is always supposed to arrive at the last second."

Despite her body feeling like it had been twisted into a pretzel and then stomped on by a horde of oni, Lilian found it within her to smile. "You've always wanted to say that, haven't you?"

"Ah-ha! You could tell, couldn't you?"

"How cliché," Iris muttered. "Don't tell me you're going to become one of those clichéd shōnen protagonists."

Kevin pouted. "That's mean, and in any case, it's better than being a clichéd harem protagonist."

"That is where you and I will have to agree to disagree."

Before their banter could go any further, Kevin was forced to dodge a wave of hellish flames. Lilian, Iris, and Kevin turned their gaze to Seth, who'd managed to climb onto one knee, though he still fiercely gripped the other. His eyes were narrowed in a hateful glare.

"You damn… human! You shot me!"

Those words caused Lilian to notice the tiny pistol in Kevin's hand, causing her to conclude that he had, indeed, shot Seth in the kneecap.

Her mate turned to the injured kitsune, his own glare matching the fierce look in the yōkai's eyes. "And you tortured my girlfriend and her sister! If you think getting your kneecap blown off is all I'm going to do to you, then you've got another thing coming! Get ready, Furball! Because we're not even close to being done yet!"

CHAPTER 12

Violent Recourse

KEVIN WAS BEGINNING TO think that antagonizing the three-tails hadn't been one of his better ideas. Oh, sure, it got the kitsune to focus the entirety of his attention on him, but that was turning out to be something of a double-edged sword, as it meant he had to deal with a constant stream of attacks sent his way. What else could he do, though? He couldn't let this person focus on Lilian and Iris, who were still recovering.

The good news was that his opponent couldn't move. Before their fight had even started, Kevin had shot the three-tails in the left kneecap. He didn't know if the kneecap had shattered, but it didn't matter. The redhead seemed incapable of standing up. That forced him to attack from a prone position and made dodging his hellfire and spirit techniques easier.

Kevin did wonder for a brief moment why Seth wasn't using any illusions, but only long enough for him to remember something that Kotohime had said to him during one of her lectures.

He was sitting on the couch as Kotohime lectured him on how illusions worked. "You already know the basics. Casting illusions is the act of supplanting a false reality within the mind of the person that the illusion is being cast on. Nothing you see, hear, or feel in an illusion is real, but the caster makes it seem real by invading your mind with youki to control your brain waves and the synapses that send signals from your brain to the rest of your body."

"Which is why it can be broken with pain, right?" Kevin asked.

Kotohime nodded. "That's correct. Kitsune excel at illusions. While some of us, like myself, prefer not to use them, they are our single most powerful ability. However, illusions are also insanely difficult to cast. While being a kitsune makes us predisposed toward using them, the amount of concentration required to envision a new reality and then impose it onto another person is insane. Therefore, if you want to stop a kitsune from casting an illusion on you, then you should inflict as much pain on them as possible."

She smiled.

"After all, inflicting pain on your enemy is much better than inflicting it on yourself."

Kevin had shot Seth in the kneecap already. That was painful. No two ways around it. Seth probably couldn't muster up the concentration needed to properly create an illusion, never mind casting one.

Not that him not using illusions really mattered in the grand scheme of things. Kevin couldn't even get close to Seth. Every time he tried to close the distance, Seth would launch a barrage of spirit techniques and hellfire, forcing him to back off. It was a vexing situation.

"You damn human!" With spittle flying from his mouth, Seth held a closer resemblance to a rabid animal than a bipedal sentient being. "I'll kill you!"

More flames rushed toward Kevin, who dodged accordingly. Searing heat caused his skin to feel singed, but he knew that was just an illusion. This wasn't a normal fire. It was hellfire, flames that were summoned from the underworld. They wouldn't burn his body if they touched him. They would burn his spirit.

A glance at his surroundings revealed that he was alone. Iris and Lilian were now behind Seth, Kevin having moved away from the pair to keep them from getting hit by a stray attack. They were watching him while they recuperated from their wounds and youki exhaustion.

Knowing that he had to keep the kitsune's attention on him, Kevin taunted the centuries-old being. "You keep saying you're going to kill me, but you haven't had much luck so far. Maybe you should just give up because it's clear to me that your aim sucks!"

"Fuck you, human! I'm not gonna put up with insults from an inferior primate!" Seth's tails stopped hurling hellfire at him and instead speared the ground. **"Spirit Art: Puppetry."**

Kevin watched warily as three pentagrams appeared on the ground. Hands emerged from within those pentagrams. Long, slender, delicate. Female hands. They were followed by more hands, then arms, heads, and bodies. Kevin felt something like annoyance mixed with apprehension as three people pulled themselves from the pentagrams, all of them women, and all of them carrying various weapons.

The one nearest him was a blonde with long hair, green eyes, and a unitard that fit her lithe figure. She carried a pair of serrated military knives. Several feet behind her, a redhead wielding a staff stood with blank brown eyes. Farthest from Kevin, a woman with hair like ash wielded a pistol of some kind, though he didn't know what type.

"These three are part of my collection," Seth said, his bloody lips twisting into an arrogant sneer. "All of them are warriors that I killed at one point and turned into puppets. Let's see how you handle them."

Without warning, two of the three women rushed at him while the other one hung back and aimed her firearm. Kevin was caught in a pincer attack that forced him to backpedal. He retreated, moving away from their attack. The two followed him.

The air screamed as a staff flew by his face. He avoided it by tilting his head back, but he couldn't avoid the aftershock, the force generated by the swing. Rather than allowing himself to stumble back, he went with it. Kevin fell backward, rolled across the ground, and jumped back onto his feet.

Red hair and brown eyes appeared in front of him, the knife-wielder, who attacked him with a series of thrusts and slashes. Kevin's breathing was ragged as he dodged. Left. Right. Back. Duck. He was a constant figure of never-ending motion. On the woman's last swing, Kevin leaned his torso as far back as he dared, and then he kicked the woman's arm to knock the knife out of her hand.

While the woman recovered her knife, Kevin was assaulted by the staff wielder.

Kevin was forced to constantly move in order to keep ahead of her attacks and avoid getting pumped full of holes. He ducked underneath a staff. His hair was buffeted by the displaced air. The scent of oil and blood filling his nose alerted him to someone coming up behind him. He spun around and was just in time to avoid having his chest carved open by a military knife.

Heavy breathing. Gasping rasps. Kevin's lungs were on fire as he moved, weaving and swerving and dodging. The two came at him as a unit, one defending and the other harassing. They worked well together. He wondered if it was because they had military training, or if they were being controlled by Seth.

Kevin changed directions, moving closer to the staff wielder. After abruptly stopping his momentum, he changed direction and took a single step into her guard, provoking the woman into attacking.

She did. It was a straight jab with her staff. Kevin turned the staff aside with his left hand and stepped into her guard, pounding her stomach with several quick hits that would have knocked the wind out of most people. All that happened to this woman was that she stumbled back. Then she came right back in, forcing him on the defensive.

"You didn't really think something like that would work, did you?" Seth asked, cackling from where he kneeled. "My puppets aren't alive. They feel no pain. Those bodies are merely containers used to anchor their souls to the earth, keeping them from crossing the Sanzu River. Your feeble human attacks won't do anything to them."

Well, that sucked. While Kevin would have loved to deny what the man said, he couldn't because his attacks clearly hadn't hurt this woman at all. She merely shook it off and attacked with renewed vigor alongside the knife-wielder who had finally reclaimed her second blade and rejoined the battle.

Deciding to try something else, Kevin began maneuvering the two girls around some more. He forced them to follow him, setting them up just as he wanted. He made sure to always position himself in such a way that neither could attack him at the same time, lest they end up attacking each other or be hit by the markswoman.

The two weapon users split off from each other and came at him from opposite directions. Kevin ducked. The staff soared over his head and almost hit the knife-wielder. If it wasn't for the woman's insanely fast reflexes, she would've had her head bashed in.

He stood up. Two knives nearly skewered him when their wielder launched herself at him and thrust her blades forward. Kevin was already moving. He grabbed the staff, which was returning to its owner's side after her swing, and yanked the woman into the knives' path.

Clang!

The knives were deflected, but it was a near thing. The staff wielder somehow managed to twirl her staff around despite the awkward position. This knocked the knives off course, but it also presented Kevin an opportunity to attack—or so he thought.

413

Out of the corner of his peripheral vision, he noticed the gunslinger take aim and put her finger on the trigger. *Bang! Bang! Bang!* Kevin dropped to the ground, rolling. His shoulders were jolted as he scrambled to his feet and tried to regain his bearings.

The gunslinger had no intention of giving him time to recover, however, and neither did the other two. The knife-wielder was already coming in hot.

Timing it just right, Kevin dodged the two knives that tried slicing him up, grabbed the woman's left hand, and placed her between himself and the gunslinger just as several rounds were fired. Thunderclap after thunderclap echoed. Light flashed from a barrel. The knife-wielder was perforated as bullets penetrated her flesh, though no blood spurted out of her body. When the gun clicked empty, he kicked the woman forward and moved away as she crumpled to the ground.

That's one down.

Spinning, Kevin was immediately forced to bend backward as a staff threatened to bash his skull in. He came back up and lashed out with a fist that knocked the woman's head back. He latched onto the staff and pulled her to him, sliding around her body, placing her between himself and the gunslinger.

He ran forward. He could feel the woman he was using as a shield jerk as she was pumped full of lead. He felt bad for using her, but he told himself that she was just a doll, that she was a puppet, not a living person. When he reached the long-range fighter, he shoved the staff wielder into her, knocking them both to the ground.

"Kevin! Watch out!" Lilian shouted.

The warning came too late. Fire seared his back as something warm and wet caked his clothes to his skin. Turning his head, he saw the knife-wielder up and ready for more. The knife in her left hand was covered in blood.

He stumbled forward, but he didn't fall. The knife-wielder was coming in hot. Kevin forced his body to move past the pain. He spun around and faced his opponent, backpedaling and weaving through a combination of thrusts and lunges.

All the while, Seth laughed like a madman. "You can't stop my puppets, fool! You can't kill what's already dead! They're invincible!"

Invincible, huh? Did that mean that nothing he did could kill them? Were they really invincible, or were they just impervious to physical damage? Dang it. This would have been so much easier if he knew the capabilities of his enemy's technique.

The two that he had knocked to the ground stood back up, the staff wielder rushing to join the knife user, while the gunslinger hung back and took aim. Kevin was given no quarter. He moved back constantly, using all of his skills to keep from being forced into a two-on-one battle with the close-range weapon users. It was a lot harder than it looked.

Seth's constant ravings didn't help any.

***

On the sidelines of the three-on-one battle, Lilian and Iris watched in frustration. Neither was in any shape to move. Just sitting up required more effort than it was worth. To top it off, they were nearly out of youki and couldn't even perform the most basic of techniques. They were, for all intents and purposes, as helpless as a human baby.

"I hate this," Lilian said through gritted teeth. "I feel so useless. Kevin is fighting to protect us, but I'm stuck here waiting until I can gain enough youki to recover."

No matter how powerful a yōkai was, without youki to fuel their techniques, they were nothing. Even a Kyūbi was useless without youki. Right now, if Lilian were to fight, she'd only hinder Kevin.

"I might be able to do something." When Lilian looked over at her, Iris bit her lip and shrugged. "I've got enough youki for at least one more technique, but I can only use one, and it will likely only take out one of those puppets."

Lilian paused for a moment, but she eventually nodded. "I don't think you need much more than one technique. Seth is only a three-tails. He's been putting on a strong front, but he has to be running out of youki by now."

A three-tailed kitsune only had twice as much youki as a two-tailed kitsune, and Seth had been slinging around more youki-intensive techniques than she and Iris combined.

"If you can take out the knife user, that would be good," Lilian continued. "She seems to be giving Kevin the most trouble right now… and she's the one who hurt him."

"You just want me to get rid of her out of revenge."

"You got a problem with that?"

"Not in the least.

***

As the fight continued, Kevin eventually deduced that the only way to get rid of these puppets was to take out the one controlling them. That was how stuff like this worked in anime, and he was going to bank on it working in this fight too. It wasn't like he had any other choice. He was already running low on options.

The problem was coming up with a plan to take Seth out. He couldn't get close to the man, and trying to approach resulted in him either being cut off by the staff and knife-wielder, the gunslinger's bullets, or Seth's hellfire. But he couldn't remain on the defensive either. He could feel his strength leaving him as the fight against Cassy caught up to him.

A step to the left allowed him to avoid the knife wielder's slash attack. Kevin spun around and struck the woman's left hand with a quick kick that knocked the knife out of her hand. She came at him again with the knife still clenched in her right hand.

Footsteps behind him made his ears twitch. He allowed the knife-wielder to get close before moving at the last second, grabbing her wrist, and redirecting the attack behind him. There was a moment of resistance, but then the knife sunk into someone's flesh. It was the staff wielder.

If there was one good thing about fighting these three, it was that they were not yōkai. Their bodies, while basically just dead shells containing a soul, were still human, with all the physical limitations that being human entailed. Having been forced to fight against Kiara's three goons in three-on-one battles several times, Kevin had become well-versed in this type of combat situation.

The key to fighting multiple opponents was to make them trip each other up. By constantly maneuvering around them so they would be in each other's way, it was possible to not only fight one on one but to also make sure they attacked each other. It was this sort of intelligent maneuvering that kept him from being killed thus far.

Kevin briefly thought about using the style he'd begun developing, but immediately decided against it. That style had been created to fight creatures beyond his ability to physically compete against, and it still wasn't complete. Cassy had managed to score several blows before he'd gotten her timing down. It just required too much focus for someone untrained in its use.

Avoiding the incoming staff thrust with a fake-out, Kevin ducked low and allowed the pole to pass over his shoulder. With his right hand pushing the pole up, his left hand closed into a fist and slammed into the woman's chin with a brutal uppercut. The sound of her teeth clacking together was audible as she fell to the ground. He didn't have much time to celebrate, because a pair of knives came in from out of nowhere to skewer him, forcing Kevin to backpedal.

He gritted his teeth as his arm was nicked. Blood poured from the wound. He ignored it and wove around her next attack, and then reverse-kicked her in the chest. The woman stumbled back, away from him—

"Void Art: Consuming Flame."

—and then dark black flames suddenly consumed her body. For the first time since this fight started, the woman screamed in pain. She dropped her knives and fell to the ground, writhing. Her mouth opened, but no scream came out. The Void fire filled her lungs and erased everything, even her ability to scream. Before long, the woman was gone. Not even ash remained. The knives were still there.

Seth and Kevin turned to see Iris kneeling on the ground, breathing heavily, her tails lying limply in front of her. It didn't take a genius to figure out who had killed that woman.

"Damn you!"

Seth's tails came up to launch a hellfire attack at Iris. With barely any time to think, Kevin reacted on instinct, grabbing one of the knives and throwing it at Seth.

He sucked at throwing things. Kevin never managed to hit a target or make a basket before. However, for the first time in his life, his aim was true.

Perhaps the desperation of his situation heightened his skills at throwing objects, but the knife smacked against Seth's head. It didn't stab him because he was hit by the handle, but it did knock his concentration off and caused his attack to sputter out.

Without giving it much thought, Kevin used this distraction to rush right at Seth. The two women remaining attempted to impede his path, but they seemed to be moving sluggishly. He guessed that Seth's control over them had loosened, or maybe something else was happening. Either way, he avoided their attacks, closed the distance between him and his foe, and snapped the kitsune's head back with a kick.

"Fucking human!" Seth screamed.

Three tails latched onto Kevin and began to squeeze him tightly. One wrapped around his neck, forcing a raspy gurgle out of his throat. They must have been reinforced with youki. Kevin could have sworn he heard his bones creak.

Seth's bloodshot eyes glared at him as he stood to his feet, heavily favoring his left leg. Blood ran down his now broken nose. "There will be no quick death for you, boy. I'm going to make you suffer!"

Kevin would have screamed as Seth forced youki into his frail human body, but he lacked the breath to shout. He could feel the foreign energy like fire burning his insides. Fire! His insides were on fire! His intestines were melting, his heart was bursting into flames, he felt the underworld calling to him. His soul was being dragged down, where it would burn in the fires of hell.

Pain turned into breathlessness as he was slammed into the ground. He would've gasped, but he'd swallowed his tongue. Kevin tasted copper filling his mouth.

Dredging up whatever strength he had left, Kevin grabbed onto the tail that was wrapped around his throat, which seemed to slacken of its own accord. It was probably his imagination, but his left hand felt a little bit stronger.

"W-what the hell is this?!" Seth screamed.

"Beloved!"

"GAH!"

Kevin blinked several times. His vision was blurry, but he eventually made out what was happening.

Lilian had leaped onto Seth's back and was clawing at his eyes. Her tails had likewise wrapped around his arms, keeping them pinned by his sides. Seth thrashed around, stumbling as he tried to throw the girl off. When that didn't work, one of the tails holding Kevin let go and wrapped around Lilian's throat, choking her.

With his vision beginning to fade, Kevin searched for a way out of this situation. Spots appeared before his eyes, his breathing was slowing down. He fought through the haze that had been cast over him and looked around. The knife that he had thrown was only a few inches to his left.

Fighting back the darkness crowding around the edge of his vision, Kevin wrapped his hand around the hilt. With one last, desperate push, he shoved the blade into Seth's chest. The blade slid in smoothly. Blood seeped out of the wound, staining Seth's shirt.

The three-tail's eyes went wide as he stared at the handle protruding from his chest in disbelief. Then he looked at Kevin. Their eyes met. Seth took a shuddering breath before his tails went slack and he toppled over. Kevin gasped, coughing and hacking as his lungs regained the oxygen they'd been deprived of.

"Beloved…" Lilian, also croaking, crawled over to him on all fours. "Are you okay?"

"Yes… I think so… what about you?"

"I'm all right." Upon reaching him, Lilian helped Kevin sit up and pulled him into a hug. She held him tightly, as if afraid that he would disappear the moment she let go. "You saved me. Thank you."

Kevin returned the hug. He took comfort in Lilian's presence and her slender arms around his waist. "I think it would be more accurate to say we saved each other. I would've been dead if you hadn't jumped on his back like that." Lilian didn't say anything to that. She only hugged him tighter.

"I'm feeling awfully left out right now."

Their moment was interrupted by Iris dropping like a sack of bricks right next to them. Kevin felt a moment of annoyance, but when he saw how exhausted she looked, the haggard bags under her eyes and the hollowness to her cheekbones, he couldn't bring himself to tell her off.

"Sorry," Lilian mumbled as the hug expanded to include Iris, who really did look close to passing out.

"It's fine," Iris slurred, her eyes slowly shutting. "So long as you let me join in, I'm good." And just like that, the cost of using so much youki and the Void took its toll. Iris fell asleep.

With the battle having reached its conclusion, the school campus was abnormally silent. The two warriors that Seth had summoned, the staff wielder and the gunslinger, were no longer present. Kevin couldn't be sure, but he guessed that, without Seth around to anchor them to the mortal plane, the two had been sent back to wherever they had come from. Maybe they'd even crossed the Sanzu River by now.

"We should probably leave," Lilian said. "The barrier disappeared when Seth died, so we don't have to stay here."

"Right," Kevin agreed.

He didn't want to stay there any longer either. The place reminded him of a war zone in a Battlefront game. Pockmarks and scorch marks covered the ground. Blood stained the cement. The school building to Ms. Vis's classroom was gutted and destroyed, a demolished wreck that looked like a wrecking ball had plowed into it...

... Seth's cooling corpse lay naught but a foot away.

Are we... going to have to dispose of the body?

"Kevin?" Lilian forced his attention onto her. "Are you feeling okay?"

"Not really." Kevin sighed before giving her a weary smile. "But I will be after a good night's rest."

Lilian worried her lower lip. "What about...?" she trailed off, and Kevin inferred what she wanted to ask through her inability to ask it.

"I... I might have some nightmares tonight, but I think I'll be okay." Kevin looked at Seth's corpse again, at the expanding puddle of carmine underneath it. He looked away. "I didn't... want to kill someone again, but he didn't leave me with much choice."

Seth hadn't left him with many options. If Kevin hadn't killed Seth, then Seth would have killed him, Lilian, and Iris. He lacked the strength to fight without killing. In the end, when forced to choose between himself and his loved ones, Kevin had done what any sentient creature would have done: He chose himself and the people he loved.

"If you need anything, don't hesitate to let me know," Lilian said.

Kevin nodded and gave her a smile. They stood up, and Kevin lifted Iris into his arms. Iris's legs swung back and forth like a pendulum. Kevin shifted, adjusting her so that her head was resting on his shoulder.

Lilian pouted. "That's the second time in one month that my sister has been carried in your arms. I think she's doing this on purpose."

"I don't know about that." Kevin looked down at the raven-haired vixen in his arms. "I think she'd rather be carried by you than me."

"Maybe." Lilian sounded dubious, but she chose not to say anymore.

"Anyway," Kevin began, "let's find our friends. Christine should still be around here somewhere, and if she's here, I'm willing to bet that some of our other friends are here, too."

"Good idea."

Together, the two set off in search of their friends. Hopefully, they were all doing fine.

***

Standing on one of the school buildings in his hybrid form, Stephen Valsiener, known as Juan to everyone else, watched Kevin and Lilian walk off.

Just as he had suspected, the fights had been most entertaining. He had been impressed by Iris and Lilian. For a pair of two-tails,

423

they were incredibly talented. The techniques they used, the way they fought. Lilian was better than Iris, but the raven-haired succubus's Void powers were frightening to behold.

Kevin Swift had also been something of a surprise. He knew that the young man was training with Kiara, but he'd not realized that training had borne such fruit. Even if that nekomata hadn't been fighting at her full power for whatever reason, it did not change how impressive his victory over her was. That he'd gone on to fight and help defeat a kitsune with three tails only showed how dangerous he was becoming.

"What a most impressive and unexpected outcome," he said to himself, not like there was anyone else around to hear him. "Though I doubt the person who sent those assassins after Lilian will agree."

Indeed, the Bodhisattva would not be happy to learn that the assassins he hired had failed. What a joy it was that the task of informing the Bodhisattva's spies of this abject failure rested solely on his shoulders. He was beginning to wonder if one or more of the eight million Shinto gods hated him.

Being an information broker really sucked sometimes.

***

Eric woke up to a headache—and a strangely musky smell that made his nose twitch, but mostly the headache. It felt like someone had slammed him in the head with a sledgehammer. His head was pounding and his ears were ringing.

As his senses slowly returned, he became more aware of his situation. He was lying on his back. The ground underneath him was hard and cold. There was also something lying on top of him, and his face was being smothered by whatever that something was.

Eric opened his eyes to get a glimpse of whatever lay on top of him.

He stared at the decidedly male crotch, covered by blue jeans, that was mere inches from his eyes.

Eric's muffled screams echoed across the campus.

CHAPTER 13

Black Cat Wanders Back

KEVIN, LILIAN, AND IRIS had met up with Christine, Heather, and Lindsay after the battle's conclusion. During their reunion, they had held a quick conference, letting each other know what had happened so they were all on the same page.

Christine, Heather, and Lindsay had been pretty shocked to learn about Cassy and Seth, the two assassins sent after their friend. Lilian was just angry when she found out that the assassin who'd gone after her in California had followed her all the way to Arizona.

With Heather's cellphone, which had survived the battle—unlike Kevin's, which he discovered had been crushed during his fight with Seth—they dialed up Kiara and Kotohime to inform them of the situation. The two had shown up a mere fifteen minutes later.

Kotohime had expressed her most sincere apologies for having not realized that they were in danger. Apparently, the barrier that Seth had put up had been a quadruple-layered illusion to fool all their senses. It even blocked out youki emissions, ensuring that not even the most sensitive yōkai could detect the release of energy during the battle.

They were driven home by Kiara after that. Heather had hung back at school, stating that someone needed to be there when the yōkai whose job was to erase any evidence that would reveal their existence to humans arrived. They would erase everyone's memories and dispose of the corpse.

There wasn't much they could do about the damage, though, as there were no techniques that could restore property to an undamaged state. They were yōkai, not magicians.

Kevin would find out the next day via the news that the property damage would be blamed on vandalism. That seemed to be a popular theme to use. Both the destruction of the gym, courtesy of Kiara and Lilian several months back, and the destruction of the office building that he had fought the gorilla yōkai in, had been blamed on vandals.

Kirihime had been quite beside herself when they arrived home. The normally demure woman had been nearly in tears when she learned about their battle with Seth. Nothing seemed to console her, not even when he, Lilian, and Iris told her that they didn't blame her for not being able to protect them.

Camellia had merely stood there during the recap of events.

The week after the battle passed uneventfully. Ms. Vis was sent to the hospital for brain damage. Seth's possession combined with an enchantment that Kotohime had placed on her to treat Lilian like her own daughter—which he and Lilian had only just learned about—had taken its toll on the woman. She'd been in a vegetative state since then, no doubt due to the undue stress that had been placed on her mind. No one knew if she would fully recover.

Ms. Vis had also been replaced by a new teacher. Yuno Valkire had a knack for teaching. Despite having only taught for a week, many of the students already loved her, especially the guys. Of course, she was gorgeous, so that was to be expected, but the girls respected her for her friendly and helpful demeanor. She was, in a sense, the perfect teacher.

She was also a yōkai sent to watch the school to make sure further incidents like this didn't happen.

Kevin and Lilian's training had been upped as well. With another threat having been barely averted, Kiara and Kotohime had decided that they needed to work harder. Four days a week, he and Lilian were put through grueling paces and unimaginable spars. They never went home without bruises.

Even Iris had been forced to train, much to her displeasure.

Alex, Andrew, and Eric had been fine. None of them could remember what happened. According to Heather, no one that had been enchanted could remember the incident. It seemed that Seth's enchantment wiped the memories of everyone caught under its sway.

That was probably a good thing, Kevin felt. There was no need to put undue stress on his friends' minds. They might know about the yōkai world, but they didn't need to become a part of it.

With Seth dead and Cassy missing, presumably gone, Kevin could only hope that his life would finally settle down. He really needed a break.

***

The potentially disastrous consequences brought about by Seth Naraka's assassination attempt on Lilian at school had been averted. Davin Monstrang had several yōkai located within local and international media channels, as well as the newspapers, and had ordered them to create a cover story for what happened at the school.

Kotohime had to admit, she was very impressed by the system set up in the United States. While the Four Saints no longer associated with each other, having disbanded decades ago, the system that they had created ensured the continued peace better than anything else she'd seen. It was no wonder that the United States had one of the lowest yōkai crime rates in the world—recent incidents caused by herself and her charge's family notwithstanding.

Now that the crisis had been averted, a meeting of the minds had been called, so to speak.

Kotohime observed all of the people stationed around the room. Kirihime was next to her, standing with her back straight, hands clasped in front of her. Only Kotohime noticed the sweat covering her forehead, a sign of nerves. Kotohime didn't blame her. She was in the presence of one of the Four Saints.

Kiara leaned against the wall, her only remaining hand stuffed in the pocket of her gray slacks. She looked rather detached, but Kotohime knew the woman well enough to know that her keen ears were listening to every word being spoken. Beside her stood Heather, the only human among their group, wearing a basic blouse and T-shirt combination.

"Ever since you kitsune arrived, Arizona has been in a state of complete disarray. I've had to deal with more disasters in the past six months than I have my entire time living in this state," Davin Monstrang said in his usual gruff demeanor.

"You have my most sincere apologies, Davin-dono." Kotohime bowed before the older and far more powerful yōkai. "It was never our intention to cause you or anyone else trouble. Truth be told, if it weren't for Kevin-sama becoming Lilian-sama's mate, I would have taken my charge and left this state when I first located her."

Davin grunted. "Well, what's done is done. There's no use complaining about it now."

"The media did a good job of spinning a believable story," Kiara smoothly changed topics. "It must have been difficult with all of the evidence that pointed toward this incident being a combat situation."

Kotohime had to agree. She'd seen the battlefield left by Seth's assassination attempt. It had been quite the disaster zone. It had also clearly been caused by a fight. Anyone with a brain would have been able to see that.

"A lot of mind manipulation was required," Davin admitted. "Several of the human reporters were a bit too nosy for their own good and had to be enchanted before they could snoop further. We've convinced everyone that this was nothing more than a vandal who got their hands on some explosives, but this incident came closer to revealing the existence of yōkai than any other we've had."

Kotohime struggled not to speak, and also to keep her guilt inside. She knew that this situation was their fault, the fault of her and the Pnévma clan. However, she'd already apologized once. Apologizing any more would only serve to irritate Davin Monstrang further, and that was to be avoided at all costs.

"That may be so, but we've still managed to successfully avert disaster and keep our existence a secret," Kiara said. "I think that's what matters the most right now. I'm more interested in learning more about those assassins."

"They come from a small village hidden somewhere in the United States," Davin said, shrugging. "They're technically not criminals, and they have no interest in revealing our existence to humans. Doing so would be bad for their business."

"They're one of many hidden villages located throughout the world," Kotohime spoke up. "I believe there is one in each major country and even a few in various third world countries that are experiencing war. I had once been offered a chance to join but declined."

"So they're like a village of hidden assassins?" Heather asked.

"More or less. They take on a variety of jobs, but assassinations are what they specialize in, and both yōkai and humans alike use their services. They're only known in certain circles, though, so I'm not surprised that Davin-dono's intelligence network has not been able to learn much about them. I only know of them because they offered me a position, and even then, I do not know where any of their villages are located."

"Actually, I do know who is involved with this particular village," Davin admitted. "And I've sent her a message telling her to cut contact with the Bodhisattva and refuse the mission to assassinate your charge. I haven't received a response back, but I don't expect one. In any event, they won't be bothering you or those under your care again."

"Thank you." Kotohime did not know how the man managed to get the assassination order on Lilian repealed, but she knew better than to ask about it. They were allies right now, but her allegiance was to the Pnéyma clan. He would not reveal his methods to her.

"How are the kids?"

"If by 'the kids,' you mean the humans who were enchanted by the one called Seth, they're doing fine," Heather said. "None of them have suffered any harmful side effects of the enchantment. The only one who seems to have been adversely affected was the math teacher, Ms. Vis, who remains in a vegetative state."

"She must have been under Seth's possession for a long time," Kotohime concluded. "**Kudagitsune**, the Kitsune Possession Technique can put incredible duress on the mind, especially if the kitsune and the person being possessed are not working as one. That assassin probably did a sloppy job possessing her, too, which does not help matters."

"Do you know if she'll wake up?" asked Davin.

"I believe she will. However, only time will tell for sure."

Davin did not seem pleased by that. He grunted but dropped the issue. There wasn't much they could do in any case.

"And what about the others? Swift and his friends."

"Most of Kevin's friends were also enchanted by Seth, including myself." Heather twitched, her hands clenching and unclenching. It must have been galling for her to get trapped in an enchantment during this incident. "They're all fine. Christine avoided being enchanted and the ones who were affected woke up without incident. Lilian and Iris received the worst of the wounds, though they won't require hospitalization thanks to Kotohime. That said, they did have a rather severe case of youki exhaustion."

"Fighting against someone much stronger than you will do that," Kiara said, wearing her feral grin. "Still, the fact that they managed to defeat Seth speaks highly of them. I hear the boya also did well in defeating both a nekomata and delivering the finishing blow to Seth, which he seems to be taking remarkably well."

"Indeed, Kevin-sama has grown into a very capable young man," Kotohime agreed.

At the mention of Kevin, Heather looked at her roommate. "Speaking of Kevin, when are you going to let me teach him advanced shooting techniques?"

"After he gets the basics down," Kiara told her. "It shouldn't take more than a month or so. After that, I'll let you teach him."

"I'm not sure I approve of letting Swift and his friends become a part of this," Davin told them all. "The yōkai world has never been a place meant for humans to tread. That five of them have already set foot into this world is dangerous. Swift's life will be especially difficult if he keeps spending time with you kitsune."

Kotohime frowned. She did not like the way he said that. "What do you mean by that, Davin-dono?"

"It's clear that you haven't heard this yet, otherwise you would have done something before now, but I've learned from several sources that the Bodhisattva is gathering forces and rallying his allies. It might not happen for a while, it might even be one hundred years from now, but sometime in the future, I have no doubt that the Bodhisattva will declare war on the Pnéyma clan."

To that, no one could think of anything to say.

* * *

Kevin woke up in the middle of the night when something small and light pawed at his chest. Opening his eyes, he was met with another pair of eyes mere inches from his face. They were familiar yellow irises surrounded by a black-furred face.

He stared at Cassy in her cat form, who merely stared back for several seconds before hopping off of the bed and bidding him follow her. A glance to his left revealed that Lilian and Iris were still sleeping. Iris was spooning her sister, who in turn was snuggling with him.

He shook his head. Iris was finally beginning to wear down Lilian's resolve. His girlfriend hadn't even cared when her sister crawled into bed with them that night. He would've complained, but he'd been so tired from training that he'd been half-conscious when Iris and Lilian climbed into bed.

Crawling off the bed, his feet pressed against the carpet as he followed Cassy onto the patio. The cool night air hit his face, bare chest, and legs. He wore nothing but boxers, which he noticed seemed to distract Cassy, as she'd not stopped staring at him since they stepped out.

When the door slid closed, Kevin witnessed Cassy transforming from a cat into her hybrid form.

He then promptly palmed his face.

"Do you really have to be naked when you transform?" he asked.

"Nya?" Cassy tilted her head, and then looked down. She blushed briefly before pulling her leather outfit from between her cleavage and putting it on. "Sorry. I would have transformed before seeing you, but I wouldn't have been able to sneak inside, nya. And yes, I do. Yōkai can't transform clothes when we change forms, nya."

Kevin did know that, but he didn't say anything and instead focused on the task at hand. "Since you didn't try to kill Lilian in her sleep, I'm guessing you want to talk to me about something?"

Cassy flinched at the reminder of what she'd done. "I'm sorry about that, nya. I never wanted to hurt you."

"I know, and I forgive you for what happened." Kevin sighed, even as he wondered if his bleeding heart would ever come back to bite him. It probably would, but he hoped it didn't.

"Thank you," Cassy mumbled softly before getting down to business. "Anyway, I wanted to tell you that the assassination order on Lilian has been revoked, nya. I'm not exactly sure what happened, but my mistress has recalled me, stating that we're no longer going after her, nya."

"Really?" Kevin couldn't keep the relief out of his voice. He placed a hand over his heart and clutched his shirt. "That's good. That's really, *really* good news."

Cassy smiled. "I thought you might be pleased, nya. Though I would still be careful if I were you, nya. Our village might have decided to renege on our contract, but the person who put the hit on your mate may decide to take the request to someone else, or even take matters into their own hands, nya."

That did worry Kevin a bit, but it also reaffirmed his desire to become stronger and learn how to fight against yōkai. He would even suggest the idea that he and Lilian learn how to fight together as a team.

Maybe I could even get Iris to join if I convince her that it's for Lilian's safety.

The battle with Seth had shown him that, while they weren't strong individually, together, he and Lilian and Iris could defeat yōkai many times stronger than them. If they combined their individual strengths, then he was sure they'd be able to defend against anyone who came after them.

"Thank you for telling me this," Kevin said, then paused as something else occurred to him. "Um, not to be rude, but why are you telling me this?"

With her hands behind her back, Cassy rocked back and forth on her heels. "I suppose you can consider this my apology, nya. It's also my way of thanking you for taking me in several years ago. I never forgot the kindness that you showed me. It was the first act of kindness I'd ever received."

Kevin hadn't known that, but, thinking about it, he could see how that might have been the case. Perhaps the village that she lived in was like those really strict places where children were trained at a young age to kill or something. He didn't know, but he didn't ask either. It wasn't any of his business.

"You're welcome." There was another moment's hesitation. Kevin scratched at his left cheek and looked away. "Listen, since you're no longer going to kill Lilian, so long as you don't attack anyone I'm close to, if you ever want to come here you can... provided you stay in cat form."

While he was all for helping others, he didn't want to open up the can of worms that would come from everyone learning that Cassy was one of the people who'd tried to assassinate Lilian.

Cassy's smile gained a melancholic quality. "Thank you for the offer, nya, but I think this will be the last time you'll see me."

Kevin didn't know what she meant by that, though he assumed it meant she wouldn't be assigned missions to this state anymore. He didn't want to admit that this didn't bother him, but, well, it didn't bother him. It sounded harsh, especially after he'd offered her a place to stay. However, Cassy not living in Arizona meant one less problem to deal with.

Cassy left after that, transforming back into a cat and leaping off of the balcony. Kevin made his way to the edge and watched as she landed on the ground, pausing to look back up at him one last time, and then scampering off.

There she goes. Well, I guess it's fine if we leave things like this.

Running a hand through his tousled hair, Kevin was about to return to his bedroom.

The door slid open, and Kevin stiffened as he realized that someone had seen him talking to the nekomata. He turned around, an excuse on his lips.

"Listen, I know what you're thinking, but it's not... Camellia?"

The excuse died when he saw who stood before him. Dressed in a simple nightgown of pure white that ended near her feet, Camellia gazed at him with a smile that Kevin had never seen before. It was kind, compassionate, and full of a tenderness that Camellia was—should have been—incapable of expressing. Also...

Were her eyes always that sharp?

"Um, is something the matter?" he asked tentatively.

Camellia shook her head. "No, nothing's wrong, Kevin-kyun."

Kevin made a face at the added "kyun" suffix. He would never grow used to the way she addressed him.

I suppose I should be lucky she's not calling me "-tan."

He was then given a jolt when Camellia gave him a fierce hug that was surprisingly not unpleasant. There was no boob smothering, no threat of death by symmetrical docking. His head gently rested against her bosoms, and her hands massaged his scalp. It was actually rather pleasant.

Kevin was disturbed by this, more so than if she had tripped and fallen boobs-first into his face.

"Thank you," Camellia said simply before letting go of the hug and blinking at him. Kevin watched as her face slowly morphed into one of confusion. She tilted her head cutely and stared at him with big, doe-like eyes. "Hawa? Kevin-kyun?"

Kevin frowned. Was something wrong with Camellia? He couldn't be sure. Still, he decided to keep an eye on her in the future, just in case.

After putting Camellia to bed—and finding out that Camellia slept with Kirihime—Kevin returned to his room. Iris and Lilian were still asleep. In his absence, Iris had snuck her hand down

Lilian's panties, which caused his mate's thighs to squirm as if suffering from pleasurable agony.

Kevin sighed before he crawled under the covers on Lilian's other side, took Iris's hand out of his mate's panties, and pulled Lilian close. Iris clicked her tongue as if she subconsciously knew what he had done. She scooted closer to Lilian and wrapped her arms around the redhead's waist.

As he closed his eyes, one last thought occurred to him.

I wonder how Lilian will react to finding out she's become a Lilian sandwich?

It would be a truly amusing reaction indeed.

To Be Continued...

AFTERTAIL

It's book six of the American Kitsune series. If you had asked me three years ago when I started publishing if I knew this series was going to keep getting more volumes, I probably would have laughed at you. The American Kitsune series has always been a parody of the harem/ecchi genre at heart, and despite all of the stuff going down in this latest volume, that fact has never changed.

Volume 6, A Fox's Mate, is filled with just as much fanservice as the previous volumes. There's still a lot of unresolved conflicts with the characters feelings toward one another. Lilian and Kevin seem happy, but Christine wants Kevin and Iris wants Lilian.

Of course, Iris being Iris has decided that if she can't beat them, she might as well join them. Her plan isn't quite on the same level as the Harem Plan concocted by one Momo Deviluke from To LOVE-RU Darkness, but when I consider how her goal has become inserting herself into Kevin's and Lilian's relationship, I can't help but fondly recall that particular manga in all its perverse, boob falling, face in crotch planting, ecchiness.

As the sixth book comes to a close, I've been looking at my recent volumes and realized that each one has been getting progressively darker. I don't think this is a bad thing. That said, I do worry about the future of this series. I still want my harem romcom because harem romcoms are my guilty pleasure and what I enjoy writing the most. However, I don't want a typical harem romcom, which I guess is why my series is getting so intense.

I've been putting a lot of thought into how I develop my characters, how I make my story progress, while still keeping the same level of fan service-filled humor. It's been tough. Randomly inserting the infamous boob fall, which turned into a Rito Yuuki-style crotch in face fall, made me realize that the art of boob falling is a dangerous and slippery slope. I'm really happy that Kevin and Lilian are at the point where they can do naughty things together or I'd never get my fix.

Out of all the characters in my series, I think Kevin Swift has definitely changed the most. Of course, he's the main character, so change is to be expected, but going from "pass out when a girl approaches" to "hot and heavy make out session with kitsune girlfriend" is a pretty big step—although it did take him a few volumes to reach that point.

This afterward isn't very big, so I'd like to take this moment to give some last minute thank yous.

Thank you, Mom, Dad, Donna, and Chuck for always supporting my writing.

Thank you, Amber and Tyler for giving me a niece to dote on.

Thank you, Kirsten for your awesome artwork. You are one of the most amazing people I've had the pleasure of working with!

Thank you, Crystal for editing my stories.

And thank you, readers. Without you, American Kitsune would have never been possible. I hope you'll join me on my next volume!

~Brandon Varnell

HAVE A SNEAK PEAK AT THE AMERICAN KITSUNE MANGA ADAPTATION THAT BRANDON IS MAKING ON PATREON!

HAVE YOU EVER EXPERIENCED ONE OF THOSE LIFE-CHANGING INSTANCES? AN EVENT SO MOMENTOUS THAT, YEARS LATER, YOU'RE STILL MARVELING AT HOW IT CHANGED YOUR LIFE?

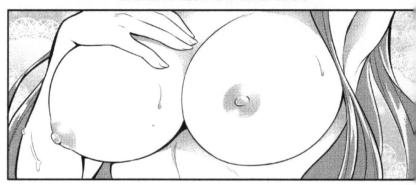

I HAD ONE OF THOSE. IT HAPPENED A WHILE AGO

EVEN TO THIS DAY, THROUGH ALL THE CHANGES THAT HAVE HAPPENED, THROUGH ALL THE EXPERIENCES THAT I'VE BEEN THROUGH, I STILL CAN'T BELIEVE HOW THIS ONE MOMENT CHANGED MY LIFE FOREVER.

NO MATTER WHAT CAME AFTER, OUR FIRST MEETING IS SOMETHING THAT I'LL ALWAYS REMEMBER.

ESPECIALLY SINCE, AT THE BEGINNING OF THIS TALE, I THOUGHT SHE WAS NOTHING
BUT AN ORDINARY FOX WITH, UNORDINARILY ENOUGH, TWO BUSHY RED TAILS.

LIFE

.

.

.

.

.

.

.

.

.

.

IT HITS YOU WHEN YOU LEAST EXPECT IT TO.

Hey, did you know?
Brandon Varnell has a Patreon
You can get all kinds of awesome exclusives
Like:

1. The chance to read his stories before anyone else!
2. Access to sketches, artwork, and more!
3. The American Kitsune Manga adaptation!
4. Exclusive SFW and NSFW artwork!
5. His undying love!

Er...maybe we don't want that last one, but the rest sound pretty cool, right?

Join Brandon and get all his exclusive content at:
https://www.patreon.com/BrandonVarnell!

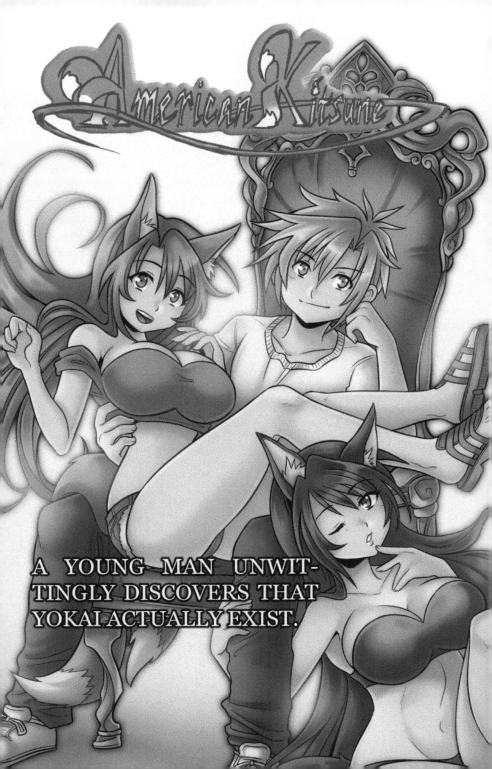

American Kitsune

A YOUNG MAN UNWIT-
TINGLY DISCOVERS THAT
YOKAI ACTUALLY EXIST.

catgirl doctor

THE STORY OF A YOUNG DOCTOR-IN-TRAINING AND CATGIRLS.

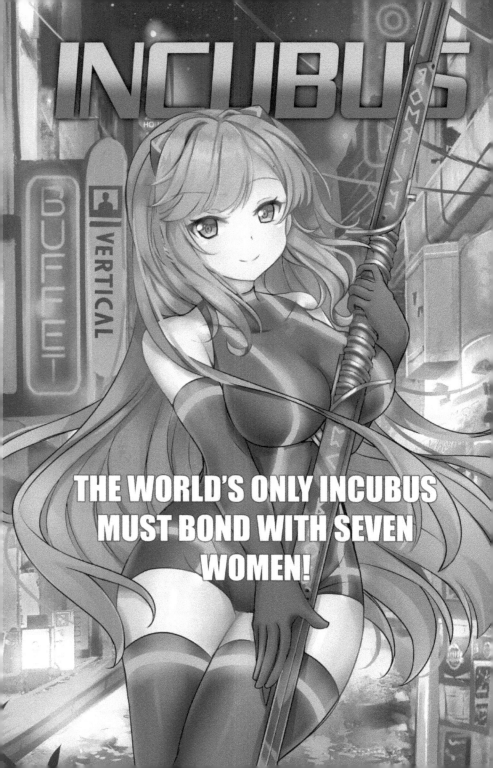

A MAN DESPERATE TO SAVE
HIS LOVER JOINS FORCES
WITH A WOMAN LOOKING
FOR A WAY OUT OF AN UN-
WANTED MARRIAGE.

MAN
MADE
GOD

He just wanted to be a hero.

She didn't want to be stuck in a loveless marriage.

A Most Unlikely Hero

Want to learn when a new book comes out?
Follow me on Social Media!

 @AmericanKitsune

 +BrandonVarnell

 @BrandonBVarnell

 http://bvarnell1101.tumblr.com/

 Brandon Varnell

 BrandonbVarnell

 https://www.patreon.com/
BrandonVarnell

CPSIA information can be obtained
at www.ICGtesting.com
Printed in the USA
BVHW062025011221
622869BV00006B/129